BAD
MOTHER

BAD
MOTHER

MIA
SHERIDAN

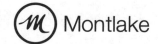

Text copyright © 2023 by Mia Sheridan
All rights reserved.

No part of this book may be reproduced, or stored in a retrieval system, or transmitted in any form or by any means, electronic, mechanical, photocopying, recording, or otherwise, without express written permission of the publisher.

Published by Montlake, Seattle

www.apub.com

Amazon, the Amazon logo, and Montlake are trademarks of Amazon.com, Inc., or its affiliates.

ISBN-13: 9781662509766 (paperback)
ISBN-13: 9781662508226 (digital)

Cover design by Caroline Teagle Johnson
Cover images: © Sidorenko Olga / Shutterstock; © LightFieldStudios / Getty Images

Printed in the United States of America

To my team. Grateful doesn't begin to cover it.

CHAPTER ONE

Reno, Nevada, the one place on earth she'd vowed never to return to. Unfortunately, that pledge had blown up in her face, an outcome that was an iffy mix of fate and her own emotionally charged decision-making.

Would you change it? Sienna asked herself for the hundredth time.

And for the hundredth time, she still wasn't certain of the answer.

Only . . . yes, yes, she *was* sure of the answer. She'd do it again if given the choice. She just hadn't anticipated the choice leading her *here*.

The cloudless desert sky—vivid blue and endless—stretched above as she pulled open the door to the police department before stepping into the blessed relief of the air-conditioned building.

"May I help you?" the woman at the front desk asked on a smile.

Sienna smiled back, though not quite as widely. "Sienna Walker here to see Sergeant Dahlen."

"Oh, hi! You're the new detective from New York, right? I'm Chelle Lopez. Nice to meet you. What do you think of Reno so far?"

"Hi, Chelle. Nice to meet you too. And I'm actually from Reno. Originally, I mean."

A look of surprise lit Chelle's round face. "Oh, well then, welcome home."

Sienna schooled her expression, even while a knot twisted in her stomach at Chelle's words, and she watched as the woman picked up the phone and let Sergeant Dahlen know she was there.

"She'll be out in just a minute."

"Great, thanks," Sienna said as Chelle picked up another call. Soon she was laughing at something the person on the other end said and lowering her voice as she chatted on what was obviously a personal call.

Sienna had barely taken a seat when a very tall, striking woman in her fifties with white-blonde hair in a spiky pixie cut entered the lobby, her eyes focused on her. "Sienna Walker?"

She stood. "Yes. Sergeant Dahlen? Nice to meet you in person."

The older woman, who was wearing a black pantsuit, a black shirt, and red high heels, moved toward her and shook her hand quickly as Sienna lifted her chin, attempting to see eye to eye with the woman and failing. "You can follow me this way."

Sergeant Dahlen led her through the station, buzzing with the midday activity of a busy police force, her long legs causing Sienna to have to hurry to keep up. They entered an office, and Sergeant Dahlen closed the door behind them. She gestured to a chair in front of her desk, and they both took a seat as she picked up her phone and asked someone to come to her office. Sienna did a quick sweep of the room, which was completely devoid of clutter and appeared as squared away as the woman who inhabited it.

She replaced the phone in its cradle, leaned back, and crossed her legs as she perused Sienna. "Your captain, Darrin Crewson, and I are both army veterans."

"Yes, he told me, ma'am."

"Ingrid." She paused, her eyes narrowing very slightly. "There's nothing I wouldn't do for my fellow brothers and sisters in arms."

Sienna nodded, her nerves tingling. "Yes, and vice versa, Darrin said." *If an icicle morphed into a person, Sergeant Dahlen is what it would look like,* Sienna thought. *Lovely in a cold, sharp way.*

Sergeant Dahlen—*Ingrid*—lifted her chin as though reading Sienna's thoughts and agreeing. "Even so, I don't need nor want a troublemaking renegade causing me headaches and unnecessary paperwork. I *hate* unnecessary paperwork."

"No, ma'am. I don't intend to cause this department—er, especially you—any trouble. What happened in New York was a . . . unique situation. I won't let it happen again." Her tone sounded *weak*, even to herself. She straightened her back, attempting to convey the message of strength with her posture where her voice had failed. Sienna had a strong feeling Sergeant Dahlen had a low threshold for weaklings.

The older woman studied Sienna for another moment, and she resisted the urge to squirm. If that was the look the detective sergeant used when she was interrogating a suspect, the department must have an insanely high solve rate. Anyone would crack under that glacial gaze. Her eyes moved to the window, and Sienna let out a silent breath. "We have a major staffing shortage right now in the Reno PD, so when Darrin requested the transfer, that made things a little easier on our end." Sienna resisted a flinch. "But," the sergeant went on, "Darrin also told me you're a damn good detective when you're not going off half-cocked and that any department would be lucky to have you."

Thank you, Darrin. For that and a dozen other kindnesses. "I'm going to do my best to live up to that generous description, Sergeant."

"See that you do."

Sienna turned at the sudden rap on the glass of the door, and a dark-haired woman opened it and peeked her head in. "Come on in, Kat," Ingrid said.

The woman named Kat came in, taking a seat next to Sienna. She had her hair pulled back in a tight bun, and her lips were red and full. She reminded Sienna of a Bond girl in a pantsuit, if a Bond girl would ever be seen in a pantsuit, fashionable and well fitted though Kat's was. "Katerina Kozlov, this is Sienna Walker, your new partner."

Kat turned, assessing her very directly but not unkindly. "Well, thank God the percentage of testosterone in this place just reduced another fraction." She leaned in slightly. "Ingrid being the biggest supplier of said testosterone." She shot a grin at the older woman, whose eyebrows rose slightly but who seemed otherwise unamused. Sienna fought the smile that would make it appear she was laughing at her boss's expense on the first day of a new job.

Kat held out her hand. "Welcome to homicide," her new partner said. "Call me Kat."

Sienna shook. "Hi, Kat, nice to meet you."

"All right, now that the niceties are out of the way, why don't you show Sienna to her desk and get her acquainted with the layout."

Kat stood. "Come on, partner. I'll show you the most important room in this building—the one where we keep the coffee."

Sienna thanked Sergeant Dahlen and then followed her new partner out the door.

The coffee lounge was small but adequate, featuring a corner kitchen area and a table off to the side, where no one currently sat. Kat picked up a paper cup and held it up to Sienna, her brows rising in question.

"Sure, thanks," Sienna said. Kat poured two cups of coffee and handed one to Sienna before turning and leaning against the Formica counter. "So what'd you do?" she asked.

Sienna let out a small, surprised laugh, then swallowed a sip of weak coffee. She hadn't expected the direct question right off the bat, though she knew well that rumors spread quickly among cops. "I neglected to follow orders."

Kat looked mildly disappointed. "Insubordination? Damn, I was hoping you had an affair with the chief or something juicy."

Sienna let out a chuckle that died a quick death. *If only.* "Well, it was a little more complicated but not very juicy. The orders I disregarded came down from the mayor."

Kat's eyebrows rose. "Ah." She was obviously considering that nugget of information. "So they did you a favor and shuffled you out of town before the mayor could demand you resign or be fired."

"They obviously don't call you Detective for nothing."

Kat smiled, nodding to the door and tossing her cup in the garbage. "Let me show you to your desk. We're going to be spending a lot of time together. If you decide you feel like telling me the details of that story, you won't have to travel far."

She followed Kat to their work area, the only privacy a flimsy partition, with two standard-issue metal desks just like the one she'd had in New York. She pulled open a drawer, expecting the squeak that followed. The familiar piece of furniture felt like one of the only things in her life that hadn't changed. *Welcome to Reno PD, Sienna.*

~

Sienna was surprised that the trailer park looked slightly less squalid than she remembered. Maybe it was due to the wash of golden light from the setting sun softening the ramshackle trailers and patchy grass. Or maybe it was because her memory had exaggerated the seediness of this place. Or *maybe* it was because at some point, someone had come along and tried to rejuvenate Paradise Estates Mobile Home Park—a true misnomer if ever there was one—and somewhat succeeded, even if minimally.

Perhaps a mixture of all those things.

In any case, here it sat, in front of her, the layout the same, though the girl she'd been, the one who'd grown up here, felt different in every way. Even though she was sitting in her car, staring out the window, she had a strange sense of imbalance as she looked down the rows toward the lot where she'd once lived, as though the world had shifted subtly beneath her.

Why were you pulled here? She'd found herself driving in this direction after meeting with her new boss and partner, without even really deciding to do so, almost as if by muscle memory alone.

The heart is a muscle too. Yes, and maybe that was the one she'd been using. She'd been raised in this trailer park. She'd left for school every morning from here, until the day she'd graduated high school. She'd had some of her happiest moments in this place and some of her worst.

She'd fallen in love here. Her chest squeezed as she turned her head to the right, gazing down the row where *his* trailer sat. Of course, it wasn't his anymore. Or his mother Mirabelle's. Someone else lived there now, she was sure. He had made it big. And though it had turned out she didn't know as much about him as she'd once believed, she knew in her heart of hearts that the first thing he would have done with the money he earned was to buy his mother a home. A *real* home, not housing made of plastic walls that swayed in any moderately strong wind.

At the thought of Mirabelle, she felt a pinching sensation under her breastbone and unconsciously brought her hand up to massage away the pain. She missed her. Still. She'd been the only real mother Sienna had ever known, her own an alcohol-drenched shell of a woman who had been generally unaware of Sienna's existence. The woman who had passed on her green eyes and her golden-blonde hair to Sienna and— thankfully—not much else had died five years before. When Sienna had learned the news, she'd felt little more than a passing sadness that might accompany the knowledge that any wasted life had ended.

She'd sent her father a check to help with the cremation costs and made a donation in her mother's name to a local charity that helped drug and alcohol addicts find recovery. It was enough closure for her. And while her father had very promptly cashed the check, she hadn't spoken to him since.

She'd left this mobile home park eleven years before without saying goodbye to either of her parents. The ache in her heart had only been for Mirabelle. At the time, that particular ache had been drowned out by a greater one, though, and it was only in the aftermath that she had realized her grief had layers.

She stared, unseeing, in the direction of what had once been her home. Her mind cast back.

~

Mirabelle pulled the door of the trailer open, wiping her hands on a dish towel. "Sienna? What's wrong, sweet girl?"

Sienna let out a quiet sob, allowing Mirabelle to usher her into the trailer, where she led her to the plaid sofa and sat her down. Mirabelle took a seat next to her, turning so they were knee to knee, and took Sienna's hands in hers, squeezing gently. Lemons and lilies met her nose, and the scent served as comfort before Mirabelle had even uttered a word. She took a deep, shaky breath. "I got invited to Amybeth Horton's birthday party, and my dad said he'd bring home some money so I could buy her a present, but he didn't, and now I can't go." Truth be told, her father hadn't necessarily forgotten. He'd likely never intended to at all or even thought twice about her request after she'd made it. He'd come home drunk that afternoon, and she hadn't "reminded" him, as it was best to steer clear entirely when he'd been drinking. He was mean in general, and liquor only enhanced that attribute. Sienna's face screwed up, the disappointment of having looked so forward to something, having been included, and then being let down—again—by her parents bringing all her misery to the surface. She couldn't go without a gift, though. That would be humiliating. The other girls Amybeth hung around weren't rich by any stretch, but they had more than Sienna's family. In every conceivable way.

Sienna wished she weren't so hyperaware of that, but she was fourteen, no kid anymore, and it was just her personality. She noticed everything. She always had. Not like Gavin, who was perpetually happy go lucky and didn't seem to care what anyone thought. He was observant, too, when he wanted to be, but his observations didn't seem to constantly hurt him in some way or another the way hers did.

Gavin wasn't currently at home. She knew that, and it was the only reason she'd come. She didn't want him to see her cry, but she'd needed a mother. She'd needed Mirabelle.

Mirabelle frowned, wiping Sienna's cheek with her thumb when a tear spilled from her eye. "Oh, darling. I'm so sorry." An expression flitted over her pretty face, part sadness, part anger, but then she set her lips together, tilting her head as she thought. "When is the party?"

"Today," Sienna said, taking a deep breath as the sharpness of the misery lessened. She still felt disappointed, but she was here, in Mirabelle's neat and orderly trailer, being listened to as though her pain mattered. She'd only come to her for comfort. She knew Mirabelle didn't have a lot of money either. She worked as the assistant to a magician named Argus, a kindhearted Greek man who called Sienna "Siennoulla" and brought home-made baklava to Mirabelle sometimes in a white box with a black ribbon, which Sienna and Gavin gorged themselves on until their stomachs were stuffed and their lips were coated in honey. Their show wasn't that popular, though, and barely paid the bills. But Argus said that the joy it brought to their audiences was worth far more than riches.

Sienna knew that to be a little white lie since he let Gavin, who was amazing at cards, play online poker under his name and split the profits, a fact they kept from Mirabelle. Sienna didn't like keeping secrets from Mirabelle, but she also knew that the extra money Argus told her had come from ticket sales and put into her earnings lessened Mirabelle's stress and allowed them to pay all their bills, even if there wasn't much left over at the end of the month.

Sienna was old enough now to know that the tricks they performed were just that, but she couldn't help watching them practice with pure delight in her heart and a gasp on her lips when an act went just right.

There was something enchanting and beautiful about the choreography alone when it came to a perfectly executed show.

"Today . . . ," Mirabelle repeated. Sienna opened her mouth to speak, but Mirabelle grabbed her hand and pulled her to her feet. "Come with me. I have an idea."

"An idea? Mirabelle . . ." Mirabelle pulled her into her bedroom at the back of the trailer. She let go of Sienna's hand and stepped up to a dresser next to the door. This room smelled even more strongly of lily of the valley, and her bed featured a quilt of yellow roses. Mirabelle opened the top drawer of the dresser and pulled out a small wooden box. She opened it and reached inside, and Sienna noticed a stack of photos, but Mirabelle covered them with her hand before Sienna had a chance to see who they were of. Her family? Mirabelle didn't ever talk about her family. She didn't have any pictures hung—except of Gavin—and she and Gavin never had any relatives over for holidays or anything else, but maybe she'd had a falling-out with them.

Sienna wanted to ask, but she also didn't want to invade Mirabelle's privacy.

Mirabelle brought something out of the box and held it up. Sienna blinked. It was a beautiful, delicate silver bracelet with pale-purple stones. "Do you think your friend would like this?"

Sienna's gaze flew to Mirabelle's. "Like it? Oh yes, but I couldn't—"

"You can, and you will." Mirabelle took Sienna's hand and pressed the bracelet into it. Without letting go of her closed fist, Mirabelle looked down, seeming to be considering what she was about to say. "I know I haven't spoken of Gavin's father," she started haltingly, meeting Sienna's curious gaze, "but he was not a nice man, Sienna. He was violent and cruel, and so I took Gavin and I left him."

"Oh," Sienna breathed. "I'm so sorry," she said, her voice small.

But Mirabelle smiled. "Don't be sorry, love. I'm not. Our life is better without him." But something shifted slightly in her expression, as though she wasn't entirely sure of what she said.

"And . . . and you have Argus," Sienna said, wanting to make the haunted look in Mirabelle's eyes disappear.

Mirabelle's worried frown transformed into a gentle smile. "Yes. Yes, I have Argus."

Mirabelle let go of her hand, and Sienna opened it, the bracelet catching the light and sparkling up at her. "It's not an expensive piece," Mirabelle said, her words rushed. "But more than that, it has . . . difficult memories attached to it. I should have given it away long ago." She stared at it, appearing troubled for a few moments before seeming to catch herself, her smile brightening. "It must be fate that I kept it and that it should belong to Amybeth. Let it make new memories. Good ones."

Sienna considered it doubtfully. It was lovely. And Amybeth was kind. Sienna would love to gift it to her, but she wasn't certain she should allow Mirabelle to give her something that—despite her words—looked valuable.

But if it was, wouldn't she have sold it by now? There were several times she'd seen Mirabelle wringing her hands, a worried frown on her face as she'd gone through her bills. "I—"

"Oh! And I have a box that will be perfect for it too." She grinned, pulling Sienna into a hug. "Say yes, Sienna, and you go to that party and have the time of your life. Nothing would make me happier."

Sienna smiled back, love and gratitude gripping her so that she could hardly breathe. "Okay, Mirabelle. Thank you. Thank you so much."

~

A little boy caught Sienna's attention, breaking her from the recollection that had tears burning the backs of her eyes. God, it'd been a long time since she'd let herself get so fully immersed in a memory. The child ran from the side of one of the trailers and ducked behind a tree, holding his hand over his mouth as though to keep himself from laughing out loud as three other children turned the same corner he had, each ducking behind a tree or the side of a porch. They were playing hide-and-go-seek. Mirabelle had never let them play that particular game. It'd made her nervous, she'd said, that one of them would hide somewhere and get trapped. And she'd looked genuinely distraught when she'd said it, so Sienna and Gavin had obeyed. At least while she was home. Sienna's lips tipped slightly, and she swallowed her emotion down as she watched the innocent game play out, the "finder" making the others howl with glee as he located them. These kids were young still. They lived and played with optimistic joy. They weren't old enough yet to realize that others would look down on them for where they came from. They weren't self-conscious of their secondhand clothes or their parents' broken-down car that would likely backfire in the carpool lane and make others nearby dive for the bushes in fear that a lunatic was firing a weapon into the crowd.

Sienna's smile melted as she reminded herself she'd be better served to stop projecting her own insecurities and cringe-inducing memories onto these children. Maybe they'd be strong enough not to define themselves by where they came from. Maybe their parents—though poor gave a damn about them. *Maybe they have mothers like Mirabelle and not like my own.*

She made a pained sound of frustration in the back of her throat, turning the key in the ignition and starting her car. She didn't have time for this right now, nor was it helpful. *Why* she had come here, she really had no clue, other than maybe to prove to herself she *could.* So, fine, now she had seen it, *faced it,* survived it, and she could go on with her life, knowing that though it now sat closer, it still had no real power over her. It was only a place. It did not live and breathe.

She turned her car, stomping on the gas so that her tires spun, and a billow of dust exploded in a grainy cloud behind her.

If it doesn't live and breathe, then why are you racing away as though it might find a way to chase you? But she pushed the whisper down, knowing there was no good answer.

CHAPTER TWO

"Nothing like jumping right in, I guess," Kat said as Sienna stepped out of her car, still slightly groggy. She had expected her body to toss and turn in tandem with the turbulent emotions churning through her system her first night back in her hometown, but instead, after unpacking a bit and eating a take-out sub sandwich, she'd fallen into a heavy, dreamless slumber. So when her new partner had called at 3:14 a.m., she'd barely had the wherewithal to locate her ringing cell phone on the floor next to the bed.

Sienna walked with Kat toward the empty street under the overpass where a couple of cops stood. There was a large building across from them that appeared to be a manufacturing facility and an empty bus stop on the corner. She looked up, to where a floodlight glowed brightly from the top of the incline that sloped to the underside of the highway. "The forensics team is already here. They're going to bag the victim up shortly, so I'm glad you'll be able to see how she was found. I called Sergeant Dahlen, too, and she's on her way but probably about half an hour behind you." Kat reached in her pocket and brought out two pairs of bootees and handed one to Sienna.

The two cops guarding the scene looked over their shoulders as they approached the base of the incline, nodding at Kat and looking curiously at Sienna. She didn't bother to introduce herself, instead heading straight to where the criminalists worked at the top, bending her head as the incline increased and the "ceiling" got lower. As they approached the crime scene, they stopped and slipped the bootees over their shoes and continued up to where three criminalists worked, two hunched over due to the small space and one kneeling in front of a woman in what appeared to be a wooden chair, the flat area at the top of the incline just high and wide enough to accommodate her in her seated position.

What the hell? A chair, sitting under an overpass? This victim had clearly been staged.

Sienna took it all in. The older woman's head was bent sideways, a gag in her mouth, eyes open, though downcast in an endless stare. The criminalist moved slightly as he used a tweezer to pluck something off her leg, and Sienna saw that the victim was wearing the short black skirt and white shirt specific to cocktail waitresses working at the casinos, although there were no defining logos or colors to help identify a particular location. If this woman had once been wearing a vest or another piece of uniform that would have helped in nailing that down, she wasn't now. As Sienna peered closer, she saw two small holes on her shirt where a name tag should have been pinned, but it had either been removed or fallen off. The woman's hands were taped together in front of her, though the tape looked loose and halfhearted, used more to secure the playing cards in her hands than to keep her restricted. *Odd.* Her legs were bound to the chair at the ankles with duct tape, and she had purple and red marks circling her neck. Sienna's blood chilled several degrees. She moved a little closer, tilting her head and bending down farther to look in her eyes.

Next to her, flashes went off as one of the criminalists shot a few pictures.

"Can you see the petechiae?" Kat asked from behind her, obviously knowing what Sienna was looking for—the telltale red dots in the eyes that indicated a victim had been strangled to death. Sienna nodded. With the combination of bright lights, the cool night air, and the adrenaline rush of coming face-to-face with a victim who had died a violent death, her clarity of mind had swiftly returned.

Sienna estimated the woman to be in her mid- to late fifties. Her dyed brown hair with two inches of gray roots was gathered in a ponytail that had mostly come loose, likely during the fight for her life. The one she'd tragically lost. Sienna noted her rough-textured, overly wrinkled, and sagging skin and thought there might have been a fair bit of "hard living" that had gone on. Her gaze moved to the woman's mottled neck. "It looks like a ligature was used," she said, noting the particulars of the marks.

"Yes." Kat gestured to a spot near the left side. "You can see here where whatever the killer used cut through the skin." It had barely begun to bleed. She'd been alive when it had happened, but not for long. Sienna hoped it had been a quick death, but either way, her suffering was over now. Still, sadness tugged. Whether quick or not, the woman had to have been terrified at the end. "Art—he's the medical examiner—will confirm."

One of the criminalists, a young woman with straight black hair and a large overbite that gave her a bit of a bunny-ish look, pulled the cards carefully from the victim's hands, peeled the tape away, and held them toward Sienna and Kat.

"It looks like her hands were bound to the back of the chair at one point," the young woman said, gesturing with her chin in that direction. "There's glue residue there and bruising on her wrists."

Yes, Sienna could see that now, pink-and-red mottling where she would have been restrained. "So why the hell did he untie her and put playing cards in her hands?"

The criminalist, obviously knowing Sienna didn't expect an answer, merely looked down at the cards, fanning them out slightly. "It looks like there's six or seven here."

"Can you turn them over?" Sienna asked. Had this victim won a game and enraged her opponent? The uniform said she worked in a casino, but she wouldn't have been playing at her place of employment. That sort of thing wasn't allowed while you were working a shift, and there were probably even rules for when you were not. No, if she'd been doing that, she would have been picked up on surveillance, questioned, and likely fired, the cards confiscated. Nothing slipped past casino security. Had she gotten off work and been playing cards with friends? But if so, why hadn't she bothered to change clothes? "These cards are a message," she murmured.

"Left by the killer," Kat said.

"Yes," Sienna agreed. "But why?"

The criminalist turned them over, fanning them out a little more. Yes, there were seven of them. An eight of spades, nine of hearts, jack of hearts, five of diamonds, jack of spades, ace of clubs, and two of diamonds. If there was some sort of message in the cards, Sienna didn't see it. Then again, she'd never been very good with cards. Anything other than basic shuffling and she was all thumbs.

If the cards were some sort of message or calling card, it wasn't one that was immediately obvious. At least not to her. "Do they mean anything to you?" she asked Kat.

Kat studied them for a moment and then shook her head. "No, but I'm no card shark. Except when it comes to Uno. That's my specialty."

The side of Sienna's lip quirked, but she didn't laugh. It never felt right to her to laugh in the presence of a murder victim's lifeless corpse. Other cops didn't always feel that way—in fact many of them went out of their way to crack jokes—but she knew it was a coping mechanism, and she didn't judge them for it.

"Bag them for us, Malinda," Kat instructed. "And by the way, this is Sienna Walker, my new partner," she said to the three criminalists, gesturing to them one by one. "Malinda Lu, Abbott Daley, and Gina Marr."

Sienna murmured a greeting. "Do you have an estimate on the time of death?" she asked Malinda, who was still the closest criminalist.

"She's only been dead for a few hours," Malinda said. She was very soft spoken and had a slight accent that Sienna couldn't place. "Rigor has barely set in. I'd guess four hours? Not more than six."

Sienna furrowed her brow, addressing Kat. "Who found her?"

"A homeless man who sleeps here sometimes. He was pretty wasted and got belligerent with the responding officers, so they took him to jail. I'll get another statement later this morning and see if he remembers anything else, but it sounded like he came up here, saw her, dropped his nightcap, and hauled ass to the convenience store a couple blocks away. This was all about an hour ago. They called us. There's no reason at this point to consider him a suspect. He could barely walk, much less haul a chair and a body up an incline while carrying a bottle of liquor." She gestured to a spot off to the side where a broken bottle lay, the concrete surrounding it wet with whatever rotgut had spilled.

Kat looked behind her, to the street below. "There's a bus that travels that street, and it would have had a direct view to this spot. I'll find out what time the last run is and get in touch with the driver. My guess, though, is that he killed her somewhere else and then posed her here."

Posed her.

"Why, though? Why sit her up in a chair?" Sienna murmured, leaning her body around the chair and checking behind it. Nothing other than some loose gravel. "Why not just dump her?"

"I don't know," Kat answered. "But it obviously wasn't to keep her comfortable if she was already dead."

"And why here?" Sienna asked, nodding down the incline. "It's weird." She looked across the street at the dark building. "What about a worker or someone there? Maybe they saw something?"

"I looked up the company, Armstrong and Sons. They make tools. But it's closed on Saturdays."

She looked back to the woman, a small shiver snaking up her spine. The cards in the woman's hands had been bagged, but she went over them in her head. Seemed it was a losing hand. The woman sitting cold and silent in front of her had been dealt more than one.

CHAPTER THREE

"Good morning," Sienna said, handing Kat the cup of gourmet coffee she'd picked up on her way in and kicking the door to the meeting room closed. Though it barely felt like morning, considering she'd only managed to grab a couple of hours of sleep after leaving the eerie crime scene and falling into bed just as the sun began to rise.

Kat practically grabbed the offered cup. "I knew immediately I was going to like you and that we'd be best friends forever and ever," she said, and Sienna laughed, setting her own coffee and the small, white paper bag containing cream, sugar, and stirrers on the table before hanging her purse on the side of her chair. She offered the bag to Kat, and they both removed the miniature cups of creamer and packets of sugar and began mixing them into their coffee as Kat nodded to the board at the front of the room. She had hung a photograph of the cards—front and back—but nothing else. "Ingrid will be here shortly. I'll get all the crime scene photos up in a minute," Kat said, tapping the folder in front of her. "And then I was going to start scouring the casino websites to see if I could at least narrow down the ones where staff wears a short black skirt and white shirt."

Sienna was worried those were the two basics for the majority of them. "We'll split the list," she said. If they could figure out where this woman had worked, they'd be able to figure out her name.

"Great."

She had to hope the ME had found something more to add to what they did have, which wasn't nearly enough but also wasn't nothing. Sergeant Ingrid Dahlen had met them at the crime scene earlier that morning and gone over what Kat and Sienna had already taken in about the victim and the props. Despite the time, the older woman had shown up looking wide awake and completely put together, as if she never slept and might have been sitting at her desk doing the paperwork she'd told Sienna she hated when the call had come in. She hadn't had any guesses about the cards, either, and didn't know what to make of them. But she'd volunteered to meet with the medical examiner first thing that morning and then let them know what he'd found. Sienna was eager to get started hunting down the person who'd committed this crime, but she was grateful not to stand in a chilled room with an open cadaver while the medical examiner pointed out all the ways she'd been brutalized. It was a necessary part of the job but one she'd rather read the report on. And if that made her a less hardened detective than others in her profession who were able to detachedly look at a dead body that had been alive and vital mere hours before, then so be it.

The door opened, and Sienna looked back, expecting to see the sergeant, but instead, a man in his early to midthirties with a short beard and wearing a janitor's uniform came in, wheeling a large garbage can. He looked up, obviously surprised to see them, bringing the hand not holding the garbage can up and removing one of his earbuds. "Oh, sorry. I didn't know anyone was using this room." He gestured to the trash can near the front of the room and then to another one near the coffee station. "Mind if I just empty those real quick, and I'll be out of your way?"

"Hey, Ollie, it's fine," Kat said, and Sienna couldn't help noticing the man seemed surprised Kat had used his name. Ollie put his earbud back in, wheeling his trash can forward, as Kat looked back at the folder of papers she had on the table. "Oh," she said, addressing Sienna, "the bus driver who drove that route yesterday will be in at eleven this morning. The last stop across from the crime scene is at eight p.m., so considering the time of death, it's likely there wasn't anything to see when he made the stop."

"And considering the spot where the victim was posed was likely chosen in advance, the killer would have known what time a scheduled bus would be driving by, right?" Sienna added.

"If he's even halfway good at murdering people and posing them, yes."

Sienna sighed. She hoped he wasn't very good at it, because that would make catching him a lot easier. "Okay. What other items are on our list?" When Kat didn't immediately answer, she looked up to see Kat watching Ollie, a thoughtful look on her face.

"Ollie," she called, waving her hand to catch his attention. At her gesture, he looked up, once again removing the earbud, and looked at her expectantly.

"You're a card player, aren't you? I've heard you talking about it with some of the POs."

He gave her a lopsided smile. "I play some blackjack on the weekends sometimes if my girlfriend wants to hit the casinos, but I only play for fun. Why?"

She tipped her head toward the board where the cards were hung. "Does that hand of cards mean anything to you?"

He looked to where she was pointing, tilting his head as he studied the suits, then shook his head. "The two jacks are a good start if you're playing poker, right? Or maybe the nine of hearts and the jack of hearts if you're looking to complete a straight flush . . . or is it a royal flush?" His brow dipped. "No, that's all face cards, right?" He shrugged. "Like I said, blackjack is more my thing, and I'm not even that great at it. Sorry."

"That's okay," Kat said. "And the suits of those cards stay in this room, okay?"

"Yeah, of course."

"Thanks for your help."

Ollie nodded, but his eyes were still on the board. "Gavin Decker," he muttered.

A spike of prickled heat shot down the back of Sienna's neck, and her gaze, which had gone back to the notepad in front of her, leaped to the janitor studying the picture of the cards on the board.

"Excuse me?" Her voice sounded strange, slightly choked. She cleared her throat to cover her reaction.

Ollie gave his head a slight shake, seeming to come out of a trance. "Sorry, sorry, I wasn't much help with the card suits, but the design on the back of those cards . . . the swans . . ." He reached down and lifted a small garbage can and distractedly dumped the contents into the larger one and set the empty can back on the floor.

"Yes?" Kat said, eyeing him speculatively.

"Yeah, so the design looked familiar, only I couldn't place why or where I might have seen it before. Then as quick as I questioned it, the answer came to me. Gavin Decker."

Sienna's heart skipped a beat. *That name again. That damn name.* And how the hell was it that it was being mentioned to her not even a full week since she'd arrived back in her hometown?

"Why does that name sound familiar?" Kat asked.

Sienna said nothing, letting them talk about Gavin Decker as though she had no idea who he was. And she supposed that—at this point—it was mostly true.

"He won the World Series of Poker two years in a row," Ollie said. "He's well known in Reno because he's from here." His brow wrinkled. "I think he might do some kind of security over at the Emerald Isle. Fans love to get photos with him and whatnot."

"Okay, so what about the cards?" Sienna prompted, making a concerted effort to regain her equilibrium. The mention of Gavin's name had just surprised her. And now that she looked closer, she could see that the design she'd thought was merely an intricate pattern of swirls was really the repeating picture of two swans, their necks positioned so that they formed a heart.

"Oh yeah, so I guess he had a tattoo on his wrist that he became sort of known for. Some company used the tattoo art to have a deck of cards printed, and they started being sold in casino gift shops."

Swans. Tattoo. She swallowed.

"So they're still sold in gift shops here in Reno?" Kat asked.

Ollie shrugged. "They're not as popular anymore, which is why I didn't immediately recognize the design. I used to see them a lot more, but yeah, I'm sure you could find them—maybe at the Emerald Isle, where he works."

"Okay," Kat said. "I'm glad you walked in when you did. Lucky timing on our part. Thanks, Ollie."

Ollie nodded, shooting a quick glance at Sienna.

"Hi, Ollie," Sienna said. "I'm Sienna Walker, by the way. I just started. Thank you for your help. If anything else comes to you about the cards, let us know, okay?"

He bobbed his head, beginning to push the garbage can toward the door. "Yeah, I will. No problem." He ducked out the door, and it closed with a soft click behind him.

Kat was writing something on the pad of paper in front of her. "We need to find out all the places in town where those cards are sold and see who bought a deck recently. Hell, maybe the perp used a credit card. Wouldn't *that* be a lucky break? What do you say we make a trip to the Emerald Isle after we meet with the bus driver? It seems like a good place to . . . you okay?" she asked when she looked up at Sienna.

Sienna forced a smile. "Of course. Yeah, that sounds like a good place to start. I'm just a little disappointed. I thought we might have a rare deck of cards that would serve as a bigger lead." And despite her being thrown off kilter for a moment there, what she'd said was true.

The door opened again, and Sergeant Dahlen walked in, a briefcase in hand, wearing a suit in a shade of pale gray blue that looked made just for her. They all greeted each other, and she set her briefcase on the table before taking a seat.

"Tell us Art had something for us to go on," Kat said.

"He still has several tests to run, but he took receipt of the body as soon as she came in early this morning and was able to do an initial report," Ingrid said, pulling her briefcase toward her and removing a brown accordion file folder. She unlooped the string holding it closed as she spoke. "First, cause of death was definitely strangulation. Art's best guess is some type of cord, as there were no rope fibers and it was thin but not as sharp as a wire." Sienna saw that Kat was taking notes, but she had never been a notetaker, unless it was information she knew she wouldn't have access to later and might forget or mix up the particulars. But some people wrote everything down. Her ex-partner, Garrod, had been that way too. At the thought of the man she'd partnered with for five years, a heaviness entered her chest. She missed him. He'd been a friend, a sort of uncle figure, and she'd become close with his family too.

She wondered how many surrogate families life would force her to say goodbye to before she was ready. And simultaneously felt a swirl of gratitude that she'd been gifted even one. She gave herself an internal shake. Her mind had only wandered for a few seconds, but she owed the victim her complete focus on this case. And time was of the essence. The first few days after a murder were crucial as far as solving the crime. And *God*, she wanted to solve the crime, not just for the poor woman who'd lost her life but because she was bound and determined to prove her worth to this department after what had happened at the last.

Ingrid removed a stapled stack of papers—the initial ME report, presumably—and began flipping through them, reading the details that might be relevant. "Art did find something odd in her clothing. I'll show you that after I go over the particulars of the autopsy so you're both in the loop about that." She paused, glancing at the paper and tapping the table with one french-polished fingernail. "She'd eaten recently. Steak, potatoes, and green beans. A more thorough toxicology report will be coming soon. But she had inhaled chloroform. There were traces in her lungs and also on her nose and mouth."

"The killer drugged her."

Ingrid gave a slight nod, continuing to read from the report. "She had bruising on her wrists and her ankles where she'd struggled against the duct tape, but other than that, no injuries, sexual or otherwise."

"So it could have been a woman who bound her to the chair and strangled her," Sienna said.

"Yeah, but it'd have to be one strong-ass lady to have carried her up the slope where she was found," Kat pointed out.

"How much did the victim weigh?" Sienna asked, thinking of the petite woman she'd seen earlier that morning.

"One hundred sixteen pounds," Ingrid said after flipping a page on the report.

"Slight, then," Sienna said. "And the chair couldn't have weighed more than a couple pounds."

"Kat's correct—it would have to be a strong woman," Ingrid said, "but I don't think we can be certain about gender at this point."

"Although," Kat pointed out, "strangulation generally indicates a personal connection to the victim. Anger. Jealousy. And the steak dinner? It could have been a date."

"Could be," their sergeant agreed. "But even so, it wasn't necessarily the person she went on a date with that killed her."

Kat made a clicking sound and tapped the point of her pen on the pad. She told Ingrid about Ollie and the design on the cards.

"It's a specific place to start, at least," Ingrid said. "But those cards could be sold in hundreds of places in the city." She pulled an evidence bag holding a piece of paper from her briefcase and handed it to Sienna, who set it between her and Kat. It was a piece of notebook paper that was creased as though it had once been folded in quarters. It was filled with writing, the penmanship neat and tidy.

"That was found in the waistband of the victim's skirt," Ingrid said.

Sienna leaned forward, as did Kat, smoothing the plastic covering the paper, and they began to read.

I was thirteen when my mother killed my father. She had to; there was really no other choice. You see, the man was a hateful bastard who didn't deserve to call himself Father. My mother had given him some amount of leeway, being that he had spent much of my life on the road, working as a salesman, and we didn't have to put up with him on a regular basis. And though neither of us appreciated his volatile presence or loathsome personality, we *did* appreciate the paycheck he dropped off before he, again, bent his tall frame into his car and drove out of town. He must have exhibited some measure of likability at some point because he'd turned Mother's head, but whatever qualities had originally lured her in, she never explained. In any case, I'd steer clear of him when he was home, lest he get it in his mind I had slighted him in some way and take out his aggression using his belt or his fists or, once, a cat-shaped doorstop that resulted in the complete loss of my hearing in one ear and a headache that lasted more than a month.

Mother fumed after that one, and though she didn't say a word, I could tell she was plotting his demise.

"Cat got your tongue, Danny Boy?" she would say when we were alone and I was particularly quiet.

"No, Mother," I would reply, sharing a secret smile. "But he did a number on my ear." And then we would laugh and laugh because, though we hadn't spoken of it, we both knew Father wasn't long for the world and that Mother was going to give him his just deserts at the first opportunity. She didn't need to say a word. I had seen it clearly in her eyes.

Kat finished seconds before Sienna and sat back in her chair. Confused, Sienna looked up at Ingrid once she'd finished reading. "Is this from the killer?"

"It could have been written by the victim, I guess, though the name Danny Boy says otherwise."

"Unless she was writing a story?"

"Anyway"—Ingrid took the letter contained in the clear evidence bag and put it back in her briefcase—"another piece of the puzzle. I'm going to search the database and see if I get any hits on missing women that fit her description, specifically ones that disappeared from work in the last few days, and any crimes that have similar elements. If we don't get any leads by the end of the day, we can consider doing a presser and asking the public for some help identifying her."

Kat slipped the notepad she'd been writing on into the folder in front of her and closed it, then slid her chair back. "We're going to compile a list of casinos where she might have worked based on her uniform, and then we'll be off to the Emerald Isle. Ready, partner?" she asked Sienna.

The Emerald Isle.

Where *he* worked.

As ready as she'd ever be, which was to say, not at all.

CHAPTER FOUR

Damn, it'd been a bitch of a day. Gavin tossed his coat over the living room chair, loosening his tie as he walked to the minibar and poured himself a generous splash of bourbon.

They'd had an upgrade on their systems, and everything that could have gone wrong had gone wrong. Not to mention he'd been locked away in a small, windowless room for most of it, which had done nothing for his mood. He took a much-needed sip of the alcohol, letting it burn down his throat. He couldn't remember the last time he'd required a stiff drink simply to relax the tension in his shoulders after a workday, but this one had been brutal enough to warrant it. He stood in front of his window, the top floor of his condo building providing a stellar view of the Reno skyline and the desert beyond. The last of the liquor was smooth going down. *All's well that ends well.* He set the empty tumbler on the side table next to him and rolled his neck, bending it left and then right. His muscles were less tight now. Better.

Of course, his mom would tell him he needed to find a good woman who would rub his shoulders *for* him so he didn't have to depend on a shot of bourbon or a good half hour in the sauna he'd had built into his bathroom to ease his stress.

Maybe so. And perhaps someday soon he'd get serious about looking. But so far, he hadn't met anyone he was interested in for more than a brief, uncomplicated relationship. If *relationship* was even the right word. He sighed and massaged the last of the tension out of his neck.

His mind wandered, the bourbon causing a pleasant fuzziness. The problem was, he compared all women to *her*. And they all came up short. Which was ridiculous at this point. He'd put her on a pedestal in his head because he felt guilty for what he'd done. Add that to the fact she'd been his first love, his first everything, and of course she was going to stand out. It was simple psychology, and he needed to get over it. Move on once and for all. Give someone else an actual chance to knock her from that lofty place she still held inside his heart.

He rubbed the bridge of his nose to ward off the dull headache he felt forming.

Jesus. Why was he thinking about her right now anyway? Gavin hadn't thought about her in a long time—at least not cognizant musings. "Stress induced," he muttered to himself as he turned away from the window, grabbed his glass, and returned to the minibar. A couple of drinks after a long day never hurt anyone. He picked up the remote control, turned on the flat-screen TV mounted to his wall, and collapsed onto his couch, where he sprawled, taking a sip of his second drink while sinking back into the buttery-soft leather.

He put his legs up on the ottoman in front of him and changed the channels until the news came on. He would have liked to have tuned into a game or something easier to zone out to, but there was nothing on. He tried to stay updated on current events in his city, though—in security, it was always good to know what was going on around you—and so the news would do.

"We go live now to a press conference at the Reno PD, where they're asking for help from the public to identify a woman found murdered last night."

Gavin swirled the last of his drink, his brow lowering as he looked at the sketch of the woman on the screen. She didn't look immediately familiar, but then again, she also didn't have any very defining characteristics. She was about his mother's age, a little haggard looking in that way that usually meant life had been less than kind or bad choices had been made consistently enough to leave a mark, so to speak.

Still . . . someone's mother . . . or maybe grandmother, sister, or wife. It'd be a kick to the gut to find out on the evening news your loved one had been murdered. He didn't think the police generally went that route unless it was a case they believed needed solving ASAP because others might be at risk.

The camera panned to the side for a moment, and Gavin jolted, pulling himself completely upright and blindly setting his glass on the ottoman.

It missed, dropping to the floor instead but not shattering on the thick area rug. He left it there, instead reaching for the remote and turning the volume up. *It can't be.*

The camera angle widened again, and Gavin stared. *Holy shit.* Sienna Walker. He felt stunned, as if somehow his very recent thoughts had come about because he'd *felt* her presence close by. He glanced at the news station logo, wondering if maybe he'd turned the TV to some national station and she was actually standing at a press conference with the New York City PD, where he assumed she still worked. But no, she was here, in Reno, standing among city cops, their uniforms ones he knew well because he sometimes worked with officers on some security-related issue or another. And more often than that, he had needed to call them to the casino due to some drunk and disorderly patrons who needed to be forcibly eighty-sixed.

His nerves were strung tight again, but he sat back, taking in the information the detective was presenting as she asked the public to call them about anyone who had gone missing in the past few weeks or days who resembled the woman in the drawing. Apparently, there were no suspects at the moment and no missing person cases that fit the victim.

He felt a little bit dizzy, his eyes trained on Sienna. Even with her hair pulled back tightly and her simple pair of gray slacks and white blouse, there was no denying her beauty. She'd been beautiful eleven years ago, and she was even more beautiful now, and he was honest enough with himself to admit that the stirring in his gut was longing. It hit him like a sledgehammer.

He'd never let go.

Even if he'd ensured she would never again be his.

CHAPTER FIVE

The bar was mostly empty, lighting low, "Fly Me to the Moon" playing softly over the sound system so it was nothing but muted background noise. Sienna picked up a fry, dipped it in ketchup, and popped it in her mouth as she turned a page on the initial autopsy report.

She'd gone over all the case details that afternoon, but sometimes something stuck out that hadn't before if you looked at a report or a piece of evidence under different circumstances and in an alternate location, and so she did that now as she ate alone.

The bus driver hadn't been able to offer them any information at all, and so they'd spent the afternoon scouring casino websites for pictures of uniforms and then narrowing it down to ten. They'd gone to each of those locations, but there were no employees unaccounted for, so that had been a dead end. Of course, there could be other workplaces—restaurants, bars, hell, *strip clubs*—where they wore similar uniforms, so it had been a crapshoot (no pun intended) to target the casinos first anyway. She couldn't help wondering how much demand there was at any strip club for a fifty-something woman who wasn't all that attractive, but decided to move on quickly from that particular line of question.

She and Kat had gone to the Emerald Isle Hotel and Casino, Sienna's nerves vibrating, but they hadn't caught a glimpse of Gavin Decker. She'd tried to prepare herself in case something within the establishment would prompt them to speak with security, but that hadn't been the case. There *were* a few of the decks of cards for sale that matched the ones that had been placed in the victim's hand, but when they'd had the manager of the gift shop check her computer, she'd told them that the only four decks purchased over the past three months had been paid for in cash. What were the odds? Sienna rarely paid for anything in cash anymore, and she figured most people were the same. "Not tourists," Kat had said when she'd voiced the thought aloud. "Tourists always carry cash for trinkets, to tip, et cetera." Good point, but unfortunate for their case.

They'd left with no leads but no sighting of Gavin Decker, a mixed bag in Sienna's mind. They'd gone to the Emerald Isle in person because of the connection between the cards and the head of security, but when the lead hadn't panned out, they'd thought it more efficient to make calls to the other casino gift shops in the area. Several of them carried the cards and were looking into the decks that had been purchased in the last three months using a trackable payment method, but that would take at least a couple of days.

Kat had mentioned talking to Gavin Decker to see if he might have any insight into the cards with the swan design, but that wasn't immediately necessary. The cards were sold all over the city. If they did decide they'd benefit from posing a few questions to Gavin, Sienna wasn't sure how she'd handle that. She'd probably have to tell Kat she'd once known him and let Kat take that job. However, if there was any conflict of interest, it was weak. She hadn't spoken to the man in eleven years.

As Sienna distractedly stuck another fry in her mouth, her gaze hung on a couple at the bar, their heads close together as the man said something and the woman laughed, crossing her legs and flipping her hair. Sienna didn't have to be a detective to recognize those cues.

She likes you, dude. I hope you're not a dirtbag.

She focused back on the notes of the case, pulling the copy of the writing found on the victim from the stack before reading it for what felt like the hundredth time. It disturbed her. Who had written it?

The killer? Had he planted it in his victim's waistband to offer a small glimpse into his life? Telling the investigators who would find it that he'd once been an abused child?

Or was it something else entirely? A piece of fiction the perp had written for reasons unknown? Or something, fiction or otherwise, written by someone else entirely—a friend of the victim? Heck, maybe it was something random the woman had picked up on the street that had no connection whatsoever to the crime committed against her.

But that didn't feel right.

No, this meant something. They just didn't have enough information yet to figure out what.

Sienna replaced the piece of writing back in the pile, then closed the folder. She needed a good night's sleep. She needed a clear brain. And hopefully a break in the case would come tomorrow.

After a day of no new leads, the press conference had been their best bet, but there hadn't been any immediate calls to the station. And so Sienna had headed out after a long, grueling day and, feeling unusually lonely, had decided to stop in this bar on her way home. She supposed she was homesick, even if, in a way, this was her home. Or it had been. But she was a stranger now, and that brought up all sorts of complicated emotions.

Sienna sighed, lowering her head and rubbing the back of her neck absently. But her head lifted when someone sat down in the booth across from her, and shock ricocheted down her spine. Shock and an odd internal stillness, just underneath the surprise. *You knew, didn't you? Somewhere deep inside, you've known this was inevitable.* She'd felt it like the far-off approach of a train—the horizon empty but the ground trembling faintly beneath her feet. He'd been approaching. All these long years, their collision had somehow been destined.

"Gavin," she said and was proud of herself for the steadiness of her voice.

"Sienna." They stared, two strangers who'd once been soul mates. And she'd believed, truly believed in her heart of hearts, that *soul mate* was not a temporary status.

"I turned on the news," he said softly. "And there you were."

As if she'd been *unfindable* for the last decade. She looked away. The couple at the bar was gathering their things, leaving together. She brought her gaze back to his and cleared her throat. "What are you doing here?" She swirled her finger in the air, indicating the bar they were sitting in. She didn't explain anything about her return to Reno. She owed him nothing.

He squinted off behind her, and she took a moment to study him more closely, her eyes doing a quick sweep of his features. He looked older, yes, but he was one of those men who got better with age. Of course he was.

She'd looked him up once a few years ago after several glasses of wine. She'd wanted to prove to herself that she was over him, once and for all. It'd hurt, but she'd survived. He hadn't been directly in front of her, though, nor in the flesh. She hadn't been able to see the texture of his skin or smell the woodsy scent of his cologne. This was . . . harder. And he still hadn't answered her question.

She'd opened her mouth to ask again when he said, "I went to the station to see you. I saw you leave and followed you here." He gave her a small, lopsided smile that reminded her of the boy he'd been. But that was also the boy who'd hurt her so profoundly. "I've been sitting outside in my car, talking myself out of coming in here," he admitted.

She did not smile back, tapping her fingers lightly on the table. "I see you were unsuccessful."

He let out a small chuckle but then went serious. "What are you doing back in Reno, Sienna?"

She shrugged. "I was offered a job."

He studied her for a few seconds. "That can't be all there is to it."

"It isn't, but it's also none of your business."

Something flickered in his expression, but she was too wound up by his unexpected presence to read it. "You're still angry at me."

A blast of indignation shot through her veins, and she leaned forward. "I'm not *angry* with you, Gavin. Why would I be? I don't know you. My life and my present circumstances are simply none of your concern."

He looked at her for a few heavy beats, and then a slow smile spread across his face.

Her brow dipped. "What's funny?"

"You're angry with me."

Sienna exhaled, sitting back and popping a cold fry into her mouth just to give herself something to do. Her jaw didn't want to work, and she practically swallowed it whole. The asshole liked her anger—it probably fed his ego—and so she'd take it away. "What do you want? A reunion?" she asked after she'd forced the fry down her throat, barely managing not to choke.

"Maybe." He paused. "But first, tell me about the cards."

"The cards?"

"The ones from your case. The woman who was murdered last night."

"I'm sorry, but I can't disclose anything to you about a murder still under investigation."

"You—or someone from the Reno PD—were probably going to question me anyway if you didn't come up with any leads to those cards, so why don't you do it now and tell me a little about them."

She narrowed her eyes. "I'm assuming the manager at the gift shop told you we'd stopped by earlier today."

"Your mind works quickly." He smiled again. "It always did."

She let out a slow breath, but her burst of anger had faded. Maybe he was right. Now that he was sitting in front of her, why not use the opportunity to question him about the cards? They'd planned to potentially do that anyway, so in essence, she'd already been granted permission. "Fine. We found several cards at the crime scene. We were later told that the design on the backs of those cards was originally inspired by a tattoo you were well known for during your poker days."

He paused a moment and then turned his arm over, pulling up his shirtsleeve to reveal the art on his inner wrist. Her stomach dropped even though she'd had a good idea what it looked like based on the card design. What *hadn't* been on the cards was the slip of lake behind the swans, the tree placement she knew well. She met his eyes. "When did you have that done?"

Gavin pulled his arm back, lowering his sleeve. The waitress approached the table and asked if she could get him anything. "A cup of coffee would be great."

She nodded. "Anything else for you, ma'am?"

"No, I'm good. Just the bill when you get the chance." Sienna wanted to be able to leave the minute she was ready.

"When I left Reno, I joined the military." He smiled a bit ruefully. "I would have started competing in cards right away, but—"

"You were only eighteen. Yes, I'm well aware."

There was that flicker again. "Yeah. Anyway, me and the guys went out drinking our first weekend off and all got tattoos. They got snakes, army insignias, leopards, and swords, and I got—"

"Swans floating on a lake. Pretty."

"Right. They still harass me over it." He smiled, and dammit, she softened. Not much, but she did.

She shook her head, the small smile she'd given him in return dissipating. She wasn't going to ask more about the *why*. It had been a pretty lake. There were good memories there, even if, for her, they'd been cast in hurt later. It was a happy part of his childhood. Something beautiful in the midst of ugly.

"I happened to drive by Paradise Estates the other day," she told him, and if he doubted the "happened to" claim, his expression didn't show it. "But I was heading east, so I didn't drive past the lake."

"Good thing you didn't," he said as the waitress showed up with his cup of coffee. She placed it down with a bowl of creamer and walked away before he continued with what he was saying. "The whole park has gone to hell. It's infested with drug dealers and even some prostitution."

Sienna let out a groan of disappointment. "God, that's a shame. I can't say I'm completely surprised, but I hoped . . ."

She didn't have to finish the statement. He nodded, obviously knowing exactly what she was thinking. *I hoped the people of the community where Paradise Estates was located would show some pride in the park they'd been gifted by a philanthropist attempting to beautify the area with good intentions but faulty logic and little understanding of poverty and human nature. I hoped they'd work to keep the park clean and well kept. Safe.* But that had been a pipe dream. Most of the people in the community barely kept their own residences livable. Why in the world would they maintain a park? They had no real ownership in either. There *were* a few people who tried their best to use the park as intended—an aesthetically pleasing, family-friendly location they didn't need to travel halfway across town to utilize. But it was an uphill battle that they'd apparently lost.

"Yeah," he sighed. "It went to ruin. Otis and Odette had babies, though, four of them."

Sienna's eyes widened with surprised pleasure. *Otis and Odette.* She'd forgotten they'd named their favorite swans once upon a time. But Gavin raised his hand as though she should temper her obvious delight. "Sadly, Odette passed away. They tried to save her, but . . ."

Sienna inhaled a sharp breath. "Oh no." Poor Otis. Swans mated for life. "Is Otis still there?"

"No. They moved him. I'm not sure where. The lake had become a garbage-filled swamp."

She opened her mouth to ask him more about the poor single dad but thought twice, pressing her lips together. How had they fallen so easily back into casual conversation anyway? She sat up straighter. "So . . . the cards. Who designed them?"

He leaned back, slinging his arm over the top of the booth. "The leader of my fan club."

"You have a *fan club?*" She tried to keep her brow from rising, but it didn't comply.

He grimaced. "Had. It disbanded when I quit playing—" He shook his head as if the very thought of a fan club pained him deeply.

"You *were* pretty famous," she conceded. "I'm not surprised you had a fan club. In fact, I was surprised there weren't pictures of you on the wall at the Emerald Isle—as an in-house celebrity and all."

Gavin laughed. "There were. I made them remove each and every one. Who wants to look at a mug like this blown up to three times its size?" He circled his hand in front of his face.

Lots of women, she supposed. It was a damn good mug. It always had been. Currently, from what she could tell, the waitress who had served them and another were discussing it in swoony, hushed tones as they stared at him from beside the bar. *Nothing's changed.* All the high school girls had wanted Gavin's attention too. In those days, though, he'd only had eyes for her. She'd believed then that he always would. She looked back at Gavin, and his eyes met hers for a beat, then two, before she again looked away.

"Anyway," he said, obviously noting her sudden discomfort, "I could probably dig up her name if you need it—the fan club president. She emails me once in a while. She still lives in town, as far as I know."

"Yeah, if you could send me her name, that would be great." It seemed like a dead-end lead, but no stone unturned and all that. "From what we can tell, the cards are sold in lots of shops across the city."

Gavin sipped his coffee. "I see them sometimes, but I doubt sales are anywhere near what they were during my poker career." He eyed her. "What were the suits?" he asked. "Of the cards the victim was holding?"

Before she could answer, her phone, sitting on the table next to her water glass, rang suddenly. *Main Squeeze* showed up on her screen, the name Brandon had jokingly programmed into her phone to identify himself. She snatched it up, but not before she saw that Gavin's gaze was lowered to where the phone had been. He'd obviously seen the caller's "name." Not that it mattered one bit.

Except that it was a private inside joke between her and the man she was dating. The man who'd called her half a dozen times today and who she hadn't yet called back. "Excuse me," she said, scooting out of the booth and picking up the case file. She couldn't imagine it would endear her to Sergeant Dahlen if she left an active case file on a bar table. "I need to take this call."

She walked toward the back of the bar, sticking the file under her arm, and answered as she ducked into the small, dark hallway that led to the restrooms. "Hi, Bran."

"Hey, babe. I just saw the news conference out of Reno."

"Yeah, it's been a whirlwind of a day."

"It sounds like it. A murder case already?"

"Yup. The body was found last night, and we hit the ground running. I was getting a bite to eat, and then I was going to call. I'm just finishing up here. Can I call you as soon as I get home?"

"Sure." He sounded a little disappointed, but whether Gavin Decker had walked in or not, she'd rather get home and talk to Brandon there than in a public bar. She owed him her complete attention, even if it was only over the phone. In many ways, their relationship had been put on the back burner while she'd been caught up in her own personal scandal and the subsequent fallout. "I'll be waiting. And hey, I miss you."

"I miss you too. Talk soon." She pressed end, then took a moment to stand in the empty hallway, where she took several deep breaths. She had this discombobulated feeling inside, as if her world were contained in a glass globe and someone had just given it a good shake so that everything she'd once known was still there but completely and utterly displaced. She squeezed her eyes shut momentarily as though that might set things back in order.

But the feeling remained.

She walked slowly back to the table where Gavin still sat, his gaze sweeping over her body as she returned to the seat across from him. His eyes were slightly hooded, his expression blank in that purposeful way of his. She shut the thought down. She had no idea what his "ways" were anymore. Perhaps she never really had. She pulled out her credit card and set it on the table where the waitress had dropped off her bill.

"I already took care of it," Gavin said.

She huffed out an annoyed breath. "You shouldn't have done that."

He gave a noncommittal shrug as though her opinion of what he should or should not do held little weight. And now her indignation was back. It seemed it had just taken a sideline briefly. She began gathering her things. "I have to get going."

"I'll need your information," he said.

"Excuse me?"

"If I'm going to email you the name of the woman who designed those cards."

Cards. Fan club president. "Oh. Right. Yes." She removed a pristine business card from the small stack she'd put in her purse from the box on her desk when she'd arrived the day before. He glanced at it, tapping it on the table for a moment and then sliding it into his wallet on the table.

Sienna slid out of the booth, hitching her purse up on her shoulder and grabbing the file folder on the table. "Thanks for your . . . assistance, and . . . it was . . . I'm glad to see you doing so well."

He looked both slightly amused and just a little irritated. "I'm happy to help. I'll get that information over to you." With a quick tip of her chin, she turned. "And Sienna." His head was turned to the side, but he didn't swivel enough to meet her eyes. When she looked back at him, she only saw his masculine profile—sharp jawline, straight nose, dark-gold lashes underneath a heavy brow. "I'm glad to see you too."

She walked hurriedly away. She couldn't read the tone in his voice, or maybe she just didn't want to try.

CHAPTER SIX

An email from Gavin appeared on her phone the next morning just as she was sitting down at her desk.

It was brief and to the point, listing the name and phone number of the woman who'd run his fan club and hand drawn the design that was on the back of the playing cards from the crime scene.

He'd signed it: *Best, Gavin.* And why that irritated the crap out of her, she couldn't exactly say and decided not to ponder.

Much.

It was still early. Kat wouldn't be in for another hour or so, but Sienna had woken at the crack of dawn, and even though that topsy-turvy feeling she'd experienced the night before had diminished after she'd gotten home and talked to Brandon, it was still there, not allowing her to fall back to sleep. She'd gotten up rather than lie in bed and let her thoughts run rampant, then gone on a run, which had helped clear her mind. Despite the early hour, she had decided to head to the office.

Was seven thirty too early to call—she glanced at her phone screen, where the email was still open—Lucia Pechero, Gavin Decker's number one fan? She copied the phone number, then closed the email and pasted the number into her keypad. If the woman was sleeping, she'd leave a voice mail.

But apparently Lucia Pechero was an early bird, as she answered on the first ring, sounding wide awake and exceedingly chipper.

"Hi, Ms. Pechero, my name is Sienna Walker, and I'm a detective with the Reno Police Department."

There was a long pause before Lucia said, in a much less chipper tone, "You're kidding me."

"Uh, no. There's nothing to be concerned about. I just have a question about some artwork you did a number of years ago that was printed on the back of playing cards that are part of an ongoing investigation."

"*Sienna*, you said?"

"Yes. Detective Sienna Walker."

Lucia Pechero expelled a long breath. "Okay, now I'm spooked. Last night when I got home, there was an envelope in my mailbox. Inside was another envelope, and on the front, it said, 'Sienna will call you. Give this to her, and only her.'"

A chill wound down Sienna's spine. "Did you open it?"

"I did, but only because I thought it was some prank or had been left at the wrong address. I wasn't sure what to make of it, and I had no idea who 'Sienna' was. Until now."

"What was inside?"

"Just a weird journal entry or something—pretty dark, actually. It's handwritten and sounds like a confession. I thought about calling the police, but again, I thought it was a prank or something."

Her pulse jumped. "Did you keep it?"

"I did, yes."

"That's great, Ms. Pechero. I need to pick it up. I'd also like to ask you a few questions about that drawing. Are you available now?"

"Um . . . I can be. I teach a spin class that just ended, so I was heading home to shower. But the letter's actually in my car, where I left it after picking it up from my mailbox. There's a coffee bar up the street that makes an amazing iced honeydew-mint tea."

"Sounds great. I can be there in twenty minutes."

Lucia gave her the name of the coffee bar, and then Sienna grabbed her purse and headed for the door she'd just walked through half an hour before. She shot Kat a text letting her know where she was going before she programmed her GPS and drove out of the parking lot.

The coffee shop smelled strongly of roasting brew and fresh baked goods. It was buzzing with rush hour activity, sleepy-eyed customers taking large gulps of coffee as they hurried past her, reminding Sienna that it was still only eight in the morning.

The woman named Lucia had obviously been watching for her, because she stood, raising her arm in a wave as Sienna stepped into the shop. Lucia was lithe and slim with wide-set eyes and a high forehead, and she gave Sienna a smile that held both warmth and a measure of concern.

"Thank you for meeting me, Ms. Pechero," Sienna said, hooking her purse onto the back of the chair and taking a seat across from her.

"Call me Lucia," she said. "And it's no problem." She nodded to two pale-green iced drinks with red-and-white-striped straws on the side of the table. "I took the liberty of ordering you a tea. They're seriously the best. But if you want something else . . ."

"No, this is great. Thank you." She took a sip of the drink. Sienna wasn't a big tea drinker, but she had to admit it was delicious, and she told Lucia so.

Lucia smiled distractedly, her expression melting into worry. "I don't need to be concerned for my safety, do I?" As she spoke, she reached into a gym bag on the floor and removed a manila envelope before sliding it across the table to Sienna.

Sienna didn't look at it right then, instead taking a glove and an evidence bag from her purse, slipping the glove on, and putting the envelope in the bag. She wanted to read the letter alone after this so she could focus on every word. "I don't have any reason to believe you're in any danger, Lucia. But if it would make you feel better, I can have a uniform car make a few trips by your home this evening and over the next few days. And if we find evidence that says otherwise, I won't hesitate to let you know," she said as she removed the glove.

"Okay, thank you. This is all just so . . . unexpected."

"I wish I could give you more answers. But right now, we're still gathering facts. Can I ask you a few questions?"

"Yeah, of course. About the design I drew for the Gavin Decker cards?" She gave a small shrug. "Those have to be the ones you were referring to. They're the only cards one of my drawings was featured on. And that was only because I was the president of his fan club.

"The design was inspired by a tattoo he has on his wrist," she explained, turning her arm over and tapping on the same place where Gavin's tattoo was inked. "I had a friend who ran a printing company, and he did a small batch for me just to use for giveaways for the fan club members and whatnot. I also sent a set to Gavin, and he posted about them on social media." A look came over her face that Sienna could only describe as adoring. "He's the best. A lot of women went gaga over him because of his looks, but he's the whole package. I started an Instagram page featuring all things Gavin Decker, and it blew up, so I formed the fan club." That adoring look increased, crossing over into the realm of *worship*, before she giggled softly. "He was always *so* generous to his fans, me included." She sighed dreamily.

Sienna figured the levels of hell were deep and full of suffering, and she didn't want to be overly dramatic, but watching someone visibly swoon over the ex who had broken your heart had to be at least one of them. "Did you have a lot of personal contact with Mr. Decker?" she asked, working to make her tone sound businesslike and casual.

"I *wish*. No, he was a busy man, and he traveled a lot in those days, but he was always great about replying online and making time to autograph items and send them. And then once he posted a picture of those cards on his social media, giving me credit, a company reached out and purchased the rights to the artwork. It was a nice little paycheck, and they sold well."

"Do you have the name of the company that bought them?"

"Yeah. They're called Mister Ace. They still print them, though not nearly in the same quantities as when Gavin was playing professionally."

Sienna typed the name into the notes app in her phone, then set it back down. There was no reason to speak to them immediately, but she'd keep their name just in case things changed. She thought for a moment. "Do you have a list of the fan club members who received those decks?"

Lucia squinted one eye as she thought about that. "I can forward you a list of the old members, but I didn't keep any information about who won the giveaways. I don't even know if their information would be current. It's been several years now."

Sienna reached in her purse and pulled out a card. "If you could email me that list, I would appreciate it. And if you think of anything else at all that might be helpful, even if it seems like nothing, please give me a call."

Lucia nodded, taking the card and looking at it before putting it in her wallet, which sat next to her drink. "I will. And if there's anything I should know about the letter, will you call me?"

"Absolutely. Oh, and one more thing—can I take that straw to rule out your DNA on the envelope?" Sienna asked.

Lucia stared at it a minute. "Oh. Yeah, sure." She plucked the straw from her drink and handed it to Sienna, who wrapped it loosely in a napkin.

"I appreciate you taking the time to meet with me." She picked up the tea and took another long sip. "This was fantastic. Thanks."

Settled back in her car, Sienna put on another pair of gloves from the kit in her trunk and brought the envelope contained in the evidence bag from her purse. She opened the outer envelope and slid the smaller white one from inside. The message, handwritten on the front, was exactly as Lucia had said: *Sienna will call you. Give this to her, and only her.* Which was eerie as hell, considering she'd only moved to Reno less than a week before. Why hadn't it been addressed to Kat or Sergeant

Dahlen? Who knew her name? Who knew she specifically would call Lucia?

She thought the writing looked very similar to that of the note found in the waistband of the murder victim, but she'd compare them side by side when she got back to the station.

She turned the envelope over, but there was nothing on the back. It had been opened hastily by Lucia, who had likely torn open the end and then dragged her finger along the top, tearing the seam. Hopefully she hadn't unknowingly destroyed DNA or other evidence.

Sienna slipped out the note and began to read.

A week after my thirteenth birthday, a stray dog had shown up in our neighborhood, and I'd been secretly feeding him on our back porch each morning before school. He was a shy mutt but obviously hungry, and I'd sit nearby while he scarfed down the offered food, one eye on his bowl and one eye on me. For the first couple of days, he'd slink away, but finally he began sniffing my outstretched hand tentatively, then allowing me to pet his head. It gave me a strange sense I'd never experienced before—the idea that I might matter to a creature I could hurt if I wanted to. It was an odd power to consider. But I didn't want to hurt the dog. Just the opposite—I wanted to care for him. I wanted to help him because no one else had bothered.

That day, before I left for school, I fed the dog I'd begun calling Jaxon, and he nuzzled my hand after his meal, his tail wagging back and forth as he lay on the porch to nap in the sun. I thought about Jaxon that day, wondered if Mother might let me bring him inside and keep him. I worried she wouldn't. Mother kept a very tidy house and liked things just so. Perhaps if I gave him a bath outside with the hose and brushed his black fur until it shone. Maybe then, Mother would let me keep him. I pictured Jaxon curled up at the end of my bed, keeping me safe as I slept, and at the image, that same unknown feeling wound through, glittery and warm. I bet you've experienced that feeling. I bet you've experienced it a lot. But it was new to me.

My stomach dropped when I arrived home to see my father's car in the driveway. I hurried inside, placing my backpack on the hook near the door just as Mother liked and lining up my shoes underneath. My heart had begun to race, my stomach lurching the way it did when Father arrived home from his travels, tired and hungry and, if business had been less than stellar, looking for someone to take his aggression out on.

I first went to the back porch to see if Jaxon was still there, curled up in his pool of sunshine. But when I looked out the window, no Jax. That's when I heard what I thought was a small, muffled whimper coming from the side of the house. I raced out the back door, rounded the porch, my socked feet skidding in the grass, a cry escaping my lips when I saw Jaxon, covered in blood, using his front legs to pull himself forward, his back legs splayed uselessly behind him as though he'd somehow become paralyzed.

Horror filled me and the world seemed to slow as I looked up, my father just feet away, a gun in hand, squinting through the sight as he aimed it at the wounded dog. I opened my mouth to yell, but my voice didn't seem to work, and only a terrible gurgle came up my throat. My arms reached forward, toward

Jaxon, who was looking at me now, terror on his face, his eyes beseeching me for help.

My father had tortured him. He was broken and half-dead, but he was still trying to crawl away. To escape. I knew what that felt like. I knew just what that felt like.

Something clanged loudly inside my head, black spots appearing before my eyes, the world rippling around me like an earthquake was erupting, but only in our yard. Beyond us, there was blue sky. There was stillness. And safety.

But not here. Never here.

The shot rang out, and Jaxon's upper body collapsed to the grass, blood pouring from the hole in his head, his body still. Lifeless. My voice erupted then, breaking through my horror, my yell piercing the stillness as all went utterly dark.

I awoke on the kitchen floor, my throat raw, my head pounding. "There, there." Mother's voice. "Take your time. You fainted, silly boy."

I groaned and pulled myself up, the room swimming as I brought my hands to my head and took a minute to get my bearings. Once the worst of the fogginess had cleared, I lowered my hands, opening my eyes and gaping at the scene in front of me. My father sat at the table, his arms and legs bound to a chair with duct tape, a gag in his mouth, and blood dripping from a gash across his skull. He followed me with his wide, glazed eyes as I came to my feet, looking at Mother, who leaned casually against the counter, a glass of lemonade in hand. She held it out to me. "Take a drink. It's quite refreshing."

I took the glass from her. Lemonade was my favorite drink, and I was very thirsty. I drank every last drop before setting the empty glass on the table and wiping the back of my hand across my mouth.

"Better?" Mother asked.

I nodded, my eyes glued to my father now, his expression changing. I had never seen him look scared or confused, and I was both mesmerized and afraid.

"I hit him with a shovel," she explained on a small, tinkling laugh. "A direct strike, and down he went like a bag of rocks." She brushed her hands together as though it had been no great effort on her part.

Then Mother pushed off the counter, crossing her slender arms over her chest, her red satin vest stretching over her bosom, the sequins on her short, black ruffled skirt scattering the light. Mother always kept herself slim and trim, and she had the figure of a swimsuit model. She sighed. "I couldn't take it anymore," she explained. "I'd had enough!" Father and I both jumped at her sudden change in tone and volume. Obviously neither one of us was used to hearing Mother yell or lose her temper. "The dog was the final straw."

The dog. Jaxon. A moan escaped me at the vision his name brought forth. His suffering. Mother wavered before me, but I fought to hang on to her, sucking in a big breath as she once again solidified.

She was calm now. Solid. As quickly as her anger had flared, she was back under control. Her patient smile returned, and she took the few steps to the table, her high heels clicking on the floor, and she picked up a deck of cards and let them cascade expertly and effortlessly through her slender fingers, the way I never could master.

When my father was away, my mother and I would play all sorts of games. Card games were her favorite, but we also played chess, checkers, and sometimes—if we had the time—Monopoly. She'd also underline words in my books to form secret messages just for me that Father would never find. Mother was a genius with games, and try as I might, I could never win against her.

No one could win against Mother.

"Danny Boy," she would tell me. "Think of life as one big game board. If you control the pieces, if you're a master of every move, you're a kind of god. If you decide to play, always, *always* play to win."

I liked the idea of controlling the board, controlling life, and creating all the rules. I had often pictured Father as a pawn, picking him up and placing him wherever I liked, moving him at my whim. Or maybe sweeping him off the board completely so that he no longer existed at all.

It seemed Mother had had the same fantasy.

And she had decided now was the time to make it come true.

My heart quickened, but this time not with fear, with excitement. My father's eyes darted this way and that, and a bead of sweat tracked slowly down one cheek, the trail of blood from his wound trickling down the other.

Mother ceased shuffling, placing the deck of cards on the table as she turned slowly before sliding a carving knife from the block on the counter and setting it next to the cards. Father's eyes locked on the items in front of him.

I watched as Mother sat, smoothing her skirt over her legs, the same placid expression on her lovely face. She picked up the cards and began to deal. Father's gaze shot to hers, and he attempted to say something through his gag. It sounded angry. He was obviously regaining his strength and his clarity after being hit upside the head with the shovel. His face reddened, and he shook his head, glaring at my mother.

"Tsk tsk," Mother said. "No need to get yourself worked up. Of course I'll set you free." My heart dropped. *"If,"* she said, "you win this game of seven-card stud." She gave him a saucy smile. "You might think I look better than I play, lover, but oh, you'd be wrong." I sucked in a breath, my heart lifting once more as she began to deal the cards.

Like I said, no one could beat Mother. No one.

Jesus.

Sienna folded the two pieces of paper, covered back and front in the precise printing, and returned them to the envelope, then dropped it all back in the evidence bag. She flexed her hands, now free of the gloves, and sat there for a moment, staring out the window. *My God.* This was clearly a continuation of the note from the murder victim's waistband. It'd been delivered to a person the writer of the note had somehow known would be questioned by the police. Which made some sense since he or she—no, *he, Danny Boy*—had placed in the victim's hand the cards that led back to Lucia. She bounced her knee, her mind racing. She supposed it would be easy enough to find out which detectives were working on a case and then address a note to one of them.

Her. There was no way this was personal. She hadn't been with the Reno PD—or in town at all for that matter—long enough for that.

What about the note itself? Was it some kind of confession? *What's the point?*

Her phone rang, and she grabbed for it, Kat's name on the screen. "Hi, Kat."

"Good morning. You got in early. What did the fan club president have to say?"

Sienna updated her on everything she'd just discovered, including her assumption that the suspect had learned the name of at least one detective—*her*—working on the case, and also the gist of the note. "There's a lot to go over and some information in the letters that might provide some clues as to who this guy is." The name Danny; potentially a man stabbed to death; his wife the suspect, whether convicted or not, if that was where this story was heading . . . the boy had lost his hearing after being struck in the head. Certainly, that would have meant an ER visit? All these potential clues ran through her mind as she started her car, heading toward the station, where she and Kat could go over the letter together and figure out the best place to start. The words Kat had said at the murder scene under the overpass raced through her head: *Nothing like jumping right in.*

CHAPTER SEVEN

"This is some effed-up shit," Kat said.

Sienna gave an agreeable snicker. "That's one way to put it. I started a list of potential clues as to his identity." She listed off the things that had gone through her mind as she'd sat in her car after leaving the coffee shop.

"We should definitely check into all of that. But . . . how do we even know this isn't complete bullshit?" Kat said, giving the copy of the note in her hand a flick of her finger.

"We don't. But until we know for sure, let's assume it's not."

Kat worried her lip for a moment. "Okay. So this killer was abused, and because of it, his psycho mom finally had enough and murdered his father? Is he trying to provide himself a defense?"

"I have no idea. Like you said, he could be toying with us. Or amusing himself. Who knows? But I'm going to get started going through the database looking for wife-on-husband stabbing victims. Whether he ended up dying or not, that would stand out."

"Unless she was bluffing and she never ended up stabbing him."

"He started off by saying his mother murdered his father, though," Sienna said.

Kat shrugged. "Maybe that was a tease to pull us in. I guess we'd have to know how the story ended. Anyway," Kat went on, "if she did kill him, she could have buried the body in the backyard."

Sienna frowned. "You're right. So there's a possibility his death—if it in fact happened—was never reported or discovered." She leaned over, picked up her phone, and added a note about checking missing persons. It might be like looking for a needle in a haystack. After all, she had no idea what year the man might have disappeared, *if* he'd disappeared, or what his description or age was. He could have gotten free and ended up murdering Danny Boy's mother. They could only go on what little they had. But if the note could be trusted, the man had had a job. Apparently he'd been some sort of traveling salesman. That could help as far as a missing person report. Maybe some guy had suddenly stopped showing up for work, and it was in the database.

In any case, all of this was an effort to lead them to the person writing the notes, the person who had taken a woman's life.

"Also . . . ," Sienna started, after she and Kat had split the list of potential leads they'd made from the note, "I told you I got the name of the woman who designed those playing cards, but I didn't mention where I got her name."

"I figured you found it online."

"No. I hadn't even started looking. I got it from Gavin Decker." Her nerves buzzed. She really didn't want to talk about this. But she had to. She owed it to her new partner to be completely transparent as far as the first case they were working together.

A small crease appeared between Kat's brows. "You went to the Emerald Isle and questioned him? Why didn't you tell me ahead of—"

"No. He actually found me at dinner last night." Sienna paused. "We have a past. I didn't mention it because I didn't know if he'd become a part of this investigation beyond . . . well . . . a few routine questions, but . . ."

"You're kidding."

"No. We grew up in the same trailer park. We dated. It ended badly, and I haven't talked to him for eleven years. So, you know, there's not really anything to tell, but I was going to mention it anyway and let you handle any potential interview if it became necessary. But like I said, he found me at dinner, so—"

"Sienna."

"What?"

"You're babbling like a guilty criminal."

Sienna let out a small embarrassed laugh. "I was, wasn't I?" She sighed. She hadn't told Kat that she'd once thought him her soul mate. She hadn't mentioned that they'd planned to marry and that he'd left her at the altar. Those details weren't pertinent, and frankly, she'd tried long and hard to forget them. "The truth is, it's a little strange for me being back here. I never thought I'd return, and for many years, he was the main reason for that. Now . . . I'm dating someone back in New York. And there's a good chance I'm going to marry him. It's not like I still have a thing for Gavin. But returning here is almost like this odd clash of past and present. I think it'll take at least a few weeks to feel on solid footing." She smiled faintly. She wasn't a secretive person. Sienna confided in those she found trustworthy, and she enjoyed deep conversations about topics that *mattered* far more than surface chitchat. She always had. But she rarely opened up to people quite as quickly. *This is an exceptional situation, though,* she reminded herself. Yes, she'd been thrust into a new job, a new partnership where they'd potentially be expected to entrust the other with their very life. And she wanted Kat to trust her, especially considering there would be an understandable cloud of suspicion surrounding her based on the circumstances of her transfer.

Kat's expression spoke of understanding. "I get it. Thank you for opening up to me." She tilted her head. "So why did he seek you out, and how did he know you were back in town? Oh, wait, the press conference?"

Sienna nodded, smiling distractedly at the way Kat connected dots a mere moment after a question had left her lips. "Yeah. Anyway, I took the opportunity to ask him about the cards, and he pointed me toward

Lucia Pechero, the *fan club president.*" There was a snippy tone in her voice that she hadn't quite intended, but Kat laughed.

"Dang, that's gotta burn when your *ex* has a legit fan club." She laughed again.

Sienna gave an exaggerated eye roll but couldn't help but join Kat in a soft laugh of her own. "It's not the ideal circumstance to have shoved in my face, I gotta be honest. You should have seen the woman swoon at the very mention of his name. I was sort of hoping for something more along the lines of him living in a van down by the river." She grinned. And damn, it felt *good* to make light of this with someone after being alone in her head with it for . . . well, since she'd accepted the transfer to Reno. She felt a sudden affection for Kat and was certain they were going to be not only partners but friends as well.

And because of the feeling, her world righted just a tad.

"So is it possible our suspect brought Gavin Decker into this case purposefully?" Kat asked. "The cards . . . and now the fan club president. *You.*"

"I don't know," Sienna answered, a strange twinge in her gut. "I just moved here, though. This can't be personal. If anything, it seems like it's been in the planning stages for longer than I've been in town."

She almost didn't notice Ingrid approaching them, but that would have been impossible, given that her boss was a six-foot Amazon with legs for days. Her smile slipped when she saw the look on Ingrid's face. "We might have a name for the victim found under the overpass."

"How?" Kat asked, standing, all laughter wiped from her expression as well.

"We just got a call from a bar slash restaurant in South Central. One of their cocktail waitresses hasn't shown in three days, and the manager caught the press conference replayed this morning. He'd assumed she was a no-show and written her off but says the sketch looked familiar."

South Central. Not the worst area in Reno but far from the best.

"I have a meeting with the chief shortly," Ingrid said, handing Sienna two pieces of paper. The top one had the name Reva Keeling written on it and, below that, an address. "That's where she lives. Her DMV photo is so old it's hard to tell if it's our victim." Sienna looked at the second printout, taking in the picture of the young woman with the vibrant smile and mostly unlined face. If it was the victim they'd found tied to a chair under the overpass, Sienna had been correct in her assessment about hard living. Because *normal* living didn't age a person this dramatically.

"At least we can do a welfare check since she hasn't shown up for work," Sienna said.

Fifteen minutes later Kat and Sienna pulled up to a ratty-looking apartment complex, garbage strewn along the curb. There was a skinny, tattooed guy smoking a cigarette leaning on a car in front, and when they passed by him, he whistled and called, "Damn, Charlie's Angels. I'm guilty! Arrest me. Take me into your *custody.*" He somehow made the word sound pornographic, pairing it with a lewd movement of his hips. *Charming.* He laughed, but they both ignored him as they approached the front of the building and headed up the outside steps to apartment 4b.

Sienna stood to the side of the window, and Kat took position on the other side of the door before reaching over and rapping loudly. "Reno PD," she called. There were some scuffling sounds inside that made Sienna frown and look questioningly at Kat. Kat knocked again, and they both leaned in as much as possible from their positions, listening. The scuffling sounds grew louder. Kat had opened her mouth to say something when the curtain was pushed aside, and Sienna leaned away from it, her hand going to her weapon but exhaling a breath when the face that peered out at them was that of a small child.

Kat took a step back, taking out her badge and holding it up. She smiled and gestured for him to open the door. His eyes were wide and scared, and he hesitated, but then the curtain fell back into place, and a second after that, they heard the lock disengaging from inside.

The child, a boy, was wearing Marvel pajamas, his hair sticking in all directions, his eyes rimmed in red as though he'd been crying. "Hi, sweetheart," Kat said. "Is your mom or dad home?"

The little boy shook his head, his lip trembling slightly.

"Is anyone home?"

He shook his head again.

"You're all alone here?"

He nodded.

"When did your mom leave, sweetie?"

"My grandmom left lots of days ago," he said, a small hiccup following the words. Sienna's heart squeezed. *Oh God, this little boy is all alone? For . . . days? Surely not.* She hoped to God the woman they'd found murdered under the overpass wasn't his grandmother, but if she wasn't, some monster had left this tiny boy to fend for himself.

"Is your grandmom's name Reva?" Kat asked, and the little boy blinked and then nodded.

"Has your grandmom left you alone before?"

His eyes welled up. "She leaved me alone when she goes to work, but not for this many days."

Her heart cracked. *Not this many days.* This small child shouldn't have been left alone for a few hours, much less an entire workday. "How old are you?" Sienna asked gently.

His eyes lingered on her a moment before he answered. "F-five and a half."

"What's your name, honey?" Kat asked.

"Trevor."

"Trevor, may we come inside? It's okay. We want to help you."

He looked briefly uncertain but then nodded, opening the door wider so they could enter. The apartment reeked. Of what combination of noxious odors, Sienna couldn't quite say—old food, dirty laundry, a pet of some kind? What she could identify was the distinct smell of urine coming from Trevor. He was obviously unbathed and had likely wet himself at some point. But even though the collective stink made her want to run for the nearest exit that offered fresh, clean air to fill her lungs with, she was grateful for one thing: it didn't smell like a dead body.

Trevor sat on the couch. It looked like he'd made a nest of sorts with three stuffed animals, a well-worn blanket, and the TV remote. The television was currently off, and there were fast-food wrappers and drink cups on the coffee table.

Sienna's eyes did a quick sweep of the cluttered room. Every surface was covered with *stuff*: piles of magazines, opened mail and other papers, a Starbucks cup with the name *Allegra* written on the side in black Sharpie, a bottle of sunscreen, a random tennis ball, an empty jar, what looked like a bracelet that had fallen apart, the beads scattered . . . *God*, there was too much *junk* to try to categorize. She didn't understand people who lived like this. Then again, she was currently using cardboard boxes as furniture, so maybe she shouldn't judge. Sienna's gaze returned to the boy.

"What about your mom or dad, honey?" Kat asked, taking a seat on a chair across from the little boy.

"I don't have a dad or mom, and my grandmom didn't never come home from work."

Oh no. Sienna's heart sank, and her muscles tensed.

"Do you have a picture of your grandmom, Trevor?" Kat asked.

The boy nodded and then jumped up and walked into a room beyond before returning just as quickly, a photo frame in his hand. He handed it to Kat, and Sienna stepped forward so she was standing over Kat's shoulder. The picture featured Trevor, smiling shyly, and his grandmother, leaning into the boy, one eye half-closed, an expression on her face that made Sienna think she'd been unprepared for the photo. An odd picture to put in a frame. But that fleeting reaction was quickly replaced by sadness. The woman in the photo was the same one she'd first seen dead and posed with a handful of cards.

Kat set the photo down gently on the coffee table. "Trevor, have you ever ridden in a detective car?"

His red-rimmed eyes widened. "No."

"Would you like to?"

He smiled for the first time, the barely there, thin-lipped expression from the photograph, and nodded. But then his smile fell. "Do you know where my grandmom is?"

"No, honey," Kat said. "But don't you worry right now. We're going to take care of you. You won't be alone here anymore."

Something nagged at Sienna, and she glanced around the room again before her gaze stopped on the coffee table where the photograph had been placed, along with the food wrappers. There was a clear plastic cup still half-full of soda and a few almost-melted pieces of ice.

"Trevor? Who brought you this food?" she asked. Because the drink had to be less than a few hours old, and the half-eaten burger next to it looked mostly fresh as well.

"The man," he said.

Kat and Sienna frowned in unison. "What man, Trevor?" Sienna asked.

Trevor shrugged, tears filling his eyes again. "I don't know. He brought me food, but he didn't stay."

Sienna's nerves prickled, and she glanced toward the door as though the unknown man Trevor had just spoken of might suddenly walk through it. But the door was closed. She looked back at the wrappers again, representing several different fast-food locations. He had to have been bringing Trevor food for days. Someone had made sure this kid stayed fed. *But who?*

CHAPTER EIGHT

Reva Keeling, fifty-four, had left for work three days before, worked an eight-hour shift seemingly without incident, clocked out, and not been seen again until she'd appeared upright in a chair, dead, and clutching a handful of playing cards.

Her boss suspected she might have gotten mixed up with drugs, as she'd recently exhibited some erratic behavior, and she'd become less and less reliable in the last few months. He looked slightly guilty when he admitted he'd been planning on firing her but had put it off, knowing she was raising a grandson by herself after her daughter had OD'd. "You'd think after what happened to her daughter, Reva wouldn't touch the stuff," the boss said. "But people are messed up."

Yes. Yes, they certainly can be, Sienna thought.

Before leaving work, Reva had used her employee discount to order the steak dinner they'd found mostly undigested in her stomach, canceling out the likelihood that she'd been on a date.

They hadn't been able to locate any family members, and so the little boy, Trevor, was currently in the custody of Child Protective Services. Sienna had dropped him off there herself, and her stomach twisted at the memory of the way the boy had resolutely taken the hand of the woman who ran the group home, his little canvas overnight bag hooked over his bony shoulder.

"Hey," Kat said, looking up from the paperwork in front of her as Sienna approached their desks. "How'd it go?"

"As heartbreaking as you might expect."

Kat nodded knowingly. "It gets worse. The victim's parents are still alive, and even though they're in their seventies, healthy from all indications, they've been estranged from their daughter for over three decades now. They live in Boulder and didn't even know the great-grandson existed, nor do they want a thing to do with him. 'I'm sure that boy's about as useless as his mother and his grandmother' is what the woman who answered the phone said, right before she hung up on me. As if they weren't her own flesh and blood at all. Cold, huh?"

Sienna made a huffing sound. That about covered it. Her job was full of heartbreaking stories involving kids, but each one still burned. Those cases simultaneously made her want to quit her job so the little faces would cease running through her head when she woke in the middle of the night and to do her job with a mad vengeance, to work until all hours of the day, to toil weekends and holidays, never taking a vacation lest she miss the opportunity to help just one.

Just *one*.

"I don't get people," she said.

"Be grateful for that," Kat answered. "The minute you start *getting* people like that is the minute you should lock yourself in your car and turn on the exhaust."

Despite the macabre statement, Sienna chuckled. She sat down at her desk, facing Kat. "Were the fast-food places able to offer anything?" Kat had taken an inventory of the fast food that the unnamed stranger had brought to Trevor over the last few days and gone to a couple of nearby locations while Sienna was making sure Trevor was situated.

"Nothing. Without a description or a time the guy might have stopped in, no one could tell me anything."

Sienna sighed. "I figured as much." They'd asked the forensic lab to rush the DNA and fingerprint report on the packaging, but that would still take several days at least. As far as which restaurant he'd purchased the food at, if the guy was smart and didn't want to be found out, he'd surely have gone to a fast-food place across town and not right down the street from the little boy he was mysteriously feeding. "Do you think the guy taking food to Trevor is the killer and was feeding him out of some sense of guilt?"

Kat tapped a pen against her chin. "Could be, but that scenario speaks more to a crime of passion. You know, lovers' spat gets out of hand; she dies; he feels remorse, panics, knows about the kid at home, and makes sure he stays alive until police find him." More tapping as her gaze moved upward. "No, Reva Keeling's body was posed. And there were no other injuries, except those made by the murder weapon. I don't think it was a crime of passion. There was purpose to her death. If it was a fight that ended badly, her body would have been hidden somewhere."

Sienna nodded. She agreed with Kat's assessment. And to add to it, Trevor had said his grandma didn't have any male friends, nor did he recognize the man who'd brought him food.

But if he wasn't feeding Trevor out of a sense of guilt or responsibility for the fact that the kid was alone and defenseless, then what was his reason? They'd questioned Trevor a little more when they'd first arrived at the station, but he hadn't been able to offer much. His description of "the man" was vague at best. He was not as old as his grandmom, closer to Kat's and Sienna's age, and he had brown hair. Or maybe black. Sienna was tempted to be frustrated by Trevor's inability to give them any additional details, but the kid wasn't even six years old, and he was traumatized.

"Forensics found her phone in her bedroom," Kat said as though reading her mind. "They're going to put a rush on it, see if anything interesting comes up."

"Do you think she just forgot her phone at home?"

Kat shrugged. "Probably. If she was getting high on a regular basis, she was probably forgetting a lot of things."

Like her grandson. For days at a time. And that was before she'd had the excuse of being dead. Sienna picked up the copies of the two notes and glanced over them yet again. They'd followed what leads they could but so far come up with squat. She looked at the photo of the cards that had been left in Reva Keeling's hand. They meant nothing to her.

What were the suits? Of the cards the victim was holding?

Gavin's question from the restaurant came back to her. She hadn't answered him because her phone had rung—and she'd considered herself saved by the bell, both because she didn't necessarily want to prolong their interaction *and* because she couldn't share information from an ongoing investigation. *Except . . .*

Gavin was good with card games. Some—like probably his *fan club*—would argue there was no one better. They needed an expert in areas neither she nor Kat was an expert in. Maybe Gavin could shed some light, if there was any light to be shed. Sure, okay, she didn't exactly relish the idea of seeing Gavin Decker again, but if it meant solving a woman's murder and obtaining justice for an orphaned little boy, Sienna was mature enough to deal with it.

"Kat?" Kat looked up from the paperwork she'd gone back to. "What do you think about asking Gavin Decker to consult on this case?" The look on Kat's face registered surprise, and Sienna understood why. She'd recently expressed interest in Gavin living a miserable life of poverty and shame in a van down by a river. "I could stop by his office in the morning. He might see something we don't in the hand of cards Reva Keeling was posed with," she said. "He might even see something in this letter." She held it up and gave it a slight shake. "I don't know," she went on. "I just have a feeling we're missing something. And he's extremely suited to provide insight we might be overlooking or not equipped to see." Not only had he been a professional poker player, but he was in security. And he'd been in the military prior to that, which must mean he had a security clearance.

"We'd have to get sign-off from Ingrid, but I think it's a decent idea. Especially since all we're doing is waiting for a lead to materialize."

Sienna stood, steeling her spine—more for herself than to prepare for her boss's response—and headed toward Ingrid's office.

CHAPTER NINE

"Gavin? There's a detective here to see you," Stef said through the phone speaker.

His hand paused and then took up again, finishing the signature he'd just been putting on the paperwork in front of him. "Detective Sienna Walker," Stef clarified, and Gavin let out the breath that he'd held momentarily, annoyed with himself at the reaction.

Get a grip. It's been eleven years. She has someone in her life. And she's likely here on business. "Send her right in," he said. Gavin stood and opened his door, waiting as Sienna rounded the corner from Stef's desk just a short distance around the bend.

She looked surprised to see him standing there but recovered quickly, her features rearranging into a polite smile. He did a quick sweep of her body. She was wearing formfitting navy slacks, a pale-peach blouse, and a short pair of heels. There was a briefcase on a long strap over her shoulder. Her hair was swept back again, and she looked both casual and fresh. Young, but not the girl he'd once known. She was a woman now, but the lines of her body and the particular way she moved were still familiar. As he watched her walk toward him, he recalled the feel of her beneath him in that old pickup truck that had creaked and swayed—

He pushed those memories from his mind, clearing his throat and stepping back to give her room to enter. "I'm sorry to stop by without calling," she said, holding her hand out. He looked at it dumbly for a moment before realizing she wanted him to shake. He did so, feeling slightly offended by her obvious effort to pretend they were strangers who'd barely met, even though he'd thought they'd spoken as people who'd acknowledged having a history at the very least in the restaurant a couple of nights before. Well, if "strangers" was what she wanted, that was what he'd give her.

"It's not a problem. I was just catching up on some paperwork." He gestured to a chair in front of his desk, and they both took a seat. "What can I do for you, Detective Walker?" he asked, his tone formal.

Her smile slipped the barest bit. If his eyes hadn't been focused on her mouth, he wouldn't have caught it. When he'd sat down at the restaurant table across from her, her eyes had flashed with anger, and he'd understood that. He'd abandoned the girl he'd loved, leaving without a goodbye. He had no idea how long she'd be in Reno, but he did owe it to Sienna to at least apologize and explain his actions, if she'd allow it. Her anger had given him a small glimmer of hope that she felt something for him. And maybe she was angry on the surface, but if she still felt any emotion at all, he had hope that something more was beneath it. He felt that same flicker of hope now. Apathy would have extinguished it, but Sienna, as much as she might be trying, was not apathetic toward him. "Last night you asked me about the cards the victim from my case was holding. I needed permission to consult with you about the details of the case, and so I wasn't prepared to share that information at the time, but I've received approval. My boss actually said the department has worked with you in the past on a few cases where the casino required police involvement. Anyway, I'm hoping you might be able to shed some light."

Gavin sat back in his leather desk chair, steepling his fingers. "I'd be happy to."

"Great. I appreciate that." She leaned down, opening her briefcase and removing a stack of papers. She chose one and slid it across the desk, faceup. He reached forward, only breaking eye contact with her once the copy of a photograph of a hand of cards was directly in front of him. "An eight of spades, nine of hearts, jack of hearts, five of diamonds, jack of spades, ace of clubs, and two of diamonds," he read aloud, his mind arranging and rearranging them in the way that came naturally to him. He felt Sienna's hopeful gaze on him, his brow furrowed as he considered. Dammit, he *wanted* to have something insightful to tell her. But he didn't.

"A pair of jacks is a decent start if the game is just beginning and you still have a chance to discard," he offered.

"What if you remove the jacks?"

"Then you better know how to bluff."

She gave him a wry half smile.

"Not much help, huh?" he asked, hating the disappointed set to her mouth.

"It's okay," she said. "You confirmed what I thought. There's not enough information to figure out what those cards mean yet, if anything. Hell, the suspect could have put random cards in the victim's hand." Her eyes flitted away and a frown tugged at her mouth as though she was saying that anything was possible, but her gut was expressing something different. He saw it. He knew it without her saying a word.

Gavin wasn't a detective. He was good at cards but not necessarily at puzzles. But he could read people. It was why—in addition to his skill with cards and numbers—he was a damn good poker player. He saw minor twitches. He noticed tiny flickers and the smallest intakes of breath, even in his peripheral vision. He *cataloged*. And he'd always read Sienna Walker better than anyone. At least once upon a time. Perhaps if that ability had changed as *she* had changed and grown, it hadn't been by much. Yeah, Sienna felt in her gut that hand of cards meant something important.

And she'd come to him for help.

"There's one more thing," she said, leaning down again and removing a few more pieces of paper from her briefcase. "It appears the person who killed our victim left a note, both at the crime scene and with Lucia Pechero."

Gavin's brows sank in confusion. "With Lucia? How's that possible?"

"I don't know exactly. It's not clear." She told him about the letter that was addressed to her and about Lucia's surprise when she'd called. "Did you tell anyone you were sending me her information?"

"No. And I sent that to you from my home computer, using my personal email address."

"Do you live with anyone?" He noted that she continued to look down at the notebook in her lap until he answered.

"No."

"Then it appears as if this person is somehow one step ahead of us, and I have no idea how that's possible unless this is all some elaborate setup. Can you think of anyone who might want to bring you into a police investigation?"

"No." He ran a finger under his lip, thinking. "I live a pretty quiet life, to be honest." Her gaze lingered on him for a moment, and she gave a nod before she reached forward, setting a couple of pieces of paper on his desk again.

Gavin took them, noting that they were copies of handwritten notes, the first short and single sided, the second two pages, both sides filled with the same neat writing.

"Do you mind looking them over?" Sienna asked. "I'm sorry I can't leave those copies with you—"

"I have time," Gavin said, picking them up and leaning back in his chair. From his peripheral vision, he saw Sienna pick up her phone and scroll through it as he read.

When he was done, he set the pages down and pushed them back across the desk. She retrieved them and set them in her lap on top of the notepad still there.

"What is this?" he asked. "Someone's diary?"

"Or a piece of fiction fed to us for reasons unknown. I'm not sure. I thought maybe the dog's name might mean something. Did anything stick out at all?"

"Jaxon?"

"Yes, but he calls him Jax in one spot." Sienna picked up the copies and scanned quickly to the place she meant, then read from the copy. "'I first went to the back porch to see if Jaxon was still there, curled up in his pool of sunshine. But when I looked out the window, no Jax.'"

"No Jax. As in . . . no *jacks*? Cards?"

Sienna huffed out a breath. "I don't know." She rubbed her temple, and Gavin had the desire to comfort her. It startled him. Not the need to offer Sienna Walker comfort from her obvious frustration but the strength of it. As if it'd been yesterday when she would have welcomed such a thing, rather than eleven years before.

But the fact remained that it had been eleven years, and regardless of the feeling's strength, it belonged to him and him alone.

"Can I see those again?" he asked, gesturing to the pages in her hand. She gave them over wordlessly, and he scanned the lines again, but there were no more numbers or card suits. He used the pads of his fingers to tap on the pages, going back to what she'd said about the dog.

"No jacks. Okay, so let's take a look at the remaining ones," he said, realizing why she'd asked him that question a few minutes before.

"I tried that, but the other cards are still meaningless to me. What about you?"

He reached his hand out, and she obviously knew what he was asking for because she handed him the photo of the seven cards placed in the order they'd been displayed in the victim's hand. Their eyes lingered for a few extra beats, and Sienna looked away first, watching as he took the picture, placed it on top of the other papers on his desk, and studied the cards. *No jacks.* So without those, the cards read: eight of spades, nine of hearts, five of diamonds, ace of clubs, and two of diamonds. Eight, nine . . . five, one, two.

Gavin looked up at Sienna to find her studying him. Her eyes widened, and she looked briefly embarrassed before her expression leveled.

"Eight, nine, five, one—if you're counting the ace as a one—two, is a zip code here in town," he said.

"Oh." She blinked twice, her gaze going to the side. "Yes. *Yes.* Where is it?"

"Over in Northeast, I think. Hold on." He opened his laptop and used a search engine to confirm what he'd said. "Yup. Northeast. It's a pretty big area, though."

Sienna was tapping her knee again the way she did when her mind was going so fast her body unconsciously attempted to play along. "He is, though," she said as if thinking aloud and only voicing half her thought.

"Giving you clues in the notes?"

"Yes." She looked slightly incredulous but also excited. She sat back in her chair, her knee stilling. "If it *is* a zip code the cards represent— which, it's too coincidental not to be, right?—then what the hell am I supposed to do with it?"

Gavin set the cards aside and went back to the note, reading through it for the second time. *Something* had stuck out to him, but he hadn't been thinking the way she obviously was—as though there were clues contained within . . . *whatever* this was. And not just clues using numbers but—"This," he said, tapping the line with his index finger. "His mother says, 'You might think I look better than I play, lover, but oh, you'd be wrong.' It's a phrase. In cards, you call a hand that looks better than it plays an Anna Kournikova."

"An Anna Kournikova? The . . . tennis player?"

"Yeah."

"Okay. So what does that mean? She looks better than she . . ." Understanding came into her expression, and she gave an exaggerated eye roll. "Well, that's rude."

He let out a small chuckle on a shrug. He agreed, but he hadn't coined the phrase.

"The real question is, What does that have to do with—" Her mouth made an O, and she went still. "There was a tennis ball at her house."

"Whose house?"

"The victim's."

"There was a tennis ball at the victim's house?"

She looked distracted as she nodded, picked up her phone, and punched in a number. Her knee started up again as she obviously listened to it ring, and Gavin watched her, his lip twitching, wanting to smile. She was clearly in her element, and an onslaught of something he wasn't sure what to call rushed through him: joy, relief, *rightness*, the knowledge that the terrible thing he'd done so long ago that had caused them both to suffer had been for good. He was sitting front and center, watching the result in real time.

He continued to observe her, living simultaneously in two separate decades—equal parts a boy and a man. Yes, what he was feeling contained joy, but there was sadness too. It had come at a price.

"Dammit, Kat," she muttered. She dropped her phone in her briefcase. "I have to go back to that apartment," she said. "I need to go get that tennis ball."

He handed her the copies from in front of him, and she dropped them into her briefcase before leaning over to zip it closed. "I'll come with you," he said.

"No. You've been very, very helpful, and I'm grateful. But this is police business."

"What if there's something at that apartment I can help with? Whoever this person is, he's obviously one step ahead. I'm not only an ex–professional card player, but I'm in security. Maybe I can spot something you wouldn't. Also, if this does have something to do with me personally . . ."

Sienna hesitated, obviously considering. "This might be a wild-goose chase. The zip code thing could be a coincidence, and the Anna Kournikova line might be nothing." But he could tell by the shine in her eyes that she didn't believe that.

"It might be." He paused. "And it might not be."

She hesitated a moment more, then stood. "Fine. Come with me and take a look around. See if you spot anything out of the ordinary. But you can't touch anything unless I say it's okay."

He stood too. "Yes, ma'am."

Gavin caught her small eye roll and grinned. "I mean it," she mumbled.

"I'll do whatever you tell me to do, Sienna. You lead, and I'll follow." And he showed her he meant it by walking behind her out the door.

CHAPTER TEN

Sienna dialed Kat's phone number, but again, it went to voice mail. She and Kat had split up so Kat could meet with the computer tech guys looking at Reva's phone while Sienna met with Gavin. She must still be with them. She shot her partner a text letting her know Gavin had spotted something in the note and they were headed to the victim's apartment. Luckily, she still had the key they'd gotten from the landlord. She'd used it to collect some clothes and accessories for Trevor once they'd secured a spot at the group home where she'd dropped him.

At the passing thought of Trevor, her heart gave a sudden pinch. She pictured him now, sitting in some strange place where nothing was familiar, little was comforting or safe, trying to process the knowledge that he'd never see his grandmother again, after he'd already lost—in some form or another—both his mother and his father.

Her grip tightened on the steering wheel. But she had to remind herself that it was better than sitting alone in an apartment waiting for someone who'd never show.

Yes, the knowing was better. Then you could move on. And she had to hope and pray that the adults who were now tasked to care for him would take their job to heart.

"How'd you end up in security anyway?" Sienna asked Gavin in an attempt to move her mind away from obsessive thoughts about children she'd done all she could for in her role and now must entrust to others.

He glanced at her, seeming surprised by her question. They hadn't spoken much on the ride, which was fine with Sienna as it had allowed her mind to go over what she hoped—believed—were intentional clues, but it hadn't been strange or awkward, either, Gavin using his phone to answer messages or send texts or whatever he was doing as he stared down at it, punching keys.

She was grateful to him and glad she'd put her pride aside and asked for his assistance. The Anna Kournikova thing . . . she never would have caught that in a million years, and it could have easily flown under the radar of even someone who knew card games well. And she had this *feeling* it was going to bear fruit.

"When I moved back to Reno, I needed a real job. I spotted the ad at the Emerald, and with my military background, it made sense," he answered her.

Interesting. She had some idea of how much he'd won in the tournaments he'd played. She'd heard passing numbers anyway. If he'd been wise with his earnings, he was rich. *Beyond* rich. She doubted he *needed* a job at all, "real" or otherwise. "I'd think you could retire early," she said. "Live the life of luxury. Sleeping in until all hours, lunches at posh clubs, afternoons at the spa, and swanky, caviar-laden parties until the break of dawn."

He groaned. "God, that sounds miserable."

She couldn't help the smile that tugged at her lips. It did sound miserable. Plus, Gavin had always been a hard worker. She didn't remember a time when he hadn't done odd jobs, even as a young kid—small repairs to neighbors' trailers, pet sitting, dog walking—and then later he'd worked delivering pizzas, anything to bring in a few extra dollars to take the burden off Mirabelle.

"What do you know about swanky, caviar-laden parties anyway?" he asked teasingly.

"Absolutely nothing," she said. "The crème de la crème of New York City don't consider public servants part of the elite." She stretched her neck out and delivered the last part of the sentence in her best hoity-toity voice.

Gavin laughed but then went serious. "You love it, though, don't you? Being a detective."

He'd posed it as a statement, not a question, but she nodded as she turned in to the parking lot of the complex where Reva Keeling had lived. *Past tense.* "I do."

"Where are you living right now?" he asked. "Did you buy a place?"

"No. I'm just renting. A condo over on Arlington with a questionably shaped cactus out front," she said on a short laugh. "It's not bad but definitely nowhere near *swanky.*"

Gavin chuckled. They got out of Sienna's car, and he followed her up the steps to the door on the second floor that had caution tape stretched across it. She glanced around as she stuck the key in the lock. It was too bad this apartment faced the side of a building and the unit directly next door was currently unoccupied. A nosy neighbor or ten might have come in handy.

Sienna opened the door, then ducked under the tape and indicated that Gavin do so too. It smelled just as pleasant as she remembered, which was to say it stank to high heaven, and she noticed Gavin drawing back slightly at the stench.

To his credit, he didn't complain.

"A kid lives here?" he asked, his eyes on the broken action figures lying on the floor.

"He did. He's with social services now." She didn't note his reaction but went for the tennis ball amid the mess.

She'd put a couple of pairs of gloves in her pocket, and she took one out now and donned it before picking up the ball. She shook it, but no sound came from within. It felt like any ordinary tennis ball. But now that she thought about it, what was a tennis ball doing in this apartment? This one looked brand-spanking new, so she doubted Trevor played with it. She knew very little about the victim so far, other than what she'd done for work and how she'd lived. But even so, the woman didn't strike Sienna as someone who had played tennis in her leisure hours or socialized with those who did. Peering at the ball more closely, she swore she could see a hairline slice that encircled the middle of the ball. *Holy shit.* If she hadn't brought the ball to a few inches from her face, she'd have never seen it. She gripped both sides and gently pulled, and the ball came apart with a cracking sound as the glue that had been used broke, one half held in each of her hands. She looked up at Gavin, who had stepped closer and was now staring at the opened ball in her hands.

"Someone cut it in half and then glued it back together," she said. She felt the speed of her pulse increasing, the way it did during a breakthrough in a case. *Excitement. Tempered victory.* She turned the two halves over so she could see inside the hollow shell and noticed the key taped to the inside of the left half. No wonder it hadn't rattled when she'd shaken the ball. She set the ball down and removed the key, then held it between her fingers and peeled the tape aside. The number 315 was written in black Sharpie on the head of the key. Sienna's eyes met Gavin's, and a prickle went up her spine. The zip code in the cards might have been a coincidence. This was most definitely not. Someone had pointed the police, and more specifically her, in this direction and then left what appeared to be a clue in the place she'd been led. Someone was playing a game. Leading law enforcement . . . *somewhere* for purposes unclear.

"Does the number mean anything to you?" Gavin asked.

"No." She looked around the overcrowded room for the second time, her gaze hitting on different items. The criminalists had been there earlier and taken a few more items—specifically, Reva's bedsheets, on the off chance they could find some DNA that might point to a suspect. They'd sprayed luminol for blood as a matter of protocol, even though Reva's murder had not been of the bloody variety. They'd tested and collected and done their necessary due diligence, even though it seemed unlikely she'd met foul play at her apartment. According to her grandson, Reva had never come home at all. On top of that, she'd been wearing her uniform when her body was found, which spoke to the fact that whatever had happened to her had occurred soon after she'd left work.

Gavin was looking around, too, leaning over this and that. She watched him for a moment, noting his curious and slightly troubled expression, though she didn't detect judgment in it. That wouldn't have necessarily been the reaction to this sty of an apartment from just *any* card tycoon who now led a security team in one of the largest and most posh casinos in the nation. No doubt he lived on the top floor in some steel-and-glass high-rise condo nearby and slept in silk sheets. Not that she wanted to think about what sheets he slept in, but the point was that Gavin Decker was a long way from those who lived like *this*.

That hadn't always been the case, although Gavin's mother, Mirabelle, had kept a clean and comfortable house. If Sienna closed her eyes and pictured it, she could still smell the strawberry potpourri that had sat on the coffee table and the lemon disinfectant Mirabelle had used to wipe her counters, humming sweetly as she did so. It was *Sienna's* trailer that had resembled the cluttered, dusty mess they were now standing in. And though Sienna had tried her best to keep things tidy, it was a fool's errand when one cohabited with those who could only be classified as—and she didn't think this was harsh or unfair, merely truth—slobs. Mostly, Sienna had tried to stay away. Being *gone* was better for her mental and emotional health than a temporarily clean trailer.

No wonder she felt so fiercely about the little boy who had lived here and now resided in a state-run group home. In many ways, she'd *been* him.

And if not for Mirabelle's influence, God only knew what would have become of her.

"Look at this cup," Gavin said, bringing her fully from her random, swirling memories. Sienna turned, her gaze landing on the Starbucks cup from the side table where the tennis ball had been, the one that said *Allegra* in black Sharpie.

"Don't touch anything," she reminded him.

"I won't."

"What about it?" she asked.

He bent closer. "There's no residue in it. It looks like it never held anything. I mean, maybe water. If it's been here awhile, I guess whatever might have been left could have evaporated. But it almost looks brand new."

Sienna leaned in, too, their heads close as she corroborated what he'd said. She picked it up with her glove, turning it this way and that. The number on the key was also written in black Sharpie. Sienna felt a twinge in her gut as an idea occurred to her. She set the cup back down. She'd bag that and the tennis ball before she left. Because she had gloves on, she asked Gavin, "Will you use your phone to see if there's a 315 Allegra Street at that 89512 zip code?"

Gavin removed his phone and did as she asked. He looked up after a moment, his gaze laser focused on her. "There is."

She let out a breath of tempered excitement. It might be something. But it might not. And if it *was* something, that something could be bad . . . or dangerous. Three fifteen Allegra Street. She took her gloves off slowly, put them back in her pocket, and removed her own phone. She dialed Kat again, and she answered, sounding slightly breathless. "Hey."

Sienna turned away from Gavin. "Hey, I've been calling you."

"Sorry. I turned my phone down while I was with the computer tech guys. I'm headed to my desk now."

Sienna wandered into the kitchen and stood on the other side of the wall. "I figured. Did they find anything?"

"Yeah, and it points to exactly what Reva's boss thought." Sienna heard a door close, and the echoey nature of Kat's voice became normal. She must have left the stairwell. "She was in regular touch with a dealer."

"Okay. Well, that could be a lead, right?"

"It could be, only it doesn't look like she'd made any specific plans to meet up with him the day she was murdered," Kat said. "The other thing that points away from the dealer," she went on, "is that if it was him who murdered her and then fed Trevor, why didn't he take the phone from her apartment? His information and specifics as to his line of work is all right there. He'd have to know that."

"Except her phone was in the bedroom," Sienna said, thinking for a moment. "Then again, if it was him who killed her, he'd know it wasn't on her person. He'd know to at least look around her apartment for it."

"Exactly. Anyway, I'll run him, and then we can bring him in and see what he has to say. What were you calling me about?"

She focused back on where she was, what had occurred in the last hour or so. "I have an address we need to check out. I have no idea what to expect, if anything. Can I explain when I pick you up?"

"Sure, that's fine. See you soon."

CHAPTER ELEVEN

"I don't even know what to think about this," Kat said after Sienna explained how she and Gavin had arrived back at Reva Keeling's house and pried apart a tennis ball that was apparently a prop left by the person she could only assume was the killer.

"I don't either," Sienna muttered, turning left where the female computerized GPS voice instructed her to. They pulled into a block of clearly abandoned houses and empty lots littered with garbage and likely used syringes. She spotted a mattress in one of the yards and looked away, choosing not to note the details of what was certainly a stained, infested health hazard.

"I'm glad we asked Gavin to consult," Kat said, her gaze focused out the window. "How are you feeling about that?"

"It's been fine," Sienna said. And that was true. Sure, his presence prompted memories to surface that hadn't in a long time, but she was a professional, and, per usual, when she was focused on solving a case, it tended to completely preoccupy her mind. Which was a gift and, according to Brandon, an annoyance. "And I never would have caught that phrase as relating to cards in any way," she said, voicing the thought she'd had earlier.

If Gavin hadn't recognized that particular wording, she wouldn't have pictured the random tennis ball . . . likely the apartment would have been bagged up, trash taken to the dump, and the clue would have been lost forever. She was still shocked about that. It was both eerie and confounding that the killer had placed it there for them to find. *Specifically, me.*

Sienna came to a stop in front of a dilapidated house, half the roof caving in and the front porch sagging. It appeared that the lawn had once featured desert landscaping—rocks and cacti—but now was weedy and trash strewn, the cacti nothing more than shriveled husks. Which went to show that sometimes even that which was right where it belonged withered with neglect.

Kat and Sienna got out of the car, squinting at the house for a moment, the lowering sun creating a molten halo. The juxtaposition was beautifully brutal, and Sienna got that strange tingle down her spine again as though someone was watching them. She looked around, but all was quiet and still. If people used this place, they did so once the sun went down and they could operate under the cover of darkness.

They both donned gloves and then made their way up the cracked pathway to the door, testing the portion of porch that looked stable before putting their full collective weight on it. The window to the side of the entry was open a quarter of an inch or so, and when Sienna looked at the door, it appeared the knob was new.

"Someone accessed the house and changed the front door hardware," Kat murmured, obviously noticing the same thing Sienna just had.

She held up the key she'd taken from the tennis ball and inserted it in the lock. It worked, as she'd somehow known it would, and she met Kat's gaze as the door swung open on a loud squeak. The person who'd led them here had installed new hardware, ensuring the key would fit this lock. The skin on the back of her neck crawled, and she looked behind herself. Wouldn't someone who had gone to so much trouble want to see his game play out? There was no movement anywhere, though, and few places within viewing distance to hide.

Kat called inside, "Reno PD. Anyone here?" They paused and listened, but no sound emerged, and so they both entered, Kat sweeping the entryway, Sienna behind her.

Kat called into the house again, but once more, all was still. There were shafts of light streaming through the uncovered windows, and surprisingly, although old and in need of about a thousand repairs, the place was free of garbage, and the structure and walls were intact, no spray paint in sight.

Perhaps the sagging roof and porch were a deterrent to those who might use the property unlawfully, when there were other abandoned homes nearby that didn't look as if they might cave in at any moment.

They went from room to room, clearing the whole house, and ended up in the kitchen at the back. The tile floor was grimy but free of cracks, only one brown cabinet door hanging askew. The busy floral wallpaper was peeling, one whole sheet slumped halfway over like a garishly dressed woman who'd fallen asleep while still on her feet but hadn't yet hit the floor.

Sienna opened a cabinet, the smell of musty captive air making her wince. Next to her, Kat was doing the same but was wise enough to stand at an arm's length as she did so. Sienna learned from her mistake and stood back as she pulled a drawer open and then another. In the bottom was an ancient-looking first aid kit. Sienna picked it up and snapped it open, but all that was inside was a bottle corroded with rust-colored liquid. She didn't imagine it was a clue—it looked like it'd been there as long as the house—but she'd make sure the criminalists gathered it anyway.

The other cabinets and drawers were empty. "Oh," Sienna breathed right after she'd opened the door to an old pantry. Kat stepped over, coming to stand next to her, and together, they peered at another piece of handwritten note, pinned to the inside of the door the way an old recipe might be. Sienna's heart picked up speed at the sight of the familiar penmanship.

She looked over her shoulder, and Kat whispered, "Did you hear something?"

Sienna shook her head. "No. It's just creepy as hell. He's leading us around, Kat."

She nodded once, picking up the note and depositing it into an evidence bag. "Let's get out of here," Kat suggested. "We can read this at the station."

"I agree. And we'll get a criminalist out here for a quick once-over." She had a feeling this guy was smart enough to wear gloves, but maybe they'd find a shoe print or a hair . . . something. Sienna felt *targeted*, and it was extremely off-putting.

They were back in the car a few minutes later and entering the station thirty minutes after that. Ingrid was out of her office, and so they used that room to spread the note out beneath the copy of the first. Sienna refreshed her memory with the final lines of the previous note and was suddenly back in the kitchen, where she pictured "Father" bound to a chair, a gag in his mouth. "Mother" had challenged "Father" to a game of seven-card stud, and Sienna had the distinct impression he was about to lose.

Father's eyes continued to convey a mixture of rage and confusion. He didn't know about the cards. Mother and I never played games while he was home, and I kept the boards and the puzzles and the decks of cards in the back of my closet under a loose board. The uncertainty in his gaze overtook the anger when my mother placed two cards down in front of him and herself in rotation.

She stared at my father, seeming emotionless, though I saw the flicker of fire in her gaze because I knew her better than anyone. Mother always played her emotions close to the vest, unlike me, who found it difficult to contain my feelings. "I like that word," she said to my father. "*Stud.* Do you like that word, Roger? No, of course you don't." Her lips tipped devilishly, and she raised her pinkie finger, wiggling it. My face burned at her insinuation. "It mocks you, doesn't it, Roger?" She clicked her tongue. "Poor pencil-dick Roger. No stud at all. Not even close."

Beneath his gag, my father let out a growl of anger.

"Danny, your father's hands are unavailable at the moment, so you'll need to handle the cards for him." I was slightly unnerved to get so close to Father, but Mother gave me a reassuring nod, and so I moved in close. "Those are your hole cards, Roger," Mother explained. "I realize you're at a disadvantage when it comes to cards. It irks you, doesn't it? But that's the way of life, right, Danny Boy?"

"Yes, Mother."

"I'll explain what you need to know to play this game, but I'm afraid the rest is up to you," she continued.

A spiral of delight swirled within me. Father was no match for Mother, and he was about to learn that truth. I wondered if it would be a painful lesson.

I hoped it would be.

The knife still lay on the table in front of Mother, its shiny silver blade reflecting the overhead can light.

She dealt him an upturned card—a seven of diamonds—and did the same for herself. I reached down, tilting the two downturned cards just enough to see that he was holding a ten of spades and a four of diamonds. Nothing. He had nothing. That spiral quickened.

I looked at Mother, signaling her silently using our special language of minute facial movements and subtle eye flickers. She didn't even appear to be looking at me, but I knew she was. She peeked at her cards and then picked up the exposed card—an ace of spades—and tapped it lightly on the table as though in consideration. "Here's the tricky part, Roger. I don't have any money because you're a miserly tightwad who leaves me nothing extra." She tapped the card again for a moment before her eyes lit up with sudden inspiration. I could tell the look was feigned, though. Mother was always two steps ahead of everyone else, though I had a special way of reading her. "How about we gamble with your *skin*!"

Father made a muffled growling sound beneath his gag.

"His skin, Mother?"

"That's right, Danny Boy." She picked up the knife. "If I win, I get to put a hole in it. If he wins, I don't."

Father made a strange howling sound that we both ignored. I was beginning to understand the game she was playing, and though the thrill increased, so did a knot of anxiety.

I breathed through it. All I had to do was relax and leave this all up to Mother.

"Ante up, Roger," Mother instructed calmly. Mother was bending the rules. In seven-card stud, players ante up before the hole cards are dealt. But Father didn't know that, and I certainly wasn't going to clue him in. Why would I? He had never played fair, and neither would I. Instead, I understood what Mother wanted of me, and so I turned the cards over, showing his lack of anything of substance. A losing hand. Mother tsked, turning over her own hand. She had two queens and three twos, the highest possible hand.

"I win," she announced, and then quick as a whip, she picked the knife up, raised her hand high, and stabbed it into my father's breastbone before pulling it out swiftly on a wet sucking sound.

Beneath his gag, my father screamed, leaning his head back as far as possible and making the chair dance and clack loudly on the tile floor. I stared, mesmerized as blood gushed from his chest wound. *I win.*

"That's for Jaxon," I whispered.

My mother looked at me, a sweet smile on her lips, pride in her face. "That's right, Danny Boy. That's for Jaxon. And we've only just started. There are still so many hands to play."

And with that, she began humming sweetly as she dealt another hand. As it turned out, my father was shit at seven-card stud. With each losing hand, his screams and howls turned more to whimpers, his head lolling on his neck as blood puddled on the floor beneath his chair, weeping from the holes in his skin. They were everywhere, those holes. On his arms and his neck. Over his stomach and across his chest.

"Should we allow him to die and put him out of his misery, Danny Boy?" Mother asked. She'd poured herself a glass of lemonade in the middle of a hand, and she took a long sip—appearing as cool as that frosty glass—as I considered her question. It seemed to me Father was mostly dead already. We certainly couldn't call an ambulance for him, so what else could we do but finish him off and bury his body in the

backyard or maybe drive him to the dump and off-
load him like the refuse he was? I suddenly felt so
tired, and my head was pounding.

"It's okay, Danny Boy," my mother said. She had
obviously noticed my fatigue, and she was understanding of it. Mother knew me as well as I knew
myself. "You rest, my darling. Put your head down on
the table and let me finish this."

I did as Mother said. I always minded Mother.

Sienna finished first, and she covered her mouth with her hand.
What if this is all true? Kat was done reading a moment later and did
the same, looking over at Sienna. "She killed him. Just like we thought.
That crazy bitch killed his father, whose name is *Roger*, by the way, not
that that helps a lot at this point."

Sienna bit at the inside of her cheek as she considered. "Is it possible
that the fact Reva left her grandson alone for hours if not days at a time
is this guy's motive?" she asked, gesturing toward the note. "He might
have found out somehow and . . . related to this kid? I realize Trevor
was more neglected, while Danny Boy was physically abused, but to his
mind, they might not be that different?"

"Or maybe he saw the neglect as a natural progression to abuse
down the line," Kat said, picking up Sienna's musings effortlessly as
she nodded.

"Okay," Sienna went on, "so he decides to kill her before she can do
her grandson any more damage. Then he realizes the kid might not be
discovered for a while, so he takes him food." She paused for a moment.
"It makes some sense as a theory."

"Yeah, I mean, think of all the things that could have happened to
that little kid left alone like that," Kat said. "The ways he could have
been hurt. Or victimized. Between you and me, maybe he's better off
where he is. At least he has adult supervision now."

"Between you and me," Sienna repeated, worrying her lip. She understood the base need to do something to protect the unprotected when no one else would. She could relate to that sort of helplessness, and the thought was troubling.

"And it's still just a theory anyway," Kat said.

Sienna paused. Yes, and that was their job—to *theorize*. She'd related to other criminals before to one degree or another, and she was sure Kat had as well. Some criminals were pure evil, but most of them were not, and it was the humanity that still existed within them that made their job—and law enforcement in general—filled with so many moral dilemmas.

Relating to aspects of certain crimes could be difficult and even emotionally crushing, but Sienna had to believe that that was what made her good at her job. She had an ability to put herself in a person's shoes—for better or worse—and figure out who they *were* so she could figure out what they'd done. And why.

"That theoretical motive might seem halfway understandable," Sienna said, "but sane people don't murder women. Sane people call the police when they have information regarding a child's abuse or neglect."

"So . . . he's not exactly sane but not so crazy that he doesn't feel some sense of twisted remorse. So that's why he's writing his personal tale of woe out for us. It's an attempt to assuage his guilt or explain why he is the way he is. His mother taught him everything he knows."

Sienna nodded distractedly. "Yes. But if that were the case, he wouldn't bother with all the games. The posing of his victim. No, he's enjoying this. He's probably even watching us," she said, thinking of the strange prickles that had gone up her spine when she'd gone to see Lucia Pechero at the coffee shop and then when she'd been at the abandoned house with Kat.

"So what should we expect next? Is this the end of his story?"

Sienna's phone lit up with a text, and she glanced at it. *Gavin*. Her heart gave an odd quiver. "One sec," she murmured to Kat, opening the message.

Just checking in. Did anything come from that address on
Allegra?

She sent a quick reply, not liking her reaction to his name on her
phone.

Yes. We found another installment. I'll follow up tomorrow.
Heading home soon.

Sienna set her phone down, glancing at Danny Boy's note and
forcing her focus back to the topic at hand. "It seems like it could be
the end of his story," she said, picking up the conversation where it'd
been interrupted. "But I think we should assume it's not and look for
the same types of clues in this letter that he put in the last." She made
eye contact with Kat. "I feel like he's one step ahead of us. How do we
get one step ahead of him?"

"For now? I think we have to follow along as he leads the way and
hope that he messes up and accidentally reveals himself." Kat's shoulders
rose and fell as she took in a deep breath. "However, a profile could
help. There's a guy who's really good, and the department has used him
in the past. He's a professor at the University of Nevada. I'll ask Ingrid
if she wants to see if he's available."

"Sounds good," Sienna said as they both stood, Kat placing the
note they'd just read into an evidence bag so forensics could process it.

"I'll make a copy of this," she said. "You and I will see if we can
make anything of it in the morning when we've gotten some sleep." She
yawned, and Sienna realized how exhausted she was too. It had been
another long damn day.

CHAPTER TWELVE

Sienna pulled into her driveway, giving a small startle as a dark shadow stepped into the light. She relaxed the muscles she'd just tensed, turning off the ignition. *Gavin. A pizza in hand. What the hell?*

She got out of her car, hefting her briefcase over her shoulder as she nodded to the phallic cactus next to the walkway, the pink flower on top sprouting in a way that made it especially . . . suggestive, if not downright lewd. "I suppose that's how you found me."

He grinned. "Arlington is a short street." He inclined his head toward the plant. "And that's quite the eye-catcher."

She suppressed a smile. "You shouldn't pop out of nowhere in front of someone who carries a weapon," she advised.

"Even if I pop out carrying pizza?" he asked, holding the box out in front of him with two hands as though presenting a case of jewels.

And frankly, at the moment, to her, it felt just as valuable. She hadn't eaten all day. The scent of melted cheese and tomato sauce wafted up to her, and Sienna's stomach growled, completely giving her away.

"Mushroom and olive, right?" Gavin asked.

"You don't play fair," she mumbled. "Also, this isn't really appropriate, you know." She scooted past him and the smell of the mouthwatering food he was holding.

"Why not?"

Sienna removed her key. "You're a consultant on my case."

"So?" he asked as she inserted the key in her lock. "Me being a consultant on your case practically makes us work partners," he went on. "You don't catch a meal now and then with coworkers?"

"Also, you showed up uninvited. At my home."

"With pizza," he repeated. "You sounded hungry on the phone."

She let out a short laugh and rolled her eyes. "It was a one-line text."

He shrugged. "I'm good at reading between the lines."

"Ha." She opened the door and then turned toward him, glancing at the pizza again. "Fine. Come in. But only because you're carrying food and I am actually starving."

Gavin grinned triumphantly, and that damn grin simultaneously made her heart do a weird flip-flop and made her grit her teeth in annoyance. She turned away from it, from him, and he entered the condo behind her as she flicked on the hall light and the overhead chandelier in the front room. Their feet echoed as they walked, Gavin following Sienna down the hall and into the kitchen, located at the back of the condo. The overhead lights flooded the space with a warm glow, and he stood in the doorway for a moment, glancing around. "I see you haven't unpacked yet," he said, nodding to the few boxes on the floor near the back door.

She shrugged, placing her briefcase on the end of the counter. "I was sort of thrown straight into the thick of things the moment I arrived," she said. And though she'd meant workwise, she realized that what she'd said probably covered the fact that Gavin Decker was standing in her condo too.

He set the pizza on the counter near where he was standing. "Plates? And would you have it any other way?"

Sienna opened a cabinet and pulled two paper plates from a stack, then grabbed the roll of paper towels near the sink. "Being thrown straight into the thick of things?" She shrugged, her lips tilting as she handed him the plates. "I guess not. I'm good at it," she said. "Unraveling clues."

"I know you are," he said, putting a large slice of pizza on a plate before handing it back. "You're right where you're supposed to be." He looked at her meaningfully, but she chose not to address that because frankly, though she did love being in the thick of things workwise, in every other way she still felt only half on solid ground. If she were right where she were meant to be, then surely she wouldn't feel so unsettled. She lifted the pizza and took a big bite, closing her eyes as she chewed. "Oh, thank you, Jesus, for pizza," she said, and he chuckled.

"I don't have a lot in the way of drinks," she said, setting the plate down and then opening the refrigerator. Inside were several bottles of water, a carton of OJ, a box of baking soda, and nothing else. She'd bought the baking soda when she'd picked up the drinks, in an effort to freshen the rental fridge. She'd planned on a full shopping trip *later*, but later hadn't yet arrived. "Water or orange juice?"

"A water would be great," he answered, and she handed him a bottle and took one for herself.

Sienna gestured back toward the front room. "There are a couple of boxes in there. It's the best seat I can offer." She walked past him, and he followed again, lifting a box from the stack by the window before setting it near the one she'd already sat down on, the plate of pizza in her lap. "Aren't you going to eat?" she asked him.

He shook his head. "I already ate. I just used that to get my foot in the door." He shot her the same smile he'd always used when Mirabelle had caught him with his hand in the cookie jar, and she resisted an eye roll, instead taking another bite of pizza. His bribe had worked, and she was grateful for the food, and so she let it go.

"So have you made any headway on the case?" he asked. "Was there anything in the latest note that moved things forward?"

"Not yet. We're not sure what to make of it. I might have some questions for you tomorrow, if you're available, but not tonight. I need some sleep and to look at everything again with fresh eyes."

He gave a tip of his chin. "That's understandable." He looked around. "Where's all your furniture, by the way?"

"I sold it or gave it away before I left New York," she said. "I didn't have a lot. The entirety of my apartment wasn't much bigger than the size of this room." She didn't mention that she wasn't planning on buying much furniture here—just enough to live comfortably. She *had* made time to go out and buy a mattress and a temporary metal bed frame the day she'd arrived. And she'd picked up a cheap coffee maker at the grocery/home store, but that was all she'd done as far as setting up house. Because she was only planning on being in Reno a year or so, long enough for the situation in New York to blow over, and so that it wouldn't appear she'd jumped from one department to another. But then she'd move back east with Brandon, and they'd buy a little house in the suburbs. She'd find a job with a smaller police force, and they'd start planning a family.

At least that was the plan she'd laid out for Brandon when he'd tried to convince her to skip straight to the part where they moved to the suburbs and started planning a family. But Sienna loved her career. She was *good* at it, dammit, and she hadn't been ready to toss it away when she'd been presented another option.

Especially given the circumstances.

They were quiet for a minute as she chewed, and he tipped his water back, taking a long drink. "How does the man you left in New York feel about you living across the country?"

She eyed him, and he stared back at her, his expression casual, though she noticed his body had stilled. He was waiting for her to speak. "He knows it was the best choice for my career." That felt like a lie, but what was she supposed to say? *He doesn't care about my career, but he knows I do, so he's going along with it. I didn't really give him any other choice.*

"Yeah? Why was that?" he asked.

She popped the last piece of crust into her mouth, taking the few moments to chew before answering. "There was a situation in New York," she said, and half of her was surprised she'd said it, and half of her wasn't at all. There was something natural about this—sitting in an unfurnished room, eating take-out food from a box, and chatting easily with Gavin. Never mind that they hadn't done anything like it in eleven years. Time was an odd thing, stretching like a rubber band and then effortlessly snapping you right back where you'd been. And though part of you felt dizzy at the sudden journey, another part rejoiced at the feeling of coming home.

Is that what Gavin is? Home?

No, no, of course not. It's just an expression.

"What sort of situation?" he asked.

Sienna reached for the water bottle on the floor next to her and took a drink before slowly replacing the cap. "In a nutshell? A woman came to me to report that her son was being molested. I looked into it and believed I had plenty of evidence for an arrest. As it turned out, however, the man she pointed a finger at was working on the mayoral campaign."

"Uh-oh," Gavin said, giving a small grimace. "Let me guess. You were asked to ignore it."

She nodded. "Word leaked out that I was investigating this guy. I had found other victims with similar stories who might have pressed charges, too, had they not been threatened. From what I ascertained, the mayor was worried that if it was made public with an arrest, his reelection campaign would take a hit. He'd be publicly associated with this creep, and it would hurt his image. So the chief called me into his office and ordered me to drop the investigation."

A mixture of emotions rolled over Gavin's face—anger, exasperation . . . sadness. "Goddamn corruption," he said.

Sienna sighed, recalling that moment in the chief's office. She'd known police work could be political, known officers and detectives—but especially the upper brass—were sometimes used as pawns and sacrificial lambs by politicians looking to run cover. And worse, that many of them were willing to go along with blatant corruption. But she hadn't realized the pure evil that could be behind it until then. She'd been ordered to look away as a pedophile continued to ruin lives and victimize innocent children. So that a man's chance at taking office wouldn't be threatened. So that *poll numbers* wouldn't dip. It felt like a bad joke.

And really, who wanted "leaders" capable of such blatant disregard for wickedness?

Sienna had decided she couldn't look herself in the mirror after following such an order. If she did, she'd be complicit, and she could not live with that.

"What did you do?" Gavin asked.

"I arrested him."

She didn't want to admit how much the look of pride that filled his expression meant to her, but it did. Oh, it did. Because truth be told, she hadn't received that look from anyone else. Not one person. Even her coworkers, some of whom had expressed support in private, had all but disappeared when push came to shove, unwilling to publicly align themselves with her. She'd told herself she understood. But in reality? It had stung. Badly. Even Brandon had looked shocked and doubtful when she'd told him what she planned to do, asking if she was sure it was worth jeopardizing her career. But Gavin was looking at her with such clear, unblinking respect in his eyes, and a sudden lump halted her breath. She hadn't realized how much she'd needed that. The fact that it came from *him* had conflicting emotions wreaking havoc in her system. "Of course you did," he said quietly, as though since she'd begun telling her story, he hadn't had any doubt it would end that way.

She cleared her throat, turning her gaze. "Anyway, it went over about as well as you can imagine it did with my bosses," she said. "They might have been satisfied with a reprimand or time off without pay, and

I might have taken either, because otherwise it would have been spun that there wasn't enough evidence and that I went rogue, libeled a man, disregarded procedure, et cetera. But the mayor called in, and he was irate. The story of his campaign worker's arrest blew up, and it was all over the news. I was just waiting to be fired."

"And then?"

"And then one of my bosses called me in and told me he could offer me a transfer to Nevada. That Ingrid, the lead detective here in Reno, was willing to take me on despite the controversy."

"*Ingrid.* That's quite a name."

"She's quite a woman, believe me."

Gavin smiled. "So you snapped it up despite the fact that you had vowed never to return to this dustbin of hell."

Sienna couldn't help the laugh. "Basically."

He smiled at her. "You did the right thing, Si." *Si.* The nickname was pronounced like *sea*, and that was how hearing it from his lips made her stomach feel—like a turbulent ocean rolled and churned inside. His tone was gentle, and their gazes lingered. She broke eye contact, looking away. She had the strange urge to reach for something and hold on, but there was nothing there. She was sitting on a box filled with the few things she'd packed up and put in the back of her car before she'd headed away from her life and back toward the Biggest Little City in the World.

"So what's he like?" Gavin asked. "This 'main squeeze.'"

"Ha." Sienna tilted her head, picturing Brandon. Why in the world was she having trouble conjuring his face? She felt herself frowning and relaxed her brow. "He's a lawyer."

"That's his defining quality?"

Sienna rolled her eyes. "No, that's not his defining quality. What do you want to hear? His name's not Main Squeeze; it's Brandon Guthrie. He's kind. He's handsome. He's well liked. He's a go-getter. He's sup-portive." *Mostly.* So he hadn't exactly wanted her to move here and take the opportunity presented to save her career. Could she blame him? He loved her, and he wanted to start their life together, not put it on hold for an unexpected long-distance relationship.

"What about you?" she asked, attempting to strike a flippant tone and suspecting she'd missed the target. "You never married?"

He paused for a beat, his gaze moving over her features, cataloging something. "No."

"Ever get close?" she asked.

"Yeah, once," he said. "A long time ago."

A prickle took up in her rib cage, and then she realized he was referring to her, and that prickle sprouted thorns. "Not funny," she said.

He gave the barest of wry smiles, but his tone was gentle when he answered, "I know." He paused for a beat. "But no, I've never gotten close."

"Why not?" It was difficult for her to believe that a man like him—gorgeous, rich, successful—didn't have a bevy of women surrounding him. And maybe he did. Maybe he just wasn't interested in marrying any of them. Maybe he'd discovered long ago—on the very day she'd waited in a chapel filled with plastic flowers—that the single life was the life for him and stuck with it.

Maybe that meant she shouldn't have taken it personally. It wasn't *her*. It was every woman on earth. And why did the thought of *that day* still make her feel bitter and sad, even now?

In answer to her question, Gavin shrugged, and she suddenly realized how large he looked sitting on the small box and that he was probably uncomfortable. It was sort of comical but sort of not, and God, there was such a clashing, rolling mix of emotions happening inside her. Or maybe it was simply exhaustion. "I was on the road for years, and then I threw myself into this job. And then there's that I just never met the right person."

"Hmm," she said, refusing to let her emotions take hold of her thoughts as they'd done a moment before. *Shut it down, Sienna.* She took another sip of water, and he watched her for a moment and then glanced around the room.

"This is what it would have been like at first if we'd moved into that house," he said quietly, causing her body to go still.

That house.

The one she hadn't thought about in a long time and yet was suddenly as clear as day in her mind. Oh, she knew what house he was talking about. "Gavin," she warned.

Something sparked in his eyes. "You never thought about it? Imagined it?"

"No," she said. "Or if I did, I can't remember." She pulled off flippant better that time, or at least she thought she did.

But when she looked at Gavin, she second-guessed that assumption. He was watching her, a small smile on his lips as though he knew very well she was lying. And of course, he probably did. He knew faces. Not just hers. But Sienna was well aware that she had a hundred tells, and if he still remembered anything about her at all, he'd pick up at least one of them.

It made her feel weak and exposed where it'd made her feel loved and known before. A long time ago.

Gavin glanced away, and she had the weird feeling he was giving her some privacy. "I told Mirabelle you're back in town," he said.

She barely held back the flinch but knew she'd failed to disguise the pain in her eyes.

"She misses you, Si," he said gently. And there was that *Si* again. She wanted to tell him to stop calling her that but didn't know how to without sounding petty. It didn't sound calculated, just like old habit, so she let it go. The better solution was to wrap up this case and never spend another moment with him. Never look into his eyes. Never hear him call her *Si* again—or anything else for that matter. And why did that fleeting thought cause even more conflicting emotions to pummel her? And why did that only happen around Gavin and no one else?

"I miss her too," she admitted, because it was true and suddenly the truth just felt easier than trying to lie when he—at least partially—still saw right through her.

"I'm sorry," he said, and her eyes met his, widening because she was surprised by the words. "I'm sorry for a lot, Si, but mostly I'm sorry that you lost Mirabelle."

Sienna made a small pained sound but shook her head. "That part wasn't your doing. It was my fault. I should have kept in touch," she said. "At first, though . . . it was better for me to cut all ties." She picked at the edge of her water bottle label. "Then later, when I'd settled into my new life in New York, when I had found happiness . . . moved on . . . it felt like contacting her—oh, I don't know—might set me back, I guess." Maybe she'd even worried it would nullify her happiness completely and she'd be right back to square one, the same spot she'd been in the day she'd knocked on Mirabelle's trailer door in a rented, dirt-stained wedding dress. Sienna shook her head. "I'd be tempted to ask about you . . . and I really didn't want to know . . ." Except she had. She had. And that had really been the problem. She let out a small laugh that held little amusement. "So I just left my life here completely behind."

They were both silent for a few moments, the space between them full of the words that had never been said, the regret they both might carry, though Sienna didn't necessarily want to get into the nitty-gritty of that. There was no real purpose, was there? They'd both moved on. She was practically engaged, and though fate had brought them back together, it was of a temporary nature.

Perhaps a small part of her really had never moved on, despite what she'd just told him. *Perhaps*, if she was going to credit fate for their reunion, the cosmic purpose—for her anyway—was so that she might work that final piece of him completely from her system. It proved to her that she could spend time with Gavin without melting into a pile of emotional goo; she could even dredge up the past and admit old hurts and still sleep peacefully that night. And then, when their time together came to a natural conclusion because her case was solved, she could go on her merry way and know that Gavin Decker no longer held any portion of her heart.

She wanted that.

Brandon deserved it. *So do I.*

"So," Gavin said after a short pause, and she saw the teasing glint in his eye as he tilted his head and peered at her, "you never looked me up? Not once in eleven years?" He asked the question to ease the tension, she knew, or perhaps to rile her up a bit, and both worked, which caused her to laugh softly.

"My God, you're still conceited, aren't you?"

He laughed too. "I was never conceited."

"You were. Totally full of yourself. I can't imagine the *fan club* helped in that regard."

They both grinned, and for a weighted moment they stared at each other, their smiles fading in tandem. "In all honesty, I did look you up," Sienna admitted with a shrug and a wave of her hand. "You know, years later. I was proud of you. Happy." And that was the truth, though it had hurt too.

She stood before he could respond, holding her hand out for his empty water bottle. He handed it to her, and she walked to the kitchen and threw out the trash. When she returned, he was standing. "You're tired. I should go."

She nodded. She'd been exhausted before she had arrived home, and she was even more exhausted now, but *now* it was more than just the physical variety. "Thanks for the dinner. As you saw, the cupboards are basically bare. I would have probably ended up eating spoonfuls of baking soda for dinner." Or ordering something that she wouldn't have stayed awake long enough to eat.

"It never has to get to that level of desperation. I'm always good for a pizza delivery when and if you need one."

There was an awkward pause, and then he moved toward the door and pulled it open.

"Gavin, wait," she said, and he turned quickly, a look she could only call anticipatory on his face. "Are you available tomorrow if we have some questions regarding that note we found today?"

A flicker of expression, but very brief and unreadable. "Absolutely." He smiled, turning away again and calling over his shoulder, "You have my number."

Sienna closed the door and engaged the lock before heading straight for the shower. She was beyond tired, so why did she have a sneaking suspicion she wasn't going to be able to sleep?

CHAPTER THIRTEEN

Sienna looked up as Kat burst into Ingrid's office, shaking something in her hand. "The closet," she said.

"And a good morning to you, Kat," Ingrid said sarcastically.

Kat gave her a glance accompanied by a fleeting smile as she took the seat next to Sienna. "Did you catch her up?"

Sienna had only arrived about twenty minutes before, and although she and Kat had given Ingrid the gist of what had been discovered at the abandoned house, Sienna had gone through the photos of the evidence, and Ingrid had taken a few minutes to read the latest installment of the note. "I'm up to speed," Ingrid confirmed.

"Okay, good. Listen, I called the criminalists who are at the house where we found the letter last night and asked them to check under the floorboards in all the closets."

Sienna's brow lowered. "The floorboards—" Her eyes opened wider with understanding. "The floorboards in the closet where he said he hid his games from his father."

"Yes," Kat said excitedly. "That seemed very specific, right? Something was nagging at me, and so I put on Rachmaninoff in the car on my way here—Piano Concerto Number Two in C Minor does it every time." She positioned her fingers in the air and moved them dramatically, as if playing the piano while simultaneously using her voice to "sing" the melody, before Ingrid interrupted her.

"Kat, what on earth are you on?"

"Not enough caffeine, that's for sure. There better be coffee ready. My point is, I needed to clear my mind, and classical genius does that. Anyway"—she waved her hand around—"the criminalists found a bag under the floorboards of the upstairs closet, and one of them is on the way here now so we can check it out."

"You're kidding," Ingrid said, her chair squeaking as she sat back. "What's the point of toying with us? Because I doubt it's to get caught."

"We don't know." They went through some of the theories they'd discussed the night before, and Ingrid agreed with their assessment.

"Have you had a chance to call Armando Vitucci and find out if he's available to give us a profile?" Kat asked, obviously referencing the profiler she'd mentioned.

"Yes," Ingrid said. "I have a call in to him."

Kat's phone buzzed, and she looked down at it, standing. "The criminalist is here. I'll go meet her at the front if you want to clear the meeting room table."

Sienna and Ingrid walked the short distance to the meeting room, where they'd begun hanging the photos, copies of the writings, and other case-specific items on the board at the front of the room. Sienna had just finished tidying up the random notepads and pens on the table when Kat walked in with a pretty young woman who had been at the first crime scene Sienna had gone to, holding an evidence bag.

"Sienna, remember Gina Marr? She's the criminalist who found the items under the floorboard."

"Yes, of course. Hi." They all greeted one another, and Gina stepped forward, placed the evidence bag on the table, and removed a box of gloves from the bag on her shoulder. They all donned the blue plastic hand coverings, and then Gina opened the evidence bag and removed what appeared to be a gold metal bee and a bottle with a piece of paper rolled up inside.

"He left us quite a bit at that house," Sienna noted. Their reward for unraveling the various clues that led to the address?

Gina tipped the bottle and used her fingertips to unroll the note. It was filled with the same concise writing. The story continued.

Kat used her phone to take a photograph of the letter, and then Gina rolled it up again and placed it and the bottle back into evidence bags. Sienna and Ingrid studied the metal bee, turning it this way and that, but it seemed like nothing more than exactly what it appeared to be. *A jewelry charm?* Sienna took several pictures of it from different angles, finishing just as Kat returned with three printouts of the note.

Gina packed everything back up and headed off to the lab to add the items to the list of things to be processed. Sienna wasn't overly hopeful.

Then Sienna, Ingrid, and Kat sat down to read.

Mother had always been a force to be reckoned with, but after she put my father to permanent rest, she was unstoppable. It's like killing him had breathed an extra breath of life into her. She didn't allow anyone to cross her, nor did she allow anyone to cross me. If something unfortunate *did* happen, she'd make it right, my mother. "Don't give them an inch, Danny Boy," she'd say, a glint in her sky-blue eyes. "Not one single inch." And then she'd smile, a melodic hum on her lips as she went back to baking a cake or folding our laundry or some other task that went toward creating a beautiful, comfortable home for us to enjoy.

Things were calm for a while, and for the first time, I felt the happiness of a life without the constant anxiety of knowing Father would walk back through our door any day. Sometimes, in the middle of the night, I would wake up and hear a car stop in front of our house and panic that it was Father. The whole bloody scene in the kitchen with Mother hadn't really happened at all. No, he was just away like he'd been so often, and now he was back.

Back to hit me and kick me and tell me how useless I was.

It didn't matter where I tried to hide.

He'd *find* me.

Somehow, Mother would always sense when this happened, and she would come to my room, shushing me softly and leading me back to bed, where she tucked me in again, stroking my hair as she sang to me softly until I fell back to sleep.

After a while, I began to trust that Father couldn't hurt me anymore—couldn't hurt anyone or anything—and I no longer listened for him to return.

Mother and I played games in the evening, her complimenting my new level of skill at Texas Hold'm, Omaha, and 2-7 Triple Draw. I'd also improved at checkers, chess, and Monopoly. Now that half of my mind wasn't focused on my fear of Father, I was able to turn my intellect toward cards, and it made quite the difference.

Unfortunately, that peaceful time would be short lived. My next tormenter showed up in a pair of khakis, a button-down shirt, and a sports coat with patches on the elbows. He appeared harmless enough upon first meeting, but I soon found out that first impressions can be deceiving.

Very, very deceiving.

I often come up with names for people before I've learned their actual one, and I had immediately called him Mr. Patches because of his attire, and in my head, the name stuck.

Mr. Patches.

He needed a lot of patches when Mother got through with him.

But I've gotten ahead of myself.

Let me backtrack.

Mr. Patches was my science teacher.

I'd never been very good at science. Like I've already told you, games were my thing. I wasn't as good as Mother, but I *was* good.

Better than most.

Worse than some.

Mr. Patches was an engaging and compassionate science teacher. If he called on you and you didn't know the answer, he would say, "That's all right. Make sure to go over page sixty," or something like that so you weren't embarrassed in front of your classmates. And then he'd wink and offer a smile and move on. And if you *knew* the answer, he would clap twice and bang once on his desk and say loudly, "Oh! Doo-dah day!" And the class would laugh and clap with him, and if it was me who got the answer right, I would feel this unusual warm buzzing in my chest and realize I was smiling, too, even though I hadn't told my face to do it.

One day, after the class had been dismissed and all the students were packing up, Mr. Patches called my name and asked if I'd stay after for a few minutes. This confused but didn't alarm me, and so I put my books in my backpack slowly as the rest of the students filed out, and Mr. Patches stood by the door, smiling and telling them to have a nice day as they left. He flipped the lock on the door and then approached me where I stood next to his desk, motioning for me to have a seat in the chair next to his. We both sat, and Mr. Patches turned to me and gave me a smile. "You've improved tremendously in this class," he said, and once again, I felt that buzzing in my chest that made me feel happy and lighter in some way I couldn't quite describe.

"Thank you, sir," I answered. "I've been working hard." And it was true. Without the anxiety of knowing Father might return from one of his trips any day, without having to make excuses and create outright lies for the bruises, cuts, and broken bones, I had been able to focus more fully on my studies. I knew I was still behind the other students, but for the first time, I thought perhaps it wasn't that I was dull or stupid but that I'd been distracted by things the others weren't and maybe it was a wonder I'd come as far as I had under the circumstances. The idea was liberating.

"Yes, I can tell you've been working very hard," Mr. Patches said. "It shows." He sat back in his chair and looked at me, and for the first time, I felt a prickle of unease. I pushed it aside, though. Mr. Patches was proud of me. That's what he was saying. "You have so much potential," he finished with a nod.

"Thank you, sir," I said again, tongue tied, which wasn't unusual for me.

But Mr. Patches smiled fondly, the way a father might smile at his son, if that father was fond of that son. "But," he said, "while you've improved tremendously, you're still slightly behind." He put his hand up as though warding off my hurt feelings, though it wasn't necessary. I was already well aware what he said was true. He leaned forward. "I have a plan, though. What would you say to some personal tutoring?"

Personal tutoring. My eyes shifted sideways, and I was suddenly nervous. My mother and I no longer had my father's income, and while Mother was extremely creative and managed to maintain a lovely and comfortable home in the absence of his money, there would never be enough for extras like tutoring. "Well, I . . . um . . . ," I mumbled.

Mr. Patches seemed to understand my discomfort, and he jumped in immediately and said, "There would be absolutely no charge. I occasionally provide this service for students I consider extra special."

I smiled, that pleasant buzzing feeling returning, though not quite as strongly. *Extra special.* "Okay, yes," I said.

"Oh! Doo-dah day!" Mr. Patches said on a wide smile, glancing at the door. Somehow, I knew in that moment I'd never like that phrase again. Outside the door, the hall was utterly quiet. Everyone on this floor had headed home for the day. "We can get started right away." He paused for only a moment. "By the way, I know someone who worked with your father," he said, and my blood turned icy, the room pulsing around me. *Oh no. Oh no.* He was going to call the police. They were going to come to our house, spray that stuff that made blood shine under their special lights. Sweat broke out on my upper lip. Mr. Patches tilted his head, watching me. "He mentioned that the son of a man he worked with—a man who *disappeared*—is in my class. He mentioned *your* name, asked if I knew you. Isn't that a coincidence?" He peered at me more closely, and I swallowed. "I'm sorry to hear about your father." He gave a grim twist of his mouth. "Sometimes fathers leave. They decide they just don't like the life they've been living, and they pack up and just . . . *go*. Start new lives, I guess. Mine did too. That's how I know what it's like to be left behind."

My shoulders dropped just a hair. He thought my father had abandoned his family, the way his had. He related to me. I let out a slow breath. "So," he went on, "how's tomorrow after school at your house?" Before I had a chance to say a word, he leaned forward, patting my knee. I dropped my gaze to his hand, which stayed on my knee, even after the patting had stopped. There was the feeling of something sinking in my stomach—something large and heavy. Mr. Patches's fingers trembled slightly, and then he raised his eyes, looking into mine as his hand began to travel up my leg toward my thigh. I was frozen. I didn't know what to do. That weight within me grew, stretching the lining of my stomach, making the contents move up my throat. Mr. Patches's hand stopped at the juncture of my thigh and moved inward slightly, but then as quick as that, he lifted it, sitting back and smiling as though I'd imagined what had just happened. Or misinterpreted it.

Which was entirely possible. I *had* been raised with a suspicious mind, after all. Father had guaranteed it.

"I'll drive you home," Mr. Patches said, and though my legs felt stiff and awkward, I made myself move to the door and out to the parking lot with him, where I got in his car and he drove me home, waving and wishing me a good evening.

My father had hit me, he'd snapped my bones and made me bleed, but he'd never touched me the way Mr. Patches began touching me after school each evening as we sat at my kitchen table, a science book in front of us, nothing but a mere prop.

"Do you like it?" he'd ask, his eyes glazed and his breath short. And if I hesitated, his expression would grow stony, and he'd say, "Don't make me *fail* you. If you don't graduate, you'll be a nobody. You don't want to be a *nobody*, do you?"

No. I didn't want to be a nobody.

But I already was.

CHAPTER FOURTEEN

It was just after lunch when Gavin opened his office door, greeting Sienna. She looked slightly harried or maybe worried, a small wrinkle between her brows. This job was obviously running her ragged, and he had the strong urge to ease her burden. He hoped he could.

"Thanks for meeting with me. I do realize you have a real job that keeps you very busy," she said as she stepped inside. "I appreciate your help, and I won't keep you."

"I have the time," he told her. He'd *made* the time.

They'd sat at his desk the last time she was in his office, but he directed her to the small seating area this time, both so she could spread out the items she'd brought if necessary and so that there wouldn't be a wide expanse of desk between them.

She'd said she would give him a call the night before, and he'd tried to convince himself he wasn't waiting like some teenager, but that would be a lie. He'd been looking distractedly at his phone all morning, disappointed each time it rang and wasn't her. Which was ridiculous on several levels, most importantly because if she *did* call, it would be to ask him about evidence for her case, nothing more. She'd finally contacted him an hour before, and he'd canceled two meetings so he'd be available—not that he'd tell *her* that, but he'd been happy, even eager, to carve out all the time she might need.

He'd enjoyed her company far too much, limited and stilted at times though it'd been. He'd wanted to stay. Dammit, if he was being honest, he'd wanted to stand up from that stupid, uncomfortable-as-hell *box* he'd been sitting on that had been caving in under his weight, swoop her up in his arms, and kiss the hell out of her. He wondered if her taste would be familiar, completely new, or some exotic mixture of the two. He wondered if his hands would know the dips and curves of her body, like muscle memory that had lain dormant but might reawaken with a single touch. But he'd forced himself to push those thoughts aside. She was involved with someone else, and he'd given up the possibility of ever having her again when he'd left without a word.

Or had he? Her reactions, the places her gaze sometimes lingered—his mouth for example—made him wonder. And Gavin was not a man who liked to leave questions unanswered.

Sienna took a seat at the end of the leather love seat, and Gavin sat on the chair next to her, only separated by a wood-and-metal side table.

She set her briefcase on the floor and bent to retrieve the items she had brought, and he took the moment to let his eyes fall on each part of her. His gaze swept the elegant line of her spine, the slender side of her thigh, and the gentle swell of her calf. She was graceful perfection, and he'd always wondered how such a beautiful girl had come from two stout, ugly creatures like the ones who had called themselves her parents. Genes were a funny thing.

Or maybe if her parents had lived lives free from addiction and meanness, poor health choices, and general disregard, it wouldn't have manifested in such physically hideous ways.

Or maybe they'd been especially ugly in his eyes because of the way they'd hurt their daughter.

Sienna set a close-up photograph of a gold bee with a penny next to it for scale on the table and removed what looked like four or five sheets of paper. Gavin recognized the same handwriting from the notes he'd read before. "The criminalists found yet another piece of Danny Boy's writing in the house on Allegra this morning." She pointed to the photo of the bee charm or whatever it was. "I'm assuming this doesn't mean anything to you, but it was found with the latest note, and I thought it might have something to do with a hand of cards or . . ." Her expression registered frustration, and she sighed. "I don't know, but there it is."

Two new notes. Wow. And a trinket. Gavin picked up the photo, looked closely at it for a moment, and then set it down. A bee? "There's a brand of playing cards called Bee."

"Yes. I found that on a Google search. Any particular significance?"

"A lot of casinos use them. They're known for their durability."

She paused a moment, thinking. "Hmm. Okay."

He gestured to the small stack of papers. "Can I read the notes?"

She nodded, picking them up and passing them to him along with a highlighter. "I also included the ones you already read, in case you need to refer back. There are a few references to card games and hands of cards in the latest ones that don't mean anything to us." She still looked troubled but hopeful, and he said a silent prayer that if there was anything he could find that would provide insight, it would jump out at him immediately. "Those are all copies that you're free to make notes on." Gavin nodded while sitting back in his chair, notes and pen in hand as he began to read.

He became immersed in the words, making note of each thing that caught his eye or stopped him for even the briefest moment. He went through both notes, line by line. They were more intense than the first ones, which surprised Gavin to some extent.

When he was done, he placed the pages back on the table, his brow knitting. "I know you had me read those for any hidden clues in the card lingo, but damn, if it's true, it's . . ." He paused, having trouble selecting just the right words.

"Shockingly depressing?"

He laughed shortly. "That about sums it up." He paused, wondering who this guy was—some maladjusted kid looking for attention in the only way he thought he could get it, or some bona fide psychopath. And really, did the differentiation matter if it meant this person posed a threat to society at large and Sienna specifically?

Sienna sat forward, crossing her legs and breaking him from his momentary musings. "You highlighted a couple of things."

He picked up the papers again. "Uh, yes. This here," he said, pointing at the first neon-yellow pen stroke, "he references Texas Hold'em, but he misspells it, without the *e*. It might just be a mistake, but I highlighted it just in case."

She nodded, taking the page he offered. "Thanks," she said. "I didn't catch that."

"Then this here," he said, pointing to another highlighted spot; "he refers to his mother's hand—two queens and three twos—as the highest hand possible. That would only be true if they were playing deuces wild."

"Deuces wild," she repeated.

"Right. She has two queens, and with three wild cards, it's five of a kind. The highest hand possible in seven-card stud." He handed her the rest of the papers. "Sorry, that's all I found." He paused. "I'm obviously not a cop, and you've probably already considered this, but what about Mr. Patches saying he knew a guy at the kid's father's work?"

"There's just no way to know who that person is, especially without knowing Mr. Patches's identity. It could've been a neighbor or a barista at his local coffee bar. Anyone really."

"Or," Gavin said, "he could've looked into the kid and realized he was the perfect victim."

Sienna appeared troubled for a moment but conjured a small smile. "I really appreciate your help."

"I wish I could offer more."

"There might not *be* more." She sighed. "There might not be anything. Maybe he's done playing games and now just wants to tell his life story."

He studied her for a moment. "But you don't believe that."

Her lip quirked. "That obvious, huh? I never did have a very good poker face."

No, you never did.

It wasn't just because Gavin was good at reading faces that he'd been able to read hers. She'd always worn her heart on her sleeve. She'd never been much good at hiding her anger or her joy.

Her sorrow.

It was why he hadn't had the courage to face her in the end.

She gathered the papers and began returning them to her briefcase. "Thank you again. The department appreciates it."

The department.

They stood, and he followed her to the door, this unfamiliar desperation clawing at him to keep her from leaving.

Cool it, Gavin. She has a job to do.

"Before you leave," he said, his words coming out in a rush, "Mirabelle wanted me to invite you to dinner. Monday."

Sienna turned back toward him, blinking. "Uh . . ."

"Argus will be there."

He saw the surprised happiness flicker over her face. "They're still together," she said.

"Are you surprised?" he asked on a smile. She'd posed it as a statement, so he knew she wasn't.

She gave a short laugh that was mostly breath but tipped her head as though conceding his point. "No, though she did put him through the wringer. Did she finally marry the poor guy?"

"Not yet. They still don't even live together, but he continues to propose."

She gave a full-fledged smile then. "He's persistent; I'll give him that."

Gavin laughed. "I don't know that *persistent* cuts it. Argus deserves a word several steps beyond *persistent*."

Her smile grew, and their eyes locked for one beat, two, before she looked away, her smile fading. "I'll think about it," she said. It wasn't a yes, but it was better than no.

"Okay. Great. Hold on just one second." Gavin walked quickly to his desk, where he tore off a sticky note and scrawled Mirabelle's address.

He walked it back to Sienna, who took it, glancing down at the small, square piece of mint-green paper. She raised her brows. "This is in South Reno, isn't it?"

"Yeah, I, ah, once I was able, I moved her out of that trailer park."

Whatever she saw in his face made her eyes linger for a moment. She stuck the piece of paper in the side pocket of her briefcase and inhaled, her shoulders rising and dropping again. "She never belonged there anyway. Thank you again, Gavin."

"You're welcome, Sienna." And with that, she turned and walked out his door. He watched until she rounded the corner to the elevator banks, and then he returned to his desk. He sat there for a moment, tapping his fingertips together as he worked to move his mind away from Sienna and young boys who watched their mothers brutally kill their fathers.

CHAPTER FIFTEEN

"You seem distracted," Kat said, scooping up some salsa with a grease-laden tortilla chip and eating half in one bite.

She *was* distracted. Distracted and frustrated. She and Kat had worked all morning before finally taking a break for a late lunch at a nearby Mexican restaurant. They'd both agreed that sitting down for an actual meal was important, not only for their mental health but so that they could update each other on what they'd individually worked on and brainstorm a little. The profiler Ingrid had called was looking over all the information they had so far, including the most recent letters and a few of their theories. Hopefully he could assist them with what they'd already speculated about and offer new ideas.

Sienna sipped from the straw of her iced tea and set it down before speaking. "I keep going over those notes. It's hard not to dwell on every small line, thinking it might be a clue pointing us somewhere." Words and phrases and snippets of Danny Boy's writings kept winding through her mind, keeping her up half the night.

"Okay, but where?"

"You mean what is the ultimate destination if it's not simply the end of his story? I have no idea." She thought for a minute. "Ingrid mentioned that the point of all this can't be for him to get caught. But what if it is? What if he's leading us to *himself* and plans on giving up once we find him? All these notes are both a stalling tactic and a way for him to tell us his story before we arrest him."

"To garner sympathy?"

"Maybe. Maybe he thinks we'll go easier on him if we understand his motive. Maybe it's just that no one has ever listened to him and he believes he has to employ extreme methods to be heard?"

"I don't know. I can't imagine any killer setting up a scenario where he ends up spending life in prison. No matter how intolerable he considers his own circumstances or what happened to him, he can't consider that *better*."

"True enough." Maybe especially *this* guy, whose past included sexual molestation.

Everyone was well aware of the things that could and often did happen behind prison bars.

"Also, for someone who might want to get caught, he's been extremely careful about not leaving fingerprints or DNA," Kat said, referencing the report they'd received from the lab on the first two notes, right before they'd left for lunch. A secondary report had let them know there were also no helpful fingerprints or DNA on the fast-food packaging brought to Trevor Keeling.

Sienna sighed and then popped another greasy chip in her mouth. *Trevor Keeling.* "I called the social worker on Trevor's case this morning," she told Kat. "Just to check in."

"How's he doing?"

Sienna shrugged. "She said he's okay. Quiet." She still couldn't get him out of her mind, kept picturing him sitting in that dirty apartment all alone, in the small nest of blankets and stuffed animals he'd set up. The only comfort available. Comfort he'd had to provide himself.

"Hey, Sienna," Kat said, her tone gentle. "He'll be okay."

Sienna nodded, looking up as their meals arrived. They both ate distractedly for a few minutes, talk of Trevor Keeling causing her mind to travel to the trailer park where she'd grown up, to the ragtag group of kids she'd hung out and played with. They had lived in close enough quarters that they all generally knew each other's circumstances. Most of them had decent parents, though not very educated and obviously poor, but there were a few, like her, whose parents were down-and-out losers in every sense of the word. It was a wonder she'd done so well for herself, really. And perhaps without Mirabelle, she wouldn't have. "There was this cat who gave birth to kittens under someone's porch in the trailer park I grew up in," Sienna said, staring into space, picturing the tiny black-and-white faces.

Kat tilted her head as Sienna met her eyes. "Sadly, their mom was killed, and the babies were still too young to take care of themselves. A group of us kids each took one and used droppers to feed them for the next several weeks. They all survived, but later, the one Timmy Lauden took would suck on the edge of blankets and clothing and even his own tail sometimes. We all knew him because he had this chronic pointy wet tip on the end." She looked off behind Kat's shoulder again, the vision of that tiny cat trying to find comfort in any way it could front and center in her mind.

"That's both gross and pitiful."

"It was." Sienna shrugged. "Other than that, he was a sweet, playful cat. None of the others did that, just him. They'd all been removed from their mother too soon, but for whatever reason, that little guy never adjusted."

Kat was looking at her knowingly. "Sienna, people aren't cats."

She gave her head a small shake, breathing out a smile. "No, of course not." She paused, picturing that needy cat again. "They're far more complicated," she murmured.

The mariachi music played softly over the speakers as they continued their meal, Sienna making a concerted effort to move her mind away from motherless boys and motherless kittens, a line of thought that was less than productive. "Any more information on the dealer on Reva Keeling's phone?" she asked after a few minutes.

When they'd run him, they'd learned he had been in jail for the past week and a half. Which eliminated him as the killer. Of course: it couldn't have been that easy. Then again, in Sienna's experience, drug deals gone wrong never ended with the victim posed elaborately under an overpass. The scene didn't fit that particular crime, and she wasn't surprised it had turned into what was most likely a dead end.

"He's a low-level dealer, in and out of jail since he was fourteen. Mostly possession, a few stolen cars. No violent crimes on his record, though. When he's not dealing, he's out getting women pregnant. He has four kids from three different women and doesn't pay child support on any of them."

Sienna sipped her tea. The fertile women of Reno who might be—inexplicably to her mind—attracted to that guy were better off with him behind bars, even temporarily.

"We can plan to have a word with him when he gets out, which should be in the next few months, but my bet is there's no connection at all between him and what happened to Reva Keeling," Kat said.

Sienna nodded.

"What did you find out about the house on Allegra Street?" Kat asked.

"It belongs to a bank," Sienna said. "Before that it was owned by a woman who died with no known relatives. Unfortunately, there aren't any neighbors on that block to ask whether they remember her. Almost all of the houses on that street are foreclosures. There was some talk about a strip mall a few years back that never came to fruition." She paused as she took a bite of food, chewed, and swallowed. "I think we can assume it's simply an abandoned house chosen because of its deserted location among other abandoned houses. It must have been easy for our suspect to enter, swap out door hardware, plant evidence for us to find, leave, and not worry about being caught on any cameras in the area or having some vagrant find what he'd left there before we did."

"So another dead end," Kat said.

"It appears so."

"Damn." She paused for a moment. "Any new insight about what Decker was able to give you as far as the notes?"

Sienna shook her head but removed the copies of the notes that Gavin had marked with highlighter.

"He only saw these two minor things." She'd said as much to Kat and Ingrid when she'd gotten back from meeting with Gavin the day before. Since then, she'd read the notes about a hundred times, and though there were a few things that sort of stuck out to her, on their own they didn't mean a thing.

Kat wiped her hands on her napkin and pushed her plate aside. "Let me look at those again, and with a full night's sleep."

A full night's sleep. Well, that makes one of us, Sienna thought. She handed the copies over and picked at the last of her burrito as Kat read through the notes one more time. When Kat was finished, she set the two pages Gavin had marked side by side. "Texas Hold'em without the *e*," she murmured as though to herself. "Do you recall any other misspellings in any of his notes?"

Sienna thought about it, wiping the corners of her mouth. "No. But I'm not the world's best speller. I could have missed one or two."

"Well, I've never won any contests, but I'm a pretty good proofreader in general. It's why Ingrid usually asks me to go over her important memos. As precise as she is about everything else, the woman can't spell worth shit. Anyway, my point here is that we've read four of his notes already, and this is the only misspelling that's been found."

"To be fair, it's more an abbreviation than a word. Anyone might make the same mistake and not consider it a spelling error."

Kat raised a brow. "Our game master doesn't know how to spell the name of a game, abbreviated or not?"

Sienna made a face, conceding the point. Even after Gavin had pointed it out, she'd sort of dismissed the misspelling as nothing more than that, but when Kat put it the way she had, Sienna tended to agree. "So what do you think it could mean?"

Kat tapped a finger on her chin. "Remove the *e*. Or . . . no *e*. Noe? Does the word *noe* mean anything to you?"

Sienna picked up her phone and opened a search engine, then looked up the word as it related to Reno. Apparently, it was a first name, and there were quite a few of them. "There's a Noe Investments," Sienna said, looking up at Kat. "But that's about it."

"That's not the name of the bank that owns the property on Allegra, is it?"

"No."

"Hmm." Kat looked back down at the highlights, her eyes moving between the two. "So the most recent two notes were both found in the same location. So maybe we should consider that the clues found in each of them are meant to go together."

"Makes sense," Sienna said. "If they are in fact clues."

Kat nodded. "Deuces wild," she said, tapping the paper where Sienna had written the term next to Gavin's highlight, the phrase that had been left out, whether intentionally or not. "What if you use *no e* as an instruction?"

Sienna took a moment to consider that. *Deuces wild, no* e. *So* ducs wild *if you removed both* e*'s. Or* duces *or* deucs wild *if you only removed one.* "That doesn't make any sense either." She picked up her phone to do a search on *ducs, duces,* and *deucs* nonetheless. "*Duces* is a Latin term," she said, reading the web page she'd clicked on. "*Duces tecum* is a type of subpoena." She read the basic definition of the term, because even though she was in law enforcement, she couldn't remember exactly what it meant. But as far as she could tell, there was no relevance to this particular case. She clicked back to the original search page and scrolled down. A moment later, her eyes widened, and she looked up at Kat. "There's a business called Duces Wild—no *e*—downtown."

Kat's expression mirrored what she was sure hers looked like. "Are you serious? What kind of business?"

Sienna clicked on the link and quickly scanned the limited copy of what was a pretty pitiful website. "It's a music store that sells records."

Kat's face screwed up. "I didn't think there were shops that sold records anymore."

Sienna shrugged. "I thought it was mostly an online item, too, but I guess not."

Sienna clicked on another page. "The guy who owns it is named Duces Reynolds, hence the Duces Wild name, and he . . ." She scrolled down the page. "He DJs on the side."

Kat signaled the server, and she came over, delivering their check. "We could go talk to him. I'm not sure exactly what to ask, but maybe he has something for us like that fan club president did. Wouldn't that be something?"

They paid the bill and were out the door a few minutes later, soon exiting the parking lot in Kat's work vehicle.

~

Duces Wild was solidly wedged between a bar and what appeared—from the multitude of chains, whips, and leather-bikini-clad mannequins in the window—to be an adult sex shop named the Back Door Emporium.

The vinyl shop was small and windowless, but the lights were bright, and it seemed clean and well organized. At their arrival, a man featuring a black pompadour à la seventies Elvis came out a door at the opposite side of the store. "Hey, my ladies. How may I serve?"

"Duces Reynolds?" Kat asked, unclipping her badge and holding it up. "Detectives Kozlov and Walker."

He looked briefly confused, and there was no recognition at their names in his expression, his hand outstretched as he approached. "Detectives? Is there a problem?"

"No. No problem. We're following a lead on a case. It might be off base, but we figured it couldn't hurt to stop by and find out if anything noteworthy has happened in your shop in the last couple weeks? Any unusual customer? Problem?"

He shook his head. "No, nothing out of the ordinary. I get a fair amount of traffic in here. You might be surprised, considering it's pretty dead today. But actually, I mostly use the space to store my DJ equipment"—he gestured toward the door he'd just come through, a space that Sienna had assumed was storage, perhaps an office—"and to have a place to meet clients, that sort of thing. Vinyl is my passion, though, so I collect them and sell the ones I have extras of or don't want." He pointed to the rows of bins behind them, and Sienna turned and glanced over the upright albums, which appeared to be organized alphabetically, with large letters written on the fronts of the bins.

"Okay, well, thank you for your time."

"Do you have a record player?" he asked.

"My parents do," Kat said. "A little too scratchy for me." She wrinkled her nose.

But Duces chuckled, obviously unoffended. "Nah, that's the whole charm," he said. "Feel free to look around, see if there's something your folks might want for Christmas."

"Sure. Thanks." Kat handed him her card. "If you have any reason to call," she said.

He looked down at it and nodded, and at the sound of a phone ringing, he headed to the checkout counter and answered the call. "Duces Wild. Duces speaking."

She leaned in to Sienna. "Listening to old records feels like sandpaper on my brain." She made a dramatic expression, squeezing one eye shut tight and lifting the other.

Sienna snickered. "Sandpaper on the brain. Lovely visual."

"Let's get going."

"Hold on," Sienna said, turning down one of the rows of records, running her hand along the tops of the artists whose names began with *A* and then using her finger to pull them forward so she could see the covers. ABBA . . . AC/DC . . . the Association. She turned back to Kat, who was following along behind her. "Were there any bands mentioned in those notes?"

"Not that I caught. I left the file in the car, but we could go outside and comb through it again." She shrugged. "I'm no music aficionado, but maybe if we're specifically looking for the name of an artist, something will pop out that didn't before."

Sienna blinked as something came to her. "Kat, what about that phrase that he said Mr. Patches used—"

"'Oh, doo-dah day,'" Kat said, wrinkling her brow. "Is that a song?"

"I don't know, but it seems like it could be." She swore she'd heard it somewhere before, though she couldn't bring a tune to mind.

Kat turned toward the counter, where Duces was just hanging up the phone. "Hey, Duces, do you know the song with the lyrics 'oh, doo-dah day'?" she asked.

"Oh yeah. That's a classic. It's called 'Camptown Races,' by Stephen Collins Foster. It's mostly thought of as a children's song nowadays, even though it's about gambling. I typically don't carry anything from the era the song was written in, but Johnny Cash did a badass rendition of it on the Bell Telephone Hour in 1959." He pointed behind them. "You'll find a copy in the *C*s, right over there."

They thanked Duces as the door opened and a girl dressed in all black with her black hair in short, curly pigtails and choppy bangs walked in and glumly greeted Duces, then headed behind the counter where he also stood. An employee?

Kat turned to Sienna, looking incredulous. "Who else would know stuff like that off the top of his head?"

"No one except him," Sienna murmured, a tingle under her skin that said they were in the right place.

"Camptown Races." She knew the song now, and the tune wound through her head as she and Kat walked quickly to the *C* section, Sienna separating the albums until they came to the one they were looking for. And on the front was a mint-green sticky note with a string of numbers.

Sienna felt a burst of triumph, quickly followed by a small stab of irritation. The two emotions mixed, making her feel slightly breathless. She turned to Kat, holding the record up. At the front, Duces was deep in conversation with the girl.

"Duces?" Kat called. "Can we ask you to look at something?" He said something to the girl, and she began taking the bag hooked around her body off and placing her things behind the counter as he headed toward Kat and Sienna.

"What's up?"

Kat pointed at the sticky note. "Is that something you put there?"

He frowned, leaning in to get a better look. "No. But I buy these old albums all over the place . . . estate sales, yard sales, thrift stores . . . so it could have been there from wherever I picked it up." He stood straight, calling over to the girl behind the counter. "Ari, did you put a green sticky note on this album?"

"A what?"

"A green sticky note with some random numbers on it."

"Why would I do that?"

"Yes or no?"

"No."

He turned back toward Kat and Sienna. "Kids," he said.

"Do you remember seeing anyone browsing this section recently?"

Duces scratched at the back of his head. "Not specifically." He turned around again. "Ari, do you remember anyone looking through the records in this section?"

The girl rolled her eyes. "No."

Duces shrugged. "Sorry."

"Do you have security cameras in here?" Kat asked.

"No. I keep meaning to get one. Not for the albums but more for my equipment." He shrugged. "But it's insured, so I guess it just hasn't been a priority."

"Okay. We're going to purchase this record and take this sticky note with us," Kat said, nodding to the note.

"Sure. What is it?"

"Maybe nothing," Kat answered.

Duces shrugged, gesturing to the counter. "Ari will ring you up."

The transaction only took a minute, and Ari handed them the album, contained in a plastic bag with the Duces Wild logo on the front.

"Thanks, Duces," Kat called. "Give us a ring if anything comes to you about who might have put this here."

"Will do. And you give me a call to DJ the next police shindig. I'll give you ten percent off."

Kat chuckled, and they pushed the door open, Sienna glancing back inside the shop quickly before the door swung closed. He'd been there. She was sure of it. Danny Boy had been there.

CHAPTER SIXTEEN

The call from Ingrid about a dead body had come in right as Sienna was putting her PJs on. It was still early, but Sienna had racked up far more overtime than actual sleep since she'd been with the Reno PD and had planned to climb in bed and attempt to catch up on some much-needed rest. The call canceled those plans, and instead, Sienna had re-dressed and headed to the scene. Apparently, the location of the DOA had been phoned in by a prostitute who'd gone behind a building to service a john. The john had seen the corpse first and taken off running, leaving the woman alone in the alleyway. A solid fellow all around, it would seem.

When Sienna and Kat arrived, Ingrid was already there, along with a team of criminalists. The bright white lights highlighted the grimy, trash-strewn area, a chain-link fence separating the small courtyard from another building behind it. The space was somewhat abandoned but clearly not unused, dirty needles and yellowed condoms littering the stained asphalt.

And sitting upright in a chair in what had certainly been a darkened corner before the crime-scene LED lights had arrived was a woman—at least fifty pounds overweight if not more—wearing a pair of leggings and an oversize T-shirt, one arm hanging lank at her side, the other duct-taped to the back of the chair, chin resting on her ample breasts.

"Strangled?" Sienna asked Ingrid, snapping the rubber gloves on. Kat had stepped aside to talk to one of the criminalists, who was taking some samples off the pavement nearby.

"Yes," Ingrid confirmed, and when she signaled the criminalist named Malinda, the young woman used her gloved hands to tilt the DOA's head just enough so that Sienna could see the ligature marks on her neck. They appeared the same as on the victim they'd found under the overpass.

As if Ingrid had read her mind about connecting this victim to the other, she said, "No cards, but this was found clutched in her untaped hand." She reached in one of the evidence bags nearby and took out a small black object. Sienna leaned a bit closer. "A chess piece?"

"Yup. The games continue." Ingrid sighed, dropping the piece back in the bag.

"I don't play chess," Sienna said. "Which piece is that?"

"The queen."

She glanced at the dead woman. She was wearing a wig that had slid back on her skull, revealing a dirty nylon cap. One false eyelash was only barely attached, giving the impression that a large spider was crawling up her eye. She might have been a "queen" in life, but in death . . . not so much. Then again, death was kind to few. Ingrid turned away as Malinda asked her a question, and Sienna walked over to Kat. "Same guy?" Kat asked.

"It has to be," Sienna said and told her about the chess piece.

"God dammit," Kat said. "I'm really sick of this. I'm tired as hell, and maybe that's the point, right? To run us ragged? Have us hopping all over town so we're too exhausted to put any real investigative effort into catching him?"

"Maybe. Or maybe he's just thoroughly enjoying controlling all of this." In any event, they were putting everything they had into solving this case. Even if they'd had to delegate some of the research angles to a few trusted POs and had reached out to the local college for an intern.

So maybe Sienna did feel like she was eating and sleeping and breathing this case, but what else did she have going on? Part of her was grateful that she didn't have a minute to spare to sit at home and dwell on things she didn't care to dwell on.

She looked around one more time, then pointed at the building on the other side of the fence, in the direction the body was facing. "What business is that?" She squinted, barely able to read the name on the front through the fence. *Med Plus.*

"I think it's a medical supply company, but they would have only been open during business hours." Kat paused, squinting herself. "Plus, I can't imagine anyone working there could have seen anything this far away."

Sienna agreed, turning to the building that let out on the alley. She already knew from parking in front that it was an abandoned strip mall. No help there.

Kat sighed, and Sienna said, "Listen, I'll make you a deal. I'll finish up here. It's going to take a while, and you meet up with the ME tomorrow."

Kat gave her the side-eye. "Sounds like sort of a raw deal." But she smiled. "I'll take it, thanks."

"Go on then and get outa here," she said, and Kat nodded, heading to her car parked on the other side of the building where the crime scene tape had been strung up. It could be a strange thing to partner up with other law enforcement officers. In the beginning, you might know little regarding the details of their homelife and yet understand completely what sort of person they were, based on how they reacted to everyday job situations. Before she'd gotten to know Garrod on a personal level, she'd known the precise set of his mouth when they'd stood over a twelve-year-old who'd been gunned down in the street. She'd known that the softer his voice became and the heavier his accent, the angrier he was. A hundred things like that, before she even knew his favorite meal or the endearment he called his wife. Sienna hadn't even had a chance to ask Kat more questions about her personal life. She knew she wasn't married but wasn't certain if she was dating someone . . . if her parents were in Reno, or even what part of town she lived in.

Once this case slowed down in one way or another, she'd ask if Kat wanted to go to dinner so they could get to know each other better.

Sienna turned and began walking back to where Ingrid was speaking with the criminalists, taking a deep breath as she focused back on her task at hand: collecting, observing, noting, and questioning anything and everything that was still part of a fresh murder scene.

By the time Sienna was ready to head home, it was almost ten. She'd walked around with the criminalists as they'd searched corners and looked under the chair the victim had been sitting in, but they hadn't found so much as a single page from their Danny Boy. She and Ingrid had also questioned all the potential witnesses they could and come up with zip. Of course, they had no real way to find the john who'd run off, but from what it sounded like, he was just some guy who'd stumbled upon the crime along with the prostitute he'd left behind.

Sienna started her car before pulling out of the mostly empty parking lot, giving a small salute to the officer who stood next to his patrol car near the entrance. She turned on her phone and saw that she had several missed calls.

Brandon.

He'd called her earlier in the day, too, but she'd been busy solving riddles and seeking out hole-in-the-wall record shops. It was almost 1:00 a.m. in New York, but Brandon was a night owl, and his last call had been ten minutes before, so she pressed his speed dial.

"Hey, stranger," he answered.

Irritation fizzled through her, and she didn't even know exactly why. It was like she felt pissed off that he was guilt-tripping her about not checking in, which was ridiculous and unfair on her part. He missed her; that was all. Didn't she want him to miss her? This case was just making her tired and irritable. She rubbed at her eye as she came to a stop at a red light. "Sorry I haven't called until now," she said, making it a point to insert gentleness into her tone. "It's been a wild day, and I'm just leaving a scene."

"A scene? You mean a murder scene?"

"Yeah, unfortunately. It looks like our gamer has struck again."

"Aw, jeez, babe. I was hoping this job in Reno would be a break from the regular murder and mayhem you saw on the streets of New York City."

"Unfortunately, there aren't many places one can go to avoid some amount of murder and mayhem these days."

"You're probably right. Hey, I'm wrapping up a few cases early next week and will probably be able to take a few days off. How about I fly out for a couple days? You can show me the lay of the land."

"I'd love that, Bran, but I don't know if next week is great for me. It seems like this case just keeps ramping up, and I'd hate for you to get here and me have to work the whole time. Things are kind of . . . unpredictable right now, and Reno PD is short staffed. It's why I've been thrown right into the fray. Which . . . I haven't actually minded. It's made the adjustment a little easier."

Brandon sighed. "This sucks, Sienna. I miss you. This feels all wrong."

"I know. I miss you too. But remember what we said? One year. This is a temporary pit stop before we get settled somewhere permanently, right? And Brandon, I already think I'm making a difference here, you know? I've been in Reno less than two weeks, and I'm already part of this team. They've welcomed me, and I've earned their trust. It's . . . well, it's what I didn't know I needed," she finished softly.

"You deserve that." So why did he sound annoyed, as though he'd made too many concessions regarding what she "deserved"?

Sienna pulled onto her quiet street, the moon bright overhead, the flickering lights from televisions glowing softly inside the homes she passed. "Thanks, Bran. Hey, I'm almost home, and I'm exhausted. I'm going to face-plant into my pillow. Can I call you tomorrow?"

"I wish I was there to crawl into bed with you."

"Me too. Soon. Sleep well, okay?"

"Okay. Good night." She'd noticed that he'd stopped telling her he loved her right about the time she'd told him she was considering taking the offer in Reno. Why hadn't she brought it up to him? *Shouldn't it matter to you more?*

Sienna hung up the phone and sat in her car for a few minutes, feeling tired but edgy and oddly emotional. *What is wrong with you?* Maybe nothing. Maybe everything. And wouldn't that be par for the course? Her whole life had been upended. She was on the other side of the country from the man she was supposedly planning on spending the rest of her life with. She'd practically had to slink out of town in shame or be fired. She'd been thrown for a loop with this case. And now she was going to enter her quiet condo alone, where there were only boxes to sit upon.

And she didn't have *time*, nor was it appropriate, for a personal pity party when she had just left a second murder scene.

Even so, she sat there for a few minutes, her head falling back on the headrest, the quiet night sounds around her barely penetrating the glass of her windows. Crickets, the distant bark of a dog, then another, a car driving by a street or two over.

She reached inside her purse and brought out the sticky Gavin had written Mirabelle's address on, flicking it lightly between her fingers. The small, square piece of paper was the same color and size as the sticky note from the record store with the row of numbers. Just random, of course. It had to be. So . . . why did she feel like nothing this suspect did was random? He was messing with her mind. How in the world would he know that Gavin had given her a green sticky? He wouldn't. They were a dime a dozen. You could buy a sticky pad at any drug, grocery, or office store in town. And they were on every other desk across America. She let out a quiet groan, dropping the address back in her purse.

She got out of the car, greeting the cactus she'd become strangely attached to. It wasn't lewd, she decided. It was pretty and unique. The poor thing shouldn't be faulted just because she had a dirty mind. She trudged to her condo and locked the door behind her.

Her purse and briefcase landed on the floor, and she grabbed a bottle of water from the still-barren refrigerator and drank half of it before setting it on the counter. The details of the case rustled through her mind, making her feel restless, frustrated. Visions of cards and notes and knife-wielding psycho mothers swirled in her brain. She should make time to buy a television and get immersed in some series or another, do something other than ponder this case and the clues that might be hidden in the words of some nut. Her brain was working overtime, and suddenly it felt like *everything* might be a clue if paired with the right combo of words or phrases or items or locations. Maybe they were all just pieces on some cosmic game board, being moved at the whim of a divine game master. Hadn't "Mother" said something similar? The whole concept was depressing, but in her heart of hearts she didn't really believe it. She rubbed her temples. Yes, the mindlessness of Netflix would do wonders. Or maybe some evening, she'd go to a park or a lake and sit and stare at the water the way she and Gavin used to do as they watched Otis and Odette gliding elegantly across the water. And suddenly Sienna found herself sitting on the carpeted floor in the front room where she'd eaten pizza with Gavin, doing a Google search.

"You bastard," she muttered a few minutes later, scrolling to his number.

"Sienna?" he answered smoothly. She could hear noise, dings, and laughter in the background. He was either still at work or enjoying a social gathering.

"You lied," she accused.

The noise grew faint, as though he'd gone into another room and shut the door behind him. "Excuse me?"

"About Odette."

There was a small pause, and then she heard him sigh softly. "I didn't lie—"

"You lied by omission. You made it sound like she'd died of natural causes. But she was *stoned* to death."

Another pause. "Yes. She was stoned to death by degenerates who were probably high on drugs or alcohol or just the thrill of hurting a creature weaker than them. It was terrible, and it was cruel, and I thought I'd spare you—"

"You thought you'd *spare* me?" She laughed, but there was no humor in the sound. In fact, it sounded—and felt—oddly like a sob. "You thought *you'd* decide what I could and could not handle and lie accordingly? Is that it?"

"Sienna." His tone had gentled as though he had realized he was talking to a crazy person and didn't want to say anything too loudly or with the wrong inflection and risk sending her over the edge. "Yes. I'm sorry it upsets you to know I left that out. It was the first time I'd seen you in eleven damn years, and I didn't want to talk about animal cruelty."

Animal cruelty. She'd seen a dead woman who'd been strangled to death tonight, posed in a used-needle-and-condom-laden alley, and it was the knowledge of a *swan's* murder that had sent her for an emotional loop. *God, I'm tired.* As suddenly as her emotions had flared, they drained away, leaving her feeling listless and defeated. Embarrassed. She sighed, sinking back against the wall.

"I'm not weak and prone to hysterics, Gavin. You didn't have to worry about me making a scene." She attempted to insert some steel into her tone but could hear that she'd barely managed *tin*.

"Are we really talking about swans?" Gavin asked softly.

Sienna closed her eyes, grimacing. No, maybe they weren't. And despite her assertion about not being prone to hysterics, she was currently acting less than grounded. Her emotions felt twisted, her thoughts convoluted. She blew out a long breath. "Listen . . . I'm sorry. I just got home, and I'm exhausted. I went online to find out where Otis might be . . . if he was still close by . . . anyway, calling you was inappropriate."

"It's okay. I'm glad you called me." She heard a man say his name, and the boisterous sounds that had been in the background when he'd first picked up blasted in the background again as though the door to wherever he'd gone had opened. "Hey, hold on a minute. I'm at work and—"

"You go. Clearly, I need to get to bed anyway. I apologize for interrupting you."

"Sienna, if you—"

"Good night, Gavin." She disconnected the call and then stood and headed into her room to put herself to bed. This day needed to end.

CHAPTER SEVENTEEN

"Her name is Bernadette Murray, otherwise known as Queen Bee, after a wig store she owned and operated that goes by the same name," Ingrid said.

"Queen . . . *Bee*?" Sienna repeated. "The metal bee, and the chess piece," she said as realization hit. "Clever."

"Isn't it?" Ingrid asked, though her tone sounded less impressed than annoyed. "Her sister called to report that she didn't show for a family event two days ago. She gave it a day, thinking she just forgot, but when Bernadette still wasn't answering her personal or work phone, she called the police."

Sienna nodded, grateful that at least putting the bee and the chess piece clues together hadn't had them running all over town.

So now they had a name. One move forward.

"Do we know anything about her yet?" Sienna asked. Ingrid and Sienna had gotten to the station a couple of hours earlier, but Kat was still at the ME's office.

"Not yet, but I'm having some information pulled on her now."

Sienna worried her lip for a moment. "He's planning all of this way in advance," she said, thinking. "We found the bee days ago. We couldn't have put it together without the chess piece, but it means he had her in his sights, even then. These are not random victims."

"No. Definitely not."

The door opened, and Kat breezed in, waving a few sheets of paper in the air. She dumped all her things—purse, briefcase, and what looked like lunch in a brown paper sack—on the table. "We've been gifted with another installment," she said, handing Sienna the papers. "Art found these folded and tucked under the victim's wig." Sienna's eyes widened as she took the papers Kat offered, glancing down to confirm they were what she assumed they were—copies of the continuation of their suspect's life story. *More.* Of course there was more. She'd known this guy wasn't done. She and the criminalists had searched the crime scene, and the criminalists had done a quick check of the victim's clothes before she'd been packed up in a body bag and driven away. But they hadn't thought to look beneath her wig. She blew out a breath as Kat handed Ingrid her own copies. "The actual notes are at the lab, but—"

"We shouldn't expect there are any more fingerprints on these ones than were on any of the others," Ingrid finished.

"Correct. This guy is careful."

"So far," Sienna murmured.

"Ah, very optimistic attitude," Kat noted. "I like it."

"I'll try to keep it." Sienna smiled. "Thanks for meeting with the ME. We have some information on the victim." And then she relayed what Ingrid had told her about the woman's name and the shop she owned.

"No shit. Queen Bee. Okay. Well, that saves us some mental gymnastics."

"What else did Art give you?" Ingrid asked.

"Everything we assumed about our victim's death was confirmed," Kat answered. "It looks like the same method and same murder weapon. Chloroform was used on this victim too. Time of death was estimated to be forty-eight hours ago, so if the sister's timing is right, this guy killed her and then held her body somewhere for a very short time before setting up his scene."

"Yes, then, most definitely the same guy," Ingrid said. "Plus, the installment"—she shook the papers she was holding—"confirms it."

"One more interesting thing," Kat went on. "There were a series of numbers written on the back of her thigh. As soon as Art looked her over, he saw them." Kat took out a photograph and handed it to Ingrid, who studied it for a moment and then gave it to Sienna. The string of numbers was as precisely written as the notes, certainly by the same hand, and it appeared that a black Sharpie had been used.

Ingrid set the papers down and tapped one fingernail. "Do either of you know anything about latitude and longitude?"

"I know it's used to find a specific location, but I don't—wait, are you thinking that's what these numbers are?" Kat asked.

"I don't know. I met this man on vacation in Miami who owned a yacht—"

"Ooh," Kat said, her brows rising. "What happened to Moneybags?"

"As it turned out, the yacht was the only impressive thing about him," Ingrid said. "I dated him for a week and was happy to hop back on a plane home."

"There might not be a man on the planet impressive enough for you." Kat smiled sweetly.

"Anyway," Ingrid went on, "he explained latitude and longitude to me, and I've forgotten the specifics but remember that each coordinate is a string of numbers. And I know someone who might be able to let us know if I'm on the right track." She picked up her phone and asked whomever she'd called to come to her office. A minute later, a stocky man wearing a PO uniform came in, greeting them. "Sienna, if you haven't met Tony Wallace, he's one of our most senior patrol officers. How long do you have left, Tony?"

"Seven months and sixteen days," he said, taking a seat in an empty chair on the other side of the table they were sitting at.

"Until you're sailing the ocean blue full-time?"

Tony chuckled. "Not the ocean, the lake, but yeah, that's the plan."

"Tony and Carol have a sweet place on Lake Tahoe," Kat said, giving him a wide smile. Tony's wife must earn a lot of money, because Sienna knew well that a police officer's salary alone would never buy a "sweet place," or even a *semi*sweet place, on Lake Tahoe.

"Which is why I need your expertise," Ingrid said, handing him the series of numbers written on the sticky pad found at Duces and the numbers found on last night's DOA.

Tony studied them. "They could be coordinates," he said, "only without the degrees, minutes, and seconds. Can I write on these?" he asked.

"Yes," Ingrid said, handing him a pen. Tony took it, writing a degree sign next to the first set of numbers on both copies, an apostrophe next to the second set, and a quotation mark after the final set, where he also inserted a decimal. He tapped his pen on the final number of the first set. "There's no direction, but if the location is here in Reno, this first one would be north and the other one west. You can program it into Google Maps."

"Thanks, Tony. I knew you were the right one to ask."

"I hope it helps," he said, standing. "It was nice to meet you, Sienna."

"You too, Tony, thanks." He gave a nod to Ingrid and Kat and left the office.

"We'll check this out," Kat said to Ingrid.

Ingrid rubbed her forehead. "The news will be clamoring to ask questions, so we might have to do another press conference. I'll let you both know. One more scene like the one last night and we have a bona fide serial killer on our hands, although I think it's safe to say we already do. And both of you be extra diligent checking this location out today. If it looks sketchy, call for backup. And regardless, watch each other's backs." She picked the printouts up off her desk. "I'll read this ASAP. Why don't you two head to that location."

Kat and Sienna stood. "I'll look up the address we're headed to, and you can read Danny Boy's next installment to me on the way, partner," Kat said. "And make sure to read with inflection."

Sienna chuckled as they let themselves out of Ingrid's office and headed for the car.

My "tutoring sessions" with Mr. Patches went on for months. My grades fell again, but none of my other teachers seemed surprised. I was deeply, deeply ashamed. I hid it from Mother.

But I could only hide things from Mother for so long.

One snowy winter day, Mother came home early.

In the past months, things had escalated quite dramatically, and Mr. Patches was no longer content with a mere hand on the thigh. Suffice to say, I was facedown on the table, Mr. Patches above me.

I won't describe the details of what was happening, but I'm sure you can surmise.

He had grabbed the back of my head, and I don't know if it was the rough contact of my forehead on the wood surface or the pain of what I was enduring, but I lost consciousness momentarily, long enough for Mother to have entered the room, taken in the scene, and smashed Mr. Patches over the head with a cast-iron frying pan sitting on the stove.

Now that I think of it, perhaps I blacked out when the force of his skull hit mine.

In any case, when I opened my eyes, I was sitting on the floor, mostly propped up against the wall, an ice pack perched on top of my head, and Mr. Patches was bound to the chair and gagged in the same manner Father had been.

Mother was sitting across from him, a pleasant smile on her lovely face, her sky-blue eyes stormy with rage. She looked over at me. "You should have told me what he was doing to you, Danny Boy. I'm cross that you didn't. Quite cross."

"I'm sorry, Mother," I choked out. Mr. Patches's eyes darted back and forth between me and Mother, pupils dilated as he blinked rapidly. His pants were still down, and I averted my eyes from his flaccid penis, swallowing down the vomit that threatened.

Mother's face melted into understanding. "It's not *you* who needs to be sorry, my precious Danny Boy, my darling. It's the lewd sack of shit sitting across from me." She sighed, noticing my surprise. Mother never swore. "Excuse my language, but in this case, I feel it's warranted, don't you?"

"Y-yes, Mother," I answered. "V-very warranted."

"Did he threaten you, Danny? Did he find out your father's gone and take advantage of that knowledge?"

"Yes, Mother." My voice rose in pitch on the last syllable, shame enveloping me.

Mother took a slow, deep breath. "It's not your fault, darling. These *people*"—she practically spat the word like a snake spewing venom—"are masters of manipulation and trickery." She pounded her fist once on the tabletop, startling both me and Mr. Patches.

That's when I noticed the butcher knife on the table next to her still-fisted hand, alongside our chessboard, all set up and ready for a game, the black pieces facing Mr. Patches and the white pieces facing Mother. Several pawns had toppled over with the force of her punch, and now she took another breath before righting them once more.

"I hear you're in charge of the chess club at my Danny Boy's school," she said. Mr. Patches looked briefly confused before the fear that had been clear in his expression took over once more. I stared at his face, drinking in his fear, letting it recharge me. I had been sagging against the wall, and now I pulled myself upright. Mother glanced at me, giving an encouraging smile and blowing me a kiss. Her lipstick was still perfect, her makeup tasteful as always. Mother was never smudged. Mother never broke a sweat. Even now.

But then she looked back at Mr. Patches, and her face hardened. "An advantage isn't fair, now, is it?" she asked Mr. Patches, who simply stared at her, wide eyed, the gag trembling in his mouth while a string of saliva hung on his chin. "You're practically a professional, and that won't do, will it? We'll have to even the playing field, so to speak, won't we?"

Mr. Patches made an odd strangled sound, something between a curse and a plea.

I liked that sound coming from Mr. Patches. It was quite satisfying.

But Mother didn't need his approval, nor anyone's for that matter. As quick as a whip, she stood, grabbed the knife, and lunged at Mr. Patches, the same way she'd done with Father. This time, instead of stabbing at his chest, she arced the weapon downward, slicing into his naked, exposed crotch.

Mr. Patches went utterly rigid, a high-pitched scream muffled behind the rag in his mouth. Mother pulled the knife out with a delicious squelching sound, and he went rigid again, his scream building once more, blood splattering onto his button-down shirt and spilling to the floor.

Mother let the knife clatter to the table. Mr. Patches was panting now, sweat beading on his forehead as tears rolled quickly down his cheeks. He swayed as if he might pass out, but Mother ignored him. "Now," she said, pushing the chessboard forward when he'd seemed to get hold of himself, though he continued to sweat and weep. And bleed. "Fair is fair, isn't it, Mr. Patches?"

He answered with a muted sob. His shoulders were shaking, and the area between his legs was a red sea of blood and ruined flesh.

"Danny Boy," Mother said. "Seeing as this disgusting excuse for a human being's hands are otherwise occupied, you'll have to help him out. I realize it's terribly unfair to ask you to assist this vile deviant in any way whatsoever, but I think you'll like where this is going. You do have the strength, don't you, darling?"

"Yes, Mother," I said, and my voice already sounded stronger.

I *felt* stronger. Better. Because I did like where this was going. I liked it very much.

"You detest vile deviants as much as I do, don't you, Danny Boy?"

"Yes, Mother."

"The world is better without them," she asserted.

Yes, Mother. Yes, indeed.

I pulled myself to my feet, inhaling a deep breath and letting it rush through my body. I walked to where Mr. Patches was tied to the chair and stood at his side, ready to make a move.

Mother smiled, sweetly, gently, her eyelids fluttering. My, but she was pretty, my mother. Pretty and perfect in every single way.

She looked at Mr. Patches, shaking and bleeding in his chair. "Let's play a game, shall we?" she asked. "Winner takes all."

Sienna set the papers in her lap. "Well." Her hands felt shaky. Was this *real*?

"Another feel-good reading experience," Kat said, obviously attempting to add some humor to her tone but falling flat. She came to a stop at a red light and turned to Sienna. "'Mother' sounds like a downright savage. I'm going to assume Mr. Patches didn't fare well against her."

"I think that's a safe assumption," Sienna said. She thought for a moment as the light turned green and Kat accelerated through the intersection. This was the neighborhood where she and Gavin had rented that tiny house so many years before. The one neither of them had ever lived in. She wondered what had become of it. After their wedding-that-wasn't, she had called the landlord and left a message on his machine telling him they had to renege on their lease agreement. She hadn't pursued the security deposit they'd scrounged up, even though she'd needed it, but she supposed the landlord could have attempted to force them to make good on the contract and pay in full, and he hadn't, so Sienna had cut her losses on that front. Sienna had cut a lot of losses that year. A few hundred dollars was the least of them.

Her mind had begun to wander as she looked out at the neighborhood, and she forced her thoughts back to order. "Do you get a strange Oedipus vibe from these notes?" she asked Kat.

Kat made a clicking sound with her teeth. "That's a good way to put it. There's definitely something off about the way he talks about his mother. That's why I still question the factual nature of the story," she said, nodding to the papers in Sienna's lap. "It has a fictional quality to it."

"Yeah," Sienna said, "I agree. It could be *fictionalized* too. Like it's real, but he's putting his own fantastical spin on it."

"Right. Because if it's *all* a head fake, what's the point, you know?"

"I still think we should assume there's something truthful to his story but continue to question what feels off . . ." Sienna's words faded as the GPS instructed Kat to turn, and Sienna realized this wasn't only the neighborhood where she and Gavin had rented the house they'd planned to live in as husband and wife; it was the very same street.

Kat pulled up in front of a ramshackle house, a large tree shading the curb. *No, this is different. It has to be.* Kat was saying something, but Sienna was only half listening as she got out of the car, following along behind her partner, trying to make sense of where she was. Surely she was mistaken. She'd been thinking about the house and confused herself. *This isn't it, merely similar.* The place they'd rented had been shabby, but it hadn't been dilapidated like this one. There hadn't been a foreclosure sign lying flat in the patchy grass. The tree near the fence had been twiggy and small. Kat and Sienna approached the house, the door open just a crack. A hum took up under Sienna's skin, and she held her breath as Kat nudged the turquoise door open with her foot, the pent-up air coming out in a harsh exhale.

She remembered this door, the way the turquoise color had seemed like such a happy omen. What would be a beautiful new start. The way the color turquoise always made her stomach sour now.

"No way," she whispered, a guttural quality to her voice.

"What is it?" Kat asked, obviously sensing her shock as, weapons drawn, they went inside the house.

She blinked at the room they'd entered, feeling as though she'd been shot back in time, a trip that left her shaky and reeling. It was. It was *the* house. "I rented this house eleven years ago," she said.

Kat stilled, turning toward her. "Hold up. What?"

"I told you Gavin and I dated, but it was more than that. We'd planned to be married . . . this is the house we rented. We never lived here, but . . ."

Before Kat could answer, music started playing from the room beyond. Kat's and Sienna's eyes met, Kat's widening before they crept forward. Sienna knew the room they were moving toward was a shoebox kitchen with yellow cabinets and brick-printed linoleum. She knew because it had almost been hers.

"How charming!" Mirabelle had said when she'd stepped inside. Even then, Sienna had known that was an extremely generous description, but the rose-colored glasses she'd worn had meant she'd agreed anyway. It would be beautiful. Because it would be theirs.

Kat gestured to Sienna to take one side of the doorway, and she took the other, calling, "Reno police! Show yourself!"

Not a creak could be heard, even though the music played softly, a children's sing-along version of "Camptown Races," a jubilant harmonica accompanying the vocals.

Camptown racetrack five miles long. Oh! Doo-dah day!

Oh no.

Kat called several more times, and they listened carefully, hearing nothing. Sienna had managed to clear her mind of the shock of where they'd been . . . lured, was that the right word? It was certainly how it felt. She couldn't think about what it meant, though. Not now.

With a gesture and nod, they rounded the corner, each sweeping the room so all corners were covered.

"Oh crap," Kat said, letting out a breath. There was a window, but it'd been boarded over from the outside, thin shafts of light streaming through. But there was plenty of light coming in from the front of the

148

house and no corners to hide in. They both lowered their weapons. The man in the center of the room wasn't going to harm them. He was all but mummified, threadbare clothes hanging off his bones. Next to him was an old crate, and on top of that sat what looked like a battery-operated radio. There was actually an extra battery next to it, as though the person who'd set this up had brought a spare in case they hadn't figured out enough to follow the clues here before the ones inside the radio went dead. Sienna leaned slightly, confirming her guess, seeing that there was no cord just as the song came to a stop and, seconds later, began again.

"It's on a loop," she said, letting out a breath.

Kat stepped forward before slowly pulling something from beneath the radio. Yet another of Danny Boy's installments, when they'd only just finished one.

Sienna stared at the decomposed corpse, bending and tilting her head. "Kat, look," she said, pointing to the rotted fabric hanging from the arm. It was difficult to tell what color the material had once been, but one thing was clear: there was a round leather patch at the elbow.

Kat bent, looking to where Sienna indicated. "Mr. Patches?"

"It could be," Sienna murmured, straightening.

"Let's get out of here and call the coroner," Kat said.

Sienna nodded. *And read Danny Boy's latest note.* Her muscles felt sore and tight, and she didn't hurry as they made their way through the house and back to the car. The man inside wasn't going anywhere.

CHAPTER EIGHTEEN

Another chapter of my life had thankfully ended.
Mr. Patches went missing. No one knew where
he'd gone when he'd left school that cold winter
day. Mother drove his car into our detached garage
and covered it with a tarp, brushing her hands and
humming as we walked away. The tune was familiar
and haunting. *Doo-dah! Doo-dah! Oh! Doo-dah day!*
Despite Mother's sweet, melodic voice, I shivered.
"How about ice cream for dinner tonight, Danny
Boy?" she asked. "I'd say we deserve it, don't you?
Mint chip?"

Mrs. Patches went on the news, her eyes red, voice
quavering, as she spoke into the microphone about
what a kind and gentle man her husband was, a lover
of learning, pillar of the community, and all that stuff
people sometimes say before they learn their loved one
is—or *was* in Mr. Patches's case—actually a demon in
disguise. There was a solemn-eyed little girl standing
next to her mother at the podium, and I wondered if
he'd violated her, too, or if he preferred boys and had
a special affinity for the fatherless ones like me who
had little protection. But when the police stumbled

upon a large stash of child pornography on his home computer, the investigation stalled. Whether that was due to a lack of leads or because the police quietly decided the world was better off if he *stayed* missing, I didn't know. All I cared about was that my "tutoring" sessions had ended. On a side note, I still feel queasy when I hear the mention of the periodic table of elements, as that's the page the science book Mr. Patches had brought to my home was open to the first time he violated me. Thankfully, conversations that might bring to mind the table don't come up that often, and maybe you'd be surprised they do at all. But they do. Oh, I should know. They do.

"*Oh, look at that sunset. It's pure gold.*"

"*Spinach is so good for you! It's full of calcium.*"

You get the picture.

Anyway, moving on. I'd been averse to being touched before Mr. Patches, but now, even though a couple of years had gone by, I still recoiled at human contact. The problem was that I wanted to like it. I noticed the girls in my school. My mouth went dry at the sight of bare legs and tight shirts. I liked it when they walked past me close enough so that I could smell the scent of their hair, but not so close they brushed against me. So when the girl in my English class who sat next to me, the one who I'd first started calling Smiles not only because she did it often but because she turned them in my direction, began chatting with me before and after class, I was happy and filled with the hope that maybe I could be normal in at least some way.

Maybe my father hadn't ruined me completely. Maybe Mr. Patches hadn't either.

No one had to know what was in my past. I'd hide it. Mother would have no reason to hurt or kill anyone on my behalf. The things she'd done could stay hidden, only between her and me. I trusted Mother implicitly. Plus, I was bigger and stronger now—no one was going to victimize me again. No one was going to threaten or trick me.

Smiles asked if I wanted to go see a movie that had been adapted from a book we'd read in English class. I didn't know if she was asking me on a date or if she just wanted to go as friends. And I wasn't sure which one I hoped for. No, that's a lie, and I'm trying my best not to lie. Are we always aware of our lies? I wonder. Don't we all lie constantly, whether meaning to or not? Whether acknowledging it or not? I see *me* in a certain light, and so, even here, even now, I'm presenting myself to you as the person I perceive myself to be. But perhaps that perception is inaccurate. Perhaps your perception of me would not be the same? Is a false perception the same as a lie? I think not. What if you hold tight to that false perception because the truth would be unbearable? These are questions I'd have liked to explore with someone. Perhaps it would have mattered. Perhaps it would have changed things.

But I digress.

I hoped Smiles liked me as more than a friend. I was just incredibly nervous. How would I know what to do? How would I know what to say? I'd never had a man in my life to teach me the things I needed to know. And I couldn't ask Mother. Boys didn't ask their mothers about such things.

The year before, I had gotten a job stocking shelves at a local grocery store, so I had my own money to spend. When the day of our movie date arrived, I met Smiles outside the theater, sporting a new pair of jeans and a crisply ironed shirt. Smiles told me I looked nice and accepted when I offered popcorn and a drink. She chatted easily, and I thought I nodded in all the right places. When we took our seats in the darkened theater, I was more relaxed. Hopeful. As the movie commenced, Smiles drew closer to me, so close that our shoulders touched and then our knees. My breath quickened, my nerves strung tight in a new way that was both pleasure and pain. She reached out and took my hand, the cool touch of her fingers startling me so that I almost jumped out of my chair, and she gave a soft giggle, squeezing my hand in hers. We sat like that for many long minutes that felt like centuries. Eons.

I was hyperaware of every breath, every movement, every soft gurgle of my stomach. I swore I could feel the molecules of my body rearranging themselves into the new person I might be knowing a girl like this wanted to hold my hand and rest her sweet-smelling head on my shoulder. I felt myself growing hard, the zipper of my new jeans pressing painfully into my swollen penis. It reminded me of the terrible pain and the confusing pleasure I'd felt in that region before. *No, no, no, no.* I tried desperately to dispel my thoughts but was unsuccessful. It reminded me of Mr. Patches, and I began to sweat, a buzzing sound taking up in my head. I didn't want to think of Mr. Patches.

Oh God. I didn't want to think of him ever again, but especially not *here*, with Smiles's curls tickling against my cheek and her smooth fingers laced in mine.

I didn't want to feel dirty. I didn't want to draw away. But my body was hot and cold, and I could feel my hands growing clammy, my erection swelling in my pants despite me trying my best to will it away. The more upset I became—the more revolted with myself—the more turned on my body got. It was misery. My heart was slamming in my chest, my balls were aching for relief, and the images in my head kept flashing, fast and furious. Nauseating. The wood grain of the table right below my face. The colored squares of the periodic table. *Nickel. Cobalt. Magnesium.* The popcorn rolled in my stomach. And so when Smiles turned her head, placing her soft, hot mouth on my neck and kissing me there, her hand wandering to my tented crotch, I ejaculated in a literal flood of pleasure and shame, a cry of confusion and disgust breaking the relative silence of the movie theater.

Smiles's head lifted swiftly and her hand drew away just as quickly, and I could feel her stare on the side of my face that was already burning with humiliation.

I heard the rustle of other heads turning, felt their shocked stares, and I stood, kicking over the half-full popcorn that had been on the floor and tripping over people's feet as I squeezed through the aisle, racing for the exit. I ran all the way home before unlocking the door and darting inside. Only then did I allow the tears to fall. Only then did I seek out Mother.

She took me in her arms and she comforted me. "There, there, my darling," she said. "Every boy needs his mother sometimes. You never have to be alone."

Smiles was still nice to me after that, but in a distant way. She greeted me cordially in class and even chatted a bit here and there. But as soon as the bell rang, she grabbed her things and rushed for the door. One day at the end of our senior year, I saw her sitting on a bench near the gymnasium. I approached tentatively, gathering my courage, forming the apology— the explanation—I knew she was long overdue. But when I stood in front of her, and she looked up at me with patient interest, the words scrambled into incoherence in my mind, and without a single utterance, I left her where she sat.

Cat got your tongue, Danny Boy? I thought, remembering Mother's old joke as I rushed away. Yes, apparently, he'd taken that too. What else was I lacking that I'd only discover in time? What else had been stolen from me that I'd never get back? And where had it really all begun?

Kat's desk chair squeaked as she sat back, waiting for Sienna to finish reading. For a moment they both were quiet before Kat said, "It's obviously purposeful that a body and this note"—she tapped the photocopy on her desk in front of her—"were left in that particular house. So now," she went on, "it's not just that our guy found out the name of one of the detectives working the case—*you*—and added your name to something he wanted the police to have. This time, he either looked into your background. Or he looked into Decker's. Or you're both involved in his twisted little game somehow. Either way, he's making it far more personal now."

Sienna let out a soft breath. She agreed with the assessment. She just didn't know how he would have found out that she or Gavin had rented the house eleven years before. But if he *had* pulled Gavin into this, *why?* Did that simply point back to her as well? She bent her neck from side to side, working out a sudden kink. "What sort of public records would contain old rental information?"

Kat shrugged. "Some of those 'people search' websites list all known addresses going back years. If you even signed a lease, it might be there. We'll check it out, see how easy or difficult it might have been to attain that address as it connected to you." She paused, and Sienna saw her assessing her from her peripheral vision. "Try not to be worried, okay? These psychos like to have a personal connection with the police. It makes them feel important."

"No, I know. I'm not worried." *Mostly.* She carried a weapon and was good with it. She could protect herself. It was more . . . *eerie* than anything to know that this person she'd come to know in an odd sense through his letters might be watching her.

Kat twirled her pen. "I have our new intern looking into who owns the house and any recent occupants."

"Okay, great." Considering the staff shortage they were currently dealing with, they were lucky to have had an intern answer their request from the local college's criminal-justice program. His background check had just come through, so now the young man was helping them follow up on leads and other information that could be obtained through computer searches—both classified and not—so Kat and Sienna could be out in the field.

Regardless, they still didn't have enough hands on deck, and crimes continued to roll in, unrelated to this killer, that still needed the attention of law enforcement. Sienna remembered what Ingrid had said about the choice to approve her transfer being made easier by the staffing shortage, but she hadn't realized the extent of the department's desperation. Well, at least she was needed, if not initially wanted.

As if her thoughts had summoned him, the young intern, Xavier, came hurrying in. "I might have something here," he said, "about the teacher you wanted me to look up? One who might have gone missing and it was later found had child porn on his computer?"

"Yeah? What have you got?" Sienna asked, a trill of hopefulness reverberating. The last installment had been decidedly . . . sad? Was that the right word? Could, or more to the point, *should* one be sad for a killer who commits brutal murders? *Probably not.* But, well, that was a moral quandary to ponder at a later date. Right now, they just needed to catch this guy so he wouldn't hurt anyone else.

He handed her a couple of computer printouts. "Okay, so Sheldon Biel, a science teacher at Copper Canyon High School, went missing twenty years ago."

Kat came up beside Sienna and perched herself on the edge of the desk. "Twenty years?"

Sienna looked up at her, feeling an internal click as though a puzzle piece had just slid into place. "That would jibe with the state of the mummified body we just found," she said before looking back at Xavier. "Great work. Anything else?"

"Look at the printout behind that one," he said, pointing to the papers in her hand. Next to her, the phone rang, and Kat turned away from them as she took the call. Sienna looked down to what Xavier had indicated. On top of the stack of papers was a photo of the school he'd just mentioned. Underneath that was the "missing" poster that had been created in the wake of Sheldon Biel's disappearance. He was a reasonably good-looking man with what appeared to be a genuine smile. But a feeling of deep distaste came over her as she looked from his buttoned-up shirt to his wire-framed glasses, the description "Danny Boy" had provided of his abuse running through her mind. She glanced over the rest of the information on the poster and then moved it behind the third printout, which was a news article detailing an update on the case. The photo that accompanied it was from a press conference when the man had first gone missing. In it, a woman stood in front of a microphone, a police officer on one side of her and a little girl on the other. The girl appeared very serious, if not frightened. *Solemn eyed.* Sienna's heart tightened. The article detailed the unfortunate fact that child pornography had been found on the missing man's computer. The investigation was taking another turn, and police were questioning whether his disappearance was related to his illegal proclivities. The words from the writing she'd recently read about the case stalling came back to her.

Whether that was due to a lack of leads or because the police quietly decided the world was better off if he stayed missing, I didn't know. All I cared about was that my "tutoring" sessions had ended.

The final printout was a photo of Sheldon Biel standing with a small group of students. The tagline beneath the photo identified them as the Copper Canyon High School Chess Team. He was wearing khakis, a button-down shirt, and a sports coat with patches on the elbows.

Sienna felt that trill again, though stronger.

Kat hung up the phone and turned back to them. "That was Art, the medical examiner," she said. "He's only given the body a precursory glance but can confirm that there are what appear to be knife marks on the bones."

"That fits too," she murmured, thinking of Danny Boy's description of Mr. Patches's violent murder. Sienna held the pictures she'd just looked at up for Kat to see.

Kat took them in before her gaze met Sienna's. "Well, hello, Mr. Patches," she said.

Sienna looked at Xavier, who was watching them expectantly. He was a cute kid, tall and kind of awkward, with smooth brown skin and watchful eyes with long lashes that curled upward. "I pulled everything I could find on him," he said, "but there might be more."

"Keep looking, if you don't mind," Kat said. "But you might have just broken this case wide open. Excellent work."

The way the kid's smile burst forth made Sienna grin as well. "Sure. Okay, yeah, will do," he said, turning and all but skipping back to the small metal desk he'd been designated over in the corner of the room.

"Sheldon Biel, you dirty, dirty man," Kat murmured, looking more closely through the printouts Sienna had just handed her.

"It's him, isn't it?" Sienna said, but she didn't really need to ask. It had to be.

"Yes, and dental records will confirm if the body we just found belongs to this man as well, but if I was a betting girl, which I'm not, by the way—gambling makes me nauseous—then I'd say absolutely."

"If this is our Mr. Patches, Kat, we're only one degree from Danny Boy himself."

"Which means those letters aren't fiction, Sienna. He's telling his story. Those things really happened. At least . . . some of it did."

Sienna tapped her chin for a moment. "If this *is* Mr. Patches, he gave him to us. Literally. He had to know Mr. Patches's identity might lead to his own. So why would he do that?"

"I don't know. But I do know that we need to go to the school and get his class list from the year he disappeared," Kat said, grabbing her purse. "One of those students might very well be named Daniel and have had a father who disappeared as well."

"Agreed. We'll ask Xavier to check and see if Reva Keeling or Bernadette Murray had any connection to Copper Canyon, which will free us up to meet with Bernadette's sister if she'll see us too," Sienna said, grabbing her things as well and following Kat to the door. She had a strong feeling they were about to make another move forward on this elaborate game board Danny Boy had set up for them to play.

CHAPTER NINETEEN

Sienna opened the yearbook on top of the short pile in her lap as Kat turned on the car, blasting the air conditioner. There was a large hand-drawn rendering of Copper Canyon High School on the inside spread, and Sienna took a moment to look at it. "It's a nice school," she said, glancing up at the corner of the building they could see from where they were parked. The inside had been nice, too, as far as old paro-chial-style buildings went. Well built. Nicely maintained. Obviously updated where needed. The district was located in an upper-middle-class area where the residents paid significant taxes and were proud of their academic successes.

The collective outrage over learning a purveyor of child pornogra-phy had taught their best and brightest must have been significant. But they hadn't read Danny Boy's writings. They didn't know the half of it.

Sienna and Kat had met with the principal and explained as much as they needed to about what they were looking for. The man had been there a little over ten years, but that still wasn't long enough to have known Sheldon Biel, a.k.a. Mr. Patches. But the principal had given them several yearbooks that they were now looking through.

Sienna started flipping the pages of the first one, from the year Sheldon Biel had gone missing, letting out a frustrated breath when none of the boys in the class pictures was named Daniel. "No such luck," she muttered.

"Danny might not be his name, though, just like Mr. Patches wasn't his. And Smiles doesn't give us anything specific to go on. Did you expect him to make it easy?" Kat asked.

"I guess not," Sienna said, her gaze moving from one boy to the next as though she'd *know* him the moment she saw his photo. But none of them stuck out at her for any particular reason. They all looked so *young*, and it broke her heart to know that a boy who—if he wasn't one of these particular children—had looked just like them had been so horrifically abused. Her eyes moved over their faces, counting the number of boys versus girls. "Twenty boys and ten girls," she murmured.

"We'll have to look into each of the boys," Kat said.

Sienna nodded, leafing through the next book in the stack. They'd figured Danny Boy might not have had his photograph taken the year Mr. Patches had gone missing. But perhaps he'd had one taken in one of the consecutive ones. Sienna had looked up the year the periodic table of elements was taught as a topic and found that it was in the ninth-grade lesson plan, which matched up with the grade Mr. Patches taught. "Danny Boy had a rough year that year," Sienna had told Kat. "But maybe he was more up for picture day as a sophomore or a junior or senior."

"Here," Sienna said, a note of excitement in her voice as her finger hit on a sophomore boy from the following year. "Daniel Forester." She tipped the book Kat's way, and they both studied the boy for a moment. He was blond with a sharp chin and an overall elfin look. His grin was big and lopsided and like nothing Sienna would have pictured, but . . . well, she couldn't let her own assumptions lead the way.

"Could be," Kat said, but there was doubt in her inflection. "He looks a little bit too . . ."

"Happy?" Sienna offered.

Kat let out a small snuffing sound. "I guess. Though happiness can be faked."

Sienna picked up the next book and found the junior class. Daniel Forester was in that class as well, appearing just as joyful, even if he'd broken out in acne that year.

His acne had cleared noticeably by the time he was a senior, and according to his smile, his joy had multiplied. When she found him in one of the club photos with his arm hung loosely over the shoulder of an equally joyful, pretty red-haired girl, Sienna figured she might be the reason. "He's in four clubs," Sienna pointed out, flipping from one picture to another.

"That doesn't sound like our Danny Boy," Kat said.

Sienna sighed, closing the book. "No, but I guess we'll find out." She put the pile in the back seat of the car, and they pulled away from the curb, heading to their next appointment.

Bernadette Murray's sister, Jasmine, lived in a single-family home in Midtown, just bordering the Reno Arts District. Sienna remembered this area as popular with young people because of its nightlife, funky clothing shops, and bookstores, and as they followed the GPS to Jasmine Murray's address, she saw that that was still the case. They pulled up to the curb in front of a white ranch with black shutters, featuring a miniature strip of yard enclosed by a low chain-link fence.

When they knocked on the door, a dog started barking loudly and maniacally, pitch shrill. "Damn. I hate dogs," Sienna said.

"Ooh, a chink in the armor," Kat said. "I might have to rescind the 'bestie for life' title."

Sienna snorted. It wasn't that she hated *all* dogs . . . exactly. There had just been lots of them that ran wild in the trailer park when she'd been growing up, and some were not to be trusted. Some bared their teeth and growled low in their throats when you walked by. Some pulled against their chains and practically strangled themselves to maul you. Or that was what their intent had seemed to be to Sienna. Maybe she just hadn't met the right one yet, but her go-to reaction to dogs was to brace for impact.

A woman in her mid- to late forties pulled the door open, slender where her sister had not been, with hair cropped close to her head and a tiny dog in her arms who let out another burst of high-pitched yelps. "Oh, shush it up now, Cookie," she said. "Detectives?"

"Yes, Kat and Sienna," Kat said, gesturing to each of them as she gave their names. "Ms. Murray?"

"Jasmine. And please come in."

They walked into the home, older, with dark-green carpet that had definitely seen its prime in every way possible, but despite that, uncluttered and clean. She showed them into the living room, where Sienna took a seat on the black leather sofa, and Kat sat next to her.

Jasmine Murray sat down in one of the two easy chairs across from them, the dog in her lap. "Thank you for meeting with us, Jasmine," Kat said. "We're so sorry for your loss."

Jasmine smiled sadly, petting Cookie's head. The dog stared at Sienna, head cocked, as though as suspicious of her as she was of it. "Thank you. I just can't believe it. It's still not real. I saw my sister every week. She started coming to church with us about five years ago, and we did a big family dinner afterward. She rarely ever missed. She had really gotten her life back on track."

Sienna frowned. "Can you tell us about that?"

"About her troubles?"

Sienna nodded, and Jasmine looked off to the side as if seeing into the past. "Well, you know, she was young when she had her first daughter, Maya. She started partying too much, got into some drugs and alcohol, and when she and Herb, that's Maya's father, split up, Maya went to live with him."

The dog, Cookie, leaped off Jasmine, ran over to Sienna, and stared up at her before jumping onto her lap. "Oh," she said, leaning back and raising her hands.

"Cookie!" Jasmine said. "Sorry, just shoo him off."

Sienna paused but then relaxed her arms, reaching out to let Cookie sniff her fingers. Cookie, apparently approving of Sienna's scent or aura or whatever dogs used to ascertain a person's worth, sat down, wiggling his butt to get comfortable. Sienna gave a small, thin laugh. "All right, then," she said, giving Cookie's miniature head a single pat.

"How old is Maya now?" Kat asked, pressing her lips together, obviously trying to hold back a smile as she looked away from Cookie.

"She's twenty-five and doing real well. She works at a bank and lives with her boyfriend downtown."

"And what was her relationship like with her mother?"

"It was good from what I could tell. I mean, Maya was bitter with her mother for a while, especially through her teenage years, you know? But in the last five, they started getting on real good. Maya would bring Trey over for dinner when they could make it, and things always seemed fine." She looked away, shaking her head before looking back. "The thing that's so hard about all of this is that Bee made her mistakes, especially when it came to motherhood, but she'd learned. She'd grown. She was happy, and her business was successful. She'd gotten her life together." She paused, shaking her head again. "She'd taken so many risks in the past, and then she gets killed when she starts living on the straight and narrow."

Sienna watched the woman for a minute, true sadness, even downright grief, etched into her features. The warm little weight in her lap wriggled, reminding her he was there and that she was unconsciously stroking his back.

"Is there anyone you can think of who might have held a grudge against her?" Kat asked. "Someone from her past, or maybe her ex-husband?"

"Herb?" Jasmine laughed softly. "Nah, Herb's an old softy, and he and Bernadette made their peace. He went to the same church we do when he lived here. But anyway, he moved to San Diego for work last year. Maya keeps me up to date on him, but he hasn't been back since he moved."

Sienna nodded. "Do you or any family members have a connection to Copper Canyon High School?"

Jasmine's face screwed up as she shook her head. "I've heard the name, but no, not that I can think of."

Kat looked at Sienna, and Sienna gave her a small nod. "I think that's all for now," Kat said. She took a business card out of her purse and handed it to Jasmine. "Thank you for meeting with us. If you think of anything at all that might help, will you contact me?"

"Oh, sure. Yes. Thank you for putting so much effort into finding who did this to my sister," she said, standing. Kat stood as well, and Sienna, unsure of how to get Cookie off her lap, remained seated awkwardly.

"Of course," Kat said, looking back at Sienna. Jasmine, obviously noticing Sienna hadn't moved, called Cookie's name, and the little dog jumped off her lap. Jasmine bent, picked him up, and placed him in the crook of her arm again.

They said goodbye to the woman and left her house, returning to the car. "You don't like dogs, but apparently the feeling isn't mutual," Kat said, raising a brow and pulling away from the curb.

"That was barely even a dog," Sienna said.

Kat laughed.

They turned the corner and started driving back to the station. "So what do you think about what Jasmine said about Bernadette's past?"

"The daughter?" Sienna asked.

"Yeah. We have a similarity between the first victim and the second. Something that links them."

"Bad mothers," Sienna said. "Or mother figures anyway." Sienna paused, looking out the side window as Kat merged onto the highway. "Neither one of them took care of their children—or grandchild, in the case of Reva Keeling—the way they should have."

"There's definitely a trend there," Kat noted. "But Danny Boy's mother *did* protect him. So was he . . . inspired by her?"

Sienna stared out the window unseeing, wishing she had an answer.

CHAPTER TWENTY

"Serial killers are typically defined as those who kill three or more people in a period of over a month, with a cooling-down time between each kill," Armando Vitucci said, his voice deep and clear, with the very slight lilt of an Italian accent. Those in the room—Sienna, Kat, Ingrid, and two other detectives who, though they were working other cases, had asked to sit in on the briefing—all watched him, riveted. The man struck Sienna as someone who had just walked out of a cigar commercial or stepped off the glossy page of an advertisement for some fine liquor.

Suave. Polished. Distinguished. His gray pin-striped suit appeared bespoke, and his thick black hair was combed back from his face, a strong cleft in his chin and flickers of gray dotting his temple. Sienna wouldn't necessarily call him handsome, but he was definitely striking.

And yet, despite his sophisticated appearance and graceful—if graceful could be masculine, because he was definitely that—mannerisms, there was warmth about him, too, in the creases fanning away from his eyes and the way in which he looked so directly at each of them in turn as he spoke.

"While our killer has only killed two people so far, it is my belief that in light of the great effort and planning he is undertaking, either there have been other victims in the past that have not been discovered yet, or"—he looked around pointedly—"there will be more."

Sienna did not disagree, and she knew Ingrid didn't, either, as she'd already said something to that effect. She would have bet her bottom dollar that their guy wasn't done yet, not by a long shot.

"So in an effort to get in front of this suspect, I am going to treat him as a serial killer and profile him as such. There are four main categories of serial killers, and I believe ours falls into two," he said, tapping the board that held up-to-date copies and photos pertaining to the case. "Perhaps one more than the other, but still both to some degree." He paused, meeting Sienna's eyes momentarily. "The mission-oriented killer's goal is to 'improve the world' by eliminating a defined group of people for a specific reason. For example, prostitutes because the killer believes them to be sinful or unclean, or gay men because the killer believes them an abomination before God. In the case of our subject, Detectives Kozlov and Walker are theorizing that he is eliminating mothers, or mother figures, who failed their children."

Sienna jotted down the phrase *mission-oriented*. It'd been a while since she'd studied serial killers, and she'd never actually worked on such a case. She planned to do more in-depth research on what Professor Vitucci was telling them here.

"Is this because he himself was abused? He's relating?" Kat asked. "Because from his writings, it seems the opposite. That his mother was his only protector."

"I cannot attest to the honesty of the writings," Professor Vitucci said. "But generally speaking, many serial killers suffered physical or sexual abuse as children."

"You'd think he'd choose to kill abusive fathers instead of neglectful mothers," the older female detective with the last name Harris said.

"Maybe since *his* mother protected him, he finds it particularly offensive that others would not?" the younger male detective named McGee guessed.

"God, I already have a headache," Detective Harris said, to which Professor Vitucci offered a soft chuckle.

"That's what happens when you attempt to enter the mind of a madman," he said, a teasing tone in his voice.

"Trust me, I know," Detective Harris said. "Have you met my ex-husband?"

Soft laughter followed her comment, and Professor Vitucci shot her an amused glance. "These killers are very rarely clinically insane or psychopathic."

"Oh, well, there goes the similarity to my ex-husband," she said to another round of chuckles.

Professor Vitucci offered a smile, but it was fleeting as he got back to business. He turned to the board, looking over the photographs for a moment. "They are often perfectionists and highly meticulous," he went on. "They plan their murders with great precision, and they are not likely to leave evidence behind, unless on purpose."

Well, that was one definite they could attest to. And it confirmed what they'd thought about the fact that Mr. Patches's body made several things easier to investigate. He was leading them somewhere, and so while the addition of clues felt victorious in a way, it also made Sienna feel manipulated. To what end, she couldn't yet guess.

"Mission-oriented killers will not stop unless they're apprehended," Professor Vitucci said. He looked around the room. "Any questions before I move on to the second category?"

There was a general murmuring, but no one raised their hand.

Professor Vitucci nodded once, linking his hands behind his back as he walked in one direction, pivoted, and walked back the other way. "The second category I believe this suspect falls into is the power-oriented killer," he said, stopping and turning their way. "This type of killer derives gratification from the dominance he exerts over a victim."

"Does that also go back to the fact that our killer most likely felt inadequate at some point?" Kat asked.

"Inadequate or powerless, yes." He paused, his gaze moving around the room. "These killers are patient, and they enjoy the process of the murder. It's him directing you. He derives intense pleasure from that. The cat-and-mouse game is part of the fun for him. This killer seems to find particular enjoyment in making a *literal* game out of the investigation, but other serial killers have done similar things . . . taunting the police by calling or writing letters to them, drawing maps as to where bodies might be found, leaving clues or notes—even cryptograms—for them at crime scenes."

"All in an effort to exert the ultimate control," Ingrid said.

"Precisely," Professor Vitucci answered.

"The press coverage must thrill him," Sienna said softly, half to herself.

His gaze hit on her. "Yes, it certainly expands his power reach."

He gave them a moment, and once the murmuring had quieted, he went on, "Those are the specific things I see when I profile our suspect. But as far as generalities, I have this to give." He linked his hands behind himself again and paced slowly in front of them, back, forth. "Generally serial killers are white males in their twenties and thirties. They are intelligent, mobile, gainfully employed, long-term residents of the area in which they kill, and their killings typically bring them into close contact with the victim, as with our killer. I would hazard a guess that he fits all of those generalities."

"So no sharpshooters," Detective McGee said.

Professor Vitucci's lips tipped very slightly. "There have been a few of those, actually. There are always exceptions, especially when dealing with the human psyche, but again, in general terms, no, and especially in the two categories I spoke of. No, this killer enjoys the hands-on. Or he's beginning to."

Sienna tapped her pen on the pad. Yes, that was true. The ME had guessed that the nature of the second victim's neck wounds indicated less hesitancy than the first victim's. If their Danny Boy hadn't enjoyed the first kill (if it *was* his first), then he had enjoyed the second far more. Or at least . . . he'd gotten better at it.

She went over the other generalities Professor Vitucci had just listed. *White male. Twenties or thirties. Drives a car. Has a job.* Sienna jotted those things down as she considered the other specifics, her brow dipping. "Professor Vitucci?" He turned, lifting his chin slightly. "You said serial killers tend to kill in areas where they've been long-term residents. The two victims live nowhere near each other. What do you attribute that to?"

"I was referring more to the same city than the same neighborhood." He paused. "But to take it a step further, the place that brought these two victims to the killer's attention overlaps somehow. This killer chose those two women because he knew their past. He knew their failures. How? Who is he or what does he do that would have brought him into contact with both? Or in what way is he connected to them?"

Sienna gave him a small smile and a nod. Yes, they still needed more information about the two women's pasts. But they were still sifting through the details of their present. *Where did they go on weekends . . . where did they get coffee . . . did they use the same gym?* She and Kat were buried in lists and didn't have enough manpower to sift through any of it quickly.

"Can we talk about the letters?" Kat asked.

"Yes. I've read through them all once," Professor Vitucci said. "I'd like to go over them again, since he left clues in the copy. It's always possible to see something on a second read that wasn't caught on the first." The professor frowned. "However, I hesitate to use the letters as a significant part of the profile. Something feels off about them," he said. "For example, what mother, while doing chores around the home, wears a sexy red vest?"

"So you got the Oedipus vibe too," Kat said.

He shot her a half smile but paused, seeming to consider that. "Perhaps it is him romanticizing her. Perhaps not. He is playing games, as we already know. To what extent, I'm not entirely sure. I'd keep an open mind. Because as we also know, there is truth mixed in."

The *truth* that they knew of was the existence of Mr. Patches and likely, considering his verifiable "hobbies," what he'd done to Danny Boy under the guise of "tutoring sessions."

"Other than playing games with law enforcement for his own amusement or as a power play," Sienna said, "do you think there are other reasons for these writings? Kat and I have wondered if he's trying to explain himself. Do they hint at him feeling remorse?"

"There is likely some of that mixed in there, yes. Or a desire to be understood. He's telling us something with his writings that he's not necessarily saying outright. In some sense I'd wager he's hoping you see through his lies, in order that you understand the truth."

Sienna worried her lip, not entirely sure she understood that statement, so she wrote it down as Detective Harris asked a question about the forensics of the notes and Kat answered.

Professor Vitucci glanced at his watch. "I'm sorry to say I'll have to leave in a few minutes as I have an appointment. But please feel free to contact me with any follow-ups. Are there any last questions before I go?"

"Just one," Sienna said. "The medical examiner confirmed this morning that the first victim, Sheldon Biel, was stabbed to death, as described in the writings. The second two, the recent victims, were strangled. Does this speak to the fact that he's trying to differentiate himself from his mother? Is there anything to deduce from that?"

"There is definitely differentiation between the killing of Sheldon Biel and the killings of the two recent victims. I would say the main difference, regardless of the two separate killers, is the rage present during the teacher's murder."

"Which makes sense since the guy was raping her son on their kitchen table when she walked in the room," Kat said, and even though Sienna was looking at Professor Vitucci, she heard the grit in Kat's tone as though her jaw was tight as she said the words.

"Yes, that kind of rage certainly makes sense given the circumstances," Professor Vitucci confirmed. "The strangulation killings, however, do not denote quite the same amount of passion. Hatred, yes; passion, no. Generally speaking, stabbings are killings of passion, while strangulation is premeditated."

Which aligned with Danny Boy's story thus far.

Ingrid stood, walked to the front of the room, and shook Professor Vitucci's hand as they each got up to thank him personally as well. Professor Vitucci bid them all goodbye, and Sienna sat back down, thinking over everything he'd said and going through the few notes she'd written. Something was racing in and out of the tunnels in her mind, but she couldn't capture it. What she did know was that if what Professor Vitucci had said about this killer was correct, there would be more victims.

And as of right then, there was nothing they could do but wait for him to strike.

CHAPTER
TWENTY-ONE

Sienna swallowed, shifting on her feet as she pressed the buzzer. The home was lovely. A Mediterranean style with two tall palm trees flanking the start of the walkway, and more palms rising behind the house. Sienna hadn't necessarily missed a lot about Reno, landscapewise, or at least she hadn't realized she had, but she suddenly realized she'd missed the palm trees, somehow casually majestic—whether an oxymoron or not, to her, it fit. *And the desert sunsets,* she thought, tilting her head to the sky, *like the one flaming above me right this moment.*

This house, this street . . . it was exactly where she could picture Mirabelle.

The door was pulled open, and the woman herself stood there, an expectant look melting into surprise and then dissolving into tears as she squealed Sienna's name, enveloping her in a lily of the valley–smelling bear hug.

Sienna let out a smothered laugh, holding the bottle of wine she'd brought to the side so it wouldn't get crushed between them. In the momentary glimpse she'd gotten, she'd seen that Mirabelle remained beautiful, her blonde hair streaked with white but still in the same upswept style she'd always worn, her figure still trim.

"Oh my God! Oh my God!" Mirabelle said, pulling away and bringing her hands to Sienna's cheeks and holding them gently. "Oh, my sweet girl. When Gavin told me you were back in town, I almost keeled over with happiness. Well, come in, oh." Despite her invitation, she enveloped Sienna in another hug, not allowing her to move for a moment before again pulling away. "Gosh, you're gorgeous. Look at you. You always were a beauty, but now, oh goodness, you must think I'm a mess with makeup running down my face." She swiped at the slight black smudges under her eyes, taking Sienna by the hand.

"Hi, Mirabelle," Sienna said, and she heard the unshed tears in her voice as a flood of comfort and the love she'd always felt for Gavin's mother overwhelmed her. God, she'd missed her so much.

Mirabelle turned, and Sienna looked up to see Gavin leaning casually in a doorway beyond, watching them, a gentle smile on his lips. Their eyes met, and he tipped his chin. "Glad you could make it," he said.

She gave him a slight smile in return, her gaze going to the photographs on the wall, the same ones Mirabelle had displayed in her mobile home so many years ago. Sienna's eight-year-old gap-toothed smile. Gavin performing in a play at school. Both of their graduation photos. She swallowed. Mirabelle had kept them up. All these years. And though the ones of Sienna and Gavin together as a couple were now gone, the ones that spoke of Mirabelle considering Sienna a long-lost yet still-loved daughter remained.

"Come in and let me get you a drink. We have so much catching up to do, don't we? Let me take that," she said, taking the bottle of cabernet from Sienna as they entered a spacious kitchen with creamy cabinets, white marble countertops, and a pearlescent tile backsplash. All the shades of white somehow blended beautifully and made the whole space feel both fresh and warm.

And underneath whatever delicious dish was baking in the oven, Sienna smelled the clean scent of lemon. Through the sliding glass doors, pool water sparkled, large rocks forming a waterfall that splashed and gurgled, emerald-green grass surrounding it, as well as those tall palms she'd seen from the front. "Oh, Mirabelle, it's just beautiful," she breathed, looking around. "You deserve this, every bit of it."

"Oh, I don't know that I deserve any of it, but that son of mine keeps spoiling me."

"I keep trying," Gavin said. He was handsome in a pair of jeans and a button-down shirt, rolled up to his elbows, strong forearms showing as he raised the glass of whatever amber-colored liquor he was drinking and took a small sip. "But she still won't let me buy her a car."

Mirabelle batted her hand in the air. "I don't need a car. Argus drives me where I need to go, or I take the bus. It's where I get my spicy romance reading in," she said and gave a small shimmy that made Sienna laugh.

Gavin gave an obviously fake grimace that then turned into a grin as he walked to a drawer, where he pulled out a wine opener.

Mirabelle gestured to a seat at the counter, and Sienna sat down. "Tell me about *you*," she said to Sienna. "You've taken a job here, so I assume you're back to stay?"

Sienna shifted her gaze away from Mirabelle's hopeful expression. "Probably not for the long term, but for the next year anyway. I . . . I'm with someone who still lives in New York."

"Oh," Mirabelle said, a line forming between her brows. "I see," she said, shooting a quick worried glance at Gavin, who was still opening the wine. But she brought forth a smile, reaching over and squeezing Sienna's hands. "We'll take what we can get. I've *missed* you," she said, and it made Sienna want to cry again because she could see the deep sincerity in her expression.

"I've missed you, too, Mirabelle. So much." Her voice hitched, and she was again overwhelmed by the same emotion that had flooded her by the door. Footsteps coming toward the kitchen saved her from an embarrassing display of tears, and when she saw who it was, she sprang up, a small sound of happiness on her lips. "Argus!"

"Sienna?"

She rushed forward and wrapped her arms around the older man. Oh, he had aged. She obviously wasn't going to say it, but she noticed, and it broke her heart because it reminded her how many years she'd missed. She squeezed him tightly. *I'm sorry, Argus. So sorry I let so much time slip away.*

No matter when I leave Reno, no matter what happens with my life and my career, I will never lose touch again, she swore silently. She let go of him and he stepped back, holding on to her upper arms as he studied her, his gaze filled with the same love and tenderness that had always been there. "Well, now, you look just fine, Siennoulla. But still too skinny." She laughed, her heart squeezing at the endearment. His hair was more gray than black, though it was still thick and shiny, and his mustache was dotted salt and pepper too. Wrinkles fanned out around his eyes, creasing his olive-toned skin, but he was still tall and broad shouldered. And he still had the same sparkle in his eye, the same warmth in his laughter, and the same strength in that booming voice of his.

"That's why I'm here," she said. "So you can fatten me up."

"Ah! Good then. It will take lots of time and many meals, so I am happy!" He reached up, making a familiar gesture as he brushed over the edge of her ear, pulled his hand back, and opened his palm. In it sat a shiny silver dollar, and Sienna's heart constricted tightly at the trick that had always delighted her as a child. "For my girl. I held on to it all this time because I knew you'd be back," he said softly.

Sienna swiped at the tears gathering in her eyes but laughed, hugging Argus again. She wanted to cry because she'd been troubled and sleepless ever since she'd arrived in Reno, and she suddenly realized that part of the reason was because she'd had no safe outlet, no people of her own to turn her mind toward, ones who provided both strength and comfort and allowed her to digest and deal with the myriad horrors her job brought forth. It had only been ten minutes since she'd walked in the front door, but it was a ten-minute reprieve to turn her mind away from brutal crime and unpaid punishment, and she already felt more centered.

Gavin came up next to them and handed her a glass of red, smiling as she took it. Their fingers brushed, and she felt the small charge between them and turned away as she took a sip, telling herself it was the wine that was causing the heated flush.

"Please tell me you two are still performing," Sienna said to Argus and Mirabelle.

"No more," Argus said. "Mira retired five years ago and me last year. I hired another assistant after her, but, eh"—he shrugged, his expression less than impressed—"she did not have the personality nor the grace of my Mira. And she was no good with the cards."

"He hired her for her other assets," Mirabelle said, cupping her palms over her apron-covered breasts.

"Pshaw. I have no need of *assets* other than yours," he said, winking at her.

"Oh, please," Mirabelle said as she stirred something that looked like gravy on the stovetop, rolling her eyes but pairing it with an obviously pleased smile. "And I'm not good with cards."

"Ah, but you are. Stop denying it."

Sienna smiled, sipping her wine. Something had always given Sienna the impression that Mirabelle didn't like cards. Or rather, she didn't like the idea of gambling with them. Sienna wondered if it was because she'd known someone who had a gambling problem—maybe that abusive husband she'd mentioned . . . maybe a parent. She'd always get a thin-lipped, disapproving look on her face when Gavin and Argus played for matchsticks or pennies, Gavin showing off by shuffling effortlessly and dramatically and winning every hand. It was why, Sienna supposed, they'd kept their little online racket a secret.

And no wonder—Mirabelle had gone ballistic when Gavin had told her he wanted to play cards for a living . . . or attempt to. She figured it was another reason he'd been so stressed right before their wedding-that-wasn't.

"Argus, help me turn this roast, will you?" Mirabelle said, breaking her from her memories.

Sienna set her wine on the counter. "I can help, Mirabelle."

"No, no, you relax. It's been too many ages since I've cooked for more than these two knuckleheads, who'd eat a pile of dirt if I presented it to them."

"That's because you'd make dirt taste good," Argus said, kissing her on the cheek.

"I can show Sienna the backyard," Gavin offered.

"Yes, yes," Mirabelle said, opening the oven door. A waft of savory deliciousness hit Sienna's nose, making her mouth water. "I think you'll like it, Si. And you'll have to bring a swimsuit next time you come over. For now, talk; drink a glass of wine. This still needs twenty minutes. Argus will help me finish setting the table, and then you will sit across from me and answer all of my million and one questions."

"Stop threatening her, Mom," Gavin said.

"Oh, quiet." Mirabelle shooed him with a wave of her hand.

Sienna smiled. "I'm looking forward to it," she said. And sure, there were a few topics she hoped not to discuss on her first visit to Mirabelle's house, but in all reality, she couldn't wait to tell Mirabelle about her life. About college, about her first job, about the pride she felt when she put her talents to use and helped someone in a way she knew had an impact and was perhaps even life changing. She was a long way from the little girl with tangled hair and worn-out shoes that Mirabelle had taken under her wing, giving her the first taste of *home* that she'd ever known. She wanted to share her new self with the woman she'd considered a mother figure, and she also found that she was willing to ponder the ways in which she was still the same, which was an interesting realization, considering she'd thought she'd spent the last decade completely shedding the person she used to be. But less than half an hour with the people who'd been her surrogate family, and she felt that girl surfacing. Strangely, it didn't feel like a negative but rather like a sort of merging, perhaps long overdue. She'd left and returned years later with an open wound. Somehow, that wound was healing, one gentle step through her history at a time. *And to move forward, I need to heal completely. Maybe that's why I never fully have.*

Gavin held the sliding glass door open for her, and she stepped through, out into Mirabelle's oasis. She stood there for a few moments, taking a sip of wine as her gaze moved from one beautiful detail to the next.

Forget miles away . . . this place felt like a different *planet* than the trailer park she'd sat in front of only weeks before. And she was happy for Mirabelle that she got to enjoy this luxury. But Mirabelle was still the same woman she'd been when her backyard had consisted of nothing more than cracked dirt and tumbleweeds. A place didn't define you, not if you didn't let it. Seeing Mirabelle here was a reminder of that, and a wonderful one.

"I bought this house for her right after I won my first big tournament," Gavin said from beside her, breaking her from her admiring reverie. She looked over at him, watching as he squinted into the dying sunset.

"That must have felt good."

"Yeah," he said, still looking at the sky. "It did. It felt great." There was a sad note in his voice that she didn't entirely understand, but she wanted to ask him about a different house.

"Gavin."

He turned, his eyes moving over her face, expression unchanging. He looked at her the same way he'd just gazed at the glowing sky. "What is it?"

"The guy who's committing these crimes put together a set of clues that led us to the house we rented. The one we were going to live in after we were married."

His expression faltered. "Bluebell Way?"

Sienna nodded. He'd remembered. "We found a body there and . . . some other things."

His face expressed utter confusion, his eyes wide with concern. "Wait. I don't understand. How did this guy know about Bluebell Way?"

She'd thought about calling him with the news about the house as it pertained to the case, but she'd wanted to look in his eyes when she brought it up. She'd planned to ask if he had any guesses about why and how she might have been led to that particular address, but that was unnecessary now. She could clearly see that he was as taken aback as she'd been. "We don't know. One guess is that he learned my name as one of the detectives on the case, which wouldn't be overly hard." He could have done it in any number of ways, and it wasn't as if it was classified information. "And then he did some sort of background check on me."

"Background check . . . how—"

"We don't know exactly. Those are just guesses. Anyway, the house is bank owned, just like the other property on Allegra, but he had to have known my connection to it. As you know, he's already called me out by name on other pieces of evidence. The only other address I lived at here in Reno was the trailer at Paradise Estates, and that's likely occupied. Maybe the house on Bluebell Way served a few purposes. It's a nice abandoned property to dump a body and the perfect way to call me out again." She paused. "But your name is tied to that house too. Not to mention your connection to the cards in the original victim's hands that then led to your fan club president."

"What are you thinking?" he asked.

"I don't know exactly, except that it's possible he either knows our history somehow and that's another callout—one that he decided to use immediately—or he's discovered you're working with us, and he's pointing out that he knows."

"Knows our history . . . how—"

She shrugged. "Maybe the old wedding announcement I put online." She felt a zing of embarrassment for that hopeful girl she'd been, the one who had devastation heading her way and didn't even know it. "A Google search would produce that. I checked." She saw his tiny flinch before she looked away, squinting out to the horizon.

He was silent a moment, and from her peripheral vision, she could see him rubbing his lower lip absently. "Or all of the above," he murmured.

"Yes."

When she looked back at him, Gavin appeared troubled. "Okay. Well, there are several maybes as far as me. But this guy definitely has you in his sights. There's no question there. Are you taking extra precautions?"

"There's no indication I'm a target of violence. He's playing games, and I'm sure using my name is one of them, but yes, I'm always cautious. I'm sure as someone who works in security, you are too."

His frown deepened. "Always. Will you keep me updated if you find out anything?"

"Of course."

The sliding glass door opened, and Argus stuck his head out. "Dinner is served," he said with a mock bow. Despite the heaviness of their conversation and the worries that swirled around it, Sienna and Gavin both smiled, and in that moment, a vision so bright hit Sienna. This could have been them. Standing together outside Mirabelle's house, talking easily, waiting to be called to dinner. Together. Lives entwined.

It could have been.

But it wasn't.

CHAPTER
TWENTY-TWO

Gavin watched as his mother placed her hand over Sienna's on the dining table, giving it a pat. "I'm worried about you, honey," she said. "This killer Gavin has been telling me about sounds scary, to say the least. Strangling women and posing them?" She drew her shoulders up in a shiver, then passed the rolls to Argus.

"You don't have to worry about me, Mirabelle," Sienna said. "I have a great partner, and I'm well trained." Gavin believed her, but no amount of training would matter if she was taken by surprise by some demented nut.

"Oh, I have no doubt of that. Still . . . it's dangerous work you do." His mom shook her head as she dished up some mashed potatoes and passed them to Gavin. He took the bowl from her and put a generous helping on his plate. "You love it, though, don't you? Your work?"

"I really do," Sienna said.

"So why leave New York?" Argus asked. "They kick you out or what?" He chuckled at his own joke, what he *thought* was a joke, and Sienna cringed slightly as Argus's face went blank. "Oh. They kicked you out."

She glanced at Gavin, and he gave her an encouraging nod. She should not be ashamed of what she'd done. In fact, she should be proud.

He was proud of her—damn proud—and he knew for certain Mirabelle and Argus would be too.

She was still the highly moral girl he remembered, and it made him smile. How she'd come by that quality—considering her upbringing and that no one had taught her not to abide injustice—was a mystery. She just never had. When she'd told him about putting everything important to her at risk so that a pedophile would be removed from the streets rather than continue to victimize children—no matter the personal cost to her—it hadn't surprised him in the least. She was different in so many ways, but she was the same in all the ways that had caused him to fall head over heels in love with her when he was still just a boy. He was a man now, but he still responded to those things, God help him.

He'd sensed by her reaction to his initial pride in hearing her story that she'd needed validation. He sensed that she hadn't had much support, if any, for the choice she'd made. *Why?* he'd wondered. So he'd looked up her "main squeeze" and found that his impression was accurate. The guy didn't deserve her. Not even close.

"Well," Sienna said, "they did kick me out. At least, in a manner of speaking." And she told them, albeit a little less haltingly than she'd told Gavin. He wondered why. Had she expected his judgment more than she expected Mirabelle's or Argus's? Or did his reaction mean more to her for some reason? He hoped it was the latter. He hoped his reaction still meant something to her. There were worse places to start.

Is that what you're trying to do, Decker? Start?

Because if you're considering pursuing her, you've gotta go all in. There can't be any half-assing it with Sienna. No wishy-washy. He'd already destroyed her trust in him once. Forget that she had a "main squeeze"; forget that the man didn't deserve her and he'd be competing with someone else—Sienna was going to be wary with a capital *W* when it came to Gavin, regardless of anything else.

But God, he missed her. She was sitting at the same table as him, and he missed her. He hadn't let himself dwell on it in eleven years because it would have been painfully pointless, but now, she was right in front of him, and he realized how vast the hole inside him had been since the day he'd let her go. She'd been his best friend, his everything, for as long as he could remember existing, and her absence had felt like the loss of a limb. He'd learned to live without her, but deep inside, he'd never felt whole.

"Oh, my sweet girl," Mirabelle said, tears shimmering in her eyes when Sienna told them about not following the order to leave their version of "well enough alone" when it came to the fate of a child. Mirabelle put her fork down, stood, and rounded the table to where Sienna sat. Sienna turned, and Mirabelle bent, pulling a half-standing Sienna into her arms and hugging her. "Oh, I'm so proud of you. So incredibly proud."

Gavin watched as Sienna squeezed her back, the expression on her face full of gratitude. He pictured her as a girl, how she'd glowed under Mirabelle's approval, like a flower drinking up the sunshine. The way she glowed now. Her own mother had mostly been a loveless shrew too busy chasing the bottle to notice anything—good or bad—that Sienna might have done. It'd made him so mad and so incredibly protective of her.

Mirabelle took Sienna's face in her hands and kissed her forehead as Sienna laughed softly. "Thanks, Mirabelle."

Mirabelle returned to her chair and raised her glass. "To my girl, who is good and decent clear down to her bones, who does the right thing no matter the cost."

"Hear, hear," Gavin said softly, meeting Sienna's eyes, watching as happy color rose in her cheeks.

"And if I may add," Argus broke in before they could take a sip, "to fate bringing you back to us."

Gavin could definitely drink to that.

~

"Before you get going, can I show you something?" Gavin asked.

Sienna looked at him sideways. They'd finished dinner and enjoyed dessert on the patio as Sienna told Mirabelle and Argus more about her life, Gavin soaking it in as well. Sienna had hugged them both good-bye, promising to call Mirabelle. It'd made Gavin happy to see the two women reunited. "I don't know. It depends what it is," she answered.

"Trust me."

"It's already dark."

"That won't matter."

She shot him a glance, but he could see in her eyes that he had her halfway convinced. "I really should get home and—"

"I won't keep you long. It's close by. I think you'll like what I have to show you. And taking your mind off the case for a little while isn't a bad thing, right?"

Sienna sighed. "Okay, fine. But no more than an hour."

Gavin grinned and led her to his car, parked in Mirabelle's drive-way, and opened the passenger door for her so she could slide inside. She was wearing a simple navy dress, belted loosely at the waist, and as she lifted her legs to place her feet on the floor of his car, her dress lifted, giving him a shot of the curve of her smooth thigh. The desire to reach down and run his hand along that thigh was so strong he had to grit his teeth as he shut the door and rounded the car.

"When you say close by—"

"Five miles, maybe less," he said. God, she smelled good, her scent even more detectable in the small, enclosed space. She was wearing perfume, something she hadn't worn when they were young—something she wouldn't have been able to afford then—but beneath that, he smelled *her*, and it was a jolt straight between his legs. He swore he could still remember how she tasted.

"Okay," she said, putting her seat belt on as the car purred to life. "Nice ride."

"Thanks." He was proud that he'd kept the sudden surge of desire out of his voice, and as he brought his seat belt around his body, he took the opportunity to adjust himself.

She was quiet for a minute as he turned the corner off the street where Mirabelle lived. "Did you ever offer to teach Mirabelle how to drive?" she asked, her thoughts obviously moving from his car to what Mirabelle had said earlier about preferring to take the bus.

"Many times," he said, shrugging. "She's stubborn about it. But I can't force her if she doesn't want to." He paused for a moment, looking over his shoulder as they merged onto the highway. "I sometimes wonder if it has to do with my father."

"How so?"

"I wonder if he eroded her confidence. She doesn't talk about him a lot, just that he wasn't a great guy."

"Yes," Sienna said distractedly, obviously recalling something. "She told me the same thing."

He glanced at her. He wasn't surprised. Mirabelle had always considered Sienna a daughter. Whatever she'd told Gavin, she'd likely told Sienna. He'd stopped asking his mother about his father when he was about twelve, as she'd always get this intensely pained expression on her face and disappear into her room for hours afterward.

Gavin got the impression that not only wasn't he a "great guy" but he'd been physically abusive. And so he could only be grateful that she'd taken him and left. They'd moved around a bit when he was a kid. They'd lived in Las Vegas for a couple of years, a town he barely remembered because he'd been so young, and then Atlantic City for a shorter time. Then they'd moved to Reno, where she'd found the job with Argus. It hadn't been long before she'd taken little Sienna Walker under her wing, the seven-year-old girl who lived three trailers over . . . the one who'd first been his best friend and later his first love.

Maybe Mirabelle had simply been trying to find the place that felt the most like home with the few material possessions or prospects she'd had at the time, or maybe she'd moved them around for a few years because she didn't want to be tracked down. But if it was the latter, apparently the man she'd been evading hadn't been too serious about doing any tracking, because Gavin was a man close to thirty now, and he hadn't ever seen hide nor hair of him.

Nor did he want to. If Mirabelle said he was a less-than-stellar person, he knew it was true.

The radio played quietly, and though Gavin's mind had drifted for a few minutes, the mood was comfortable. The quiet easy. Beside him, Sienna looked like she was enjoying the chance to lay her head back and rest, the landscape gliding by along with the blur of headlights.

He exited the highway and made a couple more turns before finally pulling off the road and stopping in front of a guard shack, where he inserted the pass he'd bought a few days before when he'd looked up this place. The gate lifted, and Gavin continued on, then stopped in a small parking lot and shut off the lights.

They both stepped from the car, Sienna standing at the door for a moment as she stared out over the water and then pulled in a breath, looking at him over the roof of the car. He smiled.

She shut the door and then walked forward, across the small paved area surrounded by trees and grass. Tall, muted streetlights dotted the parking lot, casting a soft glow over the pond beyond, the swan clearly visible as he glided across the water.

"Otis," Sienna whispered, stopping at the riverbank and sinking down onto the white wooden bench situated there. "You found him."

Gavin sat next to her, enjoying both her proximity and her awe. "He's been close by all this time," he said. Gavin knew he never would have come here without Sienna, though, even if he'd known the location. It would have felt . . . wrong, and it would have only caused him to suffer. Sitting together and watching the beautiful creatures, as they'd talked about their plans and their dreams, had been special and peaceful and intimate. It was where he'd first kissed her. Where he'd gathered all his courage and turned his face to hers, moving slowly until their lips brushed and she smiled against his mouth. Sitting here like this, a swan gliding on the water in front of him, belonged to her and only her.

"Their cygnets lived here with Otis for a while," he told her. "He was a good dad to them. And then, once they were old enough, they were moved to different locations. They're all doing well."

She smiled, tilting her head and watching Otis turn on the water and begin swimming in another direction. He was struck by how familiar this felt, how the look on her face was the same as it'd been then, how dreamy her eyes were. "I wonder if he's lonely," she said.

He watched Otis for a minute, too, before replying. "I read that they tried to introduce female swans to Otis, but he rejected them all. Apparently, he preferred to remain single." He looked over at her. "I tend to think he just never got over Odette. No one ever measured up," he finished quietly.

He watched her eyelashes flutter, and then she bit her lip, looking away, out to the distant shore, where palm trees stood unmoving in the still night air. "Whatever you're doing, Gavin, stop it," she said throatily.

But he couldn't. Being there and watching the same swan they'd watched together in what felt like a different lifetime made longing rise up inside of him. Longing for what they'd been, what they'd had together. Once. They were different but the same, and he still felt that connection that he'd felt the moment he'd laid eyes on her the very first time. He'd been nothing more than a kid then, but he'd felt it, the same way he felt it still. It was thin and fragile now, a gossamer thread, but it was *there*, and he knew she felt it too.

He was being given a second chance, and he'd regret it forever if he didn't take it.

"Sienna."

She stilled, tensed, and he heard her breath catch. "Gavin—"

"When you mentioned that house earlier tonight. Do you know what flashed in my head? I pictured what it would have been like carrying you over the threshold. I wondered what your dress looked like."

"Stop," she said again, but it was breathy. Uncertain.

"No."

She turned to him then, the look on her face so incredibly hurt, and though it stabbed at him, it gave him hope as well, just like her anger had, and for all the same reasons. "It still hurts you, too, Sienna. You're still angry. And if you didn't still care, you wouldn't be able to muster those emotions," he said, voicing his thoughts aloud. "We need to talk about it. It's long overdue—"

"I was eighteen, Gavin," she said, her voice rising. "Eighteen with no one in the world except you and Mirabelle and Argus. In one fell swoop you deprived me of all three people I considered my family! I had no one. Not one person in the world. And you didn't even have the decency to tell me to my face. You left me there. Alone. I took the bus home in my wedding dress! You want to know what my wedding dress looked like after all was said and done? It was dirty and sweaty and smelled like diesel fuel, you *fucking* asshole!"

Gavin winced. He'd wanted her anger, all of it, and he'd expected it to hurt, but not like this. The vision *flattened* him. He lowered his head and rubbed his forehead. "You had money. Why didn't you take a cab?"

"I didn't have money. I hadn't brought any *money* with me. Do you know how many places there are to *store* things in a wedding dress? I'd expected you to be there. I'd expected to go home in your truck."

He rubbed at his head again. "I'm sorry about that. I wrestled with myself up until the very final moment. If I'd thought the specifics through—"

"You wonder why I'm still angry? It's not because of the bus or the ruined dress. It's because I can still feel that day. If I close my eyes, I can still feel it, I can still *smell* it, and God dammit, I don't know how to make it stop." She stood and turned away from him, and he went after her, stopping her with a hand to her upper arm. She turned back, her expression shocked and defiant.

"I still feel it too," he said. "I still feel *you*. All these years. I haven't gotten over you. You want to know why I never married? Because no one measured up. They couldn't because they weren't *you*."

She laughed, but it contained no humor. "What am I supposed to do with that? There's too much water under the bridge. I'm with someone else."

He tensed, not able to control the bolt of pure jealousy that speared through him. "Sienna, this Brandon Guthrie that you're dating isn't worthy of you."

"You don't know anything about Brandon."

"I know plenty."

She whipped her head toward him, her stare both incredulous and affronted. "Oh my God, you did a security check on him? This is outrageous!"

"I *googled* him. And you should too."

"I don't need to *google* him. I know him!"

"Maybe not as well as you think you do. Look him up. See how loyal he is. See how closely your ideals align."

She laughed, and there was a hysterical edge to the sound. "You're one to talk about loyalty! About *ideals*?" She went to turn away again, but he put his fingers around her arm, and she stopped, turning back to him. He was encouraged by the fact that she hadn't persisted in leaving but let him stop her with the barest touch. It made him hope she wanted to stay, whether she'd be willing to admit it or not. She wanted to see this through, whatever "this" might end up being.

It had been a long, long time coming.

"I don't know what you're doing. I only know you made your choice years ago. You let me go, you threw me away, and you don't just get to take me back whenever you feel like it."

He tried to take her hands, but she stepped back, crossing her arms over her chest. "Say whatever you need to say. I can take it. But also, let me explain—"

"Explain? What is there to explain?" But again, she didn't turn away.

He took in a big pull of air. "I saw your college-acceptance letter, Si, saw the scholarship offer for the criminal-justice program."

She faltered, obviously not expecting that. "But . . . what? How? I threw that letter away."

"Not before your mother saw it."

"My *mother*?" Now she looked even more confused.

"Your mother came to me with the letter and showed me what you were about to give up. She was a miserable shrew ninety-nine percent of the time, Sienna, but she was right to do that. I think . . . I don't know for sure, but I think maybe your mother took a wrong turn at some point and ended up where she was. *Who she was.* Maybe the one decent thing she ever did was see where her daughter might make the same mistake and do what she could to stop it from happening. You'd have given that up to marry me and live in some clapboard house with a leaky roof and questionable electric work. A scholarship that you'd earned because you'd worked your ass off despite everything you had going against you."

She stood there, her wheels obviously turning, her mouth slack as she stared. He couldn't tell exactly what she was thinking, but he knew this was his opportunity to explain to her what he'd done and why and that he would not get another. "Yeah . . . ," she said, "I would have given all that up to marry you. It was *my* choice, Gavin, and you took that from me."

"What were you going to do?" he asked. "Give up your dreams to follow me around the country as I entered tournaments? It was all I had going for me. There was zero guarantee I'd ever win anything. I had no real idea what I was facing. I felt the pressure of that, Si. I didn't know how to balance my career aspirations and our relationship. I wanted to give you stability because it was the one thing you'd been denied your entire life, but I was scared. That rental house you were so excited about seemed like a variation on a theme. Almost like a trap—"

"A *trap?*"

"For both of us," he said. "I realized later that to you, that house represented potential, but at the time I couldn't see it. At the time, it seemed like nothing more than a lateral transfer. And so when your mom showed me that letter, it seemed like a weight was taken off my shoulders. It was a way out for you . . . but it was a way out for me too. I didn't have to carry the pressure of failing you."

"You couldn't explain that to my face?" she said, her voice rising.

"No, I couldn't explain that to your face. I was too weak to do that. I never would have left. I couldn't look you in the eye and break your heart. Hell, at the time, I barely had the words to articulate what I was feeling. What I did know was that you had even less support than I did, and I was trying so hard to be your rock, until I crumbled. I loved you, but I was eighteen years old, too, Sienna."

"And so you snuck away like a coward," she accused, and he saw the tears glinting in her eyes, and again, her pain crushed him, even now. He shut his eyes for a moment, took a deep breath. He'd been wrong. Or at least, he'd been wrong in the way he'd gone about breaking up with her. Very wrong, and so goddamn messy.

She had deserved the truth. He hadn't given it to her, and for that, he was truly sorry. "Yeah, I guess I did. I snuck away like a coward," he said. "But answer me this: Would you have gone? If I came to you and told you about my doubts and that I knew about the scholarship and I wanted you to take it, that your mother of all people had told me about it, would you have gone?"

She let out a shuddery breath, looking away over his shoulder. He could tell she was considering, perhaps putting herself back in her eighteen-year-old shoes and really thinking about it from the perspective of the girl she'd once been. He appreciated that she took the time and contemplated her answer honestly. It would have been easier to say, *Yes, of course I would have gone if you'd been honest with me,* but she didn't take the easy way out. That was Si. Fair to a fault. Truthful where he hadn't been. He'd wondered where she could have possibly come by her delicate beauty in light of who her parents were. But he'd also wondered about her unceasing commitment to integrity, to truth, for the same reason. Maybe the more curious question was not how she'd come by those qualities but how she'd retained them.

"I . . . I don't know. Maybe not." She suddenly looked weary, and he was sorry for it but not. She took the few steps back to the bench and sat down as if her legs couldn't hold her anymore, and he did the same. They'd needed to have this conversation. It was eleven years past due. She turned to him and met his eyes, and though the spark of anger had died, the sadness was still there. "You were my dream, Gavin. Not a college degree, not a career I couldn't picture and wasn't even sure I'd be good at. You. And maybe that was misguided. Or shortsighted or whatever you want to call it. But it's the truth. At the time I thought maybe I'd do all that . . . later, but I . . . I wasn't sure. I was only certain of one thing, and that was that I wanted you to be my future, and I wanted to be yours. I figured if we started there, the rest would work itself out."

That longing again. Because he'd had her whole heart once, and he didn't anymore. And he wanted it back. God, he did. He wanted her to want him. He wanted her to desire him the way he still desired her. The way, somewhere in the back of his mind, he always had. He'd never allowed himself to fully ponder it because when he'd made the decision to leave town before their wedding so many years ago, he'd done it knowing he was leaving her behind forever. She wouldn't forgive him, not for deserting her. And he'd told himself that he had to do it that way, leave himself no small doubt that she'd ever take him back, because if he did, he'd find her, he'd beg her to give him another chance, and then what would it have all been for?

"And now," he said quietly, "considering the life you have, the job you do, all the things that have happened between that day and this one, do you wish it had been different? In hindsight?"

She sighed. "How can I answer that? Do you want me to tell you what you did was right? That I'm grateful to you for obliterating my heart?"

He ran his hand through his hair, his shoulders dropping. "No. But I hope you can find it in you to understand." *To forgive me for the pain and loss I caused you.*

"And you?" she asked. "Would you take it back, knowing what you know now?"

He let out a gust of breath. It was a fair question. He'd asked her the same. "I don't know either," he said. "My view of the world was so different then." He'd been hotheaded, impulsive the way all young men tended to be. But he'd also been doubtful of what his future held, what the world might have in store for him. Mirabelle had dissuaded him from attempting to make a career of gambling, and he supposed any good mother would have. He couldn't blame her for that. Who wanted to send their child out on the road to follow a path that relied on such a high percentage of *luck*?

He'd believed in his own gift, though. At least enough to gamble on himself. He just hadn't believed in it enough to ante up with Sienna's future. "I used to go over it. I played the what-if game for a while and never came to any solid conclusions other than I missed the hell out of you." He paused, glancing at her profile and then away. Otis wasn't on the water anymore. He'd made it to the distant shore and shaken off his tail feathers and was doing whatever swans did as the moon grew bright in the sky. "And I wished . . . I wished I could have figured out a way to have it all without risking any of it."

Sienna let out a small sound that he thought held a note of humor but more of wistfulness. "That's not how life works." She sighed, looking over at him, and even in the dim light, or maybe because of it, he was so struck by her beauty, the outline of her bone structure, those high cheekbones, her gently sloping nose. He'd watched her turn from a girl to a woman and thought her beautiful during every stage of her life. He'd realized he was in love with her one early April day when he was fifteen years old and accepted it as naturally as the earth accepted the rain. And with just as much necessity.

And though he'd thought he'd moved on, he never really had. It was still her. Always her.

Their eyes locked, and Gavin leaned in, allowing his lips to brush against hers. He didn't even realize he'd done it until he heard her small, soft gasp. His breath halted, and she blinked at him, but she didn't move away, and so he pressed his mouth against hers more firmly, tilting his head slightly and using his tongue to lick across the seam of her soft lips. She opened, and his heart soared, his hands cupping her face as she let out another small sound—a moan this time. It raced across his mouth and down his spine to settle in his groin and vibrate there as he swelled, pressing against the zipper of his pants. Her tongue met his and she melted against him, tenderness and arousal mixing within. *Sienna. Sienna.* It was the same yet different. Past and present melded as he reacquainted himself with her taste, her textures, and the feel of her in his arms. How had he lived without this for so long? It seemed a miracle that he'd survived.

With a small, strangled gasp, she broke away, turning her head and bringing the back of her hand to her mouth. "Oh, Gavin," she breathed. "This is wrong. We're over. We've been over for a long time." She stood, and for a moment he continued to sit there, stung and stunned.

They'd talked, yes, perhaps found some understanding. Some peace. But as far as *them*, nothing had changed. He pulled himself to his feet, and dammit if his legs weren't a bit shaky. He almost laughed. Only one woman could make his legs shaky, and apparently it didn't matter if he was seventeen or twenty-nine. "Come on. I'll take you to your car," he said, and though she followed him, she kept her distance.

CHAPTER
TWENTY-THREE

"Sienna, there's someone here to see you." Sienna looked up, nodding at Xavier as she set down the can of Coke she'd just sipped from, hoping the dose of caffeine and sugar would help the slight headache she felt coming on. She wasn't in the habit of drinking soda in the morning, but God, she felt bleary eyed. Once again, she'd tossed and turned for most of the night, her mind going over the case, the letters, but with an added restlessness regarding Gavin and all they'd talked about.

Not to mention that kiss.

"The science teacher from Copper Canyon High School?" she asked Xavier. It had to be. He was the only person she'd gotten hold of who had agreed to come to the station and answer a few questions regarding their Mr. Patches.

"Yeah. I took him to your desk. I wasn't sure you wanted him in here."

Sienna stood. "No," she said. She didn't have to look at the board to remind herself it wasn't something any civilian would be prepared for. Not to mention the fact that it was evidence, most of which hadn't been dispensed to the public. "Thanks, Xavier. Any headway with those yearbooks?"

He began walking with her toward the room where both their desks were situated. "Not really. I've been able to eliminate a handful of the male students based on the fact that they no longer live in the state or whatnot, but I'm not exactly sure what I'm looking for."

Sienna sighed as they turned the corner. "Neither are we," she said. "Keep eliminating, and let me know if anything sets your Spidey senses tingling."

He grinned as he turned away from her toward his desk. "Will do."

A man in his sixties, mostly bald and wearing round glasses, sat in the empty chair to the side of her metal desk, and Sienna held out her hand as she approached. "Mr. Freehan?"

He stood, shaking it. "Detective Walker. Call me Roy."

"And call me Sienna," she said, taking a seat and blinking as a small head rush made the room spin momentarily. "Thanks for coming in. I would have been happy to meet you."

"It was no problem. It was on the way to an appointment I have in about an hour."

"I won't take much of your time. I was just hoping you could answer some general questions about a teacher you worked with twenty years ago, Sheldon Biel. You were the only other science teacher at the school at that time, so I thought you might have worked with him more closely than other staff."

"Oh, I see." His face soured. "Yes, I remember Sheldon. He was very popular with the children and with the staff too." He paused. "I never had a problem with him, per se. He seemed nice enough and from all appearances did his job well. It was only afterward . . ."

Afterward. There was a lot contained in that word. "Yes," Sienna said, "we're aware of his disappearance and what was found in his home."

Roy Freehan shook his head. "Unthinkable, really, that a man who worked that closely with children had a propensity for watching them be victimized. How do you reconcile that?"

You don't. And it wasn't only watching that had interested Sheldon Biel. "It's troubling," she said carefully.

Mr. Freehan leaned forward. "Are you looking into his disappearance again after all this time?"

"No. We've actually recently discovered a body and verified through dental records it was Mr. Biel. It appears he was murdered close to the time he went missing. His family's been notified." There had been a news story on it that morning, but evidently Mr. Freehan had missed it.

Roy sat back, his expression registering surprise. "Oh. Oh," he repeated. "And you want to know if I can think of anyone who might have wanted to harm him?" he asked. "The police questioned me about that when he disappeared."

"No, not just that, unless you can think of anything now that you didn't think of then. I know it was a long time ago. But what I'm wondering is if you remember noticing that he spent more time with one student over another or . . . well, if he seemed to favor any particular child?"

"Oh," Roy Freehan said again, obviously understanding her line of questioning in light of what had come out after he'd gone missing. "Um . . ." He scratched at his bald head, then took off his glasses and used the hem of his shirt to shine the lenses. "I parked right next to him in the parking lot," he said. "And I did see him driving students home sometimes. I think he tutored a few of them after hours . . ." Mr. Freehan looked up at her, pausing in his lens cleaning, his gaze registering understanding. "Oh." He let out a long breath, then put his glasses back on. He looked noticeably paler as he squinted, clearly traveling into the past, racking his brain. "I seem to recall seeing him on several occasions get into his car with the dark-haired kid who was always carrying around a deck of cards."

"Deck of cards?" Sienna repeated, her breath catching.

Roy Freehan nodded, squinting again. "Yeah. He . . . he was sorta tall for his age, I think, though not remarkably so. Dark haired, like I said. Quiet. I only really remember him because of those cards. They stood out. I wondered why he carried them around. No one really paid much attention to him, and for the life of me, I can't recall his name. But he'd stand around, staring into nowhere, shuffling those cards, you know, like some kind of security blanket. At the time I might've thought he was in one of the special-needs classes, but . . . yeah, I saw him get into Sheldon's car a few times. I remember because he dropped the deck of cards at my feet once, and I helped him pick them up. He met my eyes while we were down there on the pavement. It was the only time I remember him meeting my eyes. Do you think . . . do you think he was asking me for help? *Oh God.*"

~

"Hey, are you okay? You look exhausted," Kat said, sitting down at her desk across from Sienna.

Sienna gave her a weak smile, picking up the cup of coffee she'd just poured, her second in two hours. "Yeah. I'm okay. I didn't sleep great last night." *Or the night before that . . . or the night before that.*

"That's because you've been working yourself ragged since you walked in the door. And I don't mean this morning. I mean since the first *moment* you walked in the door." Kat rifled through the messages that had been left on her desk while she was out.

"Not a lot of choice," Sienna said, then took a sip of the coffee, hoping the continuing doses of caffeine would work on both her low energy and the headache she couldn't shake. She quickly updated Kat on her conversation with the science teacher, Roy Freehan. She *still* felt disturbed by the interview. *Do you think . . . do you think he was asking me for help?*

"Did you have him look through the yearbooks?"

"Yes, but he didn't recognize any of the kids as the one he mentioned." The one boy they'd found in the yearbook named Daniel

Forester had turned out to be presently living in Cleveland and working as a morning newscaster. There were enough clips of him online that he had a solid alibi going back months. Not that Sienna had thought that potential lead would pan out anyway.

"So our Danny Boy never showed up on picture day," Kat murmured.

"No," Sienna said. "Not any of them. So now I have Xavier going through the class lists and marking the names of boys who didn't appear in the yearbook."

"Good thinking. Hopefully there are only a few. We might have gotten lucky, and that will end up being a great way to narrow things down."

"Yeah . . ." And that was exactly what they needed to do. *Narrow things down.* Because right now, the information they'd gathered felt overwhelming. Sienna's mind shuffled through the evidence they possessed, the clues and writings they'd been given, and the profile Dr. Vitucci had presented as she tried to figure out an avenue they hadn't yet taken that might lead them closer to Danny.

"Oh, by the way, we got the full forensics on the items tested in that first vacant house," Kat said, handing Sienna the report. "Nothing," she said dejectedly.

Sienna took it and glanced through. No prints. No DNA. *No surprise.* She skimmed down a little farther. The first aid kit they'd found in a drawer was just that, the contents of the corroded bottle identified as iodine, a common product in a first aid kit, not out of the ordinary. "Damn," she muttered, even while something pricked at her brain. She bounced her knee. What was it?

Something . . .

She picked up her notes, scanned through them, and stopped at the spot where she'd made a note of the periodic table of elements Danny Boy had mentioned. Something about the callout had caused her to write it down, but at the time, it hadn't meant anything. "Kat, is iodine on the periodic table?"

Kat looked up from her computer screen. "Off the top of my head? You're asking the wrong girl."

Sienna smiled, then opened a search engine and pulled up an image of the periodic table of elements. It sure was. Her knee bounced faster. Its symbol was I, its atomic number 53.

He'd left that there. It'd been one of his clues. She was suddenly sure of it. But by itself, it meant nothing.

Her knee bounced, head throbbing as she desperately tried to focus. There was something to this.

That house was the second location where Danny Boy had left clues for them. The first had been under the overpass where Reva Keeling's body had been posed. She opened her notes, found the report on that scene, and skimmed through it. Nothing else had been found other than the clues left with the body.

Okay, but she'd been placed in that particular spot for a *reason*. Their Danny Boy hadn't gone to the trouble of dragging a dead woman up an incline and sitting her there randomly. What had she been facing? Sienna cast her mind back. A building that made . . . she flipped through her notes and printouts. Tools. They made tools. Armstrong and Sons. She tapped a key, bringing her computer back to life, and did a search on the company. No one had been there the day Reva had been murdered, but perhaps there was some meaning to the fact that she'd been facing that particular building. And if that was the case, the spot where the body had been left made sense, because from what Sienna could remember, two sides of the building were flanked by two-lane, somewhat busy streets and the back by another business. That area under the overpass was really the only mostly private place where a body might be positioned facing the tool company, if that in itself was meant as a clue.

Why here? It's weird.

She read through the description of Armstrong and Son's products. They designed and manufactured vanadium steel hand tools, including clamps, cutters, files, saws, and knives.

Knives . . . hmm. *Mother* had used a knife. Mother had been quite proficient with a knife.

Sienna clicked on another page and scrolled through the photos of their vanadium knives. Vanadium . . . vanadium. She brought the picture of the periodic table back up, her heart giving a small jump. Vanadium. There it was. Symbol V, atomic number 23.

Iodine was to the right. Symbol I, atomic number 53.

In order of the scenes they'd gone to, the letters were *VI*. "Roman numeral six?" she muttered.

Or possibly 2353? Another address?

Or maybe . . . the beginning of a word? Video? A name? Vincent?

Ouch. A particularly piercing pain emanated from her temple to the back of her neck.

She pulled the file for the second victim they'd found, Bernadette Murray, otherwise known as Queen Bee. Like Reva Keeling's scene, nothing had been found connected to the murder, other than that left on the victim's body. She, too, had been sitting upright facing a building, though. It was through a fence and didn't offer a great view, but it was the direction she'd been posed in, as if staring directly at it. She flipped pages. Med Plus. Again, she turned to her computer. Oxygen tanks and equipment. They sold *oxygen*. She pulled up the periodic table and found oxygen, symbol O, atomic number 8. VIO. So not a roman numeral. And 23538 was getting a little long to be an address. She did a quick computer search. There was no such zip code in the US.

VIO . . . a word? Oh Lord, her head hurt.

She glanced up, but Kat was on the phone, talking in low tones as she leafed through papers on her desk.

The fourth scene they'd been led to was the house on Bluebell Way where they'd found Sheldon Biel, a.k.a. Mr. Patches. She glanced through the forensics report, looking at the photos of what had been found, including the radio and . . . the extra battery. She brought it closer. It was a Panasonic lithium battery with the *i* in *Panasonic* scratched or worn off.

She pulled up the periodic chart again. Lithium, symbol Li, atomic number 3. 235383? Or . . . *VIOLi*. But the *i* was scratched off the battery. Did that mean the *i* in *Li* should be discarded? *VIOL*. A word? Violence, violin, violets. A name? Viola?

Wait, there'd been another scene. Reva Keeling's apartment. Her head pounded so hard she almost let out a moan. That place had been a wreck of stuff strewn over every surface. If there was something else there relating to an element, it'd probably be like looking for a needle in a haystack. They'd found the other clues there because they'd been pointed specifically to them. Certainly they couldn't be expected to catalog every button and random bottle top?

Oh God. This suddenly felt ridiculous and *crazy*. An exercise in futility.

Sienna's phone dinged, thankfully interrupting her disconnected thoughts, and her friend Nellie's name showed on her screen. Nellie was her ex-partner Garrod's daughter, just about her age. Sienna had gotten close with her over the years she'd worked with Garrod and been invited to his family functions. She picked it up as Kat did the same with her phone, making yet another call, likely returning messages. Maybe someone had called in with something useful. They could only hope. Sienna opened the text: How are you settling in in Reno? Miss you! How's the long-distance thing going so far? Lots of phone sex I hope? ;)

Phone sex. Jeez. She hadn't even thought about phone sex. The truth was, she and Brandon hadn't even had *regular* sex for months and months leading up to her move. She'd been stressed and under an extreme amount of pressure regarding the arrest she'd broken protocol to make. She'd been waiting for the hammer to drop at any moment, which didn't exactly lend itself to feelings of sexiness. Then she'd gotten the offer from Reno and only had a month to prepare to move across the country, back to the place that brought forth so many conflicting emotions. So . . . yeah, there'd been a major dry spell, and frankly . . . now that she thought about it, she hadn't really missed him in that regard. Which she supposed didn't say great things.

I googled him. And you should too.

No. No, I should not.

She'd chosen to push everything that had happened with Gavin to the back burner. There were more important things to dwell on than him. Or their conversation. *Or their kiss.* Or what he'd said regarding Brandon.

She closed the text from Nellie to respond to later when she was at home. Or maybe she'd give her a call in the car if she felt better, she thought, massaging her temple. The caffeine hadn't touched her headache, which had only gotten worse since she'd gone on a periodic table of elements scavenger hunt. She needed to go search out something stronger.

She went to turn away from her computer but hesitated.

Don't do it.

Look him up. See how loyal he is.

She clicked to the front page of a search engine and typed in his name. The most recent hit on Brandon Guthrie of Purcell, Fenwick, and Penn came up, and when she saw what it was, her stomach dipped.

She hesitated. It was a bad idea to open the article. She knew it was, and yet she was unable to resist.

This won't do you any good. You know it won't.

See how loyal he is.

The article highlighted a swanky reelection-campaign dinner for the man running for mayor of New York City, the man responsible for Sienna sitting at a desk in Reno at that particular moment. Or maybe it was *she* who was ultimately responsible, *she* who had made the conscious decision not to follow orders, but . . . whatever.

She skimmed some of the copy lauding the event's focus on sustainability . . . passed edible-flower canapés . . . entirely plant-based menu . . . hand-painted biodegradable dishes . . . bamboo flatware. *What a crock.* She'd learned a little something about the mayor when she'd been investigating his team member. In his private life, the mayor ate $900 steaks, flew to Aspen on the weekends in his private jet, and—likely, though admittedly she hadn't taken time to do any precise math—used more electricity daily than the average American in an entire year to run his twenty-thousand-square-foot home. And Sienna had nothing against luxury. What she had a problem with was hypocrites. Especially those in power. *Especially* those who covered for their child-victimizing friends. Her head pounded, and she took a sip of the now-tepid coffee from the paper cup. *Cheers to you, you piece of fake, lying crap.*

She scrolled down to a photo of . . . the dry-spell devil himself. She leaned in, her mouth opening in surprise, her heart dipping.

What. The. Hell?

There was Brandon, sitting at one of the lushly decorated tables, debonair in a tuxedo, laughing at whatever the person onstage was saying. And next to him was a pretty, large-breasted woman who worked with him. Sienna had met her at one of the company events a few months before and noticed the way she'd eyed Brandon. When Sienna had jokingly mentioned it later, Brandon had brushed it off, smiling and asking who he was going home with.

Her heart dipped further.

Maybe *Brandon* hadn't experienced quite the dry spell she had.

And truly, she wasn't sure whether the pit in her stomach was more for the fact that he looked pretty damn chummy with his coworker, who had her hand resting on his shoulder as she, too, laughed, or if it was because he was there at all. How could he attend a campaign dinner for the man who'd not only attempted to squash the investigation into a morally depraved crime but would have thrown her to the wolves if she hadn't been quickly ushered out of town to the only department that would take her because they were desperately short staffed?

Her stomach soured.

She waited for the shock and heartache to descend, but it didn't. There was only dismay. Maybe she was just emotionally drained and didn't have a drop more available for Brandon Guthrie and his dinner of disloyalty.

She clicked out of the browser and glanced over at Kat, who was still on the phone, turned away and writing something down.

She rifled through her notes. There were several things skating on the edge of her thoughts, but she didn't seem to be able to focus on any of them. With a frustrated sigh, she moved them aside.

"Hey, Sienna, you don't look so well," Kat said, placing her phone down. "Do you need to go home?"

Sienna opened her mouth to object when a particularly sharp pain in her temple made her squint her eye again. Kat was right. She felt awful, and she couldn't do anyone any good like this. Her thoughts were scattered and unfocused, and if she didn't get some sleep, she was going to fall over. "Are you sure you can—"

"*Yes.* Get out of here, now. I'll let Ingrid know."

Sienna gave her a weak smile. "Okay. A good night's rest and I should be back up and running." She stood and gathered her things, making sure her case file was in her briefcase. She'd go over it as she was resting in her bed or after a few hours of actual sleep.

"Well, don't push it. We need you at your best."

I'm decidedly less than that. She said goodbye to Kat and headed for the door.

In her car, she glanced at herself in the rearview mirror and let out a soft moan. No wonder Kat had suggested she go home. Her eyes were bloodshot, with dark hollows beneath them. She looked beyond haggard. She turned the radio on low, finally allowing her brain to relax, ceasing to force it to make connections and put clues together. A brain was a sort of muscle, too, she reminded herself. And sometimes it just needed rest.

Her thoughts turned to Gavin, as she somehow had known they would the moment she gave her mind free rein. *That kiss.* It had shaken her, confused her. And yes, it had confirmed for her that their chemistry still burned bright. She shut her eyes briefly as she stopped at a red light.

She'd had *peace*. She really had. She'd made a life in New York, immersed herself in a career she loved, and suddenly—as if from one day to the next—her entire world was shaky and unstable, and she had no idea where she should take cover.

She'd kissed the man who'd shattered her heart, and the man she was planning on marrying someday soon had donned a tuxedo to toast her bitter enemy.

The funny thing was, for years after Gavin had left her at the altar, she'd felt like she was cheating on him every time she so much as went on a coffee date with someone. It was terrible, and it was distressing, and it'd only deepened her pain. After a while, though, once the sting had lessened, she'd come to believe it was simply a by-product of the fact that he'd been her first love and her only love, up to that point. That feeling was simply due to the reality that she'd never been with anyone else, and she'd believed wholeheartedly she never would be. Yes, it was natural, and it would go away in time, she'd told herself. Because anything else was too heartbreaking to consider. And mostly, the feeling *had* receded. Brandon was the first man she'd dated without comparing everything he did to Gavin, without measuring her emotions against the way she'd felt with him. No, it wasn't the same—Gavin had been her first everything, and it only made sense that her feelings for him had flamed with the fire of newness. But she *was* attracted to Brandon. He was smart and confident, and he knew how to own a room. He looked at her like she was the sexiest woman he'd ever seen, and he made her feel wanted. She'd come to love him, perhaps not with the same scorching, all-consuming love that she'd once felt for Gavin, but maybe that was better. Maybe it was stupid to give so much of yourself to one human being when human beings were so damn fallible.

What she hadn't realized until she'd arrived back in Reno was that she was still so incredibly wounded. What Gavin had done had stabbed through muscle and bone and scratched her down to her soul. He'd been her soul mate and he'd left her without a word, and if your soul mate could do that to you, how could you ever fully trust anyone else again? How could you live in a world with no soft place to land, especially when the *world* was a place where men in positions of power put money and influence ahead of the innocence of children, where people threw rocks at beautiful creatures weaker than them, merely to watch them bleed? How?

He'd known better than anyone that she had abandonment issues, and yet he'd abandoned her nonetheless.

Your mother came to me with the letter and showed me what you were about to give up.

Her mother. The woman she'd assumed hadn't given Sienna much more than a second's thought at any given point in her life. And how did she reconcile *that?*

A sound of distress moved up her throat, and her head throbbed.

Sienna pulled into her driveway and turned off the engine just as her phone rang.

Brandon.

What great timing he had.

She sighed, accepting the call. "Hey."

"Hey there, I'm surprised you answered. I figured you'd be busy at work."

"Then why did you call?"

A pause. "Because I wanted you to know I was thinking about you. Is something wrong?"

Sienna rubbed the back of her neck. Her headache had now made its way around her head. "I saw pictures of you at the gala, Brandon."

Another pause and the loud squeak of a chair as though he was sitting up or leaning back. "Sienna—"

"You went to a fundraising event for the man who tried to cover up a sex crime? For the man who had my head on a platter and probably still does?"

"Sienna, I know how you feel. Listen, I didn't want to go, okay, but my firm all but insisted."

All but.

"Did you even push back, Brandon?"

"Yeah, of course. But there were a lot of big players there, and it was important we do some networking. Listen . . . Sienna, the polls are saying it's likely the mayor's going to win his reelection campaign, okay?" Her heart dropped before he went on. "That fact doesn't make me happy, and I don't like the politics involved in my job any more than you do, but the fact is, if I want to make partner at some point, I have to play the game."

Play the game.

The game. The one where innocent children often lost.

The *very* thing she'd been unwilling to do. Did that make them incompatible in the end?

She felt as though she were standing on a chasm, one foot on either side of the widening split. And a distant voice she couldn't quite identify was telling her she needed to choose one or the other because she couldn't choose both.

A head pang made her wince. "Listen, Brandon, I think maybe . . . we need to consider my move a little break from . . . us."

"Sienna, babe, you're making way too much of a business dinner I was forced to go to."

Were you forced to go with your buxom coworker? Were you forced to allow her to sit close enough to touch you? But she wasn't going to bring that up. She'd kissed another man.

She hadn't *meant* to exactly. And she'd pulled away. But . . . *no excuses.* She'd never been one for excuses. Gavin had kissed her, but she'd kissed him back. And yes, she'd pulled away, but not before she'd allowed herself to get lost in his taste, the feel of his body against hers, the sweet and terrifying familiarity of the flame that had once again flickered to life inside her.

Point being, this was not all on Brandon.

But she suddenly realized that the question she'd asked herself earlier about Brandon had a clear answer. The worst part of the betrayal she felt didn't come from him potentially being on a date. It came from his mere presence at that particular dinner, his unwillingness to make a stand. For her. For justice. For what was *right.*

"I think you'll realize this is for the best, Brandon." She got out of her car, lugging her briefcase over her shoulder. It felt like it weighed ten tons.

"Sienna, you sound . . . tired . . . off. Let's talk about this later, okay?"

"I am tired, but I mean what I say," she said, dragging herself to her door. "But yes, we can talk about it all later." Maybe there was more to say. It didn't really feel like it to her in that moment, but she was admittedly not exactly firing on all four mental cylinders.

"All right." She heard a female voice, his secretary perhaps. "I'm needed in a meeting, but I'll talk to you soon, okay? Sienna . . . take care."

Take care. "Goodbye, Brandon."

She flipped her lock behind her and went to the kitchen, tossed her things on the table, which she'd ordered online and which had just arrived the day before, and removed the case file.

She should be going to bed, she knew that, but Brandon's reasoning for the call—*Because I wanted you to know I was thinking about you*—was basically bullshit. He'd been "needed" in a meeting two minutes into their conversation. And he hadn't apologized for going to the dinner. He'd justified his actions. *Like the chief of police. Like the mayor.* All for future employment ladder climbing. She couldn't sleep now, despite the banging in her head. *Maybe because of the banging in my head.* Instead, she made herself a cup of tea—deciding she'd had her fill of coffee—opened the case file on the counter, and tried once more to work out this damn puzzle.

What was relevant? What had the killer given them that they had missed? *What will he give us next?*

CHAPTER
TWENTY-FOUR

Gavin held his finger on the doorbell for the third time, hearing the distant buzz from within. "Come on," he muttered, another flutter of worry heightening his impatience. He'd called Sienna several times, and when she hadn't called him back, he'd phoned her at the station and been put through to her partner, Kat, who told him she'd gone home earlier that day.

He didn't want to be a pest . . . exactly. But he also knew that she was basically alone in this city and had been called out by a killer still on the loose. Someone should be checking on her. *She's a detective trained in the use of firearms and—presumably—fighting techniques, Decker, so don't lie to yourself and pretend she needs protection.*

He thought he heard movement inside, and a moment later, the lock disengaged, and the door was pulled open. Sienna stood there in wrinkled work clothes, her hair in a lopsided updo, one eye squinted as she tilted her head to look at him. "Gavin," she whispered. "What are you doing here?"

"Hey," he said, peering at her, noticing the dark smudges beneath her eyes. "You weren't answering your phone, so I came to check on you. Are you okay?"

She sighed, gesturing that he should come inside. He did, shutting the door behind him and following her to the living room, where she'd obviously been sitting on the floor working. There were papers and files spread out around the spot she settled herself into now. She picked up her phone lying next to her and then huffed out a breath, tossing it back down. "It's dead. I need to charge it."

He glanced around, but there was still no furniture, just the two unopened boxes positioned where they'd sat the first time he'd been there. He took the same seat on the sagging box, leaning his elbows on his knees. Sienna sat back against the wall, grimacing as she rubbed her forehead. He watched her for a minute. "You're exhausted," he noted. And it appeared she had a headache.

She gave a short laugh that morphed into a pained huff of breath. "I'm aware. That's why I came home to work."

"It seems like sleep might be the better priority."

She shot him a look that said she didn't need his unsolicited advice, but the grimace that followed proved his point. She leaned forward, stretching her neck. "It's really this headache that's making me miserable," she said.

"Have you taken anything for it?"

She shook her head, and even that small movement appeared to cause her discomfort. She leaned her head against the wall and closed her eyes. Gavin pulled himself up from the cardboard box. "Do you have anything in your medicine cabinet?"

"No. I thought I had something, but I don't," she murmured. "It's been so long since I've had a headache like this," she said, her words so soft he almost didn't hear them.

His heart reached for her. She'd pushed herself so hard she'd hit a brick wall. And still, she was sitting on the floor in her house, going over case notes.

"I'll be right back." He was pretty sure he had a bottle of Tylenol in his glove box. He walked outside, leaving her door very slightly ajar, and went to the passenger side of his car. "Score," he murmured, pulling out the medicine. He closed his car door and turned toward Sienna's walkway, uncertainty making him pause.

He pressed his lips together, then stopped and took his phone from his pocket before dialing. "Mom?"

"Hi, Gavin, I'm in the middle of watching this ridiculous *American Bake-Off* show. It's the final episode, and it's tense. I can't decide—"

"*Mom,*" he repeated.

"Gavin, what's wrong?" she asked, obviously hearing the seriousness of his tone.

"I'm at Sienna's. She went home sick from work, and she has a terrible headache. Didn't she used to get them as a kid?"

"Oh dear. Yes. Is she squinting her left eye?"

"Yeah. I was trying to remember what you used to give her that worked best." He pictured a young Sienna lying on his couch, his mom sitting beside her as she smoothed a wet washcloth across her forehead. Of course, Sienna herself could probably tell him what typically worked best for her, but he was worried she'd shoo him away before he could provide her the relief she obviously needed.

"That terrible one-sided headache she used to get when she was overly stressed." Mirabelle clicked her tongue. "Give her some Tylenol. She always seemed to respond best to that. And put a cold compress on her head."

He released a breath, continuing to Sienna's door. *Tylenol. Cold compress.* "Okay, got it. Thanks, Mom."

"That's what moms are for." He heard the smile in her voice.

He went inside, locked the front door, and peeked in the living room, where Sienna was still sitting against the wall, her mouth open, as she slept. Tenderness engulfed him, his lips tipping as he watched her sleep. He considered leaving her right there rather than waking her so she could head to bed. Even in sleep, though, her expression looked slightly pained, as though the headache was breaking into her dreams. And if she slept in that position for longer than an hour, she was going to wake up with sore muscles to accompany her aching head. He retrieved a bottle of water from her fridge, shook out two Tylenols, and then returned to where she was.

"Si?" He shook her slightly, and she mumbled, her head coming forward, eyes half-open as she oriented herself. He handed her the capsules. "Here, take these. They'll help."

She did as he asked, swallowing the medication with half the bottle of water and then laying her head back against the wall with a moan. "Do you think that cactus is vulgar or . . . pretty?" she asked.

He let out a confused laugh when he realized she must be talking about the cactus outside her condo. She was so tired she was practically drunk. "Definitely vulgar," he said.

She laughed, too, though it was soft and short, more a huff of air. "We used to laugh," she said. "We used to laugh so much. I've never laughed with anyone the way I did with you."

His throat felt suddenly full. She was right. They had. They'd loved hard, and they'd laughed hard, and looking back, he'd halfway convinced himself it was just the unabashed nature of youth. But that wasn't true. Neither he nor Sienna had grown up in a way that would have encouraged an attitude of joyful abandon. They'd just brought that out in each other. Her lids drifted closed and her head began falling forward before she jerked it up again, yanking herself from sleep.

"Come on," he said, taking her hand as he began to stand. "Let me help you to bed. Even Superwoman needs to sleep sometimes."

She let out a small chuff, and for a moment it appeared she was going to argue, but then she sighed, likely deciding she didn't have the strength to fight him just then. She gripped his hand as he pulled her to her feet. She weaved, letting out a soft whimper and squinting her eye again when she came to her full height.

Shit. A head rush had to make things that much worse. "I'll leave some more Tylenol on your bedside table," he said, walking with her down the hall toward the open door at the end.

"I don't have a bedside table," she murmured.

Gavin led her to her bedroom, Sienna holding her hand at her head as they walked. "Tell me you at least have a bed."

"I do," she said, pushing the door open.

"I'm going to, ah, go get those extra Tylenol and another bottle of water," he murmured, turning as she reached for the robe lying at the end of the bed.

When he came back with the medication, water, and a cold washcloth, Sienna was already lying in bed, eyes closed, her robe falling open slightly. And he supposed, being that she was exhausted and in pain, it was less than honorable that the sight of the bare swell of one breast was arousing as all hell.

He'd seen women dressed skimpier at the hotel pool. So why did the sight of this woman in a white cotton robe make him feel off-balance? He drank her in, the shape of her body under the thin material causing a physical reaction he could not control. He'd always been so intensely attracted to her, and in one glance he remembered exactly why. It was simple, really. He was a man. He had his preferences, even if he hadn't ever defined them, and she met every one of them. The shape of her hips, the dip of her waist, even the delicacy of her collarbone and the slope of her shoulders. The way she'd been formed spoke to whatever biological quality that existed inside him to seek out the perfect mate. It was too strong and unchangeable to be anything else.

The thing that separated him from some long-ago Neanderthal, though, was that he also liked her mind. He respected her opinions and her way of looking at life. He enjoyed her sense of humor and her commitment to justice. Simply put: to him she was perfect.

Focus here, Decker. She needs you.

He wouldn't even think about the "main squeeze" right now or the fact that just the thought of him made jealousy churn in Gavin's gut.

He set the Tylenol and the bottle of water on a forensic textbook of some kind on the floor next to the bed and then set the cold washcloth gently on her forehead. She sighed but didn't open her eyes. "Thank you," she murmured.

"You're welcome," he said, adjusting the cloth, grateful she was allowing him to help her. What she needed now was sleep, and he should leave her to get some. But he didn't seem to be able to get up just yet. Didn't want to leave her when he might be able to offer even a small bit of comfort.

"I have to remind myself not to push too hard," she said, voice soft as her eyes came open halfway and she looked at him. "It's a flaw. I know. But I had to. Growing up. If I didn't . . ."

If you didn't, no one would. No one would advocate for you, and so you had to advocate for yourself. "I know, Sienna. I know," he said, moving a piece of hair off her cheek. "And it's not a flaw."

"Sometimes it is."

He paused, and even though her eyes were hooded, they speared him. He knew she was alluding to their relationship; he just didn't know exactly what she meant. And yet, as much as he wanted to talk about *them*—in any context—this wasn't the time. She was vulnerable and clearly exhausted, and he didn't want her to resent him when she got some sleep and was feeling back to herself. He didn't want her to wish she hadn't said something simply because her guard was down. "No," he said. "It's your strength, Si. It always has been. Never quitting. Pushing forward, regardless of the obstacles." He gave her a small smile. "You are still human, though, and humans need sleep."

She gave him a weary smile in return and closed her eyes. "Thank you, Gavin," she murmured.

He took the washcloth off her forehead and brought it into the bathroom so she wouldn't wake with a clammy cloth on her head.

When he returned to the room, he started to ask her if she needed anything else before he left, but when he looked at her, she was already fast asleep, mouth open. *Good. Sleep, Superwoman.* He walked to the bed, smoothed her hair off her forehead, and brought the blanket up over her legs.

The movement must have woken her, because she grabbed his hand before he could turn away, and though she didn't open her eyes, she murmured, "Stay, please stay."

Gavin's heart gave a gallop. *Stay.* He wanted nothing more. He walked around the bed and lay down next to her. She turned toward him, her body relaxing as she fell back to sleep.

He watched her for several moments. Her lashes fluttered, her lips falling open as she let out a small sigh. He felt an unexpected lump in his throat and swallowed it down. And it hit him like a ton of bricks. He loved her. He'd never stopped. He might have lived the rest of his life never watching her as she dreamed again. And this might be the last time—though hope kept him from embracing that as a reality. But what was true and known was that regardless of what came to pass, he would love Sienna Walker for the entirety of his days. Gavin rarely felt vulnerable, but in that moment, he'd never felt it as strongly. It'd wreck him to let her go again.

But she'd asked him to stay. For now. And so that was what he would do, for as long as she let him.

~

Gavin woke slowly, dawn barely slipping through the blinds, the room a hazy gray.

"My dress was an A-line gown with a scalloped hemline and had embroidered appliqués on net over Chantilly lace."

Gavin blinked at the ceiling, his mind rewinding what Sienna had just murmured close to his ear. "I don't know what most of those words mean, but it sounds beautiful."

She laughed very softly, and he turned toward her, taking her in. She looked sleepy and beautiful, the shadows beneath her eyes much less severe than they'd been the night before. He could tell just by the clarity in her eyes that her headache was gone. Plus, she'd just muttered a whole complicated string of words that he figured she'd have to be mostly lucid to have put together. Though admittedly, whether they made sense or not, he couldn't say. "It was. It was beautiful," she said wistfully.

He tucked a strand of hair behind her ear. "I'm sorry I left you there. Please forgive me. I wish I'd had the wisdom and courage to do it differently."

Though it was mostly dark in the room, he saw her gaze travel over his features. "I would have convinced you to stay," she said. "Or I would have convinced you to take me with you. And then everything would have been different."

"Different good or different bad?"

"I don't know. Probably a little of both. Maybe one more than the other. That's the thing about choices. You don't get to live two different ones. You're stuck with the one you pick, and trying to imagine the alternative isn't really productive."

"You wouldn't be a cop."

"No, probably not." She paused. "Definitely not." Her eyes went to the side, and he wondered if she was thinking about the people she'd positively affected. He hoped so. It was the thing that made the regret he felt for hurting her bearable. "I do forgive you, Gavin."

His breath released. It felt like one he'd been holding for eleven years, the hollow he'd learned to live with knitting closed.

"It was probably a bad omen that the place we picked to get married at was called the Antique Flowers Wedding Chapel," she said.

He managed both a grimace and a laugh. "Antique flowers . . ." His brows came together in thought. "What *are* antique flowers anyway?"

"Hmm . . . for me, the phrase brings to mind an old dusty, crumbling bouquet, rotting away in an attic."

He gave a full laugh then. "That's less than romantic."

"Way less." Her smile dwindled. "I knew something was wrong, Gavin. With you, I mean. I knew it, but I chose to ignore it and write it off to nerves or that you were fighting with Mirabelle about your intention of entering poker tournaments and traveling once you'd turned twenty-one. I didn't question you because I didn't want to. I thought . . . well, I thought whatever was wrong would be dealt with once we were married. I felt you slipping away, and instead of facing it and asking you why, I pushed forward. I had some growing up to do too," she finished softly.

"You are not to blame for my lack of courage, Si. Please don't think—"

"That's not what I mean. I just mean that we both played our parts, and it's important for me to recognize that."

His gaze held on her, his heart expanding. He'd thought he'd loved her before, but he'd had no idea. Impossibly, she'd become *more* of everything he'd always admired about her.

"Tell me about winning the World Series of Poker," she said, surprising him. He turned on his back. Lying with her felt familiar and new. They used to sneak out of their trailers and lie in the back of his pickup truck, staring up at the nighttime sky and talking until all hours. They'd done other things in the back of that pickup truck, too, her legs wrapped around his hips as he went half out of his mind with pleasure.

The World Series of Poker. He moved his inner eye into that large brightly lit arena, smelled the scent of cigarette smoke competing with the sour stench of adrenaline, and his body cooled, blood coursing more slowly.

"I played with this sort of . . . wild abandon. Some people wondered if I was *trying* to lose." He was quiet for a moment, remembering that time. He heard the whispers of the other players. They'd thought he was mostly crazy and that he'd be down for the count soon enough. Winning took more controlled strategy than he was displaying. "The announcers used to say I played as though I was fearless," he said, pausing again. "But that wasn't it. I just had nothing of value to lose." He turned toward her, meeting her eyes in the gauzy light. "I'd already lost the one thing that really mattered to me. You." Only worse, he hadn't just lost her; he'd thrown her away. He knew her well enough to know that was how she'd felt. But even though he'd been the one to walk away—*run away*—he'd been gutted too. Desolate. He'd wanted her with him. Her thoughts. Her touch. Her love. *Her as his wife*. And so while part of him was relieved to be unburdened by the pressure he'd felt, mostly he hated himself. Hence his recklessness.

"So if I was by your side, you probably wouldn't have won."

"Maybe. Maybe not. But I would have played differently, yes."

"So you wouldn't have been rich. You might have been living in a van down by the river."

He laughed. "I like to think I'd have figured out a middle ground." His expression became serious. "In some ways winning was awful, Si, because it felt like the thing I'd traded for you, and it didn't begin to fill your void. In fact, it made your absence starker, because I wanted to talk to you about it. I wanted to share it. With you. Only with you. And you weren't there."

She smiled, but it was fleeting. "Where do we go from here?" she asked, her voice all but a whisper.

His heart rate jumped, but he didn't really have an answer to that, because she was the one involved with someone else. That question was not for him to answer. They were so close, and part of him wanted to reply by leaning in and kissing her. But that wasn't really an answer, not one he wanted anyway, at least not only that. In any case, he wasn't going to take advantage of her, not like this, not when she was drowsy and groggy and just coming off a migraine. Yes, he desperately wanted her, but this was not the time.

"First," he said, wrapping his arm around her and bringing her close, "we get you some more good sleep, because the sun is barely up." She snuggled into him, and a few minutes later, he felt her body relax, her breath becoming smooth and even as she once again surrendered to dreams.

CHAPTER
TWENTY-FIVE

Sienna stood in the doorway, watching Gavin sleep, her lips tilting in a tender smile. She'd felt him wake several times throughout the night as he'd checked on her. He'd also gotten up once and brought her another dose of medication and a glass of water. That and the rest had done wonders. Her head felt completely clear. She was thankful he'd kept sleeping when she'd gotten out of bed thirty minutes ago. She'd wanted time to shower and clean herself up. She'd needed time to think.

No, that wasn't exactly true. She'd needed time to sit for a few minutes with the choice she'd made.

She leaned her shoulder against the doorframe, taking the opportunity to let her gaze move over him uninhibited. He'd stayed with her all night, and she'd slept more deeply than she had in months. It'd made her realize how innately she trusted him. *Still.* The room was dim, her shades blocking the early-morning sun, but she could see the crescents his lashes made on his cheeks and the dark stubble that spotted his jaw. His lips were parted slightly in sleep, his chest rising and falling rhythmically. He was still in his T-shirt and jeans, the sheet only covering his feet. He was beautiful, and she loved him. She always had. It felt so blessedly simple. After all these years away from him, shouldn't it be an epiphany? A light bulb moment that took her by surprise? *Maybe.* And yet there was something very different about acknowledging a first love, one that had never truly gone away.

Remembering what and who they'd been . . . together.

Recognizing that a man who she'd thought had carelessly abandoned her had actually grieved her loss as much as she'd grieved his. He'd made mistakes, but so had she.

Things would have been so different had they married that day. And though, in a way, she mourned the time they'd lost, she couldn't help thinking about all she'd done, all she'd realized about herself, during their time apart. The gifts that had come from her suffering. She'd traveled alone to New York City. She'd graduated college and then the police academy. She'd worked hard and become a detective in one of the most crime-ridden areas of the city. She'd been morally tested and stood her ground. She'd *done* all that, a girl who, until that point, had never left the town in which she was born. A girl who'd come from nothing. And she would have never known she was capable of all those hard things had she married him that day. There were *other*—different—things she might have known had she lived that alternate life, but she couldn't be certain of what they were. And so she'd find gratitude in the many gifts that had risen from the ashes of her heartache. What else could anyone do? That lesson was hers; she'd earned it.

Gavin's eyes opened, and he blinked at her. "Morning," she said.

He came up on one elbow and ran a hand through his ruffled hair. "Morning. Sorry I . . ." He gave his head a small shake. "I guess I fell asleep on the job. How do you feel?"

She pushed off the wall, walked to the bed, and climbed in, sitting on her knees next to him. She smiled. "Rested. Finally. And no headache."

He made a sound of relief and started to sit up. "I called Brandon," she said, her words hurried. He lay back down and watched her, wariness in his gaze. "I'd already suggested we take a break, but this morning, I made it official." She met his eyes. She could see the hope there, the longing. She felt those things too. She *let* herself feel those things, allowed all pretense to fall away and, with it, the stored hurt, the long years. Pure instinct led the way, and she leaned forward and brought her mouth to his. He moaned, deep in his throat, and wove his fingers through her hair as they kissed.

"I love you." His voice came out choked. "I always have. I always will."

"I love you too," she said back, their eyes meeting. *His eyes.* It had always been about his eyes. They'd grabbed her from the start. She'd first seen friendship there, then desire, then love. Commitment. She saw it now, clear as day. And she knew he had left without allowing her to see his eyes because she would have seen his love. She would have *known*.

She leaned back in, kissing him again, luxuriating in the feel of his mouth against hers, the way the slow movement of his tongue still drove her wild. She almost laughed, with wonder, with delight, with the curious fact she'd ever settled for less than this. *Safety, maybe. Self-preservation.* But her thoughts were fleeting. She wanted to be *here*, in this moment, and there was time for self-reflection later.

They undressed each other slowly, both of them shivering in anticipation. She pulled his shirt over his head, running a finger over the very slight scar on his rib cage, the place where he'd broken through the red rover line and fallen on a sharp rock when he was ten. He'd cried and then been embarrassed that he had. She knew. She knew all his scars, and he knew all hers. His chest was solid and smooth, a sparse patch of hair between his pecs. Sienna reached up, running her fingers over it and then using both hands to brush across his nipples. He shivered, moaned. She could tell he was holding himself still, allowing her to rediscover him at her own pace. She smiled up at him. She wanted to go slow, but she was needy, too, moisture pooling between her thighs, her nipples pebbled in anticipation of his touch.

Gavin's eyes met hers as he unbuttoned her top and let it fall open. Her breasts were bare. His mouth opened slightly, his eyes lingering, and she felt the approving heat of his stare. "You're so incredibly beautiful," he said. She *felt* beautiful. He'd always made her feel that way with his eyes, with his words, with the way he never looked at anyone but her.

"So are you," she said on a smile. She unsnapped his jeans, and he worked them quickly off his hips and over his straining erection. *Oh.* Her nerves tingled with excitement, her gaze growing hazy with lust. She had to touch him. She reached out, sliding her hand over his hot flesh, and he moaned, pressing forward, a sound that was both pleasure and pain falling from his lips. She wanted to taste him. She wanted to feel the bliss of him entering her body and watch the mindlessness of his pleasure consuming his face. She couldn't wait to see him try to hang on to control, then surrender to it, to watch him thrust and shiver, to claim her. She wanted everything he had to give and all at once.

She slowed her breathing as much as she was able, removing the PJ bottoms she'd recently put on and tossing them aside. For a moment they both lay there, utterly naked, far enough apart that they could drink each other in, their chests rising and falling, hearts beating rapidly. They moved together then, the meeting of their bare skin causing each to gasp, rolling with a laugh and a moan, both cut off quickly by the meeting of their mouths.

Oh, the splendor of kissing naked. Of limbs entwined, of halted breaths and stroking fingers. Nothing was inaccessible, and both Gavin and Sienna joyfully explored each other, slowly at first, but then with more urgency. She'd always loved to feel him tremble, and nothing had changed. Her hand stroking his erection, his mouth on her nipple, sucking, licking, and then lower as she practically screamed, her hips bucking as her pleasure crested higher. Higher. It was too much then, for both of them. It had been mere minutes, but it'd also been eleven years, and one second longer felt intolerable. Their eyes met as Gavin positioned himself over her, grasping the underside of her thigh and raising it, opening her so he could thrust inside. "Oh God," he said, his throat moving as he swallowed, his biceps straining as he held himself above her.

She gripped his backside as he began to move, directing him so he made contact with the spot that made her tremble with every quickened press. "I haven't been living, Sienna, not really," he breathed between kisses. "Not until now."

She kissed him harder in response. She felt alive, truly *alive*, for the first time in years too. Stars were dancing before her eyes, the room around her hazy and unclear, and the only thing she could focus on was the intense rapture of her body. And she loved him. God, she loved him so much. She wanted to slow it down and speed it up, and before she could do either, her body decided for her and she let go of him, gripping the comforter on either side of her and sighing his name as she climaxed.

Her climax sparked his own, and he came with a muted groan, his mouth against her neck as his hips stilled, pressing one final time to draw out the bliss.

They lay there for several moments before he pulled out of her and rolled onto his back, bringing her with him. She drew lazy circles on his stomach, and he stroked his fingers down her arm as the world came back into focus.

She smiled at Gavin, the years fading, the gap closing as though their time apart had been but a single, painful moment that now was over.

~

Sienna's eyes opened slowly, soft afternoon light filtering through the blinds. The memories of that morning came back to her, her lips tipping in a dreamy smile as she turned toward Gavin.

The place where he'd been was empty now, though, the pillow still indented. Her smile faded, and she sat up, the smell of coffee and something sweet meeting her nose. She let out a relieved breath. He was still here, and he was cooking something that smelled incredible.

She padded to the bathroom, where she brushed her teeth and tamed her hair into something that no longer resembled a windblown alpaca, and then went in search of Gavin.

She found him at the stove, just placing a final piece of french toast on a plate. He looked back over his shoulder, smiling as she came up behind him and wrapped her arms around his waist. "Good morning," she said, burying her face in his T-shirt and breathing him in.

"Technically it's afternoon," he said, turning and bringing his arms around her. He kissed her, lips lingering before he murmured, "I'm glad you were able to get a few more hours of sleep. Hungry?"

"Mm," she said. "Actually, ravenous. And that smells amazing."

He turned back to the counter, picking up the plate and gesturing to the table. "I used what I found in your fridge. And by the way, I'm glad to see you bought a piece of furniture."

She smiled, sitting down where there was already butter and syrup. She'd bought the syrup to go along with the toaster waffles in her freezer, but this was far better. "I was going to make eggs and toast, but I remembered your sweet tooth," he said, placing a cup of coffee in front of her.

She took a grateful sip of the coffee and dug in to the food. Gavin put a couple of pieces of french toast on his plate and began to butter them. She almost felt like she'd woken up in a dream. *Almost.* It felt dreamy, *yes*, but also . . . incredibly right, as though she'd taken a detour—albeit a necessary one—and was finally back on the road she was meant to travel. "Do you have a word puzzle going on?" he asked, nodding to the paper with the notes she'd made as she'd tried to determine the word the killer might be trying to spell out for them with periodic table elements. She'd worked on it in the kitchen for a while before finally abandoning it to reread the notes in the living room, where he'd found her.

She finished chewing, shrugging one shoulder. She didn't see how talking a few specifics of the case with him was a big deal. He was officially consulting, and he'd already been privy to information they weren't yet releasing, and . . . she trusted him. "I think our killer is using the periodic table to send some sort of message or spell out a word. I might be wrong, or I might not have enough letters."

He glanced at the letters she'd written in order. He took a sip of coffee before saying, "Or it's an anagram."

She sighed. Just when her brain had started feeling better. "Or that." She went over the letters as she ate, but no anagram she could come up with made sense. Olive? Voile? *Loveliness* could be in the works, but again, she didn't know what might be missing. She pushed the notes away. All of that would come crashing back tomorrow. For now? It was her day off. "Do you have to go into work today?" she asked, knowing that despite it being Wednesday, casinos—like police stations—never closed, and he might work weekends like her and have off days in the middle of the week.

He wiped his mouth with a napkin and shook his head. "I called off sick."

"Faker."

"Hardly. I'm exhausted. You kept me up all night checking on you and then had me working out—strenuously, I might add—at the break of dawn."

She raised a brow. "I didn't hear much complaining."

He laughed, hooking one arm over the back of his chair, so casually gorgeous it made her heart skip a beat. And suddenly, she felt strangely shy.

"In all seriousness," she said, "thank you. Thank you for taking care of me. For staying."

His face sobered too. "Thank you for asking."

She leaned over and planted her lips on his, and when he moaned against her mouth, she stood, put one leg over him, and sat on his lap as they continued to kiss. Only their clothes separated them, and Sienna's blood began to heat as she pressed closer, closer.

"God, Sienna," he moaned, breaking from her lips just long enough to say, "Move in with me."

She leaned back slightly, surprise causing her to still. Her eyes washed over his features, vulnerability in his expression, and her heart jolted. "Move in with you?" she repeated. "Isn't it a bit . . . soon?"

"It's years too late," he said, giving her a boyish smile. "Plus," he went on, "if you need more of a reason, I have all kinds of furniture we can do this on."

"Tempting," she murmured, leaning in to kiss him again just as the doorbell rang. They both froze, their eyes opening, lips still touching.

Sienna pulled away, looking toward the door in hopes that whoever it was would go away. The doorbell rang again, followed by a loud rap. "Who in the world is that?" she asked, climbing reluctantly off Gavin's lap.

He pulled her back, and she let out a laughing yelp as he nuzzled into the side of her neck. She could feel a smile on his face as he gave her a small push. "They seem determined," he said.

With a sigh, she headed to the front door and looked through the peephole to see Mirabelle. *Oh.* She pulled it open, and Mirabelle rushed in and set a casserole dish on the floor, a plate perched on top, covered in foil. "Oh, honey, thank goodness. You look good. You must be feeling better. How's your head?"

"Good," she said. "Much better."

"Hi, Mom," Gavin said, coming around the corner and standing in the doorway.

"Oh, Gavin, you're still here." She brought her hands together, looking from one to the other, obviously reading the situation, and Sienna blushed, looking down. When she looked back up, she saw that Mirabelle's eyes were lingering on her, a smile on her face and tears in her eyes. "Oh," she breathed. She reached forward and hugged Sienna, squeezing her so tightly Sienna laughed as she looked over Mirabelle's shoulder at Gavin, who was watching them with an amused smile. "Well, that's that then," she said as though something was finally settled, giving Sienna one final squeeze.

Mirabelle let go, sniffing and stepping back before she picked up the items she'd placed on the floor and held them forward. "The cheesy chicken casserole you always loved and a plate of baklava from Argus." She bustled past Sienna, who closed the door. She felt warm and cared for and happier than she'd been for a long, long time. "Comfort food," Mirabelle said over her shoulder.

She and Gavin followed Mirabelle into the kitchen, where she'd put the dish on the stove. "Mom, we just ate breakfast," he said.

She glanced at the table. "Oh, okay, then I'll just put this in the refrigerator for later. Sienna, do you have any Tupperware? That way you don't have to worry about scrubbing my pan. The last thing you need is more work."

Sienna's phone rang, and she reached for it on the counter, seeing Kat's number on the screen. "I've gotta get this," she said.

"Of course," Mirabelle said. "Gavin will help me."

Sienna walked into the bedroom, connecting the call. "Hi, Kat."

"How are you feeling?"

"So much better. I'll be back tomorrow."

"Okay, great, because we have another DOA. It came in last night. I was up late, so I'm just heading into the office now."

Sienna sank down on the bed. "Damn. You could have called me, Kat."

"No way. You weren't feeling well. And I was waiting for the initial pathology report, which came in about an hour ago. I thought it better to let you recover until we got more information. And thankfully Ingrid was available last night to join me at the scene." *Another scene. Another victim.* And here she was rolling around in the sheets with Gavin. Not that that made a bit of difference to this killer.

"What do you know about the victim so far, and where was she found?" Sienna asked.

"He," Kat said. "And he was found on the edge of a park in a pretty rough area. Near an old unused section of railroad. A homeless guy looking for bottles found him."

"He?" Sienna asked, frowning. "That makes no sense to our profile."

"I know. Throws things off, right?"

"Was there a note found?"

"There sure was," Kat said.

"So it was definitely our killer's work."

"Definitely. Also, same methodology, and there were clues in the victim's hand. Specifically, a pair of dice. You can read the note and see the rest when you get in."

The note. Her mind cast back momentarily as she reminded herself where the last one had left off, with Danny Boy's humiliating date with "Smiles."

"Okay," she murmured, her mind whirling. They'd thought they were dealing with bad *mothers.* "Wait, could this guy be a bad father?" she asked. That would expand things to bad *parents*, but it would still link the victims.

"If he is," Kat said, "there's no sign of it. His name's Harry Lockheed. His wife had reported him missing twelve hours before he was found. From all initial evidence, he seems like he was a good family man: three grown kids, five grandkids. Obviously, we haven't had time to interview them yet, so we'll see if it's a mirage, but on first sight, yeah, it doesn't fit. The two women victims' ages are similar, but this guy is older."

"Well, shit," Sienna muttered.

"That's for sure. Anyway, hey, I just wanted to update you, but it's your off day, so enjoy it, and I'll see you tomorrow."

Enjoy it. While she would love to do just that and spend the entire day with Gavin, the case was going to have to take priority in light of this new development. She'd made up for lost sleep, and she'd be mindful not to push herself as far as she had again. "No, I'll be in. Just give me an hour or so."

"Are you sure—"

"Absolutely. I want to be there."

"Okay, well, if you're sure, you know Ingrid will approve the overtime," Kat said, and Sienna knew she'd made the right call by the relieved note in Kat's tone. "See you soon."

Sienna ended the call just as there was a soft rap on the bedroom door. "Come in," she called.

Mirabelle peeked her head in. "I'm going to get going, honey. You make sure to prioritize your rest, okay? The world needs you at your best."

Sienna stood and went to the door, frowning when she saw that Mirabelle looked paler than she'd been, bright-red spots on her cheeks. "Are you okay? You look flushed."

"Oh yes. I'm fine. Just a little warm." She smiled, grabbing Sienna's hands and squeezing them. "You've always been a daughter to me," she said, her voice breathless with sudden emotion. "Even when you were gone. Now . . . well, I'm so glad you're back. So glad." She gave Sienna's hands another squeeze and then turned away, hurrying for the front door.

Sienna watched her open it and leave as Gavin came up next to her. "Was your mom okay?" she asked. "She sure did come and go in a hurry."

"I think she wanted to give us time alone," he said, pulling her close. Sienna smiled, giving him a quick kiss.

"I wish I could spend the rest of the day with you," she said. "But my off day is canceled. I have to get back to work." Her mind returned to Kat's phone call. *And the newest note.* "Our killer isn't done yet," she said. Of course . . . she'd known that was the case, but God, she'd hoped she was wrong.

CHAPTER
TWENTY-SIX

School ended, and I tried my best to put everything that had happened during my high school years behind me. I got a new job with a new company. I worked hard, rarely using the entirety of my breaks, never checking my phone or goofing off the way the other employees who worked with me did, and soon, I received a promotion. I kept my head down and did nothing to draw negative attention to myself. My father had taught me well.

A promotion meant more money, and more money meant more nutritious food. I even had a little extra to pay for a gym membership. I had always been tall, but now I grew in mass too. I began to notice women giving me furtive glances or fixing their hair the way I'd seen them doing when they were talking to popular guys in school. But now they did it with me.

I was still gun shy, though, when it came to women. I'd found a sort of peace, and I welcomed it. I had my job. My bosses praised me. I had a home where I felt safe. Finally.

That autumn, a new girl started at one of my places of employment. She had dark-red hair and eyes almost as blue as Mother's. I called her Dolly in my head because her skin was as pale and flawless as a porcelain doll. She was very petite, but she had large breasts that overwhelmed her frame. Though I tried to be as discreet as possible, I had a hard time not staring at them each time she passed my way, and I think she noticed because after a while, she would stop and chat, arching her back slightly and smiling a knowing smile when my gaze naturally strayed downward.

We'd been working together for about a month when Dolly finally said one day, "Why don't you ask me out? I know you want to."

I felt the heat creeping up my neck but tried my best to appear casual and only mildly interested. Inside, though, my heart was racing, and I wasn't sure if she was right or wrong. *Did* I want to ask her out? I enjoyed our chats. I looked forward to seeing her at work. I'd even practiced flirting with her just a little—or at least what I hoped was flirting—and thought it'd gone well. It made me feel more confident. It helped mute the reminder of the humiliating failure of the one and only date I'd ever been on with Smiles. Dolly was much more forward than Smiles, though, and she took my hand and placed it on her large breast, watching me as I swallowed and grew ever redder in the face. She laughed, dropping my hand and saying, "I'll be ready after work." And then she turned, blowing me a kiss over her shoulder as she returned to her post.

I could hardly focus on my work, and the next few hours saw more mistakes and fumbles than I'd made at my job since I started. Another employee asked me twice if I was feeling okay, and I told him I felt mildly ill but that I'd be fine.

Part of me hoped Dolly was only kidding about our after-work date and that when I saw her next, she'd make an excuse and beg off. I didn't see her for the rest of the day, though, and when my shift was over, I decided to leave without seeking her out because at that point I really did feel nauseated, my heart was still beating far too quickly, and my hands were sweating. But when I walked out the back door, Dolly was leaning against my car, a saucy smile on her face as she waited for me.

My heart beat ever faster and I felt light-headed. Dolly didn't seem to notice, though, even offering to drive my car, which had once belonged to my father but now was mine.

She drove us to a bar, and though neither of us were of legal drinking age, no one there seemed to care. I was thankful for the low lighting, hoping that it hid my flushed skin and the blotches that had surely formed on my neck, as they tended to do when I became anxious or worked up. Dolly ordered a beer and I did, too, and though I had never really drunk alcohol other than to try it from the stash Father had kept in our kitchen cupboard, I found the effects were just what I needed to calm my system.

I drank one, then two, and ordered a third. But I was far outmatched in the drinking arena, and Dolly not only quickly surpassed the number of beers I'd had but was also doing shots with a guy at the bar each time she placed another order. Pretty soon, her eyes were red and half-closed, and her words were slurring together. "Dance with me!" she insisted, pulling me out onto the mostly empty dance floor and pressing herself against me. Despite the alcohol in my system, my breath came short again, sweat breaking out on my brow. She wrapped her arms around my neck, her breasts large, soft pillows against my chest, and I grew hard. Dolly, obviously feeling my arousal, purred, sloppily grinding her body against mine. At her brazen touch, the anxiety poured through me like battery acid, but I forced myself not to step back, out of her grasp. She stumbled slightly, missing a step, and then laughed, falling against me and saying, "Take me home, baby."

I was so aroused it hurt at that point. So I let her lead me out the door to the car, where I took the wheel, and she turned up the music, blasting it so loud I couldn't hear my own thoughts and leaning perilously out the window so that I had to grab the back hem of her shirt to keep her from falling out.

Her apartment was only a few blocks from the bar, and surprisingly, she was able to direct me there, or rather yell "Stop!" when she saw it so that I screeched to a halt at the curb.

The alcohol was wearing off at this point, and my nerves had returned in full force. And not only nerves but doubt and a good dose of disgust toward her, even if my body hadn't yet gotten the memo, the bulge in my pants pumping with blood. I haltingly followed her up the steps to her door, and she pulled me inside before slamming it behind us. She must have been unbuttoning her shirt as she climbed the steps because when she turned, it was open, and she dropped it on the floor, unclasping her bra, which fell apart, revealing two huge, round knockers, skin pulled tight, nipples pale red and seemingly too small for the breasts they inhabited. She sprang forward, planting her mouth on mine, her tongue wet and slimy as she pushed it into my mouth, her hand clasping my erection.

It was sudden and overwhelming, and vomit came rushing up my throat. I pushed her away harshly, clapping my hand over my mouth. Dolly tripped backward, catching herself on a piece of furniture, pink spots blossoming on her pale cheeks as she gritted her teeth and raised her finger, pointing it at me.

"What the fucksh is wrong with yoush anyway?" she demanded, the words slurred. "What? Are yoush a pussy? Is that it, *pussy*?" Rage blossomed inside me then, as sudden as the sickness that had come over me at her force and the unexpectedness of my body being invaded by hers.

It was disgusting and vile and I hadn't *asked* for that.

I stepped forward, pushing her so that she fell to the side, sprawling on the floor, half-naked and bent awkwardly. "Fucksh yoush!" she yelled, attempting to get up but falling back again, her heavy breasts impeding her ability to balance. I laughed then, a maniacal sound that exploded from my throat. The sound seemed to enrage her further, and she continued to flop around like a top-heavy seal, floundering clownishly.

I spotted a checkerboard sitting to the side of the couch and grabbed a handful of checkers, tossing them at her and watching as they bounced off her forehead and she flailed some more, her tits flopping from one side to the other, a roll of pasty flab jiggling over the waistband of her skirt as she slurred epithets at me.

"Do you like *games*, Dolly?" I yelled. "You like playing your sick, twisted power games with men like me you think you can trample on? Fuck *you*, Dolly."

There was a pair of shoes by the door and I glanced at them, picturing unlacing one of the laces and using it to strangle her. I could tie her to a chair the way Mother had done to Father and Mr. Patches. I could squeeze her neck slowly, or I could do it fast. I could do it in any way I chose. I saw it again in my mind's eye. Just pulling and pulling until her life drained out and she finally shut the fuck up. It would have been so *easy*.

She was disgusting and repulsive and she shouldn't have *touched* me like she had. No one was ever going to touch me without my permission ever again.

I wound my arm back and bounced another checker off her head, hard enough to leave a mark, and she fell back to the floor, reaching up to feel the wound and letting out a sob as tears sprang from her eyes and tracked down her cheeks.

Her tears brought me back to myself, and I hesitated before finally tossing the rest of the checkers aside, my chest rising and falling harshly as I attempted to catch my breath. I watched her for another minute, spread-eagled on the floor, her tiny nipples pointed at the ceiling as she muttered and cried, and I only felt pity for her.

I turned, and I left her there before walking to my car and driving home. When I got inside my house, I poured myself a cold glass of lemonade and then stood at the counter, taking big, thirsty gulps. I was shaky, my muscles sore from having held them tightly for so many hours. I pictured Dolly lying helpless and wasted on the floor and felt a small measure of shame, but there was also satisfaction. I'd handled her myself. I'd been my *own* protector.

Dolly didn't show up at her job the next day, or the next. I went home each night, expecting the police to show up at my door, lying in my bed unable to sleep as I memorized the lies I would tell. When Dolly finally returned, she looked mostly back to normal, except for a small red mark on her forehead. I tensed when she walked my way, my pulse jumping, but she gave me a small, embarrassed smile, her eyes shifting away as she said, "I want to apologize for whatever I said or did the other night. I get a little . . . out of hand when I've had a lot to drink." She met my gaze, her eyes imploring as though she wanted me to reassure her that she hadn't been that bad or maybe clue her in to what she didn't remember but maybe suspected. Did she have flashes of me bouncing checkers off her forehead? Was she having trouble making that slip of memory align with who she believed me to be?

But I just stared and finally gave her the barest of smiles. "There's nothing to apologize for," I said, walking away. I had an extra spring in my step, however. I was off the hook after days of worrying relentlessly. But I still remembered the feeling of confidence—of power—as I stood above her, making her pay for what she'd done, even if that payment was small and perhaps less than she deserved. Yes, I'd taken care of myself for the first time in my life.

Maybe Mother knew. Perhaps she thought I didn't need her at all anymore. Maybe it's why she left. And maybe it's why I let her go.

CHAPTER
TWENTY-SEVEN

Sienna tapped her fingers on her desk, glancing at the latest copy of Danny Boy's writing about Dolly as the phone rang at her ear.

"Professor Vitucci," came the smooth voice on the other end of the line.

"Professor, hi. This is Sienna Walker, one of the detectives with the Reno PD."

"Yes, hello, Detective Walker. I saw the news this morning. I hate that I was right about the killer striking again, and sooner rather than later."

"Me too. I knew it was only a matter of time, though. It's part of what makes this job so hard."

"The feeling of powerlessness. I understand." His voice over the phone was melodic, and she felt immediately at ease. He was a professor of criminology, but she wondered if he had ever worked more hands-on in law enforcement and had to assume he had.

"Yes. I have a couple questions, and I was hoping you had a minute or two to spare?"

"Of course." She heard a door close. "Go ahead."

"This most recent victim doesn't seem to have any form of bad parenting behavior in his past," she said, referring to Harry Lockheed. "In fact, if anything, the opposite. He was a family man, a coach, upstanding in every way we were able to verify so far. And so my question is, Can our killer still be mission oriented but be focused on a *different* mission than the one we originally outlined?"

"Absolutely," he said smoothly. "The important thing to note, Detective Walker, is that *something* connects these victims. Something makes these victims abhorrent to our killer."

Abhorrent.

If they weren't bad mothers or even bad parents, caregivers, or the like, then what was so detestable about these three—*so far*—people?

"The thread is the difficult part," Professor Vitucci said. "But there *is* a thread. Somehow these three victims cross over."

Sienna thanked the professor for taking the time to speak with her and hung up before making her way to the meeting room, where she, Ingrid, and Kat had planned to gather to go over the latest murder. Because of this development, the city's fear and concern were understandably mounting, and the pressure on the police department was increasing by the hour.

Sienna took a seat next to Kat at the table and looked at Ingrid, who stood at the front of the room. She filled them both in on her short call with Professor Vitucci and what he'd said about the victims being abhorrent to their killer in some fashion. Ingrid nodded thoughtfully, using a pin to stick the photo of the close-up face of the corpse of the older man to the board that now held three current victims and one mummified teacher who'd died decades before. All of them were connected somehow—*someway*—but how?

"Harry Lockheed worked as a floor manager at Circus Circus up until a year ago, when he retired. He'd been in the hospitality industry for thirty-five years. No arrest record, clean driving record, no money issues, no concerning material found on his computer or any of his devices, even though they've only been given a precursory look. Basically, so far, nothing points to him being anything other than what he appeared to be.

"He left for the grocery store early yesterday morning, and when he didn't return after a couple of hours and his wife couldn't get hold of him, she called us. An officer questioned the grocery store employees, but it didn't appear he'd ever arrived there. His car was found ditched in a neighborhood bordering his own. His body was found a few hours after that by the man looking for bottles, another of Danny Boy's notes tucked into his shirt pocket."

"What's your take on his latest writing installment?" Sienna asked, bouncing her knee.

Kat chewed on her pen for a moment. "It seems like our Danny Boy discovered his ability to overpower a victim," she said after a moment. "And liked it."

Sienna nodded in agreement, picturing Dolly lying on the floor as Danny threw checkers at her. He hadn't taken that power in a murderous direction. Not then. Not yet. He'd first discovered the feeling with Dolly but had ultimately focused it elsewhere, and they still didn't know why. What Sienna did sense was that he was *pacing* his story in some way she couldn't understand. He had a full picture, though. She was sure of it.

"The other things he left at the scene are these items," Ingrid said, bringing three clear evidence bags out and laying them on the table. Sienna leaned forward.

The first was a coupon for a free order of chicken wings from a place called Zero Effs Sports Bar and Grille. Sienna's brow dipped. "Does this mean anything to either of you?" Both Ingrid and Kat shook their heads.

The second item was a pair of black-and-white dice. Sienna picked the bag up, turning them this way and that. "Did you check if they're weighted?" she asked, wondering if they consistently rolled to a certain number.

"Yes," Ingrid said. "They seem like regular dice."

Hmm. She set the bag down and picked up the third. Contained within was a silver coin. "A Susan B. Anthony," Sienna said, looking up at Ingrid, who gave a slight one-shoulder shrug. Sienna worried her lip. The only reason she was familiar with the coin was because Argus had pulled them from behind her ear during her childhood. He'd place them in her hand afterward as she grinned with delight, and later she'd hide them in her drawer behind her socks. They'd all gone missing one year. She didn't know if it was her mom or dad who'd taken them, just that they'd likely been spent on a pack of cigarettes or a bottle of booze.

She'd saved the ones Argus gave her at Mirabelle's trailer after that, and they'd never gone missing, though she'd left them behind the day she'd moved away.

Sienna considered the items contained in the evidence bags. She'd google Susan B. Anthony after this and see if there was something about the woman that might offer some clue. She had no idea what to make of the pair of dice or the coupon. Was there something about chicken wings that might lead somewhere?

"The place where he was left—was there anything around, specifically in the direction he was facing?"

Kat frowned at Sienna. "Why do you ask?"

Sienna opened the folder in front of her and took out the notes she'd been making right before she'd left work sick, the ones she'd talked about with Gavin that morning. She went over the items from each scene that related to the periodic table of elements. "I might not be looking at this right, or it could be mixed up or organized in some different way or combined with things we don't yet have, but . . ."

"No, this is good," Ingrid said. "Hold on." She rifled through the report she had on the table next to the two items in evidence bags and then picked up her phone to do a search. "There's a company in that direction that does mobile welding," she said.

"Welding . . . what kind of welding?" Sienna asked.

Ingrid looked back to her phone and pressed something. "Iron gates and security fences are their specialty."

"Iron." She quickly pulled out her own phone and brought up the periodic table. "Iron's symbol is Fe, atomic number twenty-six."

Kat pulled the sheet of paper toward her that Sienna had written her notes on. "Okay, assuming this order is correct, we now have *VIOLFe*, which makes no sense at all."

"Unless," Ingrid said, pushing one of the evidence bags forward, "this coupon from No Effs Sports Bar is an instruction."

"No effs," Kat repeated. "Well, shit. Okay. *VIOLE*." She paused, tapping her pen. "It's still not a word, but it's headed in the direction of these others you've written down. And it eliminates a few. *Violence* is my bet, considering his aptitude for it," she said, raising her brows.

"Why spell out *violence*, though? How does that direct us anywhere?"

"I don't know. But let's ask Xavier to print out a list of words that start with *VIOLE*. There might be a few that none of us are considering. We can then do a cross-check on street names."

There was a knock on the door, and when Ingrid called, "Come in," Xavier poked his head inside.

"Hey, your ears must have been burning. We have a short project for you," Kat said.

"Yeah, no problem. I came to let you know I'm done going through the list of boys from Copper Canyon High School that didn't show on picture day. There are only two, and I was able to dig up current photos. They're obviously not from the time they attended Copper Canyon, but maybe they'll help."

"You're kidding. How did you find photos?"

"I looked both men up online. One of them went to a trade school for a short time. I combed through their website and got lucky. This guy appeared in a photo for a community award the school won years ago and every year since. It's obviously a big deal to them, and they have all the news photos on their site." Xavier handed them the photo. "His name's Oliver Finley."

Sienna took the photograph. It was a printout, and the photo wasn't great, but when she found the student identified as Oliver Finley, her eyes lingered. He looked familiar, but she couldn't say why. "Where have I seen him?" she murmured aloud, passing the photo to Kat, who squinted at it for a moment too.

"I agree," she said, frowning.

"The second man's name is Sylvester Knox, and I found several photos of him," Xavier went on. "He's a lawyer now." Sienna looked at the picture of the handsome Black man from a law firm website.

"He doesn't fit the profile," she said. "But we'll go talk to him." She reached her hand out toward Ingrid, who was looking at the first photo. "Can I see that again?"

Ingrid handed it to her, and she stared down at it. God, he did look mildly familiar, but she couldn't place him. She released a puff of frustrated air. "Thank you, Xavier. You're a star. Would you mind looking up their addresses for us?"

He pulled a piece of paper out of the folder he was holding. "One step ahead," he said, smiling. "Although I was only able to find Sylvester Knox's information. Oliver Finley's might prove harder, but I'm on it."

"Great," she murmured. They gathered their things from the room and gave Xavier his next project. She and Kat were heading to their desks to strategize on what to look into first when one of the janitors came around the corner, wheeling a large garbage can. Sienna halted. "The janitor," she said, stopping Kat and gripping her arm. She removed the printout she'd taken from Xavier and held it up to Kat. "Oliver," she said.

Kat stared at it for a few moments. "Ollie." Kat met her eyes. "He has a beard now, but . . . I think you're right. Oh my God. Wait, you think . . . *Ollie* is our guy?"

"I have no idea," Sienna said. "All I know is he looks a whole lot like a student who used to go to Copper Canyon High School and had Sheldon Biel as his science teacher. Where do we find him?"

"Hey!" Kat called to the janitor, who had reached the end of the hall. "Excuse me."

The guy turned, giving them a slightly wary smile. "Can I help you?"

"You work with a man named Ollie?" Kat said as they made it to him. "Tallish, average weight, dark hair?" She moved her hand over her chin. "Short beard."

"Oh. Yeah. I saw him in passing. I never worked with him. But I heard he gave his notice last week."

"Damn," Kat swore. "Okay, who can I call to get his information?"

"The company we contract for is called A-1 Janitorial Staffing. They'll be able to help you."

As they rushed to their desks to make the call, Sienna thought back to their one interaction with the man named Ollie. He'd seemed normal, nice. He'd been wearing earbuds, and . . . *he'd only removed one to listen to what they had to say when they'd signaled him.* "His earbuds," she said to Kat. "He only removed one. Danny Boy sustained an injury that resulted in his hearing loss in one ear."

Kat frowned. "Yeah. Or the guy removed one because he only had one hand free and that was all that was necessary to hear what we were saying to him."

Maybe. Ten minutes later, after confirming the janitor's full name and getting an address from the owner of A-1, they were heading for the door.

As they drove, Sienna put a call in to Gavin, but the call went to voice mail. She pictured Mirabelle's flushed cheeks and the way she'd seemed a little glassy eyed. And the silver dollar and its connection to Argus had spooked her. She texted Gavin.

Hey, have you talked to your mom? The more I think about it, she seemed a little strained this morning. And would you check on Argus too? xo

She put her phone away, biting at her lip. If Gavin couldn't get hold of him, she'd pay Argus a visit after they'd checked out Oliver Finley's address.

The house they pulled up in front of was a single-family brick home in Old Northwest, several blocks away from Copper Canyon High School. They rapped on the door loudly, calling out, "Reno PD," but no noise came from inside. "Not home or not answering?" Kat asked, looking at Sienna from the other side of the doorway.

Before Sienna could form a response, they heard the very faint sound of music beginning to play. They both stilled, leaning in. *I keep my money in an old tow bag. Oh! Doo-dah day!*

Sienna's eyes met Kat's. Kat reached over and turned the knob, and the unlocked door swung open, the music inside suddenly louder and easier to hear. Kat paused. "It's coming from upstairs," she whispered. "Call backup."

After stepping away and calling for backup, Sienna leaned back slightly, looking up at the window above the porch overhang. *Obscured by curtains.* Her gut said they didn't have to rush to get inside the house, but that didn't negate the nerves. Thankfully, their wait wasn't long, and after about ten grueling, frustrating minutes, a car pulled up to the curb, and two officers joined them, a man and a woman.

"What have we got?" the male officer asked.

"We're not sure," Kat answered. "But last time we showed up to a similar situation, that song led to a mummified corpse. This time, however, we're at the home of an unaccounted-for person of interest."

"We don't know if he's inside?" the female cop asked.

"No. You two take the bottom floor, and we'll check upstairs. Take caution."

The two cops nodded, and Kat and Sienna went inside, calling their arrival and clearing the first room. The two uniforms came in behind them, and as Kat and Sienna made their way to the staircase, the voices of all four of them announcing their presence rose above the sound of the blaring repetitive song.

Upstairs, only one door was open at the end of the hall, and it was the room where the music was playing. They made their way carefully in that direction, checking the other rooms as they went, triangulating the open door and moving inside. *Doo-dah! Doo-dah! Oh! Doo-dah day!* screeched. On the bed lay another mummified corpse, shreds of clothing melded to the bones, the bedding underneath stained where he or she had decomposed over what must have been a long, long time. At one point, the stench in this room had surely been unbearable. Now it just smelled musty and dank, overlaid with the scent of rotted fabric.

The battery-operated radio was on the edge of the dresser near the door. *Doo-dah!*—Sienna reached over and clicked it off, her shoulders lowering as she exhaled.

"You two okay up there?" came a call from the bottom of the stairs.

"Yes," Sienna called back. "But call the ME. We've got a body."

"No rush," Kat murmured sarcastically, walking over to the dead . . . man. The clothes were rotted and falling apart, but by the look of them, they had once been a man's plaid shorts and button-down shirt.

"Oh, Ollie, what have you done?" Kat asked.

"If that's even his name," Sienna murmured.

"You think he's our Danny Boy?"

"I'd bet on it."

Kat pressed her lips together, looking around. "If he is, then rationally, that would make this dude—"

"Father," Sienna finished.

CHAPTER
TWENTY-EIGHT

Sienna and Kat watched from the porch as the SUV carrying the body that had lain dead in the bedroom upstairs for at least two decades drove away. Sienna moved her neck from one side to the other, stretching out her sore muscles. The sun was dipping in the sky, which made Sienna realize they'd been there for hours. She and Kat had stayed at the scene, while Ingrid had gone back to the station to pull up everything she could about Oliver Finley and the house where he'd lived with a corpse for who knew how long. The criminalists were still crawling the property, and an APB had been put out on Oliver Finley's vehicle. The one found covered in the detached garage had come back registered to Sheldon Biel, forming an undeniable connection between Oliver and the crimes being committed. It seemed there was no doubt they'd indeed found their Danny Boy.

Oliver Finley had been contracted by the staffing company to work at the police station approximately six months before. The company had done the usual background check, but it'd come up clean. At that moment, they had no idea if Oliver had purposely set about working there in an attempt to gather information about his planned crime spree or whether it'd been pure luck on his part, as he'd been working as a janitor for years at that point. They were keeping an open mind, but Sienna had trouble believing there was any *pure luck* when it came to this case.

It did explain exactly how he'd known her name as the detective working the case right off the bat, even though she'd been new to the station. It would have given him time to do a simple search on her and tie Gavin into his game immediately too. Maybe he'd even chosen her specifically because he'd believed she'd be the least likely to work out his clues. Which made her feel less personally targeted, at least.

"The house is owned by a man named Patrick Finley, who, according to tax records, fell off the grid about twenty years ago," Ingrid, who'd just arrived on the scene, told them.

"If by 'fell off the grid' you mean he's been decaying in his bed, then yeah," Kat said.

Ingrid gave her a wry tilt of her lips, moving a couple of steps to the side as a criminalist came through carrying several large plastic evidence bags that looked to be filled with bedding. "Here's the *really* interesting part. The Patrick Finley who bought this house actually died twenty-seven years ago."

"Wait, what?" Sienna asked. "How?"

"Natural causes, apparently. Something heart related. However, right before he died, his company went under. It turns out his business partner had made several extremely bad business deals and then tried to cover it up, later embezzling money. Then that business partner, Roger Hastings, disappeared."

"*Roger,*" Kat said, her eyes meeting Sienna's. "Father."

"Right. Also, when he disappeared, he took his child with him. A seven-year-old boy named Daniel."

"Oh," Sienna breathed. "Roger, *Father*, stole his son and then took on his dead business partner's identity."

"Wow," Kat said. "And then he changed his son Daniel's name to Oliver, a.k.a. Ollie."

"But he still thought of himself as Danny Boy," Sienna murmured. "At least in his writings he did." She thought for a second. "How did he get the paperwork to do all of that? I mean, if he had his partner's documents, I guess it could be easy enough. But what about his son's?"

"We're still looking into that. Roger's family owns two casinos in Vegas, though, and if you have enough money, you can pretty much buy anything. It's possible they helped him or at least inadvertently funded him, even if temporarily."

True. Sienna considered it. All he'd really needed was a forged birth certificate, and the rest would be relatively easy. "Why would his family aid and abet him?"

"Families do illegal things for family members for all sorts of reasons—false loyalty, fear of guilt by association, a way to get that person the hell away from their reputation, especially considering their very public business. But in any case, to this day, he's still wanted by police for child abduction," Ingrid said.

Well, not exactly. Roger Hastings was likely nothing but bones headed to the morgue as they spoke. "Where did he take the kid from?"

"Right here in Reno. The wife reported them both missing immediately after it happened, and they searched for them but didn't have any luck." She moved to the side again as another criminalist came through. "That's all I have for now, but Xavier and several available POs are making calls and doing information searches. We'll have a more complete picture soon. Sienna, can I speak with you for a moment?" Ingrid asked.

Surprised and a bit concerned, Sienna nodded as she stepped aside with Ingrid.

"I just wanted to say good work on this case. I'm confident we're going to unravel all of this thanks to your and Kat's collective brainpower and creative thinking."

"Thank you, Sergeant," Sienna said, grateful for the compliment but still a bit confused. *Why didn't you pull Kat aside too?*

Ingrid raised one sharp brow as though she had read Sienna's mind. "I also wanted to tell you that I looked into precisely why you were being hustled out of the NYPD."

She felt a sinking in her stomach. "Oh, I see."

"And I hired you for the very reason they were going to let you go. It's why I wanted you on our team."

Sienna blinked. "Oh," she breathed. "I see."

Ingrid's lip quirked, and she gave a quick nod. "I'll let you get back to work. I'm going to go check out the scene inside." With that, she turned and left Sienna where she stood.

Sienna watched her leave, a warm glow emanating from inside, the feeling of what she could only describe as *justice* rising within. She breathed deeply but then pushed that aside. She'd have time to bask in it later. Ingrid was right—what they'd just learned was significant. And it meant that the journal writings Danny Boy, a.k.a. Daniel Hastings, a.k.a. Oliver Finley, had given them were somewhat true.

She worried her lip, immersing her mind in the information. Although . . . if he'd been abducted, how was it that his mother was with them too? Had his father remarried? Was "Mother" his stepparent? Kat was near the porch railing, writing something in her notebook. She looked up as Sienna joined her. "Is everything okay?"

Sienna smiled. "Yes, all good." She was sure Ingrid would repeat the compliment she'd given Sienna about their work to Kat later. She leaned against the porch railing. "Regarding this case, you know what's weird?"

"What *isn't* weird?"

Sienna let out a small agreeable chuff. "What's weird is that the bed the dead body upstairs, presumably 'Father,' was left in, the place where he rotted and turned to bones, it was a single bed."

Kat cast her eyes to the side. "Hmm. Yes, I see what you're saying. If he shared a room with Mother, where did she sleep?"

"Right. I mean, there are a couple of other rooms upstairs, but from all appearances, Father was a single man."

"Then again, if you were Mother, would you have shared a bed with that dude?"

"I don't know. It seems like Mother did whatever Mother wanted to do at a certain point, but before that?"

"Detective Kozlov?" one of the POs who'd helped them clear the house earlier called as he approached. "Can I get you to sign off on a few things?"

"Sure." Kat accompanied the officer back inside the house, and Sienna brought her phone out. There were two texts from Gavin that she hadn't seen, as the last several hours had been spent trying to figure out what the heck they'd walked into.

She stepped to the side of the porch, out of the way of the steady stream of law enforcement and criminalists going in and out of the house, and dialed Gavin's number.

"Hey," he said, picking up right away. "I saw on the news there's something going on in Old Northwest. Are you okay?"

"Yes, I'm fine. We're pretty sure we found our suspect."

"Danny Boy?"

"Mm-hmm."

"You apprehended him?"

"No, he wasn't here, but he left plenty of evidence."

"Oh." There was a pregnant pause. She knew he wanted to ask for more details but was glad he didn't. She couldn't share all of them anyway, but she also didn't have the clearest picture of what was going on. "I get it if you can't—it's been a long day. But if you're up for dinner, I'd love to have you here. You haven't seen my place yet."

She smiled, letting out a soft breath. *My place.* The sudden yearning to be at this unseen *place* immediately, snuggled up in his arms, almost knocked her off her feet. She steeled her spine. There was work to do, and they had time for that. So much time. "I'd love that," she said, glancing at the door, where Kat and the PO she'd been signing paperwork for were coming out. "It might be a little late. Will you keep it warm for me?"

"As long as it takes," he said softly.

She smiled again. "Okay. Oh, hey, have you talked to your mom?"

"I texted her earlier after I got your message, and she texted me back, but I haven't spoken to her. Apparently, she came down with a bug or something. I haven't gotten hold of Argus yet."

Her brow dipped, but she felt better. No wonder she'd seemed flushed when she'd left Sienna's house earlier. She'd try Argus shortly. Right now, she needed to focus on work and on apprehending the man who'd already murdered three people and might be setting up the clues that would lead them to another. "Okay. Will you text me when you do talk to them?"

"Yeah, of course."

"Okay . . . see you later."

"Hey, Si . . . I love you."

"I love you too." The words came as easy as an exhale.

She ended the call and turned back toward the doorway. Kat was still chatting with the PO, but it didn't appear to be related to work this time, Kat's head tilted as she smiled at something he was telling her, using his hands to gesticulate. He was cute too. *Go, Kat.*

The criminalist named Malinda Lu came out of the house, carrying a pile of board games in her hands. Sienna blinked, hurrying over to her. The woman came up short. "Hi, Malinda."

"Detective Walker."

"Where did you find those?" she asked, nodding to the pile of games in her arms, contained in a large plastic bag.

Malinda glanced down at them. "Under a floorboard in the closet in the first bedroom. It was pretty obviously loose, and I remembered finding evidence in a similar spot in that abandoned house we worked. We're bagging as many things as possible in that room because it looks like the only one that was occupied. We took the bedding and—"

"Can I look through those real quick?" God, she hadn't even thought to look in the closet for his games, even though he'd said that was where they were in his letters. Thank goodness for thorough criminalists with good memories.

"Oh . . . sure. Do you want me to set them on the table in the kitchen?"

"Yeah, that'd be great." She followed Malinda back inside, and the criminalist used her gloved hands to open the plastic bag and remove the games, setting them on the table where, presumably—and if the gouges in the wood were any indication—Mr. Patches and Father had been sitting when they'd taken their final breaths.

This room and, from what she'd observed, the entire house, was neat and orderly. Their Danny Boy was definitely the detail-oriented perfectionist Professor Vitucci had guessed him to be.

"I'm looking for one that's missing the dice," she said, and Malinda nodded, setting the box of checkers, which didn't use dice, aside and opening the top of the second in the pile, Monopoly.

"It looks like the dice are missing," Malinda said after she'd swirled her finger through the small cup that held the player pieces. The Chance, Community Chest, and Property cards were neatly stacked in their respective holders.

Kat came up beside her. "Did you find something?"

"I don't know," Sienna said. "But this one is missing the dice."

"The dice in Harry Lockheed's pocket."

"Yeah. Will you pick up the board?" Sienna asked Malinda, and when she did, there was a short portion of a note beneath, written in their Danny Boy's hand. They both leaned forward, reading quickly.

My life was peaceful again. There was no reason to lie in bed concocting lies. But I mourned Mother. I mourned the absence of her potpourri, her homemade doughnuts, and the lemon-scented spray that made our house smell clean and fresh.

I couldn't conjure them anymore. I couldn't conjure *her*. No matter how hard I tried.

I lived. I worked. I went about my life. I read books. I watched news programs in the evening so I was well versed on world politics and current affairs on the off chance someone spoke to me about such things, so that I could provide an intelligent reply. But people rarely spoke to me, and for the most part, I avoided them as well. When they did engage me in conversation, I made up stories about who I was and the things I did. Maybe I was imagining who I would have been. *If.*

In any case, I was mostly at peace, I suppose, but I was lonely.

I was so incredibly lonely.

And I had to come to terms with the fact that I always would be.

Sienna straightened. "Thank you, Malinda. Will you bag that up separately?"

Malinda nodded and began bagging the games and the note back up as she and Kat walked out to the porch again, where they'd be out of the way.

"What are you thinking?" Kat asked.

Sienna crossed her arms, tapped her fingers against her skin for a moment, and just as quickly uncrossed her arms. She felt antsy, troubled. "Kat, do you think it's possible *he's* Mother?"

Kat frowned. "The whole *conjuring* wording?"

"Yes." She paused, thinking. "But also, both times Mother killed for him, he lost consciousness right beforehand." She scraped her teeth over her bottom lip. "I'd have to look back at the exact wording of the notes, but when he came to, Mother already had the men tied to the chair."

"Do you mean he has a split personality or something?"

Sienna's frown grew deeper. "Not exactly . . ." She let out a frustrated breath.

They were both quiet for a moment as Malinda exited the house for the second time, heading for the city vehicle.

"The thing that goes against that theory," Kat said, "is that the two crimes *Mother* committed are very different. Stabbings are incredibly violent and bloody."

"Because he was being actively abused, actively *hurt*, in those two instances," Sienna said. "Maybe he snapped, and the only way he could follow through with protecting himself was if he created this fictional 'Mother' who actually never existed at all."

"A modern-day Norman Bates."

"I'm not suggesting he really thinks he's *her* or is even under the impression she's real. But in the moment, she helped him do what he needed to do to stop his tormenter."

"Plural," Kat reminded. "*Tormentors*. Some people are monster magnets."

Sienna winced. What a horrid thought that those easy to victimize had a smell to them, easily detectable by human beasts. She moved her mind away from that terrible possibility. "Okay. So why is he strangling others now?"

"That's the million-dollar question. It's not because they're abusing him. He planned these murders well in advance."

Sienna thought back to Professor Vitucci's profile, filtering through it in her mind. *What are we missing?* "Professor Vitucci was helpful when I called him earlier," she said. "We could see if he has some ideas about this."

"Sure. The more help the better. We're going to be here for a little while longer anyway," Kat said.

Sienna nodded. They would stay until the criminalists finished their initial collection. She dialed Professor Vitucci's number, and he answered right away.

"Hello, Professor. It's Detective Walker. Again. I feel like I'm becoming a pest."

He laughed softly. "Not at all. It's good to feel useful. And it's nice to feel part of a team again. I received the most recent pieces of writing you emailed and read through them earlier. What can I help you with?"

"Well, we're almost positive we found our suspect," she said. "He led us straight to his house, where the body we are assuming belongs to his father was found in an upstairs bedroom."

"Oh, I see."

"Anyway"—she glanced at Kat—"Detective Kozlov and I were theorizing, and a question arose. Can I put you on speaker?"

"Absolutely."

She pressed the speaker button, holding the phone between her and Kat. "Hi, Professor."

"Detective Kozlov," he greeted.

Sienna paused for only a moment. "Professor, is it possible that Mother is really *him*? He seems to have 'lost consciousness' both times she showed up to save him."

He was silent for a moment. "So Mother doesn't exist?" he asked.

"Right. He kind of . . . conjures her when he needs protection. It's him, only he's playing a role so he's able to follow through."

Professor Vitucci was silent for another long moment, and Sienna swore she could hear his brain clicking over the phone lines as he obviously pondered her question.

"There are oddities in his story regarding Mother," he said. "Things that don't add up."

"What did *you* see?" Kat asked.

"She's too perfect. Her reactions aren't in line with what's happening. She's a sort of Stepford wife. It was my original assumption that he was idealizing her, but what you say is possible too. He's inserting her as his savior because he either cannot accept or does not *want* to accept that he did the things he did."

"Or maybe," Sienna said, meeting Kat's eyes, "at the time he wasn't ready to take responsibility for those crimes, and so he created this Mother figure?"

"It's definitely plausible," Professor Vitucci said. "I would hasten to guess, though, that if she did not exist in those particular instances, Mother is still based on someone very real."

Sienna and Kat thanked the professor and ended the call. Kat saw someone she knew and excused herself for a moment, which gave Sienna time to filter through what the professor had said and everything they'd learned since they'd arrived at this house. *Father. Mother. Danny Boy. Mr. Patches. Oliver. Ollie.* She walked to the porch railing and looked out to the residential street beyond.

She tapped at the wood, thinking about what she and the professor had just talked about, then she considered the portion of note in the Monopoly box. Another thing about it bothered her too. Her personal familiarity with the mention of potpourri and lemon-scented spray.

Mother-ish things, she supposed, but they reminded her of Mirabelle, and she couldn't shake the feeling it was a clue she was meant to recognize. Although he'd mentioned homemade doughnuts, too, and Mirabelle had never made those to her knowledge.

Either way, she knew one thing for certain. They were *there*, at his house, because Danny Boy wanted them to be there. His game wasn't yet over.

CHAPTER
TWENTY-NINE

Mirabelle's hand shook as she set the pen back down on the counter. She'd been trembling all day, ever since she'd left Sienna's. Ever since she'd seen her notes on the kitchen table.

She'd immediately felt sick and distraught, and yet . . . underneath that, a wild hope had also flapped its caged wings. Not knowing what to do or even if she was right, she'd come home and re-created the notes so she could go over them, evaluating whether she was jumping to conclusions.

But no. No, she *knew*. Her gaze returned to the notepad where she'd rewritten what Sienna had jotted down as she'd apparently tried to work through some clue in her case.

Vanadium, Iodine, Oxygen, Lithium. VIOL

Violets, Violence, Violent.

Mirabelle had done a search on vanadium and iodine and the rest and found them all on the periodic table of elements, each one apparently relating to a letter in a word being spelled out, though not yet complete. Sienna had obviously been trying to guess where it might be going. Mirabelle was almost certain she knew what the word was, though, and what the final two letters would be.

The names Reva Keeling and Bernadette Murray had been written down as well. And she recognized them. She'd heard Reva's name on the news, but it hadn't been familiar. Reva must have gotten married at some point, because when Mirabelle had known her, her name had been Reva Lilly. They'd mostly called her Lil. Other than the few details that floated by when Argus was watching TV, Mirabelle hadn't paid attention to the news other than to know Sienna was working a dangerous case. As she didn't necessarily *want* to know the details, she tuned the news out as a matter of course. Specifics about violence upset her. She'd had enough violence for one lifetime. Her ex-husband had been a monster.

Could it be him? After all these years? Right here in Reno? In the same town they'd once lived in together?

She looked up Reva Keeling's photo from the press conference, checking and rechecking her assumptions. She looked so different. So *old.* Although Mirabelle hadn't heard mention of the name of the second victim, she'd known it immediately when she'd seen it scrawled in Sienna's handwriting. Bernadette. It was a unique name, and Bernadette had been a unique woman. Funny as hell. She'd had Mirabelle practically peeing her pants with laughter some days.

Reva and Bernadette. Lil and Bee.

There'd been another victim found just the night before. She'd looked online but hadn't seen his name anywhere yet. Maybe they'd already identified him and didn't need help from the public. But maybe they were still contacting family members. She had to wait. She had to find out the name of that third victim.

Her phone rang, startling her and practically making her scream. She grabbed for it, taking a deep breath, attempting to slow her racing heart.

"Gavin," she greeted.

"Hey, it's good to hear your voice. How are you feeling? You still sound a little weak."

Weak. That was one way of putting it.

"A little. But I'm better. I'm getting there. How are you? How is Sienna? I saw on the news there was another murder. It's terrible."

"You don't usually watch the news," Gavin said, a smile in his voice. "You've always said you're allergic to it."

"Oh. Well." She let out a small laugh. "Now that Sienna's back in town . . ."

"You're going to watch the news to make sure you shouldn't be worrying about her. I get it." She heard the tenderness in her boy's voice—he'd always be her boy, even though he was a man now—and her heart constricted tightly. Oh, the joy she'd felt when she'd looked between him and Sienna and realized they were together again. The way it should be.

The world had seemed to grow ten shades brighter. She'd felt such a sense of hope, the likes of which she hadn't felt in so long. She'd seen the love in Gavin's eyes and the happiness in Sienna's.

"Do they have a name?" she asked Gavin. "For the newest victim?"

"Yeah, they just put it out, actually, a few minutes ago. Harry something, I think they said . . . why do you ask?"

Her stomach dropped again, bile moving up her throat. She swallowed it down. "Oh . . . no reason," she managed.

Gavin was quiet for a moment. "Hey, Mom, have you spoken to Argus? I tried to call him earlier, but he still hasn't called me back."

"No. He might have been sleeping. He teaches that class Tuesday nights, Hocus-Pocus and Sleight of Hand? It usually goes until almost midnight." And Argus, the old fuddy-duddy, didn't even own a cell phone. She glanced at the clock, though. It was almost six now. Even if he'd slept late and then gotten busy doing errands, he was usually good about calling back once he got home.

"Oh . . . right. Okay, well, when you talk to him, tell him to call me."

"I will."

They said their goodbyes, and Mirabelle ended the call, then immediately dialed Argus's number. She'd been in her own world since leaving Sienna's house, but . . . she hadn't spoken to him all day, either, and that was unusual. Often they went a few days without seeing each other during the week, when she caught up on errands and he taught a couple of classes, and then he basically moved in on the weekends, but they usually spoke every day. Their arrangement wasn't typical, she supposed, but it worked for them. *It works for you,* she told herself. Okay, yes. But she had reasons for that. Her independence, the control over her own environment, was still highly coveted, even so many years later.

The buzz of panic that had been vibrating under her skin ever since she'd seen those notes increased as Argus's phone went to voice mail.

She hung up without leaving a message and then called for a cab.

Let me buy you a car. I'll even teach you how to drive myself. She heard Gavin's voice in her head.

But Mirabelle already knew how to drive. That wasn't it, but she couldn't tell him that.

The cabdriver dropped her in front of Argus's house fifteen minutes later, and Mirabelle made her way quickly to the door of Argus's small, neat house.

That buzzing sensation increased, and she almost turned back. *Something's wrong.* She suddenly knew it in her gut the same way she'd known when she'd seen that car driving away, out of sight, so many years before.

Danny. Danny. Danny.

She took a deep breath and blew it out slowly, steeling herself. She had a key to Argus's door, but it was unlocked. Somehow she'd known it would be.

"Argus?" Her voice sounded small and uncertain. Shaky.

The curtains in the front window were still closed, dust motes floating lazily in the shaft of light filtering through the gap where the fabric barely met. She called his name again, the click of her footsteps loud in her ears. Something was wrong. Something was very, very wrong.

A startled scream broke from her lips as she dropped the things she was holding. Argus was in a chair, facing the doorway, his head lolling, his skin purple and mottled.

She rushed to him, even knowing he was already gone, the scream turning to a cry as she choked out his name. She put her hands on his cheeks, attempting to lift his head and seeing the cord still wrapped around it, the flesh there bloody and swollen. She let go of his face. He was cold. Oh, he was so cold. And stiff. He'd been dead for a while.

Her Argus. Her sweet, gentle Argus, who had made her believe in magic again.

His phone rang, startling her, and her eyes shot to it, sitting on the edge of his counter. His outgoing message came on, a spear of agony stabbing through her to hear his beloved, accented voice filling the same room where his dead body sat before her. The beep filled her head and seemed to linger there, and then Sienna's voice came on, asking him to call her. Mirabelle heard the slight lilt of worry in her tone and clenched her eyes shut. *Oh God, no, no. God, please, no.*

She sank to the floor in front of Argus, her shoulders hunching as sobs racked her body. *Who? Why? No. No. No.* She didn't know how long she stayed there, shaking with grief, but after a time, she forced herself to her feet. There was a silver watch on Argus's wrist that Mirabelle had never seen before. Argus didn't wear a watch. She stared at it, under-standing dawning. The watch was made of titanium. She'd been right about the word—the *name*—being spelled. *Oh God. Oh no.*

Harry had been the *E*, and Argus was the *T* in *Violet*.

She clenched her eyes shut. Small moans climbed her throat, but she felt almost numb as she walked toward her purse and her phone.

That was when she spotted the red vest on his counter. Her eyes lin-gered, recognition and horror gripping her. Another moan burst forth, this one louder, and she spun around. No one was there, only Argus's still, lifeless body. Her hand shaking, she reached out, running a finger over the satiny material, dread spiking.

The room wavered as she picked the garment up. She felt as though she were in a nightmare she could not—and would not—escape.

Not this time.

Another small noise behind her made her whip around again.

And there he was. A dark-haired man with a very short, neatly trimmed beard, standing behind her, his smile growing. "Hello, Mother," he said.

CHAPTER THIRTY

Twenty-seven years ago

Violet gave the pot of spaghetti sauce a stir and then cracked the oven open to check the breadsticks. A loud metallic sound rang out, making her wince against the headache that had plagued her all day, and she brought her fingertips to her brow, pressing lightly on the bandage covering the spot where the crystal decanter had hit her.

The decanter he'd thrown at her with so much force it'd broken, slicing into her flesh and causing her to see stars.

She bent, taking the metal spatula—the one Gavin had just used to strike the pot—out of his tiny hand as he protested with a loud cry of dismay. "Here, honey," she said, giving him a plastic spoon. He struck the pot but seemed disappointed in the hollow sound, his tiny, expressive face screwing up in consternation. Despite her aching head and the anxiety that rested on her chest, she smiled with affection. He was only two years old, but he was still a spirited little thing. As if in agreement with her thought, he went back to gleefully pounding on the pot, the vigorousness of his strikes making up for the muted sound of plastic on metal.

Gavin was full of life. But it was her Danny Boy she worried about.

She walked over to where he sat at the counter, coloring a picture of a fire truck. She ruffled his hair, leaning in to take in the scent of her precious little boy—apples and hay. He smelled like everything good and pure in the world.

"I like that," she said. "What's the dog's name?" she asked, pointing to the dalmatian sitting next to the truck, his tongue out, ears perked.

Danny paused. "I don't know," he said.

"How about Spot?" Violet suggested, leaning in closer.

"I like Jaxon," he told her shyly, his eyes meeting hers, looking for approval.

"That's a wonderful name for a dog. Maybe one day we'll get a dog and that's what we'll call him. What do you think?"

Danny gave her one of his sweet, gap-toothed smiles, and she smiled back. But then his gaze moved to the bandage on her head, and his smile faltered, faded. He looked back to the drawing, moving his red crayon back and forth.

Her heart gave a painful squeeze. "Hey, Danny Boy, how about I make those doughnuts you like for dessert?"

His lips tipped, and he nodded. "Then doughnuts it is." She hadn't made them in a while because last time she had, Gavin had eaten one and broken out in a rash from some ingredient or another. But they were Danny's favorite. "And then, how about we play a game?" she said, trying to infuse some optimism into her voice, hoping he'd give her another smile. Danny loved it when she played games with him, giving him all her attention. His eyes would widen with delighted happiness when she let cards cascade through her fingers like water, the skill that came so easy to her. *Effortless. Second nature.* "Checkers or—"

"Jesus Christ, shut that kid up."

Violet jumped as the back door slammed. She whirled around, bringing her hand to her chest. *Oh God.* She hadn't heard him coming over Gavin's banging. She ran to her toddler, grabbed the spoon from him, and turned back around. "Roger! I didn't know you'd be home early," she said, her words spilling out in a rush. Her gaze flew around. Dinner wasn't ready. The boys weren't cleaned up, and neither was the house. Neither was *she* for that matter. She ran a hand over her dirty, lank hair and then picked up Gavin, propping him on her hip. She'd meant to do so much more by this point in the day, but her head ached so badly, and she still felt mildly nauseous. Out of sorts. She likely had a concussion, but she didn't dare go to the hospital. There would just be questions, and she wasn't up for spinning lies. Not today.

"Clearly," Roger said, loosening his tie and looking around in disgust. At the counter, Danny sat stock still, staring at his father with wide, fearful eyes. Violet swore she felt her heart splinter. Roger's gaze hung on his seven-year-old for a moment, and then he looked away as if Danny were nothing more than another appliance in the kitchen. "I need a goddamn drink." He tossed his briefcase and his tie on the counter and walked into the living room.

Violet released a slow breath, then set Gavin back down and rushed to the stove, where she took the breadsticks out of the oven. Thank God they weren't burned. Depending on what type of day Roger had had, things like burnt breadsticks could result in broken bones.

Only hers, so far. Thank God. But her worst fear was the day when hurting her wouldn't be enough. Or he'd kill her, and then he'd turn to their sons.

"Danny, will you grab the napkins and help me set the table?"

Danny climbed down from the counter stool and headed to the drawer where they kept the linens. She'd turned back to the stove when she heard Danny let out a small gasp, but before she could turn to see what the problem was, she was grabbed harshly by her hair, her head jerking backward. She let out a shocked, guttural cry as Roger pulled her brutally and then pushed her so hard that she fell to the floor, going down on her hip, pain exploding up the left side of her body. She scrabbled backward and turned just in time to see him lunging at her. She screamed again as he yanked her up by the front of her shirt and pushed her against the counter.

He got right in her face, his hot breath gusting over her skin. "Did you think I wouldn't see his number on the phone? Did you, whore?"

Oh God. Oh God. The phone. She hadn't deleted his number. She'd meant to . . . she'd just lost track of time, and her head had ached so badly, and she'd napped along with the boys, so grateful that they'd been tired, too, and had let her rest as long as they had. "He's my friend, Roger. Not even really that. Just my ex-boss. He was only calling to say happy birthday."

He looked very briefly confused before his eyes flared with anger again. *You used to remember my birthday, Roger. You used to buy me presents.* She was wearing one now—the silver bracelet with violet amethysts he'd said had reminded him of her, his violet girl.

But apparently telling him that another man had remembered her birthday when Roger had not was a bad move. His fist tightened on her shirt, and he let out a low growl, raising his other hand and slapping her. She cried out, her head whipping to the side, hot tears coursing down her cheeks. In the background she heard Gavin crying, and when she opened her eyes, she saw Danny standing still as a statue behind his father, eyes wide, skin as pale as milk.

She couldn't let them see this. Not again. Roger's eyes were practically glowing with hate. He'd always despised her boss from the casino where she'd worked when they'd met, even though it was Roger's family who *owned* the place. When Roger had swooped in and "saved" her from her life of menial labor and hardship. Of course, he'd been different then. His eyes had looked at her hungrily in her tight red vest and short, short skirt, and it'd made her feel sexy and beautiful. *Special.* He'd wooed her, charmed her. Because she'd been nothing more than a wide-eyed girl who saw only what he'd wanted her to see. And for whatever reason, Roger was *still* jealous of the men she'd known in that life, creating some relationship between her and Harry that didn't exist and never had.

His hand moved to her neck, and he grabbed hold, squeezing. She gripped the counter behind her, seeking leverage, but he was too strong.

"What about those whores you used to call friends, Violet? You think I don't know that you meet up with them? I followed you, Violet. Nothing but loser whores, and you're just like them, aren't you? You'd give up your children for them, is that it?"

Oh God, oh no. She'd taken such a risk. Why had she done it? *Because seeing other people who used to know the old you has kept you sane. Given you hope that maybe you can be that girl again.* Yes, yes, she knew why, but oh, it'd been foolish to get together with Lil and Bee.

He'd thrown a decanter at her head the night before when she'd misheard something he'd said. He was going to kill her over the fact that he knew she'd been meeting up with the girlfriends she'd had at the casino and the birthday phone call. Maybe it'd be an accident, maybe not. But surety filled her—this was the night she was going to die.

No, no, I can't leave my boys alone. Not with him.

Her head tilted to the side, white dots clouding her vision as he squeezed harder and she fought for breath. Out of the corner of her eye, she saw the red pasta sauce, no longer bubbling but surely hot. *Scalding.* She turned her face back to his, allowed him to watch her struggle to breathe, saw the enjoyment in his eyes at viewing her suffering up close. Slowly, blindly, she reached for the pot, grasped its handle, and lifted it. With the last of her waning strength, she swung it around Roger's back and tipped it, the contents spilling out as she simultaneously whacked it into the back of his head. He let out a piercing yelp, letting go of her neck and jumping backward—away—as he shook off the burning sauce in an absurd type of dance that might have been funny if she had had the ability to laugh. Red sauce flew out around him as he shuddered, finally ripping his shirt over his head and flinging it away, his skin red and already blistering beneath.

In the time it'd taken Roger to shake off the sauce and remove his shirt, Violet had sucked in enough air that she was no longer seeing spots and grabbed the largest cleaver out of the butcher block on the counter. She held it out in front of her now, shaking with fear.

If he hadn't looked completely murderous before, he did now. Rage rolled off him like toxic fumes.

"You want to play, bitch? Is that it?"

Gavin was wailing now, sitting on the floor near the door to the living room, and Danny had walked backward until he stood near the refrigerator, stealthily trying to slink as far from his father as possible. Next to the refrigerator, another doorway led to the back of the massive house. "G-get out, Roger," Violet said. "Leave."

He eyed her, his gaze moving to the knife and then back to her face. Something sinister was in his expression. Dark and malevolent, and she swallowed down her terror. *Someone, help me.* But there was no one to help her. In fact, there were two innocent little boys who needed her to help them. Gavin's wail rose, calling her name—"Mama!"—and she brought her shoulders back, slicing at the air with her knife, her arm shaking so badly she almost dropped it. Roger's mouth tipped as he silently laughed at her.

He took a step closer. "If you wanna play, then let's play, bitch. I'm going to make it a fair game, though, because even with that knife, you don't stand a snowball's chance in hell. I could knock it out of your hand like batting away a fly." A tremble went down her spine, the knife shaking in her hand, punctuating his statement. It was true. She knew it was true. She was so weak she was about to fall over, her head was pounding, and she was so scared her muscles had all but seized up. "I'll give you to the count of ten to hide." He glanced at Gavin, still crying near the door, and over to Danny, standing by the fridge, and then back to Violet, who was positioned between them both, backed up to the counter. "I'll even let you take one of them with you and get a head start," he said, his smile growing, though there was no humor in his eyes, only cold malice. "Pick one."

Pick one? What was he saying? Her gaze shot from one boy to the other. Choose one of her sons to hide with? Her mind spun, trying desperately to figure a way out of this, to de-escalate the situation. But there was no doing that now. She'd enraged him, had scalded him, and was now threatening him with a knife.

She could try to run for the front door, but the neighbors were too far away, and she couldn't run fast enough with one child, let alone two. Plus, she was injured, pain reverberating down her leg where she'd fallen. He'd be on them in a heartbeat. He'd use a rock on her head, strangle her again as she struggled in the dirt. *No, no.*

The cordless phone. He'd looked at the phone in the living room where she'd left it, but when he'd come back in the kitchen, he hadn't had it with him. It must still be there. If he was going to let her hide, she could grab the phone and lock herself in the bathroom upstairs, call the police. "Pick one!" he said again, so loud it made her jump. "One!" he yelled, beginning his count.

Violet's gaze darted again between Gavin—his tearstained face red and blotchy from crying—and Danny, eyes wide with fear, imploring her. "Two!" She needed the phone. She had to call for help. "Three!" A sob moved up Violet's throat, and she forced herself to *move*, half running and half limping toward the door, where she scooped up Gavin and darted as fast as she could into the living room. "Hide, Danny!" she yelled behind her. Roger didn't want to hurt Danny anyway, not really. He wanted to hurt her. He'd come after her. But Gavin was still practically a baby. He didn't stand a chance without her. Danny was clever. Quiet but so very clever. He'd find a good hiding spot in this big house, and he'd stay put until help arrived.

"Four!"

Hide, Danny, hide.

She ran into the living room, a cry of defeat falling from her lips when she saw that the only thing on the coffee table where she'd left the phone was a stack of magazines. "Five!" Roger hadn't brought it into the kitchen with him, but he'd hidden it somewhere. And she had no time to search. "Six!" She dropped the knife in the pocket of her apron, Gavin holding on to her shoulder, his little body still shaking from his recent sobs.

She gripped the banister as she ran up the stairs as fast as she could, then turned the corner and raced down the hall. "Seven!"

Hide, Danny, hide. There were so many good spots for him to fit, and she knew he was good at it because she often played with him, tickling him until he giggled when she found him, pretending she hadn't known where he was all along. "Eight!"

Maybe if she hid long enough, Roger would cool down. *Just give him time to cool down.* "Nine!"

She ran into the guest room, opened the closet as quietly as possible, and then closed it behind her. "Ten!" There were several garment bags in there, formal wear that had gone unused for a long time, and she scooted behind them, Gavin's sobs gone now, faded into the occasional shuddery breath and small hiccup. He'd been saved. In his mind, he'd already been saved because he was in his mother's arms. He put his head on her shoulder, exhausted, calm.

Violet waited, every muscle tensed as she sat in the dark with her toddler, rocking him gently, ever mindful to go still if she heard Roger's footsteps coming closer. Maybe he'd search the house for a while and grow bored, realize how irrational he was being. He'd always had a quick temper and been prone to sulk and seek retribution when he didn't get his way. He'd turned downright mean and unpredictable after Gavin was born, but it was only recently that she'd seen the shine of something more sinister in his eyes.

Stay hidden, Danny, somewhere your father would never look. Stay quiet as a mouse, baby boy.

Their breath merged, hers coming out in quickened pants of dread, Gavin's evening as he fell asleep, his body going limp in her arms. Carefully, so carefully, she laid him on the carpeted floor, stopping in her movement every few seconds to listen. But there was no sound of Roger approaching.

Where are you? Oh God, where are you?

Again, she waited, her ears pricked to every creak of the house, every small noise. Was he walking quietly from room to room, dragging this terrible game out to make her suffer? To heighten her fear to a fever pitch? Was that his ultimate goal? Would he be satisfied with her terror, or would he try to hurt her? More permanently this time. Perhaps he wouldn't kill her, but what if he punched her again, so hard she sustained brain damage? What if he threw her down the stairs and she spent the rest of her life in a wheelchair, her ability to speak or move gone? Completely at his mercy. A deep tremble moved through her. Oh yes, there were fates worse than death, and she'd pictured them all. She still had the knife. She'd use it if she had to, but without a phone, she was back where she'd started in the kitchen.

Outmatched.

Violet blinked in confusion when she heard the faint purr of a motor from beyond, and then the sound of crunching gravel. *A car.* A car had pulled up in front of their house. How had she not heard it approaching?

Oh my God. Oh my God. Help.

Violet came to her feet, moving as quietly as possible, holding her breath as she opened the closet door, half expecting Roger to lunge at her. But if *she'd* heard the car, he certainly had, too, and he'd be heading to the driveway, trying to get them to leave before she came outside.

Before she screamed for help.

Run. Hurry.

Violet ran to the window, ready to fling it open and scream for whoever it was that had arrived. But her hand faltered on the lock, a confused gasp emerging, eyes widening. It was Roger's car, and it was leaving. For a moment, relief flooded her body, so intense she sagged under its power. But as quickly as the relief had descended, it vaulted into alarm. And then horror.

A little face looked out the back window, eyes terrified and haunted. Violet screamed, waving her arms, but the little boy had turned away. She ran for the hall and bounded down the stairs, skipping several at a time, a wonder she didn't land on her head and do to herself what she'd just feared from Roger. She flung open the door, screaming Danny's name, but the car had turned the corner in the long drive and was already out of sight.

Violet ran anyway, arms waving, heart pounding, screaming Danny's name over and over, but it was no use. It was dark now, and the car was already too far away and quickly picking up speed, just a wavering dot of light in the distance.

Oh God, oh no, bring back my baby. My little boy.

Violet fell to the ground, weeping and shaking, calling Danny's name until her throat was raw.

CHAPTER
THIRTY-ONE

"I'm headed home to shower and change quickly, and then I'll be on my way to you," Sienna said.

"Finally." She heard the smile in Gavin's voice. "Long day, huh? I have just the thing to relax you. It's very large and very hot."

"Mmm, tell me more," she said, adding a dramatic, suggestive purr to her tone.

"And very meaty," he added.

"Ooh."

"With extra onions."

She burst into laughter. "In-N-Out?"

"Of course. Paired with a fine Pepsi-Cola, extra ice. I'm going to call DoorDash as soon as you tell me you're on your way."

She sighed happily. It was way past dinnertime, way past *bedtime*, actually, but she was starving. There simply hadn't been time to eat. "You still remember all my favorites."

"Of course. I'm sure you have more than a few new ones too," he said, his tone becoming serious. "I'm dedicated to learning them all."

She smiled. In fact, she did have a few new favorites. Her taste and her world had . . . expanded since she was eighteen and very poor, but she loved that he knew the person she used to be before she could afford fine dining and top shelf, because that person still existed, too, and as it turned out, not all the finer things in life cost more money.

"Do you still get extra butter on your popcorn?" she asked.

He laughed. "No, but only because my arteries aren't in their teens anymore."

She grinned. "See you soon. Oh, hey, Gavin, give me a few extra minutes. I'm driving right past your mom's exit, so I'm going to stop in and check on her in person. I know it's late, but if she's been sleeping all day, maybe she's up. I won't be long."

"Oh. Yeah, sure. She's usually up past eleven watching those reality shows she loves." He paused. "Argus never did call me back, but hopefully my mom's spoken to him. Maybe a bug passed between the two of them and he's laid up now."

"Maybe. I'll text you in just a bit."

"Okay, sounds good."

Sienna took the exit, followed the route she'd driven the week before, and pulled up in front of Mirabelle's house. She shut off the engine, letting out a breath when she saw the light of a TV screen from within the house. She continued to stare at the large structure, her brows dipping. Maybe Mirabelle had fallen asleep in front of the TV, because other than the small flicker, something about the house felt *strangely* dark. No porch light was on, not even the smallest glow from a lamp within.

If Mirabelle *was* still sleeping, in front of the TV or otherwise, she obviously needed the rest. Sienna hesitated before ringing the bell, going back and forth between not waking her and offering assistance. But then she remembered Gavin's persistence at her door and how much she'd needed his caretaking, whether she'd known it or not, and pressed her finger to the doorbell. *What if Mirabelle's bug has gotten worse? What if she's feverish but doesn't have any Tylenol? What if she's dehydrated? What if she hasn't eaten all day and just needs someone to heat something up for her?*

What if simply helping her out of her TV chair and into bed means she doesn't wake up with a painful kink in her back?

She waited a minute, pressing her ear to the door, but no sound came from within, not even the quiet sound of whatever TV show was on, and a wave of worry rolled over her. And when she tried the knob and it turned . . . opened . . . that worry increased.

"Mirabelle?" she called into the dark house. "Mirabelle, it's me." Her weapon was still in the holster at her waist, and out of habit, she put her hand on it as she reached inside, flicking on the hall light. She called her name again to no answer, inching forward.

She's just at Argus's house, left the TV on, and forgot to lock her door. Or she's going to come out of her room, drowsy and disoriented from some cold medication, and you're going to scare the bejesus out of her.

She leaned into the open doorway of the spacious living room, but there was no one in it, just the muted television playing an infomercial from QVC. She moved on, rounding the corner to the kitchen slowly before flicking on the overhead light. Everything was spick-and-span, and Sienna smelled that familiar lemon cleaner that always conjured memories of Mirabelle.

Her shoulders relaxed slightly, but she called her name again. When she peeked her head in the open bedroom doorway, the bed was empty. Frowning, she flicked on that light, too, but Mirabelle wasn't there.

Sienna did a quick walk-through of each room, calling Mirabelle's name, and then returned to the kitchen. Mirabelle was definitely not home. But she also wasn't collapsed on a bathroom floor like Sienna had half feared.

Why did you fear that? Listen to your gut.

Was something off, or was it just this *case*, this guy, wreaking havoc on her mind, causing her to see games and clues and messages in every small thing?

But I mourned Mother. I mourned the absence of her potpourri, her homemade doughnuts, and the lemon-scented spray that made our house smell clean and fresh.

She pulled in a deep breath. That was what was still nagging at her mind. And yet she kept talking herself out of it because talking of a mother in relation to potpourri and lemon cleaner was like someone saying their mom liked to burn candles and save gift bags.

Every mother did that.

Well . . . not *hers*, but lots of them.

Those things were not particular to Mirabelle.

But they reminded you of her, didn't they, Sienna? a small voice whispered.

How could Danny Boy possibly know that, though? There was simply no way.

She was lifting her phone to text Gavin and tell him she was leaving and that Mirabelle wasn't home when she saw the pad of paper on the edge of the counter with Mirabelle's handwriting.

She approached it, her brow furrowing as she looked down. "What the hell?" she muttered.

They were *her* notes, only . . . rewritten by Mirabelle.

Vanadium, Iodine, Oxygen, Lithium.

And then beneath that, she'd added to Sienna's brainstorming with apparent *E* and *T* words from the periodic chart.

Europium?

Erbium?

Einsteinium?

Titanium?

Tantalum?

Thallium?

Tellurium?

Thulium?

VIOLET

Sienna stood there for several moments, trying to understand. Mirabelle had obviously seen the notes from the periodic table at her condo. That was why she'd rushed out of there looking peaked? And then she'd come home and rewritten them with her own additions. Why? Mirabelle had gotten the *E* right, even though there was no way she could have known about the company Harry Lockheed's body was facing or the clues the killer had left that had led them to the same letter. And why did Mirabelle think the word would end up being *Violet?*

Her eyes moved downward, to the bottom of the page, where Mirabelle had written three names. *Reva (Lilly) Keeling, Bee Murray, and Harry Lockheed.* The three strangled murder victims who'd been elaborately posed.

Below that was a rough sketch of a crown, done in red ink, almost as if Mirabelle had been doodling while going over the notes. *What the hell is going on?*

Something occurred to her, and she brought her phone out to call in to the station. Kat was long gone, home to get a good night's rest, but maybe Xavier was still there, despite the late hour. She used the automated system to type in the extension of the phone at the desk where he was working, and he answered right away.

"Hey, Xavier. You sure are burning the midnight oil. But I'm glad you're still there."

"I was actually just packing up. What's going on?"

"Ingrid said that you're pulling information about Roger Hastings and his son's abduction?"

"Yeah. I'm still working on it, though. There's a lot."

"That's okay. I just need to know his wife's name, if you have that. The one who reported their son's abduction in the first place."

"Ah, hold on." She heard rustling as though he was going through notes or printouts. "Violet. I thought so but wanted to confirm. Violet Hastings, former cocktail waitress turned homemaker, reported that Roger left with their son, Daniel, aged seven, in the back seat of his car and never returned. According to police, she claimed it was a spousal disagreement and he'd taken the boy to punish her."

Punish her?

Sienna's heart was beating rapidly, her stomach suddenly queasy.

"Does it say where she waitressed?"

"Um." She heard papers rustling again. "Yeah. Casino Royale? That's the one that closed last year, right?"

Casino Royale. She couldn't picture any casino with that name. She stretched her brain, trying to picture it, but came up short. It'd been so many years since she'd lived there and known every building in every corner of the city. "I don't know," she said distractedly.

"It was a classic casino close to downtown but more off the beaten path," Xavier went on. "I mostly remember it because of that giant red crown on top of the building."

Her rib cage squeezed. *Red crown.* Yes, yes, now she remembered it too. She'd never gone inside, but she'd driven by. Her gaze locked on Mirabelle's rough sketch. She felt breathless. "Thank you so much, Xavier. You've helped a lot. In fact, when this is all over, I'm nominating you for employee of the year."

She could hear the pride in his voice when he said, "Wow, thanks. It's no problem. I love this stuff. See you tomorrow."

She hung up, her eyes going to the notes again, her brain attempting to merge and arrange all the information she had.

"Oh, Mirabelle," she whispered. Was *she* Violet? Had she worked at Casino Royale with the murder victims? Violet . . . Danny Boy's *mother?*

The inspiration for the infamous "Mother"?

She didn't understand. How could this be? Had Mirabelle had another son?

A son who was now strangling people to death? The writer of the notes? Oliver. Ollie. *Daniel.*

He'd been a child when his father had taken him.

She suddenly remembered something and headed to Mirabelle's bedroom, where she opened the top drawer of her bureau. The box where she'd once kept that long-ago bracelet was near the back, and with trembling fingers, she pulled it forward.

Sienna set it on the bureau and opened the top, the tiny hinges giving the quietest of squeaks. The pictures she'd glimpsed so many years before were still there, and she pulled them out, moving the one on top to the back, looking at each in turn. They were photographs of a baby, then of a toddler, a little boy, all with the same dark hair and wide dark eyes and a timid smile. She turned the one that had been on the bottom over and read the back: *Daniel, 7.*

A tiny moan escaped her lips. She saw Gavin in him, but mostly, she saw Mirabelle. A little dark-haired version of Mirabelle. *Oh God.* She clenched her eyes shut, reeling. When she opened her eyes, she saw that underneath the place where the photos had been was a purple fabric drawstring bag, and she set the photos down, already knowing what was inside by the feel of the bag in her hands. She pulled the string and tipped the purse, the silver dollars she'd once given to Mirabelle for safekeeping spilling out onto the wood of the bureau. All of them still there, every last one. Mirabelle had kept them safe for her all these years, because she'd told her she would. Even before she'd moved to this house with the palm trees and the double oven and the en suite bathroom and the pool. Even when Sienna was gone, and surely, she'd needed one a time or two to make final ends meet.

Oh, Mirabelle.

She returned the photos and coins to the box and walked dazedly back to the kitchen.

She stopped in the doorway, her eyes going to a cookbook on a stand on the counter, closed but with a bookmark sticking out of the top. Her breath halted, and she moved toward it and flipped it open to the marked location, her breath gusting out in a sudden rush when she saw what was contained within. A folded piece of paper. Her heart hammering, she unfolded it, already knowing what it was and who had written it. *Him.*

He'd been here.

Sienna's eyes flew over the words, her heart sinking like lead.

Yes, Mother was gone for good, or so I thought. And then one day, I turned on the television and there she was. Mother.

She was in the audience, cheering for another boy as he dominated in poker. I stood, watching. Absorbed. My mind whirled. Buzzed with . . . memories. *Not dreams.* And then, understanding dawned, like a black sun rising over a colorless sea. She was real, not the figment of my imagination I'd convinced myself she was. No . . . she'd been very real. Alive. She'd been living a double life. She'd been hiding, and she'd never stopped.

Once I found Mother, I could no longer pretend. I had to come to terms with the way things had really been.

The way things were.

It took me a long time. Years.

I looked for Mother in the audience as the other boy played his game, so much pride glowing in her eyes. I went to an event the big winner himself was advertised to be at, and Mother was there too. I followed her to a dingy little trailer, where she'd been hiding. How long had she been there? So close and yet so very far away.

There were pictures inside of both the boy and a girl growing up through the years. Mother was in the pictures too. Hugging the boy. Arms wrapped around

the girl. Smiling. So much smiling. There were pictures of the boy and the girl together, the boy staring
at the girl like she'd hung the moon and all the stars.
Where was she now, I wondered. Where had she gone?
Mother had obviously loved her like her own child.

Loved her in a way she hadn't loved me.

No photos of me hung on her wall or decorated
the table next to the sofa. Not a single one. It was as
if, to Mother, I'd never existed at all.

Later, the big winner bought her a huge fancy
house. How happy she was. How satisfied with her
life. How little she missed me or felt sorry for what
she'd done.

Oh yes, I understood now. And I grew angry.

I realized that maybe Father was right about
Mother. Maybe *I* was the one who'd been wrong.

I thought about it all the time. I thought about it
when I went home at night, eating dinner alone at the
table where I'd once been raped, sitting in the chair
where Father and Mr. Patches had sat as I stabbed
them to death. I thought about it when I cleaned
other people's toilets and emptied their trash.

And I began planning.

I kept tabs on Mother, my anger and confusion
keeping pace with my loneliness. The big winner, my
brother, achieved more and more success as he strate-
gized and built his empire.

I had no empire. I had no success. I had nothing
and no one. I had only memories that still sometimes
made me scream in the middle of the night. Screams
that went unheard by anyone other than the decaying
bag of bones in the room three doors down.

I watched Mother, the pride in her eyes as she gazed upon her son. The one she'd chosen over me. The one she protected.

In some ways I understood why she'd chosen him. She must have seen in him all the things I lacked. He had her sky-blue eyes and her easy laugh. He was a master of cards just like her. He'd inherited the ability to effortlessly keep track of the ones that had already been played and intuit the likelihood of what would be drawn next. I watched him—I recognized what he was doing because I'd watched Mother do it too. Once upon a time. Long ago. I had tried. I'd practiced. But I simply didn't possess that talent.

He was a game master.

He was a big winner.

He was who I wanted to be.

I was nothing but a hack.

An embarrassment.

Yes, no wonder Mother had chosen him and left me behind. But I had something he didn't. I had Father's ruthlessness. Or I could if I tried hard enough. I knew I could. Because the boiling heat I felt inside me was *rage* at her abandonment when I'd still needed her. Rage at the man who'd lived the life I should have lived.

I'd start by punishing the very first ones Mother had chosen over me, the ones who'd helped her sneak and lie. And then I'd move on to the big winner and his detective. I'd make them pay. And I'd make her watch it as I did.

Oh yes, I'd make Mother see me. I'd make her look my way. I'd remind her that mothers who abandoned their children to monsters didn't deserve to live.

Oh no. Oh God. She went to reach for her phone in her back pocket. She needed to call Gavin. She needed to call Kat. *He has Mirabelle. He must.*

Strong arms wrapped around her from behind, and she jerked, reaching for her weapon as a strong chemical smell invaded her airways. She smashed her head backward, making contact with the man holding her, and he let out a grunt, tightening his hold. She struggled, taking in big gulps of the chloroform-laced rag, her muscles growing heavier and heavier, tears stinging her eyes as she tried desperately to stay awake, to *fight.* Her weapon was so close . . . so close. She couldn't make herself move. *Oh God. Gavin.* She folded, drooping to the ground, the words coming to her just before she lost consciousness.

"I knew you'd come here, Detective. I gambled on it."

CHAPTER THIRTY-TWO

Gavin pressed end and tossed his phone on the counter, his concern ratcheting a notch higher. Sienna had told him she'd text when she left his mom's. He'd second-guessed himself, thinking maybe she'd meant she'd text when she left her house after showering and changing, and so he'd given it a little more time, but that had been an hour and a half ago. He'd tried Mirabelle's number several times, too, to no response.

Had something come up regarding work? Still, though, wouldn't she have let him know? He understood the nature of her job was that she dealt with *emergencies*, however, so he'd tried not to worry. And wasn't succeeding.

His phone dinged as a text came through, and he grabbed for it when he saw Sienna's name. His breath gusted out as he opened the message, his brows knitting.

Can you meet me at Argus's? Come quickly. Come alone.

What?

He attempted to call her, but again, it went to voice mail. Was something wrong with Argus? Or with his mom?

But if so, Sienna would call him. She wouldn't send a cryptic text message.

He paused, trying to figure out what to do, and finally went to his safe and removed his gun and holster.

Come alone.

Sienna's partner's name was Kat, he was pretty sure. Should he try to call her? Or the police? The problem was, the police wouldn't just meet him there and follow his instructions to stay out of sight and park three streets over in case he needed them.

Come alone.

What if not doing so put Sienna in danger in some way? If it wasn't her texting him, then someone had her phone. Someone had *her*.

And potentially his mother, too, because that was where Sienna had been headed. God, he shouldn't have listened to his mom earlier. There'd been something in her voice. He'd passed it off as sickness, but . . . he should have gone there himself and checked on her whether she'd asked him to or not.

This isn't helpful, Decker. Move.

Gavin grabbed a sweatshirt and headed for the door.

He made the twenty-five-minute drive to Argus's in nineteen, his hands gripping the wheel, forcing himself to stay as calm as he could, knowing he needed to be quick but that it would do no one any good if he got into a car accident because he was in a state of panic.

He parked a block away and walked through the backyards to Argus's house, his hand on his weapon. The house was dark, but the moon overhead was full and bright. He could see that the back curtains were closed. His heart pumped quickly as he stole around the front, stopping every few steps to listen for any small noise, but all was still and silent.

The unlocked front door opened, emitting a soft creak as it swung on its hinges. He drew his weapon, holding it facing downward as he put his back to the wall and moved inside.

He smelled the body before he found it—the very early stench of decay—his heart slamming in his chest. *Oh fuck. Argus. Oh Jesus.* His throat burned, his chest aching as he stared, back pressed against the kitchen wall, at the remains of the only father he'd ever known, the man who had taught him how to shave, how to tie a tie, and how to look another man in his eyes when you shook his hand. A painful lump filled his throat, but he swallowed it down, his breath coming short. *Oh God. No time, no time for that.* Argus was gone. Sienna and Mirabelle were his priorities right now.

He forced his eyes from Argus and glanced around the room. There were two phones on the edge of the counter, and Gavin walked to them. One belonged to Sienna. He recognized the red phone case. And the other was his mother's. Sitting next to those was a note in the handwriting he recognized from the letters he'd been asked to read, looking for clues that might turn the police in the right direction.

Danny Boy.

Danny Boy had killed Argus, and now he had Sienna and his mother.

A jolt of fear and adrenaline tensed his muscles. He blew out a sharp breath, looking down at the note.

> Gavin—Don't call the police if you want to see your mother or girlfriend again. I've left you all you need. Ask Violet about me; she has the key. If you involve anyone else, it will be game over. You play fair, and I will too. You're such a big winner, Gavin. I have all the confidence in the world that you'll find us. But time is of the essence. Soon the countdown will begin. Danny

A surge of pure rage went through him. This psycho had the two women he loved most in the world, and he expected Gavin to play some sick game in order to find them?

Anger gave way to frustration, laced with fear, and underneath that was still the grief over Argus that he could not address, not now. Later, but not now, even as his body scented the room with death.

What was he meant to do, search this house for some small trinket that would lead to another trinket? Where would he even start? The only thing Danny had left him was the note and the two phones. He read through the note again, forcing himself to do it more slowly. Who the fuck was Violet? He tossed it down, cursing, his eyes moving to the phones. He picked up Sienna's first and brought it to life.

The image on her screen was of two palm trees, one bent in front of the other, a red sunset behind them. It reminded him of something, and he had to stare at it for a few moments before it clicked. It looked like a photo version of the Paradise Estates logo. Just to be sure his memory wasn't playing tricks on him—though he didn't think it was; he'd looked at that logo almost every day for the first eighteen years of his life—he brought his phone out and did a search. He made a concerted effort to still the shaking of his hands. The mobile home park's website came up, and Gavin stared at it. The logo had been updated and now featured some type of tropical plant with a swish of water behind it. Which made absolutely no sense, but then neither did the name of the community. Sienna had always made fun of it, called it ironic. Which of course it was, and the fact that it wasn't purposeful irony made it all the more cringeworthy.

His chest ached. *Sienna.*

No, he was pretty damn sure this screenshot was a very close representation of that old logo, the one that had been on the sign at the entrance of the community they'd grown up in. And he was also fairly certain it hadn't been on her phone when he'd seen the text from "Main Squeeze" come through.

He brought Mirabelle's phone to life and saw that the picture on her screen was the same one that'd been there for months, if not a full year: Mirabelle and Argus sitting in lounge chairs beside her pool, glasses of lemonade in hand. He'd taken it himself.

He had to stuff down the ball of grief that rose up inside him at the sight of Argus smiling next to Mirabelle. *Not now, not now.*

He went to her text messages, but nothing seemed unusual. He opened her web browser and found that the only page open was the front page of a local news station. He frowned. Mirabelle didn't look at news. Although she had said she was paying more attention now that Sienna was in town. Was this related? He let out a frustrated growl low in his throat, tossing the phone on the counter. *This is insanity.*

He opened Sienna's phone and found the text that had been sent to him, the one he could only assume had actually been sent by the man who had her.

Helplessly, he looked around the kitchen, keeping his gaze purposely averted from Argus's body, but nothing was out of place that he could see. The only clues were the phones.

"Jesus," he muttered, his hand on his firearm as he once again left the house, took the same route he'd taken from his car, and got inside.

He steeled his resolve as he drove away, hating that he couldn't even call the cops to notify them about Argus's murder. *I'm sorry, Argus. But I know you would be telling me to focus on our girls now.*

It took him fifteen minutes to get to the trailer park, and when he got there, he had no real memory of the trip, his mind so preoccupied with what he'd found himself in the middle of and how this all might end. He parked near the new sign, with the new logo, a large boulder sitting next to the signpost. That was new too. Gavin walked to the sign and circled it once, running his hand along the top in case something flat that he couldn't see was there. But there wasn't. He moved his attention to the rock and attempted to push it aside, but it was too large and too heavy. He'd need a damn crane to lift the thing. God dammit. If he wasn't meant to be *here*, where was he supposed to go? He swore, falling to his knees and desperately moving the sand around the base of the boulder aside to see if something might be buried in the dirt, but there was nothing.

He knelt there for a moment, listening, as a dog barked, then another and another as they all answered each other. A few yells rose in the air—owners telling their hounds to shut the hell up. He smelled the lingering scent of charcoal and meat. Someone, or several someones, had grilled their dinner, as many did rather than smoke up the small spaces inside their trailers.

He had to have been led here. Of all the people picking up that phone, only he would know that the picture on the screen was not Sienna's and that it was a photo depiction of the old Paradise Estates logo.

He brought his phone out and shone a light on the rock, and with the additional illumination, he could see that there were etchings and writing on the surface of the stone. He moved the light around, his heart beating swiftly. It wasn't graffiti; this looked very intentional and themed, done in shades of brown and gray, so he hadn't immediately spotted any of it in the low light. There were outlines of children's hands with inspiring words that declared, *Faith!* and *Believe!* and *Grit!* It looked like the owner of the trailer park, or whoever had redone the sign, had had the children who lived here participate in some feel-good art project that blended into nature and that they could be encouraged by as they passed it at the beginning and end of each day.

As a poor kid who'd grown up in a trailer park and gone to a public school system lacking in funds, Gavin was well versed in this type of project, some big like a man-made lake with swans to beautify a downtrodden area, others smaller like this rock of positivity. They were the projects that made others feel good but that typically did little to change lives.

Cynical, Decker. And not the time. His mind was just in a free flow, and he was so damn scared he was running out of time in some specific way he didn't know how to measure.

He moved his phone flashlight over the rock hurriedly, looking for anything that stuck out or—

There. There it was. One word written near the bottom in black Sharpie. He did a quick sweep of the rock again to confirm that it was the only word written in black. Just like the number on that key Sienna had found inside the tennis ball and the name written on the coffee cup. The handwriting here looked the same, too, the word printed carefully: *Renew! 4:2.*

His breath was coming short now, his heart beating so rapidly he swore it was coming out of his chest. What the hell was he supposed to do with the word *renew* and the numbers next to it?

He did a quick Google search of the word. There was a medical spa he'd never heard of nor been a patient at with the word *renew* in its title, but that was about it. He opened a thesaurus site and looked up the word. *Extend, prolong, reaffirm, revive.*

He was at a loss. *Fuck!* He wanted to raise his face to the heavens and shout. What else did he have to go on?

4:2. Was that a Bible verse? He searched for it and found one option from Ephesians. *Be completely humble and gentle; be patient, bearing with one another in love.*

Okay, that didn't help. And there were too many other biblical options to wade through. No, it had to be something else. Something more logical and less time consuming.

Right? Or was the *point* to keep him tied up in thousands of pages of Bible passages?

His mind reached, grabbing at possibilities.

Relax. You won't help them if you don't relax. Approach this as you used to approach cards. All in, but calm, controlled. It's how you win. He took a moment to even his breathing.

The news website. It suddenly came to him. The one that had been left open on Mirabelle's phone. But probably not by Mirabelle. He opened the news website on his own phone and scanned the front page. *There!* One of the bars at the top said *Renew Reno*, and he clicked on it. There were several listed stories, mostly regarding revitalizing old buildings, cleaning up parks and other public areas, and the like. 4:2. It appeared that there were four pages on this subpage, and Gavin clicked to the last one and scrolled down to the second article.

It was a story about an old casino, the Casino Royale, being brought down by controlled demolition. The blast was scheduled for the following morning at 5:00 a.m. Gavin stood slowly, paused only a moment, and then ran for his car.

CHAPTER
THIRTY-THREE

The road that led to the old Casino Royale had been closed, construction vehicles parked here and there, large warning signs that demolition work was in progress. Gavin left his car in an empty parking lot across the way, ducked under the fencing, and jogged toward the dark structure.

Caution tape was strung between cones, blocking off the parking lot in front of the building, and Gavin could already see that the windows had been boarded up. For a moment he stood looking at the old casino. Was Sienna inside? His mother? Fear arced through him, the terror that his search was going to lead to their lifeless bodies, heads lolling on their bruised necks the same way Argus's had. *Argus.*

Don't think. Just act.

He forced his body to move, hurrying between objects he might use as cover if necessary, as he made his way around the large structure.

There was a service door at the back, halfway open, and surprised at the sight, Gavin shrank back, positioning his body behind the corner of the building before sticking his head out. He couldn't see inside, only blackness beyond, but it was a way in.

And he knew that it'd been left open for him. Which meant he'd come to the right place.

Sienna.

Inside, a song began playing.

Doo-dah! Doo-dah!

What the hell?

He slipped through the door, turning his head—*shit.* A spotlight turned on, blinding him. Instinctively, he ducked, anticipating a hit of some kind as he struggled to see. His hand went to his holster, but a voice came from just beyond. "Don't. I have a weapon, too, and I can see you."

Gavin lowered his hand as the voice came again. "Congratulations, Gavin. I'm not surprised you made it here. Not surprised in the least. All my bets seem to be paying off. I guess I'm the big winner tonight. We'll see."

The spotlight moved to the side, and Gavin straightened, squinting into the gloom, the song rising merrily in the background, the mood at complete odds with the situation, adding a frightening element of unreality.

A man walked toward him, with what he could now see was a flashlight in one hand, held pointed away, and a gun in the other, trained on Gavin. "Danny?" he asked.

The man's lips tipped, though Gavin wouldn't call the expression a smile. As he came closer, Gavin could see that his nose was red and bruised as though someone had hit him. "Ah. You know my name, of course. My real name. Detective Walker brought you my writings. I guess you wouldn't call them my autobiography, considering some information was . . . left out." He gave an exaggerated sigh.

Gavin stared. He . . . recognized him. *Danny.* He searched his mind. "You work in my building," Gavin said. He'd seen him before. *The janitor.*

Danny smiled but didn't confirm or deny. "Anyway, I hoped she would," he went on as though Gavin hadn't spoken. "Bring you my writings, that is. A combo of the card design and her own desire to see you, I imagined, if the photos on Mirabelle's wall and the way you two looked at each other once were any indication. Slide your gun across the floor. And your cell phone too."

Gavin paused, calculating the chance of him getting a shot off before Danny did, but Danny's weapon was held steady, and he had the upper hand, holding the light. Plus, Gavin still didn't know where his mom and Sienna were, and if he managed to kill Danny, he might never know. Slowly, he took his gun from his holster, slid it across the floor, and then removed his phone from his pocket and slid that over too. Danny bent, his eyes trained on Gavin as he put the phone in his pocket and then used one hand to open the chamber of the gun, remove the bullets, and put those in his pocket as well. He stood, using his foot to kick the gun to the right of him. It slid into the darkness, worthless now. "One weapon is enough for me," Danny said, nodding at the one in his hand. "Plus, this is the gun my father used to kill Jax. You read about Jax, didn't you? It seemed apropos that I should use it now, here, at the end of my story."

The end of my story.

"Where's Sienna?" Gavin asked. "My mom?" His nerves were strung tight, stomach muscles clenched in preparation for the worst. Mirabelle in a chair, a cord around her lifeless neck. Sienna . . . no. *Those thoughts won't help.*

But if that was the case, he would attack Danny with his bare hands. Because then, he'd have nothing left to lose.

Oh! Doo-dah day!

"Your mom. Ha. Don't worry," Danny said, taking a few steps to his left, where he flicked a switch. "They're right over there." Gavin's head swiveled, and he saw the two women, sitting on the floor, their hands tied behind their backs, gags in their mouths, but their eyes wide. His gaze flew over them. They appeared scared but okay. *Alive.*

"What do you want with them?" Gavin asked. "What do you want with me, and why?" It was clear now that he'd targeted them both from the beginning. But what goal was he moving toward? And how were they part of it?

"Oh, I already told you that Violet would answer all your questions," he said, looking over at the women. "You were always a loud little shit," Danny said as he began backing away. "Loud and happy. You got to stay that way. Good for you, Big Winner." Gavin's muscles tensed, primed to both run to the women and react to whatever Danny might be doing, whatever nonsensical things he was saying. But Danny simply backed away toward a door Gavin could see behind him now that his eyes had adjusted. Danny opened the door and then pulled it closed behind him, and Gavin heard the flip of a lock and what sounded like the loud clanking of chains.

He moved then, rushing toward Sienna and his mom, going down on his knees when he got to where they sat, pulling the gag from Sienna's mouth and then Mirabelle's, his fingers flying quickly to untie their bound hands. Their breath released on loud exhales, Mirabelle leaning her head forward as she sucked in big mouthfuls of air. "Gavin," Sienna said, tipping her chin, her eyes cast over his shoulder.

He turned quickly. The door he'd used to enter had closed behind him, but now he could see a red light flashing on a panel on the wall. He turned back to Sienna, who was finishing the job of removing the ropes from her hands. "Help her," he said, gesturing to Mirabelle. Sienna nodded, and he jogged back over to the door to look at the flashing light and the words beneath the panel:

You will only have one chance to input the correct code. If the incorrect code is entered, the system will be permanently disabled, and the door will remain locked. The blast is set for 5:00 a.m. on the dot. Good luck.

The blast.

He tried to turn the door handle, but it just rattled in his hand. He followed the wires from the alarm-looking box upward, but they disappeared into the darkness overhead. *Goddamn, it's tall.* At one point there might have been an escalator in this large, open space, but now, from what he'd seen when he was talking to Danny, it was just a massive empty room. He couldn't see a damn thing up above, nor did he have any form of light. He lowered his head, looking from one corner of the door to the other. Reinforced steel. Just like every casino. They'd need a bulldozer to get through it.

Or the unknown code they had one chance to enter.

Or a technician who knew how to dismantle whatever system this was and a light by which to work.

They had none of those things.

He ran to the exit Danny had gone through—another damn steel door—and found it locked as well, and when he shook it, he could hear the chink of the chain moving against itself on the other side. It was locked, and it was chained.

They were well and truly trapped.

CHAPTER
THIRTY-FOUR

Sienna watched as Gavin returned to them, holding his hand out to his mother. Mirabelle took it before standing and embracing him. "Oh, Gavin. I'm so sorry. So very, very sorry." Her voice was choked with tears, and though Sienna's adrenaline was rushing with the fear of having woken bound and gagged, her heart clenched for Mirabelle.

Gavin let go of his mother and turned to her. God, she didn't think she should be so glad to see him, because it meant he was in danger, too, but she was. She was. "Are you okay?" he asked, his gaze moving over her face and down her body, quickly assessing.

"Physically, I'm fine," she said. "I just want to get out of here."

"We will." He pulled her to him quickly, giving her a tight squeeze and then letting her go. "There's some kind of system hooked up to the outer door that requires a code," he said. "The door over there"—he nodded to the place Danny had disappeared through—"is locked and chained from the other side."

He stopped, looking back and forth between the two of them. "What's going on here? What do you know that I don't? And who in the hell is Violet?"

Sienna shot a worried look at Mirabelle, who took a big, shaky breath. "I am," she said. "My real name is Violet."

Gavin's face screwed up with confusion. "Your . . . *what?*"

Sienna grabbed Mirabelle's hand. "She'll tell you, Gavin. But first, we need to explore our surroundings. Mirabelle, you used to work here. Can you think of a way out?"

Mirabelle bit her lip, looking distressed. "Those are all inner rooms without windows," she said, pointing in the direction opposite the locked door.

Suddenly, the music that had been playing cranked up, a light coming on overhead. A gunshot fired, and plaster exploded somewhere to their left. "Holy *fuck!*" Gavin yelled, pulling Sienna into him, going low and covering her head, while next to her, Mirabelle ducked down too.

As quickly as the light had blinked on, it blinked off. "One!" was heard shouted from beyond. "Two!"

"Hide," Mirabelle said, her voice desperate.

"Hide? There's nowhere to hide."

"There is. There's a pile of boxes near the corner," Mirabelle said. "He's re-creating that day. That last day. Oh my God."

"We need to do as she says," Sienna said, and Gavin must have heard the certainty in her voice because he gave a quick nod. She didn't know what *that last day* entailed, but she knew more about Mirabelle and Danny's past than Gavin did, even if she didn't understand the entirety of it. Also, they'd been sitting in this room longer than he'd been here, and they'd had a chance to note some of the layout.

Gavin grasped both Sienna's and his mother's hands, and they all crouched as they ran for cover. They ducked behind the boxes, barely illuminated in the low light, and then the lights blinked on. A gunshot sounded, hitting the spot where they'd just sat.

Sienna's pulse spiked, her heart pounding as Gavin's breath gusted against her neck. Danny was really *shooting* at them.

Three pairs of eyes met in the near dark as they knelt behind the cardboard barrier. "Tell me what we're dealing with here, Mom. I want answers," Gavin said, his voice hushed, even though the music was playing loudly enough to cover any noise they made. "I think it's important. This isn't a game." He paused, and Sienna sensed his momentary indecision. "Also, Argus . . . Argus is—"

"I know, Gavin," Mirabelle choked. "I went to his house. I know."

Oh. Sienna brought her hands to her mouth. "No," she breathed. *Argus. Oh no.* Gavin put his arm around her shoulders, and she leaned into him, trying desperately to hold back tears. She couldn't cry now, though. Not now. Because if she started crying, she feared she wouldn't stop, and she'd be useless as far as figuring a way out of this locked building. *Come on, Sienna. Now's the time to use your training. Pull forth your inner professional.* And so she allowed herself only a brief moment of comfort in Gavin's arms before pulling away.

"Who is Danny, Mom?" Gavin asked.

"He's my son," Mirabelle said.

"Your . . . son?"

"Yes. Your older brother. Your father abducted him from me when he was only seven years old." The pain etched into her features was so profound that Sienna's hand itched to reach for her, to offer comfort, but she didn't. She didn't want to risk halting Mirabelle's will to tell her story to Gavin, her second-born son.

The lights blinked off again. "Three!" came loudly from beyond. "Four!"

Mirabelle screamed as Gavin hissed an expletive. *We need to keep moving.* "There's something leaning against the wall about a hundred feet to our left," Sienna said. "I think we can all fit behind it."

Again, they ran, then ducked behind what appeared to be large sections of drywall that had been torn down but not carried away. The lights came on, a gunshot sounding and then what seemed to be the noise of the boxes they'd hid behind toppling. Gavin swore.

"Why didn't you ever tell me this? Why didn't you ever mention Danny?"

Mirabelle released a breath, her shoulders lowering. They were standing so close Sienna could feel Mirabelle trembling. And she appeared smaller somehow. Breakable. "I was afraid. *Ashamed.* At first, I couldn't talk about it at all, and you were too young to understand anyway. Too young to carry the burden of having to look over your shoulder. And so I did it for you. For us. And then . . ." She gave a small, listless shrug, her lips tipping in a sad smile. "And then it was too late. You had a life, such a bright future. What good would it have done to ask you to carry my heartache?"

He gave his head a small shake, his features still set in confusion, and Sienna could see him working to see the picture she was painting. The one he'd never known he was a part of until this very moment. "I might have been able to help," he said.

"How, Gavin? Years had passed. Decades. I'd hired private detectives right after Roger disappeared with Daniel. Initially they traced him to Las Vegas, where his family lives, and then they lost him. It was believed his family had helped Roger gain a new identity, though that was never proved."

"That's why we lived there," Gavin murmured. "Even though I was born here." A muscle jumped in Gavin's jaw, and he peeked out from the place they were hiding. "There's a large cabinet of some kind over there," he said, nodding in the direction of the wall that was now close enough to see in the dark. "We go there next."

She and Mirabelle nodded, and when the lights went out again and two more numbers were shouted, they sprinted behind the cabinet, pressed their backs against the wall, and sat down.

"There's a room over there," Mirabelle said, gesturing toward the place where Sienna could now see a soft light emanating from beneath what looked like a door. "There aren't any windows or exits inside, though."

The lights remained on, but no gunshot sounded.

"It's our best choice," Sienna said. Because Danny had obliterated all their other options for cover. "We need to crawl to the door."

"What if it's a trap?" Mirabelle asked.

They raised their heads in unison when they heard the faraway echo of footsteps overhead. Danny was somewhere, but he wasn't in that room. It might be a trap, but it might lead to a way out. And at the moment, it was the only possibility. "Let's go."

They crawled quickly to the door, pushed it open, and ducked inside. It was another large room, what appeared to have once been the industrial-size kitchen. There were still long steel counters on one side and open ducts where appliances had been. Sienna looked up. At least there was nowhere from which Danny could shoot them.

Both Gavin and Sienna immediately rushed to the door on the opposite side of the room, Gavin holding up the large cylindrical lock with a combination code. He leaned closer and peered at it. "It's a number-code lock, requiring five digits," he said. He jiggled it, but there was no give on the lock, and he dropped it.

"So we're meant to use some unknown number code to exit this door?" she asked, looking around for a place to start.

"It appears so," he muttered, using his hands to feel around the door. With a look of frustration, he dropped his arms. He stood there for a minute and then brought his foot up, kicking the door. It shook but didn't give. He kicked at it several more times, yelling in frustration as the lock held soundly. He was breathing hard, his jaw clenching. *"Fuck."*

"I found a box," Mirabelle said from where she was standing at one of the counters against the wall.

She was holding a plain metal box with a key lock holding it closed. Mirabelle shook it gently, and whatever contents were inside slid from side to side.

Gavin took it from her and examined it, turning it upside down. "We don't have time for stupid games. I'm going to smash this lock on the ground."

Sienna put her hand on his forearm. "Wait, what if whatever's inside is breakable or . . . gets ruined in some way?"

Gavin looked around. "Fine. Is there something we can use to pry this open?"

Sienna walked to one of the long counters and leaned over so she could see behind it. It was bolted to the wall. *Great.*

"I think it's worth spending a few minutes looking for the key," Mirabelle said. "If Danny locked us in this room, then the key's here somewhere."

Gavin stared at her for a moment, placing the box down on the counter.

"Tell me all of it, Mom, from the beginning, but fast. I need to understand what we're dealing with."

Mirabelle leaned back against the counter as though she needed it to hold her up. Maybe in some ways it was also a relief, to off-load the weight that had been resting on her shoulders for so long.

"Wait," Sienna said. "Help me push that"—she pointed to a metal cabinet—"in front of the door we entered through. At least that way we know he can't surprise us." They could go back that way and stay in the large, open area, but that was where they were sitting ducks. He had the advantage of darkness and higher ground.

"Good idea." She and Gavin first examined every side of the cabinet, opening the doors and running their hands over the inside, but there was nothing to find. They pushed the heavy object in front of the door and returned to Mirabelle. She took in what seemed to be a fortifying breath of air. "I met your father," she began, "Roger Hastings, when he was sent by his family to open a new casino here in Reno. Long story short, he wooed me. I'd lost my parents young, was hungry for love, validation . . . stability, a family. Anyway, we married quickly. I was already pregnant with Danny. And things fell apart very soon after Roger fouled up the opening of the casino in every way possible. He hit me for the first time when Danny was four. That's also when he began isolating me from my friends."

"Reva Keeling, Bernadette Murray, and Harry Lockheed," Sienna said quietly.

Mirabelle nodded, her eyes downcast. "Yes."

"The . . . victims? The ones who were strangled?" Gavin gripped his hair, turning away and then back again. "Oh, Jesus."

"Yes," Mirabelle said.

Sienna thought of the letter she'd found in Mirabelle's kitchen. He'd believed his mother had chosen them over him. "Do you think Roger spoke about them? Is that why Danny went after them too? I mean, we're talking twenty-something years ago, Mirabelle."

"I guess so. Roger was . . . very violent. Danny heard and saw everything. Roger accused me of choosing my friends over him and my children." Her last words ended with a shuddery intake of breath as though she was trying desperately not to cry. Sienna could only imagine how hard this was for Mirabelle to reconcile. That a child she'd loved deeply—mourned—could become a killer.

Gavin's expression was stony. But Sienna saw the pain in his eyes and the confusion. He didn't know how to feel, and she didn't blame him one bit. She didn't either.

"The rest," Gavin said, and though the words were demanding, his voice was laced with the same pain Sienna saw in his eyes. "What else do we need to know to get out of here?" Gavin picked up the box and began bending the lock back and forth. It wasn't likely to work, but Sienna had a feeling he needed to occupy his hands in order to control his emotions.

Mirabelle sniffed back another sob. "That day, Roger played a sick game of hide-and-seek. He hit me. He threatened me. He made us run. I was standing between the two of you, and he made me choose." Anguish altered her features before she again got hold of herself. "I chose you because you were too little to hide on your own." She hung her head, and they gave her a minute to compose herself. That was why. That was why Danny had started shouting numbers as they hid. That was what Mirabelle had meant when she'd said he was re-creating that day. That day he'd never really moved past.

"I reported the abduction, of course, and the police issued an arrest warrant. The Amber Alert wasn't even a thing back then." She gave her head a small shake. "And I think because it was a parent abduction, the investigative motivation wasn't quite the same as it would have been had a stranger taken Danny. Anyway, they searched for Roger for a while. But with all his connections, who knew where he might have gone and who could have helped him."

Mirabelle took a staggered breath. "Anyway, everything was repossessed. The house, my car, all the furnishings. I was left penniless and still in fear for my life. I'd received several threatening notes from Roger, telling me he'd come and take Gavin too. I gave them to the police, but as far as I know, they simply filed them away. It was then I hired the PI with the very last of what I had, and only because I'd been able to sell a few pieces of jewelry Roger had given me in the beginning, but that ended up being fruitless too. No more notes arrived, and that was both a blessing and a curse because while I wasn't being threatened, I had no proof that Roger hadn't driven himself and Danny into a lake somewhere." She offered a completely mirthless laugh, which ended in a terribly pained grimace. "The things I imagined . . . the scenarios that went through my head . . . it was hell on earth."

And oh God, Mirabelle had no idea how horrific it had really been for Danny. Sienna's heart broke to know that she'd find out if—no, *when*—they survived this; it would be inevitable.

"The police provided some protection for a short while, but that went away quickly too. And anyway, what they'd offered was so weak. And so I put myself into my own protection program. I changed my name. I never contacted anyone I had known in my previous life again. I didn't change your first name, but you were so little. You weren't even in school yet." Her eyes met Gavin's. "I'd already lost one son; I could not lose two."

Mirabelle looked down, exhausted. "I was always wary Roger was going to come after me and Gavin," she said.

She'd protected Gavin by staying unattached with no driver's license. Untraceable. Mirabelle hadn't known that Roger had been dead for years. No longer posing a threat. It was all so heartbreaking.

"I searched for such a long time. Anywhere I knew Roger might go to earn money under the radar."

"That's why we moved around when I was young," Gavin said, setting the unopened box back down on the counter. The lock would not be broken by mere twisting and turning and pulling. "To Las Vegas and then to Atlantic City and then back to Reno. All places where gambling was plentiful."

Mirabelle nodded. "In the early days, I would walk the strips, hat pulled low, looking for Roger. I didn't dare gamble anywhere myself. He also knew I was good and could earn money that way." She chewed at her lip for a brief moment. "But I also found it hard to stay away from cards. They had always been a draw for me. Something that had always . . . lured." She looked up at Gavin. "You have it too. You know what I mean."

He nodded slowly, hesitantly, but admitted, "Yes. Yes, I know." He had been a natural with cards all his life. Sienna knew it as well as he did. They had pulled him, all the way out of Reno. All the way to the World Series of Poker.

A small smile lit Mirabelle's face, a real one, but her eyes were still filled with sadness. "And so," she said, pulling in a shuddery breath, "I took a job as a magician's assistant to a kindly Greek magician who knew I had secrets, who paid me under the table and understood that I couldn't marry him but never stopped asking anyway. And I convinced myself Danny was dead because the alternatives were too agonizing to live with." Grief took over her features, but she went on, her eyes meeting Sienna's. "And I met a seven-year-old girl, watchful and sensitive like my Danny had been. I protected the all-but-motherless child, and she helped fill the terrible vacant hole in my heart. And life became bearable again."

Mirabelle's eyes were beseeching, and Sienna's heart ached to hear the torment she'd lived with for so many years. She let go of Gavin's hand and stepped forward, wrapping her arms around the woman who had mothered her when her own had not. And yet she couldn't help the low hum of guilt that resonated within her. She'd benefited from Mirabelle's mothering, while her own son had suffered so intensely without her.

And because of it, lives had been lost.

Even more devastating was the fact that all this time Danny had been right *here*, not thirty minutes away. Roger's family might have helped him initially, but apparently, their help had been temporary. They'd helped him to disappear and then wiped their hands of him. And Danny.

And Danny had suffered. But he'd remembered his mother, possibly only vague recollections that felt false and unreal as time moved on. He'd imagined her. Dreamed her. *Become* her when he'd needed to. The soft place he barely remembered except in the way she'd *felt*. His protection. His savior. It was all too awful to consider. Especially now, when their lives were perched in his terribly troubled hands.

Sienna stepped back. "So what does he want?" Gavin asked. Sienna looked at him. His eyes had softened, though the pain was still there. "Vengeance?" he asked. "Vengeance for what? You were a victim too." Mirabelle gave him a sad but grateful smile, reaching out for his hand. He took it, and they shared a moment, mother and son who had never truly known each other until that moment and yet knew all the things that truly mattered.

"He doesn't see it that way," Sienna said. She told them about the final note, about Danny's loneliness, his suffering, his blame, keeping it short and very simple.

"He's on the other side of that wall," Gavin said, gesturing to the door with the locks. "If we can get to him, maybe there's a part of him we can still appeal to. It's gotta be getting close to three a.m. We need to hurry."

Mirabelle nodded, a light of hope entering her eyes for the first time. "Let's get through that door," she said. "To Danny."

Sienna reached for the box Gavin had only managed to scuff and scrape with the lock itself. "Maybe you're right about breaking it rather than searching for the key," she said.

Gavin nodded, but he looked as though something was bothering him. "The key," he murmured. "'Ask Violet about me; she has the key.'" He looked at his mother. "Search your pockets," he told her.

Her brows knitted, but she did, reaching in the one on her right and coming up empty handed. She reached in the other pocket, and her eyes widened as she pulled something out and held up a small silver key. "He planted it on me while I was unconscious," she said. "How did you know?"

"It was in his note to me," Gavin said hurriedly, reaching for the key and the box. "I just remembered it now."

Sienna's breath came short. If Gavin was right about the time, they had a little over two hours before the blast went off.

CHAPTER
THIRTY-FIVE

Sienna's heart beat rapidly, and she stepped forward, watching as Gavin stuck the key in the lock. It opened with a tiny click. Their eyes met very briefly, and then he set the box down, tossed the key aside, and lifted the lid. Three items sat inside, and he pulled them out one by one. A magnet of what looked like a flag, but not one Sienna recognized—though admittedly, she had never committed them all to memory—a small china doll; and a pin with a blue ribbon on it and the number ten, with the zero crossed off to make it a one.

Gavin set them in a row, and they all stared down at them in silence. "What flag is this?" he murmured. Neither Sienna nor Mirabelle answered.

"Isn't Texas the Lone Star State?" Mirabelle asked, looking down at the red, white, and blue flag with a white star in the center of the blue portion.

"Okay. Yeah. It is," Gavin said. Not being a Texan, Sienna couldn't picture their flag, but that seemed logical. Then again, lots of places had stars on their flags, even internationally.

She had the urge to laugh, but as much as she knew if she cried she wouldn't stop, she knew the same would be true if she gave in to laughter.

"What about this?" he asked, picking up the china doll. It had dark-red hair and fine porcelain skin.

Sienna took it from him, studying it, and tried to rub the small red smudge off its forehead with her thumb, unsuccessfully. Whatever had stained the doll's skin was permanent, and likely purposeful. She frowned down at it before setting it back on the table.

For a minute they were all quiet as they tried to puzzle out the contents of the box. "Why don't we do a more thorough search," Gavin suggested. "Maybe there's more that goes along with this. I'll check the undersides of the counters."

They split up, each searching over and under and behind, looking at the walls and the floor but not finding anything. Sienna rubbed her head. Something was niggling at her about the mark on that doll's head. That doll . . . "Dolly," she breathed.

Gavin turned, joining her as she walked back toward the box and its contents. "The girl he threw the checkers at," Sienna said. Mirabelle approached, looking at her with confusion. "It's from one of his writings," she explained. He'd thrown checkers at her head. He'd left a mark.

"Okay," Gavin said. "So the—maybe—Texas flag and a girl from his story named Dolly. And this?" He held up the pin, turning it over. It was one of those pins you might buy for the birthday boy or girl, but the blue ribbon made her think of a first-place winner, especially considering the ten had been turned into a one. "Number one," Gavin said, setting it back down. "So the number one has to be part of the code, right? Maybe each of these items represents the other four numbers. What number state is Texas in the Union?"

Sienna let out a sound of frustration. "Does anyone know that kind of thing off the top of their head?"

"Maybe a Texan."

Sienna let out a small chuff.

"It has to be somewhere near the middle, though, right?" he said. "All the states on the East Coast were founded first. We could try everything between twenty-five and thirty-five," he suggested. Which sounded sort of hopeless, but what else did they have? Nothing.

"Okay, so the ten numbers between twenty-five and thirty-five, the number one, and then whatever this might represent," he said, picking the doll up. "Can you think of a number the person named Dolly from his writings might represent?"

Sienna took her bottom lip between her teeth, looking down as she attempted to recall everything about Dolly, the drunk, large-breasted coworker. What had they been drinking? Beer . . . some sort of shots. Sienna shook her head. "Unless you can think of a number that goes along with checkers? I don't recall him mentioning a number."

"There are two colors, two players," Gavin said. "Maybe the number two."

"Possible." But she could tell that he heard the tone in her voice saying that didn't feel quite right. *Anything* could have pointed to the number two. He'd put Dolly in there for a specific reason.

Mirabelle looked back and forth between the two of them, clearly at a loss. She was at a disadvantage, though. She hadn't read any of Danny's letters. A mercy for her but one that did not help them now. Gavin stared down at the items again, clearly frustrated.

Sienna picked up the star and the doll. "Maybe a word combination," she said, attempting to work some out aloud. "Star Checker Winner. Texas Winner Doll. Dolly Star—"

"Texas Dolly," Gavin said. He raised his head, his eyes opening wider. "Texas Dolly."

"What does that mean?" Sienna asked.

"It's a poker hand. No, I mean . . ." He ran his hand through his hair, ruffling it. "Okay, no, I mean yes, but . . ." He took in a breath and blew it out. "Doyle Brunson, otherwise known as Texas Dolly, won the World Series of Poker in the seventies. He had a starting Texas Hold'em hand named after him."

"What is it?"

"The 10-2. It's a trash hand, but it worked out for him twice."

"Ten, two?" Mirabelle repeated. "If you break each of those numbers into two digits, it's . . . one zero, zero two," she said, picking up the number one pin. "But even then, it's still one digit short."

Gavin was staring down at the items, his brow knitted. "No, I don't think that's it. I think it's referring to me."

"Why?" Sienna asked.

He raised his head and looked at her. "Because it's the hand I was dealt when I won the series the first time. The Doyle Brunson, ten-two combo. And I played it." His eyes went over her shoulder for a moment as he obviously recollected. "The flop was K-Q-ten, with two of diamonds and one spade. A two on the turn, and then, on the river, I spiked another ten for a runner-runner full house." His eyes focused back on her, and though she had no idea what he'd just said, something inside told her he was onto something. *I think it's referring to me.*

She picked up the number one pin. "You played it, and you won," she said, pinning the pin on his shirt.

He glanced down at it and then back at her. "My first winning hand," he said. "Ten, ten, ten, two, two." He paused only briefly. "That's too many digits, though, so"—he looked at the pin again, tapping it with his finger—"you have to remove the zeros to make it one, one, one, two, two."

"Try it," Sienna said, sucking in a quick breath.

They all raced over to the lock, and Gavin lifted it and put in the numbers. He met Sienna's eyes again as he gave it a small pull, and it opened with a click. They both exhaled, and Gavin unhooked the lock and pushed the door open.

The room beyond was dark, the only light the dim illumination spilling in from the room they currently occupied. Gavin stepped forward, and Sienna and Mirabelle followed close behind. Sienna squinted, her eyes adjusting so that she could see that the ceilings were as tall as the first one, though there were windows on the second story of this one, most of the glass gone. Sienna's head turned as she looked at the walls. There was writing all over them, spray-painted as though some-one had left graffiti in this room and only this room, but it was too dark beyond the doorway to see what it said.

"Congratulations, players," came a voice from above. Startled, Sienna raised her head. A light clicked on in one of the open windows, and Danny was sitting on the ledge with one hip, his feet on the other side of the short wall as he stared down to the place where the three of them stood. He smiled slowly. "This is fun, isn't it?"

Sienna did a quick sweep of the room, looking for something they could take cover under should he pull out a gun. But the room appeared somewhat small and empty, though it was mostly dark beyond where they stood. The best they could probably do was to run around the room in a zigzag pattern to make it hard to hit them. But that could only last so long. She looked up and met Danny's eyes.

"Hello, Detective. You have no idea how happy I am that you're here. I didn't expect it. I took that job at the police station so I could monitor my game from the inside. Imagine my surprise when I heard your boss mention the new detective that would be coming to work for the department. Imagine my shock at hearing *your* name, the girl Violet loved like a daughter, the one she'd raised instead of me." He leaned forward very slightly, his head tilting as he looked upward as though in memory. "It doesn't happen often . . . at least not for me. Being given that final card to complete a winning hand . . ." He smiled, and it managed to be both wistful and slightly sinister, his gaze landing on Gavin. "You know all about that, though, don't you, Big Winner? Fortune smiling down upon you?" Before Gavin could answer, Danny went on. "I added you to my game board, Detective, even though I only had a month to rearrange the pieces. But I had to. I'd just been given the opportunity to take out three opponents in one fell swoop." He swept his arm to the side as though sweeping the board from his perverse imagination.

"Danny," Mirabelle said, stepping forward. "This isn't a game, Danny. It wasn't then, and it isn't now. Let us out. Please. I tried, Danny. I tried to find you."

"You didn't try hard enough!" he said, raising his voice. "And then you stopped trying altogether."

"Mom," Gavin said softly, putting his hand on her arm, but she ignored him, continuing to appeal to Danny.

"I was scared," she said. Sienna swallowed, looking back and forth between the two of them, the tension in the air so thick she could *feel* it vibrating around them.

"It wouldn't have happened at all if you'd chosen me," he said, his gaze going to Gavin and then returning to Mirabelle . . . *Violet*, but Sienna had never known her by that name and couldn't think of her that way now. "Why didn't you?" His voice broke slightly, but he seemed to catch himself, his back going straight and that same distant smile returning to his face. Before she could answer, he went on. "I hid in the cupboard in the playroom," he said. "In case you wondered. Did you ever wonder, Violet? Did you ever weep when you thought about it? About how terrified I was. How I shook . . . about the moment he opened the door and found me there? The murderous look on his face. And he did murder me that day. Or close enough." Sienna clutched Gavin's hand in hers.

Mirabelle's head lowered, her shoulders drooping for a moment before she looked back up at Danny. "Of course I wondered. Of course I wept," she said, a tear tracking down her cheek. "Danny . . ." He stood and walked from one window opening to the next, where he flicked on a light and put his palms on the sill, leaning forward. *His hands are empty. He's not holding a weapon . . . for now.* Mirabelle stepped farther into the room, her head still raised as she followed him from below. "I can only imagine what you survived and how," Mirabelle said. "There wasn't a day that went by when I didn't think about you and wonder where you were. When I didn't say good morning to you and then good night. You've been here"—she tapped her heart—"every moment since that day. Please know. Each time someone asked me how many children I had, I acknowledged you, even if only in my mind. I didn't forget you, Danny. Never, not for one day."

He stood there for a moment, looking down at them, and though he was still and silent, he appeared unmoved by Mirabelle's words. "It doesn't matter, though, Violet. Because what's done is done. You caused it, and because of that, I paid, and now they have to too. And you'll be here to watch it happen."

"You're angry at me, Danny. Don't punish them," Mirabelle pleaded.

"It's *always* about *them*, isn't it, *Violet?*" The inflection in his words was strange, as though he was expressing ten emotions all at once, and they blended together, jerky and unclear, all while his expression remained neutral. A shiver crept down Sienna's spine.

This man had planned this elaborate game, over many, many months. Maybe even years. He'd held on to his anger, his twisted misery. He'd killed in self-defense, and he'd murdered innocent people. *Who are you really?*

"Let's walk out of here, you and me," Mirabelle said, still attempting to appeal to him. "You're not all bad, baby. You tried; I know you did. I'm your mother. And I see that part of you is still there. I see that."

Danny just smiled, though. And Sienna realized that, yes, he was still that scared little boy hiding in a cupboard, abandoned and terrified. *He's Danny, the horribly abused and neglected child who cared for the homeless mutt he called Jaxon, and he's the lonely teenager who raised himself. He's also Ollie, the reserved janitor who fed the little boy named Trevor he knew had been left alone, because otherwise the child would have starved.* But he was also *Mother*, wasn't he? His own version of an unflappable protector. Cool and calm. Ruthless and murderous, yet sweet and loyal. And now he was channeling Father. Cruel and sadistic.

He was each identity. The killer. The caretaker. The monster. The victim. A mixture of them all.

He'd become whoever he needed to be.

"Walk out of here?" he asked. "So you can visit me in prison? No, I don't think so." He leaned casually against the edge of the window, looking directly at Sienna once more. "I set up all kinds of paths, different clues you might have followed. It was fun to see which ones you discovered first and which ones you did not. I was prepared for every move. But they all led here. This was always the final game." He scratched his chin. "So many options. So many veering roadways. Do you think life is like that? Do you think God himself sets us up to watch us fall because we're so stupid and fallible? How much fun he must have. The ultimate game master. *Don't give them an inch,* he must think. *Not one single inch.*" He smiled and clicked his tongue. "There's little time for philosophy, though. Time is ticking." And Sienna suddenly knew they were not getting out of here if they played by his rules, because he was trying his best to play his version of God, and he, too, had set them up to watch them fall.

Danny stood straight, then pushed off the ledge and turned away. A few more lights blinked on overhead when he flicked a switch, illuminating the room below, and then he turned and walked out of sight.

"Danny, no. Come back," Mirabelle sobbed, her agony obvious. "Please, please come back." But Danny was gone, at least for now, and once again, they only had each other.

CHAPTER
THIRTY-SIX

Gavin gave the room a quick once-over before tipping his head back again and walking to the far wall so he could see more of the top floor where Danny had just been. It appeared empty, though. Wherever he'd gone, he was no longer watching them from above. Where was he? Off to set up another room? No. No, this had all been done far in advance.

He walked to the door on the opposite side of the wall and picked up the lock, identical to the one that had been on the previous door. A five-digit code.

Gavin lowered his head, massaging the back of his neck. He'd attempted to swallow down the shock and deep sadness at what his mom had divulged, but it was catching up with him. Danny Boy was his *brother*. He'd been reading his brother's notes. *Jesus.* He breathed in and let out a long exhale. He knew he had to hold his emotions at bay for now so he could focus on the predicament Danny had forced them into, but he needed a moment. Just one.

You were always a loud little shit. Loud and happy. You got to stay that way. Good for you, Big Winner. Danny's words from when he'd first arrived came back to him, along with a ripple of pain. He'd remembered Gavin, while Gavin had no memory of him.

He turned away from the door and met Sienna's eyes. There was so much understanding in her expression, and it washed over him. A balm. A blast of strength. Just the one he'd needed.

With regained focus, he walked back to the middle of the room and stood looking up for a moment, calculating whether or not they could climb on each other's shoulders to make it to the window, but he didn't think so. What were these? Private gambling rooms? Had there been felt-covered tables in here once where high-stakes bets were made? The offices had been situated so that security could view the room from all angles at all times but were far, far removed from the games going on. Even if they stood on each other's shoulders, the person on top—his mother since she was the lightest—would have to jump for the window and then pull herself up and over the ledge. It wasn't going to happen. Plus, Danny was up there somewhere, and if he knew they were attempting to climb and jump, he'd only have to reach his hand out and push, and they'd all go toppling over, someone's back likely breaking.

Gavin walked over to Sienna, who had approached his mom where she was still standing by the wall and taken her in her arms. She let go, and Mirabelle wiped a tear from her eye. She looked shaken and grief stricken. Hollow. He put his hands on the sides of her shoulders. "Mom. Listen to me. We're going to get out of here, and then we're going to get help for Danny."

"He doesn't want us to get out of here, Gavin. He's just running down the clock with all of"—she swept her hand around, and Gavin glanced briefly at the graffiti-like scrawls, all in orange paint, on the walls—"*this.*"

"Maybe," Gavin said. *Probably.* "But we have to keep going, because through one of these doors is going to be an opportunity."

"Gavin's right, Mirabelle," Sienna said. "Maybe he assumes we won't make it through in time, but he's also giving us an opportunity. If he wanted us to sit and wait for this building to explode, he'd have simply tied us up and left us. Maybe part of him hopes we'll make it out. And if that's true, then Gavin's right: we can't give up."

His mother nodded but looked unconvinced. Gavin tipped his chin to Sienna, who gave him a small smile.

You play fair, and I will too. The line from Danny's letter came back to him. If he even halfway meant it, he'd set this all up with the possibility—no matter how small—that they'd make it out. *Maybe.*

Gavin spotted something on the ground. He took the few steps to it before bending and picking up the penny. He held it up to the two women, who both looked at it in confusion. Gavin stuck it in his pocket. For all he knew, Danny had dropped it when he'd been in here creating this orange artwork. But it might be relevant.

"Let's do a full search of the room first," he said. "Maybe he hid another container of clues."

They each went in an opposite direction, feeling over the door ledges, looking in corners and along the baseboards. There was a loose floor tile near the wall, and they spent several minutes pulling at it, but though it was coming up at a corner, it seemed mostly adhered. They'd need a pry bar to remove it completely or feel underneath. "Damn," he swore as they walked toward the wall with the most graffiti on it. It seemed their clues would be contained to the sloppy drawings.

Sienna stood back so that she could see the entirety of the main wall, and Gavin came to stand next to her. "It sort of looks like a map," he said, his gaze going from one intersecting line to another.

"That's what I thought too. And look, there's an *X* there."

"*X* marks the spot," he murmured. "But what spot?"

"Could that be a bridge?" Mirabelle asked, pointing to an arched shape near the bottom of the wall to their left.

"It could be," Gavin murmured.

"If that is a bridge," Sienna said, "then those are probably waves." She pointed to the small swooshes beneath the arch.

"There are several bridges here spanning the Truckee River," Gavin said. "Do any of them mean anything to you?"

"No. You?" She turned. "Mirabelle?"

He and his mom shook their heads. "The bridge is off in the distance, though," Mirabelle said. "It seems like this"—she pointed to the intersecting lines above them—"is the main focus."

Gavin agreed. But what were they supposed to make of a bunch of intersecting lines, with the only landmark a distant bridge?

They all stood there for a while longer, looking at the details of the lines, the swooshes. Gavin did a few more searches of the room, mostly to keep himself active so he wouldn't get so overwhelmed with frustration that he became useless. Sienna huffed out a breath, walking to the other side of the room and then leaning against the far wall as she took in the map. "Oh my God," she said.

"What?"

She walked forward, her head tilted as she stared at the orange drawing. "It's the Bayonne Bridge in New York City. It connects Staten Island with New Jersey."

"Are you sure?"

"I think so. Because this shape way over here looks like Yankee Stadium." She used her finger to point to the rounded sort of triangle to Gavin's right.

"And see," she went on, pointing to two narrow channels on either side of them. "That would be the East River," she said, pointing to their right, "and that would be the Hudson." She moved her finger to the left.

"Okay," Gavin said, a buzz of anticipation giving him a small burst of renewed energy. "So what would this be?" he asked, pointing again to the *X* that was obviously the focus of this massive, scrawled, unlabeled map.

"Well, the Financial District would be all the way down there," she said, pointing to their feet. "So this up here would be . . . Harlem."

"What does Harlem mean to you, Si?"

Her head moved back and forth over the map as though she was orienting herself. "It was where I worked," she said. He was silent as he watched her, obviously figuring something out. Just like the box in the previous room had been for him, this map was for her? Danny had broken up the rooms—thus far—focused on one individual?

"The orange," she said, turning to him and his mother, her eyes alight. "This is all in orange." She swept her hand over the wall.

"Why? Why is it in orange?"

"Because it was the color of the day." She gave her head a small shake. "The NYPD uses a color-of-the-day system to identify under-cover cops working in high-risk areas. It's meant to prevent friendly fire. I was wearing orange for my first big arrest."

"In a nutshell," he said, trying to hurry her along without compromising details they might need.

She spoke more quickly. "I was undercover. I watched a big drug deal go down. There was a kid in the back seat, or I might not even have noticed. But I saw that kid, and I kept my eyes on the car. In all honesty, I got lucky, Gavin. Anyway, the arrest led back to a big kingpin. I got an award. It was all over the local news. It's one of the reasons I was fast-tracked to detective."

She hadn't gotten lucky. It was always about kids for her. She couldn't tolerate seeing them victimized or uncared for. And he'd tell her later how much he fucking loved the hell out of her. "Okay, so it was a big arrest . . . here?" he asked, pointing to the intersecting lines.

She nodded, her eyes glued to the spot. "Yes. Yes, right there."

"Five digits. Do you remember the zip code of the neighborhood?"

She put her hand to her forehead, looking away. "God, there might be a dozen. It's a big area, and I don't know the one in that specific spot. It'd start with one zero zero."

A zap of frustration sizzled through him. *Damn.* How many potential combinations was that? If he were better at math, maybe he'd know.

As it was, they were just going to have to start trying one by one. "Okay, let's get started then," he said, turning for the door.

"Wait," she said, putting her hand on his arm. "The penny."

He reached into his pocket, removed it, and held it in his palm.

She took it from his hand and held it in her thumb and index finger, studying it momentarily before obviously seeing, as he had, that it was just an ordinary penny. She handed it back. "Copper," she said.

"What about it?" he asked.

"The first shields of the NYPD were made of copper," she said hurriedly. "It's how the name *cop* came about. My shield number in New York was five digits."

Their gazes held for a moment, and he started to move toward the lock but then halted as an idea came to him. "What?" she asked. He turned his head, making eye contact with his mother, too, as they both drew closer. "Turn to the wall and keep pretending to discuss the map," he said. He had no idea if there was some small hidden camera where Danny was watching them. He didn't see one, but there were a million places something very obscure could be hidden. He was in security; he knew that well. Sienna pointed to a place to their left, and he tilted his head as he spoke as quietly as possible, with as little lip movement as he could. "Listen, the first room was geared toward me, toward my first big win. If that lock opens with your first shield number, he'll have done the same, only directed toward you."

"Which means that if there's a room beyond this one, it will be for me," Mirabelle said very quietly.

"*If*," Gavin said. "But if we can open this lock and rush straight for the next one without stopping to work out clues, we might be able to take him unaware. He won't expect that. What's beyond these inner rooms, Mom?"

She frowned. "An open three-story lobby. There's an escalator that goes down to a lower floor."

Gavin nodded once. At least he knew what he'd be running into if he got that far.

"So we're assuming the third lock has to do with something positive that happened in Mirabelle's life," Sienna said, pointing at another spot and turned slightly away from him. "A *win* of sorts. But one he could know about."

Neither one looked at Mirabelle, but she obviously knew they were waiting for her to offer ideas, because she made a small sound in the back of her throat that let them know she was considering. "I don't know . . . my happiness is you. You and Sienna and . . . Argus." Her voice cracked on Argus's name, but she cleared her throat softly, pulling herself quickly together. "I love my house—"

"Your *house*," Sienna said. "He mentioned your house in his note."

"The zip code?" Gavin said. *No, wait.* "Your street number is five digits too." That buzz again. Anticipation. Anxiety. Anger that their last moments might be spent solving puzzles that never ended, all to make a man feel powerful and that he was controlling the board—just once. Fear that whatever plan they came up with would not work.

But Gavin was a gambler. He took risks. He played hard hands, and he was going to attempt this one. He had to because they were running out of time.

"The street number is more specific," Sienna said. "More personal."

Gavin agreed with a minor tip of his chin. "We're going to go over there and enter your New York shield number," he said, "and then you stay inside the doorway as I run for the other lock, where I'll input your address." He looked at Sienna, and he could see she was considering the plan and what, as a trained officer, her role should be. "We both know how to fight," Gavin said. "But my size more closely matches Danny's." He didn't relish fighting the man he'd just found out was his brother, but his brother was a murderer. And if it meant their survival, he'd do what he had to do. He had no idea what was going to be on the other side of the door, if anything. But they had to try because he could not think of a better option. Sienna looked at him for a moment and then gave a quick nod.

All three of them moved to the door, and Sienna picked up the lock, her hands shaking as she began putting in the numbers. Her gaze lifted as she clicked the last one into place, and she met his eyes, mouthing, "I love you."

"I love you too," he mouthed back, taking his mother's hand in his and giving it one squeeze as Sienna pulled the lock and it opened. With a flick of her wrist she removed it and pushed the door open. Gavin burst through, sprinting for the other side of the dim room, the outline of another door barely visible. When he got there, his breath rushed out in a relieved gust as he saw the third lock. He felt the way he'd felt when he'd gotten a two on the turn during the game he'd described in that first room.

Necessary for a win but not quite there yet.

His hands were steady as he input Mirabelle's address. There was a lifetime and an instant between the time he pulled upward on the lock and the moment it pulled free. Gavin's heart slowed, then sped up, and he tossed the lock aside, yanking the door open and barreling through.

Danny stood several feet away on the other side, his expression stunned as he stumbled back before catching himself on the rail of the ledge behind him.

They both froze, brother facing off with brother, staring for several breathless seconds.

"I tipped my hand, didn't I, Big Winner?" Danny finally said, reaching for his waistband. "The problem is, there's only fifteen minutes left. Ticktock. Too late."

Gavin didn't bother to answer, instead lowering his head and rushing forward, straight at Danny, as the gun appeared and his hand began to rise.

CHAPTER
THIRTY-SEVEN

Sienna and Mirabelle stepped through the door just as Gavin made contact with Danny, both of them flying backward, a cry falling from Mirabelle's lips as they hit the railing and bounced off it and onto the floor. It was a terrible, nightmarish twist on the play fighting the brothers might have done had they grown up together, loving each other and hating each other as brothers did. The rushed, far-off thought zipped through Sienna's mind even as she stepped toward them, instinctively reaching for the weapon at her hip that was not there.

They were fighting in front of a portion of ledge that held a railing, but the rest of it was open to the floor below, a nonoperational escalator in front of them.

Gavin gained the upper ground, rearing back and raising his fist, and Mirabelle screamed, a sound that made both men jerk, and Danny used the momentary micropause to raise the hand still holding the gun. Gavin reacted, slamming his own hand down on Danny's wrist, but not before Danny pulled the trigger, the gun firing, the sound of the blast making Sienna's ears ring as her leg caught fire. Or that was what it felt like as she went down on one knee, crying out in pain.

"No!" Mirabelle raced forward and barely caught Sienna before she fell over. She supported Sienna's weight as she reached for her wounded leg.

"It's okay, Mirabelle." Sienna's breath sawed in and out, agony moving through her leg in surges. She could see the hole where the bullet had entered, shattering her bone. It was bleeding profusely, but at least he hadn't hit an artery.

The two men were still fighting, and Gavin made eye contact, his expression registering shock and rage. He hauled Danny to his feet and smashed his fist into his face. Danny got a hit in, too, as they continued to fight on their feet.

Mirabelle was crying as she wrapped what Sienna thought was her shirtsleeve around her wound and tied it off. "Thank you. I'm okay," she choked, soothing the woman even while her fear and debilitating pain wound higher, watching as the two men fought their way toward the gun that had slid closer to the edge of the platform.

Danny dived for it, Gavin following, and they rolled precariously close to the edge. Sienna's heart rose in her throat as they moved in the other direction before both came to their feet, their grunts ringing through the large, open area as they fought to overpower each other, to grab the weapon.

Outside, lights blinked on, the high, boarded windows overhead illuminating the cavernous space in streaming rays. Sienna heard the distant sound of vehicles. The demolition crew had arrived, or perhaps they were just now gearing up. *I can't walk. Oh God, it hurts. I can't even stand.*

Even if Gavin got the gun, would holding it on Danny work to force him to give them the code to the exit? Did they even have time to make it to that faraway door? Was there another they could make it through? There was no time to search. Sienna panted with both pain and terror.

Danny swung his arm back and lost balance. His bloody expression registered startled fear as he almost caught himself but lost his footing, falling backward and down the escalator. Mirabelle cried out his name, and Sienna grimaced as she heard his descent, his body pounding off the metal steps as he fell to the bottom.

Mirabelle screamed, letting go of Sienna and then rushing forward as Gavin came to his knees and then his feet and rushed to where Sienna sat, her blood soaking into the plywood floor.

"Oh God, Si, your leg," he said breathlessly. "We have to *go*." He leaned down and scooped her up. From the higher vantage point, she saw Danny lying below, his body limp, one leg bent backward. And she saw his eyes open, heard his pained moan. He was still alive.

Mirabelle was standing at the top of the escalator, her shoulders shaking with sobs as she stared down at Danny. "Mom! Let's go!" Gavin said, turning back toward the room he'd burst through minutes before, surprising Danny. Sienna reached up, lacing her hands around his neck, her heart pounding so harshly she could barely breathe, pain making the room throb around her.

Outside, over an intercom, a voice came. "Twenty."

Oh God. A countdown. Just like that long-ago day when Father had begun calling out the numbers, when Violet had been forced to choose. The realization came distantly. Her thoughts were staggered, seemingly disconnected from reality. The pain in her leg was sharp and overwhelming.

Mirabelle—*Violet*—turned, a small, sad smile on her lips as once again she stood between her two boys.

"Nineteen."

And even in her disconnected state, Sienna *knew*. "Mirabelle," she whispered. A goodbye.

Below, Danny moved, pulling himself backward with his arms, his leg dragging uselessly as he cried out in pain. He slumped against the wall, chest rising and falling with stilted breath.

"Eighteen."

"Mom!" Gavin called, panic in his tone.

"I love you both so much," Mirabelle choked, stepping onto the escalator. And before Gavin could even step forward, Mirabelle began moving rapidly down the narrow set of steps, toward Danny.

"Seventeen."

"Sienna," Danny called from below, his voice weak and shaky and so soft she could barely hear it over the escalating activity outside. "Violet Whitney Hastings," he said, his head going back and hitting the wall.

"Sixteen."

"Twenty-three, seventy-four . . ." Danny grunted. *What are you saying, Danny?* He tried to take in a breath, but it ended in a coughing fit, his neck bending to the side.

"Fifteen."

Gavin made a growling sound of frustration and panic in the back of his throat, adjusting Sienna in his arms. He took one step toward Mirabelle but then pivoted, his growl turning into a sob as he kicked the door in front of them open, Sienna gripped tightly in his arms as they moved forward. *Away.*

"Fourteen."

Sienna understood. She knew. If they stayed and attempted to force Mirabelle to come with them, they'd all die. Mirabelle had made her choice. Once again, she'd stood between her sons, and this time, she'd chosen Danny, because the first time she had not.

Gavin's breath gusted against her cheek. Sienna could no longer hear the countdown from this inner, enclosed section of the building, but she said the numbers in her mind.

Thirteen.

Gavin ran through the room they hadn't taken the time to explore, the one that held the clues to Mirabelle's address. The room that, had they taken the time to work through it, would have been their grave, all of them buried under rubble, just as the game master had planned.

Twelve.

Gavin burst through the second door, heading to the outer one through which he'd entered. What was he going to do? Tear the alarm from the wall? Then they'd never get out. Use a battering ram? They didn't have time. Her mind grew cloudy, pain rolling through her like a red wave.

Eleven.

Danny had called numbers to her. What had they been? *Twenty-three,* he'd said. *Seventy-four.*

Violet Whitney Hastings.

Mother.

It all came back distantly, flitting in and out of her mind.

Ten.

Gavin ran through one door into another, entering the room that had once been the kitchen, lifting his leg and kicking the cabinet they'd put in front of the door.

"The periodic table," she murmured. He'd used his mother's name . . . the code to it all. *The final answer.* The world was closing in around the edges. She was so cold, so incredibly cold. Her jaw didn't want to move. Violet . . . *V* . . . atomic number twenty-three. That was right, wasn't it? She'd thought it was a moment ago. She tried desperately to bring forth the picture of that table she'd studied so hard, but her mind wouldn't cooperate. *So cold. It hurts. God, it hurts.* Whitney . . . *W* . . . She couldn't remember what that stood for or even if its atomic number was seventy-four.

Nine.

Gavin's breath came out in sharp exhales as they ran through the kitchen, the pounding of his feet causing her leg to bounce and throb with horrible pain. But he had to. *Hurry. Hurry.*

"The initials relate to the numbers from the periodic chart," she slurred. "Violet. Twenty-three. Whitney. Seventy-four." He ran into the tall open area he'd entered through, the one where Danny had made them play a sick version of hide-and-go-seek as he'd shot at them from where Sienna could now blearily see was an open second story, and Gavin sprinted for the door.

Eight.

Violet Whitney Hastings. *H* . . . Hastings . . . *hydrogen.* "I think it's the first one at the very top," she managed as he skidded to a stop at the door, the panel blinking. His breath came out in sharp pants. "Twenty-three, seventy-four," he repeated. "What are the last two digits, Si?" He sounded desperate, panicked, and she knew she should be, too, but instead, she was floating . . . drifting. *How much blood have I lost?* Hydrogen was at the top of the chart. The very first one. She squinted, reaching for what her mind had retained. *Please.*

Seven.

Or was hydrogen on the other side? "Si," he practically shouted. "Si!" He needed her. Gavin needed her. *No, no, the other side is* He. *Helium. Hydrogen is number one.* "One," she managed. *It has to be.*

He huffed out a breath. She could smell his sweat. His fear. She saw it sparkling on his forehead. "One," he repeated. "Two, three, seven, four . . . zero, one, because it's six digits, Si."

She didn't answer. She couldn't lift her tongue.

Six.

He raised his hand. It was shaking. Gavin was afraid, so afraid, and though her heart was beating so slowly, so very slowly, if these were her last, they'd each be for him. *I love you.*

With a strangled sound and a whoosh of breath, he typed in the six digits. *One chance. One chance.* It was all they had.

The alarm made a long beeping sound and the red light went off as the door clicked open. Gavin let out a short cry, shouldering the door as he shot out into the night, Sienna held tightly in his arms.

Five.

He sprinted, his feet pounding the concrete, the sweet night air hitting Sienna in the face as she felt him throw his body forward, clenching her so tightly it hurt, and she gasped out a tiny cry as the world blinked out.

CHAPTER THIRTY-EIGHT

Violet stepped off the escalator and moved toward Danny. Her son. His eyes, the left one already beginning to swell, came open. He blinked at her, and even though his face was bloody, his features distorted from his injuries, she saw disbelief . . . then wonder . . . *relief*. It was naked and raw, the look he might have given her had it been her who'd opened the cabinet that day instead of the devil who had. She rushed the final steps and went down on the floor next to him. "I'm here," she said.

"Four," came the voice over the megaphone outside.

Run, Gavin, run!

Danny slumped toward her, and she brought her arms around him, lowering his head to her lap, stroking his hair. *Soft.* It was as soft as she remembered.

Gavin and Sienna would make it out. She knew they would.

She wouldn't leave Danny, not this time.

"Three."

"Mom," Danny whispered, turning toward her like a child, gripping the hem of her shirt in his fist, burying his face in her stomach.

Violet rocked him. He was her Danny. Whoever else he'd been, whoever else he'd had to be, he'd die as her boy. In his mother's arms, the arms he'd been torn from far, far before he was ready.

"Two."

He turned more fully to her, and she felt the wetness of his tears soaking through her shirt. She held him tightly, humming softly, and rocked him as she'd rocked Gavin that long-ago day as they'd sat in the closet, hiding together.

She bent forward, gripping his body to hers, shielding him. "I'm here," she whispered again.

"One."

EPILOGUE

Four months later

Sienna's gaze hung on the little boy sitting all alone on a short rock wall at the edge of the yard, using a stick to draw what appeared to be random shapes on the ground. The woman who ran the group home said he was often out there, all alone. Sienna understood it, though. The boy had learned to find some solace in his isolation. He'd had to, and now, perhaps, he didn't know another way. Sienna, Gavin, and Kat approached him, his head coming up as they drew closer.

"Hi, Trevor," Sienna said, giving him a slight smile, butterflies fluttering between her ribs. She didn't want to make him nervous, but she was nervous too. She wanted to do this right. She wanted to put him at ease. For that reason, she'd asked Kat to come along, the two of them having formed what she hoped was a comforting duo the day they'd entered his grandmother's apartment and found him alone. *Rescued him.* Sienna's leg only ached mildly as she squatted in front of the boy. He ceased the movements with the stick, looking at her curiously at first, but that expression quickly faded into what she figured was a practiced detachment. "Do you remember me? I'm Detective Walker." She looked back over her shoulder. "And that's Detective Kozlov."

Kat smiled. "Hey, Trevor, nice to see you."

His eyes hung on her for a moment before they moved to Gavin, wariness creeping in. "That's my husband, Gavin," she said, giving Gavin a smile. *Husband.* The word still made her catch her breath. They'd married only a month after that horrible night at the Casino Royale. *Let's not waste another minute,* he'd said. And she'd agreed wholeheartedly. Minutes were precious. *Seconds.* Who knew that better than them?

Gavin stepped forward, offering his hand. "Hi, Trevor." Trevor stared for a moment before reaching out and shaking. Gavin let go, flexing his hand in the air as if the boy's handshake had been tight enough to cause pain. "Wow, you've got quite a grip on you," Gavin said. Trevor's lips tipped the barest bit, and Sienna's heart lightened. *Breathe in. Breathe out.*

"Are you here to move me somewhere else?" he asked, his gaze going to the scratches he'd made in the dirt. *Always moving. Never staying. It must be how he feels.* He dragged the stick listlessly, back, forth.

"We're here to ask you if you'll come live with us. Permanently."

His gaze shot up, large eyes meeting hers. "Live with . . . you?" He looked behind her, first to Kat, then to Gavin, and back to her.

She nodded. "With me and Gavin. Kat would like to visit you at our house sometimes too."

"They have a really nice house, Trevor. I can vouch for it," Kat said on a smile.

His little forehead dipped, but she swore she saw a light of hope in his eyes, small and distant, flickering, but there. "You . . . want me?"

Her breath released, heart constricting, and she reached out, taking his hand in hers. "Yes, Trevor. We do. We want you. We want you to come live with us. We want to give you a home and be your family if . . . if you want us back. You don't have to answer now. You can decide. We've spent the last few months setting up what we think is a really nice home. You can come see it and decide if you like it there or not, okay?"

He blinked, nodded. "O-okay."

Tears burned the backs of Sienna's eyes as she looked over her shoulder at Kat and Gavin. He smiled, stepped forward, and squatted next to her so he was at Trevor's height. "Thank you, Trevor, for giving us a chance." He took Sienna's hand in his, squeezing. "That makes us really happy. We know you've lost people. We know it's been hard. We've lost people too." He cleared his throat but not before Sienna heard the pain. "But we're hoping . . . well, we're hoping we can all help each other heal."

Sienna and Gavin had supported each other through the worst of it, the grief, the funerals, the way the media had pounced on the story filled with murder and sacrifice, trickery and terror. Kat had been a loyal friend and a sounding board for Sienna, and Ingrid had had her back professionally, every step of the way. Only four months later, there was still healing to be done. But Sienna and Gavin were stronger for it, too, each picking up where the other left off, both deciding that it was time to welcome a lost little boy into their home and their hearts. Sienna had a deep feeling Mirabelle would approve.

Trevor nodded, his expression grave. Understanding in a way no little boy's expression should be. They all stood, and Trevor took Gavin's hand in his. "I can help," he said.

"Great," Gavin answered. "We're betting on it. And I'm pretty good at that—making winning bets. I'll tell you about it when we get home, okay?"

Home.

"Okay. Can we go now?"

"Yes," Sienna said. "Let's go." And she took Trevor's other hand in hers, Kat joining them as they walked across the lawn together.

Sienna didn't see life as a game, at least not the way Danny had. She didn't believe they were all pawns to be toyed with. Life could be hard and unfair, but as Mirabelle and Argus had taught her, life held magic, too, and love in the most unexpected of places. She linked her arm with Kat's, holding on tightly to Trevor's hand as she shot Gavin a smile. She supposed there wasn't always an answer when it came to the greater questions of why. Sienna knew one thing for certain, however: that whether you were given one or you had to create your own, there was nothing more important than a really great team.

ACKNOWLEDGMENTS

There are many types of teams. I'm lucky to have the best of the best when it comes to both a home team and a professional one.

To Kimberly Brower, who has my back in all things. Every author should be lucky enough to have an agent like you.

To Marion Archer, who helped me organize and polish the first drafts of this story. Thank you for knowing what I mean to say even when I don't and helping me find the right words.

To my Amazon editing team, who I worked with for the first time, Charlotte Herscher, Maria Gomez, Riam Griswold, and Bill Siever. I stand in the presence of greatness. You challenged me and inspired me, and my appreciation knows no bounds. All four of you are so incredibly *smart*. I can't wait to do this all over again!

To my precious readers. You make this all possible. Thank you from the bottom of my heart for picking up my books when there are so many out there.

To all the book bloggers, Instagrammers, and BookTokers who are so incredibly generous with your time and your talent. I value each and every one of you.

To my husband. Partnering up with you was the best decision I ever made.

ABOUT THE AUTHOR

Mia Sheridan is a *New York Times*, *USA Today*, and *Wall Street Journal* bestselling author. She lives in Cincinnati, Ohio, with her husband. They have four children here on earth and one in heaven.

Sheridan's other romantic thriller novels include *Where the Blame Lies* and *Where the Truth Lives*.

Connect with her on her website at www.MiaSheridan.com or on Facebook at www.Facebook.com/MiaSheridanAuthor. Follow along on Instagram (@MiaSheridanAuthor) and Twitter (@MShcridanAuthor).